The Midnight Carousel

The Midnight Carousel

FIZA SAEED McLYNN

MICHAEL JOSEPH

PENGUIN MICHAEL JOSEPH

UK | USA | Canada | Ireland | Australia
India | New Zealand | South Africa

Penguin Michael Joseph is part of the Penguin Random House group of companies
whose addresses can be found at global.penguinrandomhouse.com

Penguin Random House UK,
One Embassy Gardens, 8 Viaduct Gardens, London sw11 7bw

penguin.co.uk

Penguin
Random House
UK

First published by Penguin Michael Joseph 2025
001

Set in 12/14.75pt Bembo MT
Typeset by Falcon Oast Graphic Art Ltd
Printed in Great Britain by Clays Ltd, Elcograf S.p.A.

The authorized representative in the EEA is Penguin Random House Ireland,
Morrison Chambers, 32 Nassau Street, Dublin D02 YH68

A CIP catalogue record for this book is available from the British Library

HARDBACK ISBN: 978-0-241-71520-8
TRADE PAPERBACK ISBN: 978-0-241-71521-5

Penguin Random House is committed to a sustainable
future for our business, our readers and our planet. This book is
made from Forest Stewardship Council® certified paper.

MIX
Paper | Supporting
responsible forestry
FSC® C018179

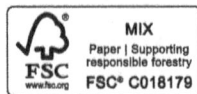

For my father

In years from now, when petals fall
And Mother's seed-heads form in place,
Touch fingertips upon my mouth,
Blow softly, softly on my face.
Sweet breath of yours, my wild delight,
Doth scatter me as Nature's sail;
Released to dance on winds of Fate,
I wait for you beyond the Veil.

Contents

Prologue

Paris, France, 1900

On the outskirts of Paris, where factories and foundries bustle by day, there is silence at night. From the city's port to a patch of wild scrubland near the shabbiest slum, fog creeps between deserted industrial buildings. Tools hang on hooks; looms lie idle. Furnaces and carts, pulleys and cogs, are shrouded by dark and an eerie stillness.

Halfway along a gravel track flanked by large wooden sheds sits the carousel workshop, the single source of light for a quarter-mile around. Inside, hot air roars like dragon's breath as Gilbert Cloutier guides the flame of a blow torch. Metalwork is not his speciality, but soon lengths of hollow pipe are welded into shape. The burning steel smells; grey smoke fills the air. Taking an oak-handled engraver, he leans in and begins to etch a pattern of swirls on the cooling surface.

After hours of intense concentration, Gilbert is groggy; his eyes droop. With a clang, the tool falls to the stone floor, disturbing a party of squeaking rats from behind the drilling machine. Nausea rises in his stomach as the room spins. The wood pile blurs into the mahogany filing cabinet. A pile of paint tins judders.

Waiting until the dizziness clears, Gilbert shuffles to the tap. He splashes his face, rubs trickles through his hair. Cold, the water wakes him. He would like to unroll his sleeping mat and curl up in the corner, but he needs to push through the exhaustion. Gilbert made a promise to his son, and he intends to keep it.

With Liliane lying dead in the room next door – thankfully never aware that she had transmitted the influenza to their beloved child – Gilbert had perched on Théo's bed, silently praying for a miracle.

I

Despite being pale, drenched in a feverish sweat, the boy was as fascinated as ever by the special carousel his father was building for the Exposition, and he summoned the strength to half open his eyes.

'Please, Papa,' he whispered hoarsely. 'Please could you name one of the horses after me?'

Such a simple request. Simple, yet Gilbert discovered yesterday morning that time was running out.

Machines were being powered up when he was alerted by shouting to a meeting between his foreman, Antoine, and a handful of the workers. Keeping out of sight, Gilbert had listened in through the open doorway between his office and the main work area.

'Right, let's get down to business,' Antoine announced. 'Is the platform any nearer to completion, Olivier?'

'So-so.' Olivier's deep voice matches his stature. Well-built and imposing, he heads up the mechanics team. 'We still have to work out how the pieces slot together. This new design of Monsieur Cloutier's is more complex than we're used to.'

'All I need to know is whether you'll finish in time.' Antoine sounded tired. 'We received a letter from the Director of the Exposition this morning. He says that the carousel is expected there ten days before opening,' Antoine continued. 'The morning of April 4th. Will you be ready?'

There was a ripple of concern amongst the men. When Gilbert initially spoke with the Exposition Committee, he had been told that the exhibits would be installed one week before the inauguration ceremony. With less than a fortnight to go, segments of the carousel platform still needed to be welded together, the canopy painted and the controls wired. Moving the schedule forward by three days could lead to the project's being botched.

'If the men work longer hours, possibly,' Olivier responded. 'But we will expect a fatter wage.'

'I'll see what I can do. But we do expect maximum effort to get it done.' Antoine's voice was clipped, as though he was trying to stifle his irritation. 'It's a matter of professional pride, after all. And don't forget how important this is to Monsieur Cloutier. Under the circumstances.'

Gilbert was grateful for the foreman's tactfulness. He did not need to hear the details spoken out loud.

'We're doing our best, Antoine, but we're not miracle workers.'

'And all we want is your best.' Antoine's voice softened. 'Because your best is nothing short of perfection.' He cleared his throat. 'So we're agreed. The platform is to be completed and at our Trial Ground for testing by April 2nd. Not a day later.'

This means Gilbert's own deadline is also April 2nd, nine days from now. Only if it is fully carved and painted will his horse be taken with the other parts, the components for the carousel of all carousels, to the Trial Ground situated at the furthest end of the track. Tested, faults fixed, triple checked, the carousel will be disassembled, then reassembled at the Grand Palais in Paris, one of the sites of the Exposition. Opening to loud applause on April 14th, 1900, delighting crowds for seven months, it will later be returned to the workshop. Or sold off by creditors.

Gilbert is up to his neck in debt. The opportunity to build the finest carousel in the world to outdo his fiercest competition – the Savage factory in England – for a once-in-a-lifetime event had seemed too good to miss. It was his big chance, his one shot, to prove what the country boy was made of.

What a waste, he now realizes. The money, the stress, those overtime hours lost to the project – all that pushed his wife and son away, and can never be regained. His fists clench at the thought, squeezing until his nails dig into flesh and relieve the pressure, like air being released from a bicycle tyre.

As the pink salute of dawn crawls through the dusty windows, Gilbert stumbles to his office, hiding away before the workforce arrive. He nods a greeting to the portrait he painted of his family, hung above his desk, and salutes Théo's tin soldiers. Whereas they once pushed forward the glorious red, white and blue of the French Empire by fighting off barbarian hordes on the boy's bedroom floor, all ninety-nine pieces of moulded metal – eleven for each year of his son's short life – now stand silent guard over Gilbert's work. The scrutiny of their eyes is unwavering, and perhaps explains the unsettling sensation that he is always being observed.

He sits on a stool in front of a piece of woodwork. As the owner of the enterprise, he long ago rose above the task of carving. But this creation is a horse for his child. Eyelids closed, his sensitive fingers explore the velvet folds of an ear, the hollows of nostrils, the curve of a forelock, finding bumps, sanding them down, fine sawdust falling to the ground.

Next, Gilbert unfolds the cloth protecting the chisels. They stare up, glinting. He selects the quarter-inch blade, perfect for refining details of the eyes and mane. With tiny, gentle hand movements, he carves grooves around the pupils, creating a small circle less than a hair's-breadth deep. It is delicate work but needs only patience and a steady eye, nothing his ailing muscles can't bear. Sawdust builds up in crevices and he blows it away, his dry lips cracking and his tongue tasting blood. But he persists. Each scratch, each scrape, brings Gilbert closer to the final tasks: decorating the horse with paint, marking the individual hairs of the coat, the swirling mane, the vibrant saddle, followed by layers of lacquering. It brings him closer to the finish line.

Suicide had been his first plan.

It was the priest at both funerals who convinced Gilbert it was not the way. As he stood by the gravesides watching Théo's tiny coffin being lowered next to his mother's, Gilbert had clawed his hands, punched his thighs. Through sobs that shook his body, he shouted that he was glad Liliane was dead, cold, and could feel none of this.

Concerned, the priest asked Gilbert to stay. They sat in the parlour, the priest letting him weep, uninterrupted. When afternoon turned to twilight, Gilbert was ready. Sugared tea soothed his throat and made him able to ask the question.

The eyes of that priest had been so kind, and now rounded like butter crêpes; then he frowned a frown so intense his eyebrows overhung his eyelids.

There was one answer, as clear-cut as the question: there was no way to end it all by his own hand. Only natural causes of death would satisfy God. Any other means and Gilbert would lose his place in Heaven, his only way back to his family. It meant Gilbert was stuck here, festering, maybe for decades while his wife and only child waited.

Anger boiled inside Gilbert. Thwarted by God, thwarted by the priest as holy messenger, he had roared as he struck teacups, pulled books from the shelf, kicked out at the priest. The commotion caused the housemaid to fetch two burly gendarmes, who hauled him to a night in the cells. Still fuming after his release the next day, Gilbert had stormed to the factory, dragged a huge lump of timber from the storeroom to his office and slammed the door shut.

When he sat on the stool in front of the hulk of wood one week later, the rough structure of a horse had already been formed. Over the next few hours, he crafted a raised diamond shape on the forehead, then painted the letters of his son's name, one along each side. With his right wrist steadied by his left hand, he stilled the tremble and, holding his breath, marked the accent on the *e* with the fine hairs of the brush. There: the horse was christened Théo.

It was then that a thought popped up like a jack-in-the-box, both frightening and exhilarating: Gilbert would need another plan.

Choosing

I

Paris, France, 1914

With a twist and a flip, Detective Laurent Bisset folds the corners of a single-page report on the theft of several bottles of eau de cologne from the Galeries Lafayette department store. After another six creases and the fanning out of the flaps, the work is completed. He props the folded paper, now shaped as a dove with wings and a beak, between a pair of origami parakeets. Although he is tempted to fashion a peacock next, this is not the day for dallying.

Soon he and the Chief Inspector will be speaking to the press. There will be photographs taken on the steps of the Préfecture de Police, Inspector Barbet promised, *so you'd better look your best*. With dark circles under his eyes, Laurent looks nothing close to his best. It cannot be helped, however. Teething is natural, and Amélie is not to blame for keeping him up for the third night in a row.

He moves to the mirror affixed to the wall behind his desk and straightens his tie, his face staring back. Despite his worn-out appearance, he knows he is a handsome man. 'The child will break hearts,' Tante Brigitte once announced to assembled family members, peering with such sternness through her monocle that Laurent took fright and ran to hide behind the grand piano. That was then. At thirty-five years of age, he has grown quite accustomed to women, and sometimes men, noticing his grey eyes fringed by dark lashes, and the athletic gait of his long-limbed frame.

'Do you need anything else, sir?'

Laurent turns as the pretty receptionist Suzette enters the room. She hurries to the desk, and he catches a glimpse of her legs as she leans over to position the newspaper next to the paper knife, four inches below the ink holder, parallel with the blotter. Just as he likes.

'No, thank you, Suzette. I'm just preparing for the Big Event.' He stands with his arms out and rotates on the spot, the corners of his mouth twitching with amusement. 'How do I look?'

Since adolescence, Laurent has never been able to help himself when it comes to having the attention of a pretty young woman.

Suzette's eyes narrow and she grips her skirt. 'You look fine, sir.'

Intriguing. This is new. Evidently, the tiredness is taking an even greater toll on his looks than he had thought.

'Most kind, Suzette.'

He watches her leave, then peers at the newspaper. They say the Germans are rumbling, spoiling for war. But it is conjecture. No one has the appetite for military antagonism, not in the twentieth century, when advances in technology have made us all civilized. Tomorrow's headlines will be different. Unless there is a grand calamity such as an explosion at the Eiffel Tower, the newspapers will talk of Laurent.

He checks his silver watch, tucked in the pocket of his best waistcoat. Four minutes to noon. He leaves to saunter along the rambling corridor, past the rooms where the constables jostle cheek by jowl, and out of the main door, arriving on the steps of the building at ten seconds to noon.

'*How did you catch him, Detective?*'

Pop! The flash is so bright that Laurent winces.

More practised at these occasions, the Chief Inspector speaks up first.

'It was a simple matter of deduction, gentlemen.'

Not so simple for Laurent, who did the legwork. After supper each evening, while Odette took to her darning then retired to bed alone, he would pull the file from his briefcase, which grew thicker every day, and hunt for clues until the early hours of the morning. From the moment the case of a missing child first crossed his desk, Laurent had the feeling that it could be the one he would make his name with. Besides, Chloé Fourtou was just eleven years old when she disappeared from Bastille Market late morning on a blustery, October day in 1913, and Laurent was determined to see justice done for the girl. What he had not anticipated was discovering other victims.

'*What took you so long to find him?*'

Another *pop*! This time Laurent forces his eyelids to remain open.

'Here in Paris, we have the best detectives in the world.' Quick off the mark again, the Chief Inspector throws out an answer as if he has prepared for every question. 'And we have proved today that we will never give up.'

In truth, no one even suspected the guilty party when he came to the attention of the police fourteen years ago. Back then, Laurent was a junior constable, sent to acquire background information from Victor Cloutier as the sole living relative of a missing factory owner. Lost to grief-stricken madness over his dead family, poor soul, the uncle, Gilbert, had disappeared from his workshop one night in April 1900.

At the time, it was assumed by Laurent's superiors that the man had drowned himself in the Seine, given his obvious suffering. That his acquaintances all agreed he had become too feeble to wander very far, as well as there being no trace of his body anywhere else in the near vicinity, bolstered their theory. This explanation bothered Laurent, since those same acquaintances knew Gilbert as a God-fearing man, a person who would naturally shy away from a self-inflicted death. He had hoped Victor would be able to shed some light on his uncle's state of mind, but Laurent received a surly 'How would I know?' in response.

Soon his concerns were dismissed by the officer in charge, and the file closed, giving him no choice but to push the case from his mind, however much it nagged at him. That is, until many years later.

It took Laurent several hours to recall why he recognized the Cloutier name in the notes on Chloé Fourtou's disappearance. There was a small carnival at Bastille Market that week, and the girl was last seen talking to the owner of the carousel. When Gilbert was declared dead by court order a decade after he vanished, Victor inherited his uncle's workshop, personal possessions and the carousel. It was a suspicious windfall for an individual with a string of convictions for theft.

On a hunch, Laurent began piecing together the route Victor

took when the carnival toured, scouring the archives and digging for unsolved disappearances in other districts. It was painstaking work over many weeks. But, lo and behold, he unearthed two cases similar to that of the missing little girl: Nathalie Moulland, described by her Aunt Mathilde as a sensible child, suddenly vanished from the annual Nantes Fair in the middle of a particularly warm day in the summer of 1911; and Gérard le Blanc the following March. Gone in a poof, his fiancée said, from a fairground they had strolled through on their way to lunch in Montpeyroux. So out of character to leave his widowed mother alone, struggling to make ends meet, according to the family. Like Chloé, the last sighting of Nathalie and Gérard was with Victor, who was collecting centimes for the ride.

Through perseverance or luck, call it what you will, Laurent had established the man's connection to four strange disappearances. He probed Victor's history next: there were domestic disputes, reports of bad blood between him and Gilbert. And then another break in the case – a nightwatchman recalled seeing Victor skulking near the carousel workshop the night his uncle vanished.

Laurent dreads to think how many other disappearances there would have been, if not for these discoveries.

'*What did he do with the bodies?*'

Laurent fiddles with his pocket watch. From the corner of his eye, he can see the Inspector staring at the ground. This question is impossible to answer because, search as they have, there is still no sign of the victims. No one saw how or where Victor took them, it seems.

It would be a different story if the man had cooperated. But he has never cracked. Not on the day he was taken to the empty cell with constables Pouliot and Mallet, the burliest gendarmes in the arrondissement, only returning when his face was properly bloodied. Nor the day Inspector Cantin organized a group of constables to help him dunk Victor's face in the horse trough, until the spluttering drew complaints from the tavern next door. Not even the day several weeks ago when Laurent attempted bribery with a small square of opium gum.

But, in the end, it made no odds to the judge that there were no bodies, since Victor was, by way of common-sense deduction, the missing link that connected each case to the next.

'Victor Gabriel Cloutier,' he rasped. 'You have been found guilty of the most heinous of crimes known to humanity. And, for that, you are sentenced to the ultimate penalty. Death by beheading.'

Bang!

Victor screamed as he lunged towards a small boy, his miniature double, sitting in the public gallery. 'I love you, Henri!'

No more than five years old, Henri – wide-eyed and sucking his thumb – shrank behind a weeping young woman. Dragged back by three constables, Victor fell silent as swift jabs with many pairs of elbows winded his lungs.

At last, the case was closed. All those hours, days, months, spent attempting to make sense of senseless acts was finally rewarded. Laurent was toasted with beer by the constables, with Bordeaux by the Inspectors, and promised his new office and promotion.

'*What did he do with the bodies?*' the reporter repeats.

The Chief Inspector is now bobbing on the balls of his feet. 'Gentlemen –'

'May I, Chief Inspector?' Laurent interrupts.

'Please be my guest.'

Pop!

Laurent exhales slowly to steady his nerves.

'What we should focus on, gentlemen, is that, with Victor Cloutier due to be executed by the guillotine in two hours' time, the citizens of Paris are now safe from such disappearances, and the victims are at peace.' He waits a moment for a rattling cart to pass. 'Each of them should, henceforth, be remembered not for the circumstances of their last moments, but for the joy they brought their loved ones.'

The Chief Inspector smiles his approval. Laurent returns the smile, but beneath the surface he suspects that the absence of bodies and no motive established will always haunt him. As the reporters drift away, he calculates there is just enough time to make a detour before he is expected at La Santé prison to witness the execution.

'See you there,' he tells the Chief Inspector and hurries off before there is any objection.

The evidence warehouse is crammed with ill-gotten gains, mainly acquired from various corners of the Paris slums – crates of wine, murder weapons, a stuffed black bear stolen from the National Museum of Natural History. At the back of this huge space is the carousel, the individual components assembled as a visual aid for the judge and jury.

Chloé Fourtou's disappearance provided the most detailed eye-witness statements, the other cases offering patchy information at best. Thus it was decided by the prosecution team to re-enact the known movements of both the little girl and Victor at around that time, using police officers and members of the court as extras. The jury was instructed to observe carefully from the sidelines. There was clapping when the carousel music began, pointing at the painted soldiers that appeared to march across the canopy as it spun. Finally, the entire room burst into cheers as a spectacular pattern of lights flashed above the horses. And not a single person noticed the stand-in Victor whisking away the actress playing the part of Miss Fourtou.

The exercise clearly demonstrated the ease with which it is possible to lose sight of someone – and the difficulty in noticing a crime – when faced with the excitement of the ride, and the bustle of the crowds.

With the trial over and the execution imminent, the carousel will be taken apart later today, leaving Laurent with only a few hours for a final look at the place where Chloé, along with Gérard and Nathalie, were last seen.

His shiny boots tap between aisles of shelves crammed to the ceiling with boxes. Past the large container of black-market cigarettes, Laurent stops in his tracks. Naturally, he has viewed the carousel in its fully formed state before. He remembers glimpses through the captivated crowds at the Exposition all those years ago. There it stood as a wonder of modern engineering in a glass-domed building, surrounded by exotic palms and marble sculptures. And, again, several weeks ago, as a part of the court proceedings. But Laurent has never seen it alone, and he is awestruck.

A circle of early-afternoon sunlight illuminates the structure like the star of the show in a theatre production. Steel gleams – the platform, steps and struts – crowned by a painted canopy decorated with familiar scenes from French history. The storming of the Bastille. The Napoleonic Wars. With reverence, Laurent draws closer to it.

Ascending the three steps, he admires the intricate metalwork – fleurs-de-lis cover everything, including the poles supporting the twenty-four carved horses, which are paused mid-motion, manes flowing and hooves kicking, each one centred above a large hexagonal shape engraved on the platform. A horse the colour of light fudge stands out amongst the others, distinguished by a raised blue diamond on its forehead. Although the paintwork is universally skilled, it is obvious that extra care has been taken with this creature; stroke by stroke has been applied with such precision that each hair, every feature, looks real.

An inexplicable compulsion overtakes Laurent. He pounds to the central cylinder. Curious, Laurent had watched as the jury was shown the spot where eyewitnesses spied Victor lurking during the rides, and he knows where to find the controls. He opens a metal flap, pulls down a lever, races back to the horse and leaps on.

The carousel glides into motion. Laurent peers into the dark depths of the control cylinder. It is the perfect hiding spot, and, yes, large enough for both Victor and a victim. The man could easily have darted out and in, unseen.

As the ride accelerates, Laurent is struck by the sleekness of movement, smooth as a knife over soft butter. My, this is wonderful! With the rise and fall of the horse, he feels his heart pounding as he clings on. Soon, however, the initial thrill is replaced by wistfulness. This reminds him of the summer afternoon three decades ago at the Parc de Belleville. In those days, it was rare for his mother to feel up to an outing. But there she was, perched beside him on the park's pretty blue-and-white carousel, the rush of the ride loosening her neat chignon. 'Oh, to hell with it,' she laughed, and, with a flourish, pulled out the clasp, setting those rich brown curls free. Never having known her to be so bold, so alive, Laurent was captured by the moment.

He can almost see her here now, sitting on the elegant grey pony next to him with her hair flowing back. He can almost reach out and touch her. Almost. As the ride slows to a gradual stop, Laurent stumbles off the horse and staggers to the edge of the platform, where he sits, his head between his hands.

A crowd is already assembled on the pavement outside La Santé Prison when Laurent takes a seat opposite the guillotine. He is just in time to witness Victor's scrawny neck being positioned beneath the sharp blade. The man screams, protests his innocence, but it is too late.

After Victor's body is placed on the ground, the young woman from the court steps forward, clutching the hand of the little boy, Henri. Both mother and son stare at the lifeless man. Laurent knows from interrogating Victor that the boy is a bastard, and, therefore, entitled to nothing from the estate.

Discomfort pricks Laurent. A pauper's life in the slums is what lies in store for the boy: starvation, begging for scraps, beatings, being taken advantage of by unsavoury types. But Laurent's hands are tied. After all, he doesn't make up the rules.

Henri escapes his mother's grip to grab a long stick from the ground. Not fully grasping the situation, he begins running around, lost in innocent play. In that moment, Laurent pictures Amélie, delicate and vulnerable. To hell with it, he thinks. There must be a way to help the boy.

Gaining Speed

2

Canvey Island, Essex, England, 1910

At first, Maisie pretends she can't hear the whimpering. She is crouched, her fingers loosening the sand, digging in a circle. With a squelch, she releases a cockle from its home and moves on to its neighbour. Last night's gusts stripped a layer from the beach, and a month's supply lies like a field of crops inches beneath the surface. Easy pickings. Though not so easy that seawater doesn't sting Maisie's skin, made raw by the Essex climate. Perhaps one day she will become as polished as the smooth stones scattered along the shoreline, rubbed new by the tides.

The distant whimpering of what sounds like an animal rises to a scream as Tommy returns from his toilet break further up the beach. It would be easier if he could wade into the waves to relieve himself, but Maisie won't let him dirty the sea. He scratches a sore on his leg, his shins like twigs about to snap.

'There's something hurt – I saw it,' he lisps.

She tosses a handful of cockles into a bucket of seawater and straightens up, patting her knees clean.

'Show me where,' she replies, sounding braver than she feels.

Maisie follows Tommy up the escarpment, using spiky marram grass as steps to the top, and along the ledge to the dunes. They weave along their usual path, dodging driftwood as large as a man's torso, and arrive at a thicket of sycamores. It's as she feared: a writhing squirrel is caught fast in the fangs of a poacher's trap, with no chance of survival.

'What do we do?' Tommy asks.

'Dunno,' says Maisie, shrugging.

They both know exactly what next steps to take, but neither

likes to say. Tommy shuffles while Maisie stares at her bare feet, the dirt beneath her toenails like the speckled patterns of a snail's shell. Their awkwardness is interrupted by a piercing shriek, and she can bear it no longer. Gritting her teeth, Maisie picks up a small rock and ends the creature's misery.

Both children turn to the sea, their arms upstretched.

'Dear Lord of the Water, please care for this soul,' Maisie murmurs.

'Amen,' Tommy agrees.

There's one thing left to do before the squirrel is at rest. With the rock as a headstone, they arrange a collection of leaves over the body.

Life on this spit of an island is precarious, and the two children often come across dead crabs washed up after a storm, rabbits lured by the poachers' traps and, once, the half-skeleton of a young deer with its neck snapped in two. They have had so many near-misses of their own that Maisie has always feared it could be her or Tommy next. Tumbling from branches, being caught out by rising tides and slipping on wet rocks are all commonplace. Then one day she strayed into a graveyard.

They have never been to church, not officially, but she and Tommy were blackberry picking on the other side of the island four autumns ago. Hungry for the plumpest fruit, they were balancing on the wings of a stone angel set upon a tomb when a priest surprised them. 'Dear Lord, our Saviour,' he'd exclaimed, taking several paces back. 'Have mercy on these heathen souls.' He made a sign across his chest with the fingers of one hand while clutching a line of beads that looked like pebbles from the beach.

Here was a man of God showing Maisie a path to safety. She had been fascinated. And so now Maisie and Tommy had their own customs to protect them. Blessing the dead animals they find. Taking fifteen steps sideways after getting injured. Drawing circles in the air before climbing trees. Arranging stones in small piles to ward off bad luck.

Their duty done, they continue foraging for cockles, moving up the beach until the lengthening shadows of the sand dunes tell Maisie it's time to leave. Worried about crossing paths with the unfriendly locals, she takes a circular route home. Sometimes they throw sticks at Maisie, or give chase.

Heaving the half full bucket, the children cross a stretch of mud that is sometimes land, sometimes sea; then they pass a rise of land where a misty view of the mainland appears, and plunge into the darkening forest.

There's just time to check their treasure is safe. Stored in the hollow of a dying copper beech, wrapped in a washed-up rag that looks like it's torn from a sail, Maisie knows the contents by heart, each piece buffed and admired and held to the sun to catch its sparkle. The tooth from a large shark. Five stripy seashells. A giant crab's claw. A collection of pebbles. A copper coin that isn't English. And their favourite: a bright coloured picture, which is possibly a page from a book, that they had rescued as it bobbed along the current last summer. Attracted by the flash of colour, they had waded up to their chests to pluck it from the water before the wind got there first, their feet mashed by stones. It was worth every ounce of pain. There have been other scraps of paper, of course, discarded from ships, swept from lands on the other side of the sea. But nothing like this.

'What d'you think it is?' Tommy asks for the umpteenth time as they remove it from an empty gin bottle, lay the paper on a rock and weight it down with stones, the corners flapping in the breeze like the wings of a flightless bird.

Maisie examines the image. A landscape of a thousand tiny houses forms a sprawling city sliced in half by a river. Yet it's the foreground that captures her heart. A silver circle supports a group of beautiful horses with sticks poking up from their necks – not like the farmer's plough horse, or the muddy wild ponies, or the heavy-hooved drays that pull the beer cart. No, these horses are delicate, painted the colours of a rainbow, protected from the elements by what looks like the top of a patterned tent, out of which rises a gold-and-blue flag flapping in an imaginary breeze.

The writing running across the top could perhaps explain this wonder, but means nothing to two children who can't read a word.

'I don't know but it's pretty,' Maisie whispers, unable to tear her eyes from the scene.

The picture is crumpled, torn along one edge and spotted by black mould, but is also a symbol of hope – imagine if something this glorious were actually to exist in the world?

They roll it up again, stuff it back in the gin bottle for safe-keeping and arrive home seconds before sundown.

Indoors, the air is thick with the reek of gin. In the semi-gloom, Tommy pulls the bucket towards the kitchen table, while Maisie focuses on the opposite corner, as though splitting up makes them a smaller target for the Sixpences, who occupy the only seating – a long platform that turns into their bed – where they lounge, humming whichever tune Mr Sixpence is fiddling.

Of course, Sixpence isn't their real name. Long ago, Maisie heard the new postman call out 'Parcel for Heaton'. But everyone else on Canvey Island knows them as the Sixpences because six pennies are what they charge each month for every orphan and forgotten bastard who is sent away by whatever family they have left to somewhere that is one step up from the workhouse. *So you should count your blessings*, Mrs Sixpence says.

Arriving at the hearthside, Maisie crouches. There's insufficient wood for a proper fire, but, if she's able to coax a few embers in an earthenware pot, they might not freeze to death in their sleep.

The glow from the match brings three toddlers nearer, as well as Tommy, who scoops up the baby to settle him on the floor nearby. Maisie senses danger when the smallest child reaches for the poker. Pinning his hands to his sides, she mouths for him to keep very still. This is a rare interlude of Sixpence contentment that could fracture for the slightest reason. A wrong look. Fidgeting.

At last, when darkness seeps through the crooked window, Mrs Sixpence heaves her bulk up and attends to the gruel, while Maisie's stomach grumbles in anticipation.

When the children are lined up in ascending age order, she's the last to be served, and deserves the biggest helping. But Maisie's bowl is only a quarter full, which is less than even the toddlers received. Mrs Sixpence stares at Maisie with a sneer.

'Your sort can get lazy if you have too much food,' she remarks.

The sort with darker skin than everyone else, Maisie understands her to mean, having heard this sentiment a thousand times before.

Assembling her confidence, she states, 'Thank you, Mrs Sixpence,' in a loud, clear voice, then resumes her place on the dirt floor.

Mrs Sixpence half grunts, half laughs, as though she's seen through to Maisie's disappointment. It takes seconds to wolf down the meagre ration, followed by the usual ache of watching the Sixpences consume second and then third helpings. Finally, Mrs Sixpence lights the stub of a candle and shuffles to the hearthside. All of the children flinch as she looms over them to pluck something from the mantelpiece.

'A letter come while you were out,' she announces to the room in general. 'From your aunt. Says that, due to a change in circumstances, there's space for you after all.'

Maisie has never heard of an aunt, and neither has Tommy, it seems, because they exchange looks as if to say *Which one of us does she mean?* Her heart is pounding. This is the grand prize, what they have all dreamt of since they set foot in here.

Like a miracle falling from the sky, the letter is thrust at Maisie. Breathless with excitement, she stares at the swirls of blue ink on white paper.

'Aren't you going to read it aloud?' Mr Sixpence guffaws, and Mrs Sixpence cackles along.

Maisie doesn't care that they're laughing at her inability to pick out the words. She's leaving them – and soon, with any luck.

'You're a rum one, Maisie. We'll miss your quiet ways,' Mrs Sixpence claims, though it's obvious she'll miss the sixpence each month most of all.

Maisie turns to nudge Tommy, a silent message to ask *Did you hear that woman's nonsense?*, but he's shuffled to face the wall, the baby left on the floor. He's rocking back and forth, his dirty fingernails picking at a patch of bare scalp. Putting the letter aside, she wraps her arms around him. With all her heart, Maisie is desperate to leave this place. At the same time, the thought of being separated from Tommy brings a lump to her throat.

★

Maisie's aunt arrives on a day that smells of smoking pilchards and wet rope. Tommy is at the shoreline, scraping lard from the cauldron when he spots a tall lady picking a careful passage over the mud, one hand clutched to her straw hat as if the sky will fall in if it blows off.

He bounds across the scrub to tell Maisie. Since she got the letter, he hasn't let her out of his sight, as though he worries that she might be whisked away at any moment without a proper goodbye. Maisie feels the same way. For the past week, she's made the most of every second with Tommy, teaching him how to light the fire and pluck cockles and forage for berries on his own, hugging him more than usual when he gets it right. Though he's only a few months younger than her, Tommy has always relied on Maisie.

Together, they watch as the lady almost slips on damp pebbles before righting herself. Maisie knows this can only be her aunt, because no one ventures this far up the estuary path, with the exception of the dock boys in search of iron rivets lost from ships or the wild dogs chased off by Mr Marley, the local farmer.

There is a tightness in her chest. Heat flooding from her head to her limbs makes everything spin. After all those years of hoping, she's minutes away from freedom.

Mrs Sixpence lumbers to join them in the doorway. Her face is a picture, her expression twisting like everything she's ever known is turned upside down.

'Now then,' she says, removing her stained apron. 'If someone had bothered to tell me you had the distinction of being born from a white mother, I would have been a little kinder, given you more food.'

Mrs Sixpence shakes her head, tutting, as though Maisie is to blame for having been ill-treated. But Maisie has lived on Canvey Island for a decade, a lifetime for a twelve-year-old, brought from the mainland on the back of the greengrocer's vegetable cart 'like a lumpy potato', Mr Sixpence enjoys telling everyone – and she possesses not one single memory before then.

It means that she's as surprised as anyone by the appearance of the woman now navigating the path alongside the rocks: a creamy-skinned, golden-haired princess – so unlike Maisie, with her beige complexion and brown hair, that the two don't appear to be related.

Her nerves tingle. All the children at the Sixpences', including Maisie, create imaginary stories about their parents – they are kings and queens of faraway lands, explorers, ballerinas, brave soldiers – but this is her chance to know who her mother and father really are, and why they have left her in this place all these years.

'Your pa must be one of them dark spice traders from the East,' Mrs Sixpence tosses out, bustling to the washstand to prepare herself for refined company.

A desire for justice overcomes Maisie like a storm erupting in her mind. She knows that Mrs Sixpence would like nothing better than to entertain her aunt, offering her stewed prunes on chipped china, so that she can tell Mrs Dalrymple, her sister-in-law from Leigh-on-Sea, of her important, new acquaintance. To deny her foster mother this pleasure, Maisie hugs Tommy and whispers that he can keep all the treasure to himself if he doesn't cry.

As she bolts out of the door, she hears the crash of the copper water jug and swearing.

She skips over the stones near the riverbank and along the row of dark green poplars. Her aunt is as elegant as a silver birch, willowy, with delicate features and a wide smile. Now that she's in front of her, Maisie finds herself holding back, suddenly shy.

'You must be Maisie,' her aunt says, stooping to shake hands. 'I'm your Aunty Mabel and I'm very pleased to meet you.'

The magic of this moment makes everything sparkle. The sun glints. The river gleams. Her aunt's eyes are filled with shining tears as though there's no person more wondrous than Maisie. It's a look she's never seen before.

Shouting in the distance breaks the spell, and they both turn around. Mrs Sixpence has appeared at the mound of fish guts piled near the washing line, shaking her fist. With surprising speed, she lopes across the patch of tall grass and is soon close enough for Maisie to see the grimace on her face.

'Shall we go?' Aunty Mabel asks.

Maisie hears Tommy crying in the distance. She imagines him wanting to run after her, but too frightened of the Sixpences to stray from the shack. There's a wrench in her heart, an urge to race back and rescue him. But Aunty Mabel tugs her hand, and, before she knows it, they are scarpering across the stepping stones that lead to the mainland at low tide, both silent, not stopping even when they're out of breath. In their haste, Aunty Mabel loses her hat to a gust that takes them by surprise at the turn of Mr Marley's farm gate, and she doesn't even try to follow it back down the path.

'There are plenty more hats in this world,' she puffs.

Past the fork in the road, Aunty Mabel helps Maisie into a waiting carriage. As the driver cracks his whip to encourage the four white horses to set off, the knot in Maisie's stomach uncoils. She is safe. No one can take her back now.

Aunty Mabel's smile returns, and she wears the same expression as before, like Maisie is the most interesting person in the world. It helps Maisie to lose her shyness.

'Where are we going?' she asks.

'To Jesserton.'

Maisie opens her mouth to ask what Jesserton means, and whether her parents will be there. But an uncomfortable prickle that the answer might not be what she wants to hear encourages her to hold her tongue.

Pressing her nose to the window, she soaks in the patchwork landscape of corn fields streaming past, tiny villages with smoke curling from chimneys, dark green forests merging into the distance. With each circle of the carriage wheels, everything she's ever known is left further and further behind.

Dusk is descending like mist by the time the carriage pulls on to a long gravel driveway, at the end of which the tallest, widest residence she's ever seen rises like a giant sandcastle on rolling countryside. A cosy cottage is what Maisie was expecting, not a building a hundred times larger than the tavern on Canvey Island.

'This is Jesserton. I've a new position as head housekeeper,' Aunty Mabel says, as though that explains everything. 'Welcome to your new home, Maisie.'

3

Seven chimes reverberate through the walls and all the way up to the tiny attic room with its sloping ceiling and postcard-sized window, where Maisie is making her bed, smoothing the blankets and plumping her pillow. This is the signal to find her way downstairs.

Jesserton is a maze of dark corridors lined with portraits of stern-faced dead people. The ancestors. They observe Maisie descend the staircase and take two wrong turns before locating the central corridor. Passing two maids and a footman who all fail to return her greeting, she finds her aunt in the large linen room on the ground floor, where the air is filled with the perfumed scent of bedding stacked floor to ceiling on oak shelves.

There is so much washing in this house. Washing clothes. Washing skin. Maisie suspects that Tommy wouldn't recognize her scrubbed clean, and with straight hair as soft as cotton-grass. Then there are the almost new hand-me-downs from Miss Catherine, the daughter of Sir Malcolm, Jesserton's owner, the thick cotton hanging snugger than it did in her first few days thanks to the regular mealtimes.

Aunty Mabel looks up at Maisie and smiles. Maisie's heart leaps. Being in her aunt's presence is like bathing in warm sunshine after years of winter.

'Let's get your hair tidied first,' Aunty Mabel says. 'Then we can make a start on the darning before morning inspection.'

Maisie has learnt that this is when nine chimes ring through the house. In her four months here, Maisie has become familiar with the new routine. Ten chimes – the coal man arrives. One chime – soup and buttered buns. Four chimes – afternoon tea for the grown-ups, a glass of milk and three biscuits for Maisie. Six chimes – supper alone in her loft room. Eight chimes – Maisie prays to the Lord of the Water before Aunty Mabel arrives to tuck her in for the night. For all the pretence that Sir Malcolm Randolph is the master of Jesserton, Maisie believes that the mahogany-and-brass grandfather clock in the entrance hallway holds the real power.

Maisie kneels in front of the stool on which Aunty Mabel is perched. Closing her eyes, she imagines that it's her mother now combing through her hair. Though she's very fond of the woman who rescued her from the Sixpences, an aunt isn't the same. There's been no sign of either parent since her arrival at Jesserton, however, and no explanation from Aunty Mabel, despite Maisie's questions. All she's learnt is that her mother's name is Eliza, along with a handful of anecdotes about the five Marlowe siblings growing up in a small flat above their parents' haberdashery shop in Chelmsford.

Maisie keeps quiet because her aunt has a tendency to share stories when they sit like this. Sure enough, she soon begins to talk.

'It's funny, your hair is the exact same texture as your mother's at that age,' Aunty Mabel observes, plaiting. 'Although much darker. As is mine, you might be surprised to hear. Eliza always was the blondest of us all.'

Maisie's eyes snap open, her pulse races. Any details she uncovers are precious, and quickly stored in her heart.

'Is she as pretty as you, Aunty Mabel?' she asks, hoping to build a clearer picture of her mother.

She feels her aunt's fingers freeze.

'Looks aren't everything, Maisie. A person's character counts for more,' is the brisk reply.

'Then is she a nice person?' Maisie persists.

Aunty Mabel clears her throat.

'What sort of question is that?' she responds as she ties a ribbon to secure the plait. 'There, all done.' She kisses the top of Maisie's head, as though this signals the end of the subject. 'Now let's get started on our work.'

Maisie is left wanting more, as usual. But she knows from experience that she will have to wait until Aunty Mabel is in the mood to talk about her mother again. She follows her aunt to the shelves, where they run their fingers over sheets, looking for nicks and tears and either refolding the piece of fabric or setting it aside in a pile. Outside, the rhythmic *thud, thud, thud* of the gardeners constructing a protective fence around the vegetable patch provides a soothing backdrop.

Her mind drifts to Tommy. She can't remember a time before him. A time when they weren't exploring Canvey together, or huddling together at night, or helping each other scrub barnacles off the boat, or untangling fishing nets, or foraging for food. Sometimes she catches herself talking to him out loud as if he's here. 'Look, Tommy, I've got a real bed' or 'I found this kingfisher feather in the garden.' But he isn't here. He's by himself now, and the thought makes her heart hurt.

Presently, the clock chimes eight times and the pile is waist high. Aunty Mabel removes a needle and bobbin of cotton from a wicker basket and shows Maisie the technique of threading.

'If we finish this task by lunchtime, I've got a special treat for you this afternoon,' she says, her eyes gleaming with mischief. 'The cook saw her sister in Clacton yesterday, and it's the last day the funfair is there before it heads to Margate,' Aunty Mabel continues. 'Sir Malcolm has given us special permission to go. Isn't that kind?'

Maisie nods, though, never having heard of a funfair, she has no idea whether this is a kind gesture by Sir Malcolm or not. Jesserton's owner is a distant figure who spends most of his days alone in the study. Nevertheless, he always takes the time to ask Maisie how she's getting on in her new home, listening to her answers with a caring expression, on the rare occasions they come face to face.

Seeming to pick up on Maisie's uncertainty, Aunty Mabel gives a gentle smile. 'Your mum always loved the funfair as a child. We both did.'

'Then couldn't she come with us today?' Maisie counters, pouncing on the opportunity to reopen her favourite topic.

Her heart beats extra fast as Aunty Mabel's smile falls away. 'Well . . . it's not . . . it's just . . .'

Staring at her hands, Aunty Mabel lapses into silence. Maisie hesitates for an extended moment; her aunt's reaction is beginning to magnify the niggling sense that she might not like the answer to her most burning question.

'Where's my mum now?' Maisie pushes out the words she's repeated many times over since coming here. 'And what do you know about my dad?'

Aunty Mabel looks up slowly. 'It's a long story,' she responds after a pause. 'I know you keep asking because you want to learn everything, and I will explain – but when you're a bit older, so you can understand.'

This is the same answer as every time before. Later. Another day. Not now. Maisie's face flushes red. Clearly noticing, Aunty Mabel lays down the darning to wrap her arms around her niece.

'I'm sorry your mum isn't around. She would be here if she could. And I'm sorry it took me so long to collect you. It's not that I didn't want you, because I did.' Aunty Mabel strokes Maisie's arm. 'But my husband, Bertie, thought different. He cares too much what other people think when he oughtn't. We're apart now, and I've built myself a new life. A bright future for us both.'

Maisie hugs her aunt. It goes without saying that she's grateful for this bright future. At the same time, the lack of information troubles her like a splinter under the skin.

The odour of burnt sugar. Loud, cheerful music. Yellows and pinks and scarlets and greens. Maisie feels like she's lying amongst spinning wildflowers, their perfumed petals closing in.

'Do you like the funfair?' Aunty Mabel is smiling, watching Maisie's eyes grow rounder. Maisie nods, overcome. 'Well, we decided you should receive a monthly allowance. You might as well spend it here.'

Aunty Mabel presses eight copper pennies into Maisie's palm. This is more money than she's ever seen, a greater sum than Mrs Sixpence receives in a month for each of her charges. Before Maisie can recover her wits to thank Aunty Mabel, Sir Malcolm speaks.

'I suggest we adults tour the promenade and leave the children to explore the stalls. We can rendezvous back here in one hour and enjoy the rides together.'

When Aunty Mabel had suggested an outing, Maisie assumed she meant just the two of them. But here they are, accompanied by Sir Malcolm and Miss Catherine.

'As you wish, Sir Malcolm,' Aunty Mabel answers, smoothing her pretty, blue dress. She's smiling, but Maisie can't help but notice that there's a slightly strained look to her face, as though she's in physical discomfort.

Maisie wants to tell her aunt to stay here, but she is already disappearing with Sir Malcolm, arms linked. Suddenly finding herself alone with Miss Catherine, Maisie is struck by a bout of coyness. While her own time is taken up by household tasks, the older girl spends every day with a governess or reading alone in the library, her dark blonde hair draped over a book. The two have enjoyed limited interaction thus far – a quick greeting if they happen to pass on the stairs or smiling at one another in church from opposite ends of the pew.

'I thought we might try hoopla first, then you can choose your favourite,' Miss Catherine proposes, breaking the silence.

The older girl must know that Maisie would not have had the chance to form a favourite but is too kind to say. Grateful, Maisie smiles. 'Good idea.'

By the time they've won a bag of sweets on the hoopla, then wasted a penny each on the coconut shy, Maisie feels comfortable with Miss Catherine. Nice in a quiet sort of way, she seems quite taken with the stories about Canvey Island, encouraging Maisie with her smile and clapping in delight at Maisie's retelling of the bold escape with Aunty Mabel. They pass amusement after amusement, lost in non-stop chatter. When Miss Catherine asks what Maisie wants to do when she grows up, however, there's a long pause; survival was the main preoccupation of her previous life. Managing to eat enough, keep warm and dry, avoid the Sixpences in order to live another day.

'I haven't thought about it,' Maisie answers eventually. 'What about you?'

'A crime novelist,' Miss Catherine replies without hesitation. 'I want to write stories about a lady detective who solves murder mysteries. The female answer to Sherlock Holmes.'

Maisie keeps quiet. No one at Jesserton, not even Aunty Mabel, has guessed the shameful secret that Maisie can't read, let alone write, and she prefers to keep it that way.

'I'm glad you've come to Jesserton, Maisie,' Miss Catherine says with warmth, as though she means it. 'Since my mother died, the house has seemed terribly empty.'

Maisie feels a growing kinship with Miss Catherine. Despite their different starts in life, they have the absence of a mother in common.

They are passing a red-and-white tent when Miss Catherine stops partway through an explanation of where to find the strawberry bushes at Jesserton. Maisie notices irritation pinching the older girl's face as she stares at a gang of mid-teen boys some way off. Pointing at passing ladies, they laugh uproariously. To Maisie's surprise, the tallest boy waves at them.

Miss Catherine pulls Maisie towards the tent.

'My annoying cousin, James,' she explains. 'His school term won't have started yet. Let's wait in here and hope they go away. We can watch the show.'

Inside the tent, a circle of light bathes a vacant chair, above which is a large, painted sign. Ten rows of benches crammed with paying customers are arranged in a semicircle. Miss Catherine leads them to an empty place in the third row. There isn't long to wait before loud applause erupts. Through the spectators, Maisie can only just make out the figure of a wide-hipped woman approaching the chair, with her back to the crowd.

'Lift up your skirts, love, and show us if your other beard is just as long,' a man in the audience shouts, standing up to bow as everyone roars with laughter.

The lady ignores him as she settles on the chair. Her spine straightens and she removes a handkerchief that Maisie can now see has been covering her lower face.

There's a collective gasp, and someone shrieks. The woman holds still, unflinching as everyone stares. Maisie is spellbound. There she is: a lady with a thick, brown beard down to her chest, gazing out with cat-shaped eyes.

By the time they leave the tent, Maisie has seen the double-headed serpent man, a leopard woman, Siamese twins from Russia, and she doesn't quite know what to think.

'Looks like she should be in the freak show with the others.'

Maisie looks over to where the voice originates. A freckly boy in a straw boater – part of the rowdy group from earlier – is pointing at her while his friends snigger.

'Dirty little scum,' he spits. Malice glints like sharpened knives in eyes that are locked on to Maisie.

But I washed this morning, she says to herself. Without thinking, Maisie touches her face to check. The boys jeer, nudge one another.

'That's not going to help your dirty, scummy skin,' a second boy scoffs.

Like mist clearing, the truth dawns on Maisie. They mean her complexion. She feels sick to her stomach. Having noticed the side-ways glances from the crowd this afternoon, she was too absorbed in the fun of this place to grasp that it's because hers stands out as the one dark face in a sea of paleness. It's exactly how she was treated by everyone on Canvey Island, apart from Tommy.

The next thing she knows, Miss Catherine rushes forward to spread her hands on the freckled boy's chest and drive him backwards. 'You ought to know better, Edward,' she says with surprising forcefulness.

Maisie could hug her new friend for sticking up for her. James rolls his eyes as though he can't see what the fuss is about.

'It was just a bit of harmless fun, Catherine.' He breaks off from his friends, watching as they head towards the dodgems. 'Boys just trying to get the attention of a pretty girl.'

He redirects his stare at Maisie. The way his bright blue eyes take her in makes her tingle uncomfortably and she looks away. That's when she sees it.

In the corner of her eye, an object of unparalleled wonder appears: a circle of horses rotates like a spinning top, galloping to nowhere.

Some soar in the air and come down again. Others edge forward. She pinches herself. There's no waving flag, the colours aren't exactly the same, but, yes, this dazzling ride is remarkably similar to the picture she and Tommy found on Canvey Island. If only she could rush back and tell him that such a wonder really exists.

'What's that?' Maisie asks, so overcome with awe that she isn't sure if she spoke out loud.

Miss Catherine follows her gaze.

'The sign says THE SAVAGE FACTORY'S OLDE ENGLAND CAROUSEL.'

A carousel. The word has the taste of mystery, of faraway places. Transfixed, Maisie is unable to tear her eyes from its beauty. Drawn closer, she pushes past dawdlers, not caring about the buzz, the chaos of crowds, even forgetting the recent incident with the boys. She's walking in a dream, a dream that is real.

'Would you like a ride?'

Aunty Mabel is back, her cheeks glowing the colour of the heart-shaped ruby brooch she's wearing. Coughing, she produces a lace handkerchief and wipes her nose.

'Yes,' is all Maisie is able to say.

'Let's all have a turn,' Sir Malcolm declares as if he too is enraptured. 'You as well, James. What a coincidence to find you here.'

James shakes hands with Sir Malcolm. 'Yes, Uncle. It was a bit of luck that Catherine and I bumped into one another.'

Maisie notes Miss Catherine making a face.

They wait for the ride to slow and the current riders to dismount, then choose their mounts. Picking the most beautiful is difficult: the ginger horse with the yellow mane or one that is striped purple and pink? But there's shoving and a panicked rush; both those horses are quickly taken; and Maisie worries that if she's too slow there will be none left. Miss Catherine is already sitting on a dark cream stallion, next to which is a dainty, pale brown pony. Yes, this is a good choice. She plants one boot on the footrest, swings the other leg over, sits in the saddle. Gripping the brass pole, Maisie pats and strokes the painted coat. Magical.

'Giddy-up, boy, or you'll end up down the knacker's yard,' James jests from the other side of Miss Catherine.

In the row behind, Aunty Mabel and even Sir Malcolm laugh. Maisie has an inkling that it isn't normal for a master of the house to mix with staff like this, but she's too excited to pay further attention to it. There's a gentle hum, a vibration up her spine. They're moving, slowly at first, then speeding up. Her hands tremble as she feels the lift of the pole, the sensation of rising and surging forward, the sea breeze streaming past her face.

Rising, falling, rising again, she whips past the group of waving spectators, a view of the pier, dodgems, then her eyes return to the spectators.

She couldn't imagine anything better than sneaking off with Tommy in Mr Sixpence's boat, or pelting over the flats from Canvey Island with Aunty Mabel, or riding in Sir Malcolm's carriage with her face stuck out of the window. Until now.

Too soon, the ride slows, jerks to a stop. Maisie is breathless, her cheeks flushed. If she could remain here for a second, third, fourth turn, she would, but the others are already clambering off. With a final pat of her horse, she reluctantly dismounts.

On the way home in the carriage, she is jubilant. There's talk of Maisie spending more time with Miss Catherine and even becoming her companion now it's been shown that the two girls get along.

Leaning in, Aunty Mabel whispers, 'And let's ask the governess to help you with your reading.' She says this with eyes so full of affection that Maisie thanks her lucky stars she's ended up at Jesserton.

As they enter the house, Aunty Mabel coughs violently, then stumbles as if her knees have turned to blancmange, knocking over the vase of chrysanthemums on the console table. Her cheeks are beetroot red now, a colour so unnatural that Maisie can't help staring. Sir Malcolm calls for one of the maids to clear up the mess while Aunty Mabel composes herself, tells everyone not to fuss and retires to her bedroom for a lie-down.

Maisie herself feels the beginnings of a sore throat and struggles to swallow her supper. After eating, there's just time to creep to the bathroom and turn on the taps. She pours bath salts under running water. and soon fragrant lemon steam clouds the room. Usually, Maisie would perform her evening ritual to ward off bad omens while she waited for the tub to fill, arranging a handful of dark and light stones from the gravel driveway on her bedroom windowsill. But she is tired tonight. Besides, after a such a glorious day, she can't imagine that anything bad will happen in this fancy house. For the first time in her life, she feels safe, protected.

Undressing, she clambers into the tub. Her body aches as she uses the scrubbing brush to remove every speck of dirt. Scrub, scrub, scrub, until her skin glows. But once the redness fades, she's still left looking beige.

Dressed in her nightgown, Maisie sits on her bed, waiting to have her hair brushed. Her face begins to feel burning hot. It grows dark outside, owls hooting from the branches of the sycamores, ten chimes of the grandfather clock, and still Aunty Mabel has failed to turn up.

4

The scarlet fever creeps across England like a thief in the night, stealing babies from mothers, husbands from wives, friends from one another. For three weeks, Maisie drifts in and out of consciousness, haunted by strange images of the ancestors climbing out of their portraits and dancing in her room. Her only visitors are faceless people wearing masks made of handkerchiefs who bring food and water, provide bed pans. Even Aunty Mabel stays away.

One day, a stout gentleman in a dark suit arrives to peer down her throat.

'You're in the clear,' he announces, and departs the bedroom.

Quarantined alone for so long, Maisie is bursting to see everyone, but she waits until seven chimes of the clock. Her limbs weakened, she battles to bathe and dress herself, yet the effort is worth it to feel cleansed of the illness. Clutching the banister, she takes each flight of stairs carefully, resting between floors. Even so, her legs are shaking by the time she reaches the entrance hall.

A thick film of dust covering the antique console table is the first sign that something is amiss. Uncertain where anyone is, she follows the sounds of the household along another corridor.

Two footmen hurry past, laden with tall piles of sheets.

'I wouldn't go that way if I were you,' one of them advises without stopping.

Not heeding the warning, Maisie continues, using the wall to support her weight. There's a moaning noise, as if an injured animal has found its way indoors. Alarmed, Maisie peeks through the doorway of a room she now remembers is the library.

Sir Malcolm is sitting in a leather armchair, his body convulsing as he sobs. His sandy hair is in upright tufts, his chin unshaven. The sight is so startling that Maisie can't pull herself away.

'This way.'

A person Maisie recognizes as Miss Catherine's governess beckons her to the music room, which hosts an upright piano topped by a vase of wilted flowers. Curled petals spill on to the dusty rug. Maisie has never seen such dishevelment in this grand house, and she can't understand why Aunty Mabel has let the usual standards drop. The governess's hair is flowing, she now notices, free of its usual tight bun, and stains adorn her blouse. Maisie wonders if she's seeing a trick of the fever.

The governess avoids eye contact. 'I'm sorry to tell you this, but Miss Catherine went five days ago, and Mabel the night after.' She sighs. 'They were buried at St Margaret's yesterday morning.'

Slammed by a rush of dizziness, Maisie slumps on the piano stool, her head between her hands. She thinks of the squirrel caught in the poacher's trap, the young deer in the forest. Both dead. Like Aunty Mabel and Miss Catherine.

It can't be real. The funfair was less than a month ago with everyone returning in high spirits, planning the future. What about Miss Catherine's novels about the lady detective?

Maisie bitterly regrets not having laid out the good-luck stones when they returned from the funfair that evening. Look what happens when her guard is lowered.

Dear Lord of the Water, please bless their souls.

She feels a comforting tap on her shoulder, then hears the governess leave the room.

For a while, Maisie is still, numbed like a rose that bloomed too early, frozen by the frost on a winter's morning. Eventually, she's able to sit up without the room spinning. Lady Lydia smiles down from her portrait above the fireplace with the same kind eyes as her daughter, Miss Catherine. Her expression is like a beam of light thawing Maisie's heart. Hot tears stain her cheeks. Gentle Miss Catherine, who had never harmed a soul, didn't deserve to die. Neither did Aunty Mabel.

Trembling, Maisie remembers the first time she ever saw her aunt, holding on to her hat, with her face set in determination. It's difficult to believe that she'll never see Aunty Mabel's smile again, never hear her laugh like a lark at sunrise, never hold or be held by her aunt. Never be held by anyone in this great, big house.

With a fright, Maisie comprehends that she's all alone here, having been brought to Jesserton by a woman who now lies cold in the ground. Rising panic overpowers the sadness. What's going to happen to her now?

Maisie quickly works out that her fate lies in Sir Malcolm's hands. Lost, she spends her days in limbo, sitting on her bed and brooding on what lies ahead for her now. Only venturing downstairs to eat, she takes great care to avoid being noticed by the servants. 'That girl is cursed, like all them half-castes,' she overheard them agree amongst themselves on the first evening without her guardian. Before, she believed she was welcome here, had found somewhere she belonged, at last. But it now occurs to Maisie that the staff have always kept their distance from her, and Aunty Mabel was shielding her from the same hostility she's faced throughout her life. Jesserton was never really her home, she understands with an ache like a punch in the gut. It isn't safe, and she's no longer protected.

The alternatives are even more frightening. Maisie worries that she'll be banished to the workhouse or forced to return to Canvey and the Sixpences. She can't decide which is worse. Though a reunion with dear Tommy would be joyous, Maisie isn't sure she could survive the beatings or starvation after experiencing the gentleness of a life with her aunt. She briefly contemplates running off to find her parents, but has no idea how or where to even begin looking for them.

When a footman informs Maisie one week later that Sir Malcolm wishes to see her, a sense of trepidation makes her stomach somersault. She follows the liveried man to the first floor, her palms moistening. As he indicates a doorway, then departs, she wipes her hands on her skirts.

Maisie steps into a spacious room that smells of cigars. She's never been allowed in here before, never seen the fineness of the patterned rug nor the bright paintings that are nothing like the dull portraits of the ancestors. Sir Malcolm is sitting at a wide desk, writing. They've had no interactions since she saw him sobbing in the library, and Maisie can't extinguish the image from her mind.

'Has the governess commenced your studies?' he enquires without looking up.

His vowels are rounded, his *t*'s like stones hitting glass.

She feels it best for everyone not to tell on the woman. 'Yes, sir.'

'Good,' he replies.

He lays down his pen, reaches for a tumbler containing an amber-coloured liquid and downs it in one. His eyes search the room and alight on a decanter containing the same kind of drink. He stands and goes to pour himself another glass.

'My brother, Hugo, lives in America, and I'll join him there. I'm selling Jesserton. Some rich Californian made me an offer I couldn't refuse. I leave in ten days.'

Maisie's eyes flick up briefly to see if he's joking. But he seems deadly serious, no trace of a smile appearing. With Sir Malcolm leaving, and so soon, her own departure from Jesserton is probably imminent. A fresh wave of fear makes her heart skip a beat.

'So will you join me?' he asks, his expression impossible to read.

He puts the proposition in such a casual manner, like he's asking if Maisie minds passing him the letter opener, that it takes several seconds before she understands that Sir Malcolm is offering her the chance to accompany him.

She is reeling. 'To America?' she blurts, wondering if everyone in the household has been asked.

'You're Mabel's niece, and I promised her I would take good care of you.'

Maisie's mind swirls while Sir Malcolm taps the rim of his glass, clearly expecting some sort of reply.

'I –'

'This is a big decision, I understand, and we can make other arrangements for you should you prefer to remain in England.'

Maisie dreads to think what other arrangements he means.

He hasn't mentioned Miss Catherine, but it's obvious from the dark circles under his eyes that the loss of his daughter weighs heavy on Sir Malcolm. If he wishes it were Catherine standing here instead of Maisie, he doesn't show it, though she wouldn't have blamed him. Didn't she secretly want it to be her mother rather than Aunty Mabel who brushed her hair every morning?

A thought crosses her mind.

'Shouldn't we tell my parents, Sir Malcolm? They might want to know what's happened.'

Or be able to provide a home for Maisie, she refrains from saying, in case she appears ungrateful.

Sir Malcolm's eyebrows shoot up. He opens his mouth, closes it, opens it again, like a goldfish offered as a prize at the hoopla stall.

'Do you know where they are?' she continues, desperate to learn something. 'Or anything about them?'

Sir Malcolm takes a gulp of his drink.

'Your aunt never shared any details, I'm afraid,' he responds in a tone of regret. 'All I'm aware of is that it won't be possible to inform them of anything. I wish it were.'

His eyes are filled with a look of such sympathy for her that Maisie is hit by a sudden realization. The clues were there, and part of her always knew: Aunty Mabel choking up whenever she talked about Eliza; why her aunt and not one of her parents, collected Maisie; the mystery of their whereabouts. *She would be here, if she could.*

Her mother and father are dead.

It feels like the ground is giving way. Maisie clutches the edge of the desk to keep from sinking to the floor. A tightness in her chest makes it difficult to breathe. She is all alone in the world, helpless like a piece of driftwood at the mercy of the currents. It now falls to Maisie to safeguard her own future. To find a protector.

As tears threaten to spill out, she squeezes her fists and swallows down her feelings, placing them in an imaginary bottle, like the picture she left behind with Tommy.

'Then thank you for the invitation, Sir Malcolm,' she replies in a shaky voice. 'I would very much like to go with you.'

He sets down his glass.

'America will be good for us, Maisie,' he reassures her before moving back to the desk to resume writing. 'Besides, I need to get away.'

Maisie is still awake as dawn streams through the window. Realizing that sleep is impossible, she dresses and creeps outside to say good-bye to Jesserton. This is her last day here. Her last day in England.

Skies tinged purple and pink mirror the colours of the flower-beds – lavender, trailing roses, rhododendrons, wisteria – a snapshot of England she knows she will miss. Maisie imagines a vast land-scape of craggy mountains and bone-dry deserts is awaiting her, with the only plants spiky cacti that grow tall enough for outlaws to hide behind, based on what she's overheard the servants say this past week. Not that any of them have ever seen America for them-selves, or will do so any time soon. It transpires that Maisie is, in fact, the sole person from Jesserton honoured with an invitation. A question stirs at the margins of her mind. Why just her, and none of the others?

Passing the pond and cluster of mulberry bushes, she follows the path to the weeping willow that drapes like a fainting lady in a quiet corner of the grounds. She sits with her back leaning against the trunk and stares up at morning sunlight seeping through an interwoven pattern of green.

A face peering through the trailing canopy of leaves gives her a start. It takes a moment to recognize James.

'Sir Malcolm summoned me,' he explains. 'He wanted to say goodbye, in person. I arrived last night.'

As he sits beside her without an invitation, Maisie remembers Miss Catherine's disdain for her cousin and she feels herself shrink-ing away from him. Up close, he's wider and looks older than she recalls, with a trace of blond stubble on his cheeks.

He drills into Maisie with his blue eyes. 'So where does his departure leave you?' he probes. 'Are you staying on here?'

It's obvious that James has no idea that Maisie is leaving with Sir Malcolm. Made uneasy by the intense expression on his face, she decides not to set him straight.

'I came from Canvey, so I might go back,' she lies.

He considers her answer for a second. 'Perhaps I could come to visit you there,' he suggests.

She stares at him. Why would she want that? Why would he? Before she understands what's happening, James's mouth is jammed on her own. She tastes coffee, feels his breath on her face. Using the full force of her disgust, Maisie shoves him away. Leaping to her feet, she strides towards the house.

'I'll have you one day, Maisie,' he calls after her, laughing.

You will not, Maisie resolves. Soon, she will be living on the other side of the ocean, far away from him, away from this house, which has lost its fairytale-like quality. As she catches sight of the luggage being loaded on to the carriages, Maisie knows she is ready to move on.

Steaming Ahead

5

Paris, France, July 1914

Laurent walks along Rue de l'Université, passing the Palais Bourbon, and enters a four-storey, double-fronted establishment with a pair of potted olive trees outside the front door. He would prefer to be heading home to see Amélie before her bedtime, especially since he is visiting Le Havre tomorrow and will probably return late again. But he has been summoned for a meeting this evening.

Nodding to a silver-haired man behind the reception desk, he ascends a grand staircase and reaches a dimly lit hallway, which takes him to an enormous room filled with oil paintings of military vessels, where scores of gentlemen sit huddled in small groups, talking and drinking and smoking. In the very far corner, sprawled on a green leather couch, is a rotund man with a bushy beard and greyish complexion. It is not for nothing that Laurent's father is referred to as 'the beast' by his fellow politicians.

'What's all this Claude has been telling me about your arriving late for the Cloutier execution?' he asks before Laurent has a chance to sit down. 'It looked most unprofessional, apparently.'

Monsieur Charles Augustin Bisset is referring to the Chief Inspector, with whom, most naturally, he is on first-name terms. Laurent takes a seat on a springy velvet armchair.

'Not to worry, Father, I was there for the main event,' he replies, refusing to rise to the bait. 'The most important thing is that I managed to secure the conviction in the first place.' He notes his father's eyes drift around the room. 'And my promotion. It's official now, by the way,' he adds, hoping that this might earn the man's attention, and a modicum of praise.

Monsieur Bisset gives a dismissive wave of his hand as his focus snaps back to Laurent.

'You should be Chief Inspector yourself by now,' he states. 'Honestly, Laurent, I had hoped that you would take your work more seriously.' Monsieur Bisset curls his lip. 'You get this flightiness from your mother, of course. Geneviève once spent a full month going on about traversing the world in a hot-air balloon. It was all poppycock, as usual.'

Laurent grips the armrests. He is saved from making a scene by the appearance of a stick-thin individual who shakes hands with his father. Laurent is introduced to Monsieur Varenne, and is then promptly ignored as the pair discuss the upcoming vote on the increasingly serious situation in Europe. The gentlemen's club sits a stone's throw from the centre of political life, and Laurent is accustomed to these interruptions.

After several minutes, it seems that an agreement is reached, because Monsieur Varenne wanders away with a satisfied look on his face.

'And what does that wife of yours think of you not living up to your potential?' his father continues, picking up where he left off.

'Odette is satisfied with her life,' he answers through gritted teeth.

Of this, Laurent is uncertain. During their courtship and in the months after their honeymoon, Odette's face lit up whenever she saw him, but now there is a constant tension to her expression, as if the marriage has not lived up to her expectations either.

'Hmph,' his father retorts sceptically. 'To be honest, Laurent, I don't know why you chose such a mousy creature. It's not like she has money or a title. You would have been better off remaining unmarried, in my opinion.'

Evidently, the man has a selective memory. Laurent was sitting in this very seat when he was told in no uncertain terms that his wayward bachelor days were an embarrassment to his father, and that he was to pull himself together and settle down. 'Cast out your net and see what you can get' was the command.

The words might not have packed such a punch without

Monsieur Bisset's parting disclosure: his doctor had diagnosed him with heart disease, and it was imperative that he was provided with a grandchild by his only offspring. Laurent already felt shame that he had let down one parent. He couldn't face failing his father as well.

When Odette arrived to start a job at the police station that same week, her eyes soon filled with adoration for the charming, popular Sergeant Bisset. The timing could not have been more perfect. And Laurent really did believe that the burgeoning fondness he felt for the quiet, easy-going receptionist with her shy smile would be the glue to hold them together.

Three years later, his father remains in fine fettle, and Laurent is beginning to question this line of thinking. Guilt prickles him; it is not his wife's fault that the deepest emotion he is able to feel for a woman is fondness.

He stands up, seething. 'Odette is always nice to you, Father,' he answers. 'And Amélie is fine. I shall tell her that Grandpapa sends his love.'

His father rolls his eyes.

'Before you go off in one of your huffs, there was a particular reason I asked you here.' His father indicates the armchair, but Laurent remains standing. 'I know you've turned down club membership before, but it would be good for your career to reconsider.' Monsieur Bisset rests his hands on his vast stomach. 'Meeting Claude in these more relaxed surroundings, as equals, gives you a chance to persuade him that you are not as mercurial as you come across.'

In this moment, Laurent does not know why he expected the conversation with his father to be any different.

He is still brooding the next afternoon as he arrives at the port of Le Havre and strides up the *SS La Touraine*'s gangplank.

'The wind is in our favour,' Captain Lavigne tells him. 'Though your cargo has given us some trouble. It's bigger than we're used to, heavy too. You sure you don't want it to stay here?'

Shaking away all thoughts of his father, Laurent nods. 'Quite sure, thank you.'

It took several days to devise this plan, and he has no intention of backing down now. Victor's assets are being sold off by the French state. Through his seniority at the precinct, Laurent has taken charge of the carousel – the most valuable item – to ensure that it fetches the best possible price.

Taking care that no one else is watching, Laurent reaches into his jacket pocket to retrieve a letter to Mr Fraser, the owner of the auction house, who will be dealing with the sale. Detailed instructions are included on how to skim off a portion of the proceeds, which are to be sent directly to Laurent himself. It is not ideal, but the thought of young Henri Cloutier receiving not one single franc is too much for Laurent to accept. And the risk of being caught is minimal if Mr Fraser does exactly as instructed.

'I'll see he gets it,' Captain Lavigne winks, accepting Laurent's ten-franc note.

As he returns to dry land and watches the ship depart, Laurent is afflicted by an uncomfortable sensation. It is too late for second thoughts – but what if his plan backfires?

6

Chicago, Illinois, August 1914

'Pardon me, ma'am.'

A middle-aged gentleman lifts his hat while he reviews Maisie from under thick black eyelashes. He is smiling, his teeth gleaming in a face that is darker than her own, dark like so many here.

Alighting from the *RMS Oceanic* on her arrival in America four years ago had been a revelation to Maisie. There was the towering goddess of New York with her flame held aloft in welcome; the city rising heavenwards; the noise and hustle at the port, passengers pouring like ants from the huge hulks of ships; languages from all over the world; the smell of steam and sugar-coated peanuts. But nothing beat the sight of varying degrees of brown skin. Tan and ebony, bronze and sand.

The surprises had continued. Far from being the land of barren deserts she was expecting, the journey by train from the east coast to Chicago offered a view of evergreen forests and rolling prairies, interspersed with thriving towns. Then there was her new home. Maisie took to it at first sight. A colonial-style residence situated on a large estate on the eastern borders of the city, Fairweather House is filled with light, and the scent of apple and cherry blossom or the earthy richness of fallen leaves, depending on the season.

Admittedly, living in close quarters with a man she barely knew took some getting used to. Sir Malcolm was probably equally discomfited to find himself responsible for the welfare of his dead housekeeper's orphaned niece. They have never talked about the subject, but it didn't take long for Maisie to work out that her new guardian was almost certainly entangled in some sort of romance with her aunt. It explains their friendliness at the funfair, why

Maisie was allowed to live at Jesserton, why she alone was favoured with an invitation to America, and assigned a governess here.

How different her life would have been if not for the good fortune of being taken in by this generous man. He treats Maisie well, provides her with a home, food, even continuing the monthly allowance that Aunty Mabel started. Most likely she would have been an illiterate pauper living on the streets by now, scraping a paltry living harvesting cockles or scrubbing floors, had he not helped – assuming that she'd survived. And yet knowing her position is based entirely on Sir Malcolm's feelings for her aunt makes it seem all the more tenuous.

It makes Maisie careful and as watchful as she was at the Sixpences', always doing as she's told, agreeing to Sir Malcolm's requests, such as accompanying him here to the station today when she would rather be at home.

'Hugo says Nancy has bought up half of New York, so it's all hands on deck,' were his exact words after he received a telephone call from his brother requesting assistance with the transportation of a large quantity of his wife's luggage.

She spots the back of Sir Malcolm's head through the crowd. Chicago's Grand Central Station is swamped, and Maisie became separated from him after being shoved aside by a family of five rushing for a train. Everyone is impatient here, she finds, always in a hurry to reach somewhere else.

'Excuse me, please,' she says to the middle-aged gentleman.

His gaze is latched on to Maisie. She turns around, aware that he's still watching as she elbows a path away from him.

The fragrance of fried onions from the hotdog stand follows Maisie as she struggles through the thousands of passengers milling about. Sidestepping a pile of luggage, she narrowly avoids colliding with a porter pushing a cart piled high with leather suitcases.

She is about to catch up with Sir Malcolm on platforms 5 and 6 when it happens: one second, their lives are progressing in a certain direction; the next everything changes, as though fate's hand slips on the tiller.

Two burly station hands are manoeuvring a large wooden crate from the freight train alongside Platform 5, grunting with the strain. Swinging like a pendulum on a series of ropes, it needs steadying by another couple of men, who rush over. Together, they begin lowering the load, then leap back as the base of the crate collapses under its own weight. There's an almighty crash. Sir Malcom and Maisie dive aside just in time to avoid being knocked out by a large object hurtling to the ground.

Sir Malcolm's face turns puce, his eyes bulging. 'Does no one know how to do their job around here?'

Nudging each other, one of the station hands is pushed forwards.

'Sorry, fella, I'll just be taking this here out of your way,' he says in a broad Irish accent.

As the man tugs the bundle, the protective wrapping rips at one corner. Underneath the dull exterior of burlap, canary yellow bursts through like sunshine. The rip extends and tears away a large chunk of the covering to reveal something so unexpected that at first Maisie thinks she must be imagining it.

Without thinking, she kneels down amongst cigarette stubs and discarded gum, pulled by some sort of magnetic force. Deep brown eyes staring up at Maisie are framed by a toffee-coloured face and auburn mane. Reaching out, her fingers stroke smooth skin as excitement tingles through her body. She can't stop looking, can't help admiring the beautiful form of a carousel horse.

She glances up at Sir Malcolm and spots a rare softening of the hard lines around his eyes, as though he's as enthralled as she is. Perhaps he's also reminiscing about that magical day at Clacton, riding the carousel just weeks before their worlds collapsed.

Another helper arrives to lift the other end of the wooden horse, and the two men begin carting it off.

'Wait!' Sir Malcolm calls, halting them. 'Where is this item going? It's part of a carousel, I presume.'

'It is, sir. The carousel will be sold at auction. Mr Fraser, the owner of the auction house, is over there, checking the cargo,' one of them explains, pointing to the rear of the train.

Sir Malcolm's brow furrows; his mouth twitches. Maisie is alert enough to the play of his expressions to know that this is his contemplation face.

'I shall buy it,' he announces to the station hand. 'Take me to Mr Fraser. And here's a dollar for your assistance.'

Maisie is speechless. Sir Malcolm is never this impulsive with money. Or anything. Even deciding on a new tie involves days of deliberation. In fact, moving to America is the only hasty decision she's ever known him to make.

He hurries away, leaving Maisie alone with the horse. Her fingers trace around a blue diamond on its forehead surrounded by four red letters – E O T H. Gold-flecked eyes study Maisie as she tries to work out what it means. As the horse stares, everything seems to melt away – the crowds, the noise – and she is transported back to the funfair at Clacton, circling around and around on the ride. She thinks of the picture she found with Tommy on the sea off Canvey Island, the excitement they always felt extracting it from the gin bottle and dreaming of the outside world. All that's been wonderful in her life, she realizes, is centred around a carousel.

While they wait for the 6.47 p.m. from New York, Maisie uses an advertising leaflet for Sapolio soap as a makeshift fan. Courtesy of the American governess, she can read the slogan. CLEANS, SCOURS, POLISHES AND WORKS WITHOUT WASTE. She flaps the paper frantically, finds there's a little relief from the moisture-drenched heat. Chicago in August must be the hottest place on earth, she thinks to herself.

'It's like a damn inferno here,' Sir Malcolm grumbles, echoing her thoughts in his own way.

He has returned from buying the carousel, and is frowning at the large clock suspended on the north wall of the station. Clearly impatient for his brother's return, he repeatedly checks his pocket watch as if that will make the hands tick faster.

Hugo is younger, jollier, than Sir Malcolm. Having met his second wife by a Renoir painting in the Met while visiting America, he followed her to her home state of Illinois soon after. At twenty-seven, Nancy is nine years his junior, with the self-assuredness of someone much older. *A breath of good luck for my brother*, is how

Sir Malcolm describes his sister-in-law, *and well deserved after poor Charlotte*, he always adds, referring to the death of Hugo's first wife from a burst appendix.

The current Mrs Randolph is a regular visitor to Fairweather House, accompanying her husband there for dinners and drinks. Unfortunately, she took an obvious dislike to the little girl from England from the moment the pair were introduced to one another at this very station, minutes after Maisie and Sir Malcolm had arrived in Chicago.

Maisie tears the leaflet in two and offers half to him to fan his face.

'Try this,' she says.

He shakes his head. 'Your need is greater than mine.'

His shirt is damp, and his forehead is shiny with sweat.

'I don't need both,' she persists.

Directing the scrap of paper closer to him, she wafts it around his face. Sir Malcolm grunts.

'Very well,' he concedes and takes it from her.

The train puffs alongside Platform 6 bang on time. It's another twenty minutes, however, before there's any sign of the Randolphs. The carriages are almost fully disembarked when a door is finally flung open and out steps a vision in sapphire blue. She gambols towards them, her shiny, brown ringlets bouncing, her arms out-stretched like she's a famous actress from the moving pictures.

'Malcolm, dearest, we've just had the most thrilling conversation with the Maharaja of Lahore. He has his very own carriage and was recounting the tale of how he rode a wild elephant across India and, would you believe it, we didn't realize the train had stopped!'

Without a sidewards glance in her direction, Nancy thrusts a silk stole and a small bag at Maisie and plants a red lipstick kiss on Sir Malcolm's cheek.

'Delightful to see you, Nancy,' Sir Malcolm says as if he means it. 'You too, Hugo,' he adds.

'It's good to be back,' Hugo says to his brother. 'The eastern seaboard is perfectly lovely, but, if we'd stayed any longer, Nancy would have bankrupted us.'

'Malcolm, your brother thought I was very naughty in New

55

York,' Nancy giggles. 'In fact, he told Mr Bloomingdale that under no circumstances was I to be allowed an extension on my credit. What do you think of that?'

Maisie never hears Sir Malcolm's opinion, because Nancy sinks her fingers into his arm and whisks him ahead. Hugo uses the opportunity to relieve Maisie of his wife's items and carry them himself.

'Apologies for the wait, Maisie, that was selfish of us,' Hugo says gallantly. 'Were you here long?'

Hugo is easy to talk to: all smiles and with the same interest in people as Miss Catherine.

'Quite long. But mainly because we were here early. So early that your brother even had time to purchase a carousel,' she answers with a trace of humour. 'It's being delivered to the house tomorrow.'

Hugo's eyes widen. 'Good God, don't tell my wife. I'll never hear the end of how Malcolm is frittering away his money. Nancy is convinced that, as his closest, living relative, I stand to inherit the lot.'

They stop at the news-stand for the men to buy a newspaper each. WAR IN EUROPE, the headline screams. Three little words that are like an icy hand squeezing Maisie's heart. Though the front-line is a long way away, she worries for Tommy. She thinks of him still, funny little Tommy who was her shadow for all those years. A big part of her will always regret not daring to ask Aunty Mabel if he could join them at Jesserton. He must be sixteen years old – the same age as Maisie – if he escaped from the Sixpences alive. She prays he did, prays he didn't just make it out only to then be dragged into a rich man's fight.

The brothers and Nancy lag behind, their eyes fixed on the newspapers, conferring. Maisie follows the seven luggage carts as they wobble across the street. It's a race to reach the opposite side-walk without getting mown down. Horns blare, and a streetcar crosses her path, so close that Maisie's skirt swirls in its wake.

Nancy catches up to Maisie, eyeing her belongings, now in Hugo's hands.

'I hope you're more helpful towards Sir Malcolm than you've been to me today,' she says curtly. 'What would become of you otherwise?'

Maisie chews her bottom lip and turns her face to hide her unease. With an uncanny ability, Nancy has honed in on her insecurity.

The Daimler is waiting in a side street, along with the separate horse-drawn wagon that Sir Malcolm has arranged for the luggage. Somehow the porters squeeze in every last item, though Hugo and Maisie are laden with hat boxes in the back seat.

Twilight is falling as they finally set off. Maisie is quiet while the adults talk, gazing at Chicago streaming past. The city sparkles in the evening. Streets lined by buildings three times the height of Jesserton teem with pedestrians; bars and restaurants overflow. On Michigan Boulevard, a small parade slows traffic. Marching to the tune of 'Yankee Doodle', a brass band is followed by an enthusiastic troupe of young women twirling batons in formation. Maisie is amazed that there are so many people out and about at this time when she herself rarely ventures out, even during the day. Is this what every night is like? A whole world happening without her?

Sir Malcolm is a natural at driving an automobile, and he weaves through the streets, and on to greener suburbs. Presently, they turn into Albany Avenue, the row of boxy townhouses where Hugo and Nancy live.

Nancy hops out first, peering into the distance for the plodding wagon. When finally it arrives, she begins issuing her instructions without lifting a finger herself.

'Hugo won't let me do a thing, you see,' she explains, unable to hide the delight in her voice. 'Especially now.'

As she pats her belly, Hugo pauses halfway up the steps to the house, his expression cautious.

'I thought the plan was to hold off on informing anyone until we're certain,' he says.

'Nonsense, third time's a charm,' she replies breezily.

'Then it seems congratulations are in order,' Sir Malcolm says, and he sets down four hatboxes to clap his brother on the back.

Everything is changing again, Maisie thinks, her mind drifting to the carousel. She can't explain why or how she knows, but it feels like its arrival in their lives is the start of something momentous.

7

Early the next morning, a loud bang like a shotgun disturbs the air, causing sandpipers to scatter; they glide past the drawing-room windows and over the glassy surface of Lake Michigan, towards the cresting sun. As Maisie peers out, she notices a cloud of dust near Hutton-Bellamy House. 'Vulgar nouveau riche,' Sir Malcolm always mutters whenever the neighbours are mentioned: namely Mr Hutton-Bellamy himself, the labourer-turned-lumber-magnate; and Mr Janssen, the once penniless Dutch immigrant who now owns the largest papermill in Illinois.

Though all the houses in this neighbourhood seem anything but vulgar to Maisie, Fairweather House is especially refined. With white ship-lap walls and large windows framed by navy shutters, it sits majestically on forty acres of land that includes flourishing orchards. Inside, crystal chandeliers and cream marble floors continue the elegance. The space is airy in a way that Jesserton never was, helped by pared-down furniture and the bright paintings from Sir Malcolm's study in England. The ancestors were left behind: no eyes follow Maisie as she navigates easily between the living spaces on the ground floor and the five upstairs bedrooms, each with its own bathroom.

The main attraction, however, is the view of the lake from the rear of the house. In her spare moments, she sits at her bedroom window, mesmerized by water the colour of steel, which teems with warblers and blue herons and salmon larger than her arm. At night the surface sparkles as though it's covered in fallen stars, stretching without end to the distant horizon. From here, she prays to the Lord of the Water every evening without fail while rearranging a line of pebbles collected from the shore along her windowsill. After the tragedy that befell Aunty Mabel and Miss Catherine when she lowered her guard, Maisie is taking no chances.

The grey cloud of dust created by a procession of vehicles rolls up the road like a wave. Since this is the last estate before the land becomes too boggy to build on, Maisie knows it's heading their way. This must be the carousel arriving, though delivery is earlier than she thought. Sir Malcolm has yet to emerge from his bedroom – and, if the two empty wine bottles discarded on the drawing-room floor are anything to go by, they won't be seeing him any time soon.

She collects up the evidence before the staff arrive for their morning duties. There are fewer servants here than at Jesserton, all employed at Fairweather from before Sir Malcolm purchased the place from the previous owner. Their number complements the modest size of the house.

Likeable for the easy-going way he turns his hand to tasks most butlers would consider beneath them, Arnold is responsible for the other three: Eric, the footman, a man in his late twenties who rarely smiles; Clara, the maid, a shy young woman with a round face; and the cook. Widowed when her husband was killed dynamiting a tunnel for the railroads, Peggy Mae moved from Alabama in search of work with her three young children, and the entire family lives in staff quarters near the main gate with the others.

Maisie often wonders who they think she is to Sir Malcolm. It must be obvious she isn't blood, because ever since it was decided last month that she had outgrown the governess, she has occupied her time with household chores. Yet neither is she one of them, since she resides in the main house. Her deep-rooted sense of not belonging has travelled with Maisie to America.

The vehicles snake past the cherry trees that flank the driveway. An assortment of burly labourers piles out.

A dark-haired man with a long beard eyes Maisie. 'The name's Corbett. Where d'you want the carousel set up?'

Where? She remembers no instructions from Sir Malcolm about which part of the estate had been selected for the carousel. Silent on the way home from his brother's house, within seconds of returning he had procured a sizeable quantity of Burgundy from the wine cellar before holing up in the drawing room. Maisie is torn between facing his wrath by waking him early, and his fury at the carousel being sited in the wrong spot.

'This way,' she instructs.

She knows the perfect place and can only pray Sir Malcolm agrees. The vehicles follow, trundling between the swathe of apple trees, out to a clear, flat area with direct sight of the lake.

With clanging and shouting, the work begins. A circular platform emerges first, hauled off the biggest truck by every pair of hands. It's an enormous structure, twenty feet in diameter and three feet deep, fashioned of engraved metal that rattles as it's lowered into position. Sweating, the workers drag out other components to attach to this central piece, slotting in steps, fastening pipes and tightening bolts, adding the beginnings of a brightly painted canopy.

There are figures near the house – the servants starting their workday – which means that Sir Malcolm will soon be roused by the chatter and the noise of breakfast being made. Waving at them in the distance, Maisie tears herself away from the carousel to fetch him, and is about to step inside when the *ting, ting, ting* of a cowbell stops her.

A sturdy woman with jet-black hair and a strong jawline is steering a cart towards the house. As the wheels grind to a halt, Maisie approaches.

'Good morning, Mrs Papadopoulos,' she says. 'We need milk and butter, please.'

Maisie makes a special point to be up early enough to meet the dairy cart every morning. There's a comfort in knowing that Mrs Papadopoulos will always turn up, as reliably as the sun rising in the east. Besides, she likes the woman. Maisie can't help admiring anyone who was forced to leave behind everything in their home country, then musters the enthusiasm to start over. 'Occupation by Ottomans is Greek tragedy like Euripides wrote,' she once said, but there wasn't a trace of self-pity in her voice.

Mrs Papadopoulos clambers from the cart, pokes her head under the canvas protecting the produce and offers Maisie a small package. 'You have this too. Feta.' She cups Maisie's face, studies her. 'Greek cheese for Greek girl.'

If only Mrs Papadopoulos knew that Signora Maronelli, the seamstress, is convinced that Maisie is part Sicilian, and Bobby Whitefeather from the general store is sure she has Navajo blood. She considers admitting that her ethnic origins are a mystery even to herself, but it's a rare chance for Maisie to feel like she fits in somewhere. There's no harm in it, as far as she can tell.

'Thank you. Your other clients are going to think you have favourites,' Maisie laughs.

Her wide smile makes Mrs Papadopoulos appear younger, pretty even. 'Maybe I do,' she winks.

A labourer rushes past, reaches inside one of the vehicles, and retrieves a toolbox and what looks like a large poker before racing back to rejoin the crew near the lake.

'Early for visitors,' Mrs Papadopoulos states.

'It's our new carousel,' Maisie explains, but the older woman looks blank. 'It's a ride for children. They go around and around,' she adds, moving her hands in a circle.

'What you do with child's toy?'

It's a question that should have been asked at the train station. Now the carousel is here, Maisie can see how ludicrous its presence must seem to outsiders.

Mrs Papadopoulos rolls her eyes as if she understands. 'Crazy rich,' she mutters as she hauls herself into the cart, leaving Maisie to search for Sir Malcolm.

She follows the scent of cigars to the morning room, where Sir Malcolm is usually to be found before he sobers up and hides away in his study for the rest of the day. What he does in there, Maisie isn't certain, but it seems to require a decanter of Scotch on a drinking day, a pot of black coffee otherwise, a large bundle of daily newspapers and the telephone. Every so often, he receives a call from Mr Duke Deveraux, his stockbroker, or one of the handful of acquaintances introduced to him by Hugo, and he dashes off to a meeting in the city, all spruced up. In the early days of living in America, he had attended church every week, taking Maisie with him, but those outings came to an abrupt halt after the minister informed the congregation that the death of their loved ones was

God's will. Since then, he has spent Sunday mornings in his study, reading the Bible. 'I don't need a middleman to communicate with God,' he claimed.

Engrossed in his activities at all times, Sir Malcolm continues to read a newspaper even while eating lunch or dinner in the dining room. Rather than enduring mealtimes without any conversation, Maisie prefers to join the informal staff supper in the big kitchen, listening to all the news while she helps to prepare vegetables and wash the dishes afterwards. Everyone else is too busy in the day for socializing, which wasn't so noticeable when she was occupied with her studies. Now these evenings spent with the servants are all that stands between Maisie and crushing loneliness.

She knocks. It's impossible to tell what sort of mood Sir Malcolm might be in. Most of the time, he's gruff but vaguely approachable, although after a night of fierce drinking, he is best avoided. But the carousel's arrival is a big event.

'Yes?' he answers with a resigned sigh.

Entering the room, she can see there are purple circles under his eyes. He lounges in an armchair, puffing away and still in his dressing gown.

'Excuse me, sir,' she says quietly. 'But the carousel is here and –'

He winces. 'Keep the noise down. I feel a migraine coming on.'

Maisie would raise her eyebrows if Sir Malcolm wasn't glaring at her. He must have no idea that she can identify a hangover blindfolded after years of witnessing the gin-induced afflictions of the Sixpences.

'How about sweet tea and a boiled egg? I'll get Clara to bring it.'

'Indeed. And please deal with the carousel. I'm not up to much today.'

Or most days. What a waste of a life, she thinks. On the other hand, she's glad for his fragile state, for this gives Maisie the perfect opportunity to show Sir Malcolm how indispensable she is.

By the time Maisie returns outside, the canopy is complete, rising in the sky as a gigantic, multicoloured parasol. With one hand shielding her eyes from the sun's glare, she can make out the painted figures of a red, white and blue army marching towards a fleet of golden ships that float on a turquoise ocean. Following the curve of the carousel, Maisie realizes that the picture morphs seamlessly into an intricate scene of a city under siege. The artwork is so beautiful that her heart sings.

Enthralled, she watches as the carved horses are next unwrapped. There are copper manes, silver chevrons, saddles that blaze gold. A ginger pony with purple hooves and striped mane is carried past. It seems that whoever designed these glorious creatures went to great pains to make sure that no two were alike.

Mr Corbett is bellowing instructions, gesticulating wildly. His face is now as red as a ripe tomato, his cheeks puffed up. There seems to be some difficulty in positioning the correct horses on the correct poles, the mention of a certain order. His labourers struggle, switch horses, try again. With a rush of adjusting, there's success at last. Just as Maisie thinks the work is completed, one of the men races up the ladder to screw a flag at the top.

A shiver runs down her spine. It can't be. As though Maisie has been carried off to the past, she's sitting near the copper beech tree on Canvey Island, unrolling the picture she and Tommy treasured. The multicoloured horses. The patterned, tent-like covering. The silver disc. The gold-and-indigo flag. The similarities to the carousel standing right in front of her are startling.

There's cheering and clapping as the workers congratulate themselves.

'Finally finished. Almost had us beat,' Mr Corbett declares, wiping sweat from his forehead with his sleeve. 'There were all sorts of newfangled parts to place right; horses that wouldn't slot in on the first go. Now I just need to show someone how to work the controls.'

Maisie has no choice, she supposes, but to be that someone. She follows him, listens to his lengthy instructions about how to work the lever, the switches, some rambling about oiling the parts.

'You got an automobile?' he asks.

Maisie nods. 'The master of the house does.'

'Good. This ain't one of those old-fashioned rides running on clockwork or steam. It's different. I don't know much about these matters, but it has an engine like an automobile, Mr Fraser says, so it needs gasoline like an automobile. There's enough in there for a couple of turns, but it'll need topping up occasionally.' He hands her a folder. 'Not sure what use this is since it's in a foreign language, but here you go.'

Apparently satisfied that Maisie has absorbed enough of the instructions, he rallies his crew and they disappear up the driveway. Relieved to be rid of them at last, she removes her boots, which are like vices after standing for so long.

Perched on the metal platform, she opens the folder. Mr Corbett is quite correct – the papers are written in a language Maisie doesn't understand. There are diagrams of mechanisms, perhaps instructions. Rifling through, she's at the point of giving up on making sense of anything when she spots something poking out of a page at the back. She pulls out a poster. It's an advertisement for an event, similar in style to the advertisements for Hershey's chocolate. She can hardly believe it. This *is* the same carousel. PARIS EXPOSITION – and the date APRIL 14TH, 1900.

Maisie shakes her head in wonder. It's like being reunited with an old friend. This picture sustained her through the bleakest times of her life, gave her hope when all seemed lost. How many hours had she sat with Tommy, memorizing every brush stroke, absorbing the exact shade of every horse? And now she's holding a pristine version in her hands. How is that even possible? Perhaps she's a conjuror, drawing her wishes, her dreams, from the other side of the sea.

Soon Sir Malcolm appears through the trees, dressed in shirt and pants with a trace of colour to his cheeks. He heads straight to the carousel, his eyes fixed ahead like he's sleep walking, climbs on to the platform, metal clanging under his brogues, and examines the nearest horse. He moves to the next horse, then the next, and so on as if he's inspecting an army. Maisie is relieved he makes no irate comment about where the carousel is situated. Perhaps he's even pleased.

'Should we have a turn?' he asks abruptly, gazing down at the complex pattern etched on the platform, a labyrinth of inter-connected lines.

She thought he would never ask.

He chooses a brown horse with an emerald saddle, while Maisie pulls down the control lever, then leaps on the one nearest to her, a dappled grey stallion. They move off, the wind in their faces.

She feels it immediately. There's none of the clanking or jerking of the Clacton carousel, no roar. This machine purrs, gliding with every rotation. It's faster too, cutting through the air at such speed that Maisie can barely catch her breath. For a moment, there's a pang in her heart for that special day at the funfair. She pictures the joy on Miss Catherine's face, Aunty Mabel laughing. The image is so clear in her mind that it suddenly feels as if they're really here. A surge of exhilaration courses through Maisie as a show of sparkling lights appears above. Gripping the pole, she pulls herself up. Two rows in front, Sir Malcolm also rises to his feet. They both whoop in delight.

8

The big idea appears early the next morning, soon after watching Mrs Papadopoulos's sons playing a game of cowboys on the stationary carousel. The two boys jump on and off the wooden horses, firing imaginary pistols. Seeing their delight, Maisie finds her head beginning to spin. Could she invite some of the local children here for a ride? Though she doesn't know many people well, Maisie feels confident enough to ask the neighbours, as well as the tradesmen supplying Fairweather House.

Two days pass before she decides to test the water. As though he was suspended in a bubble of euphoria that popped the second that he dismounted from the horse, Sir Malcolm's pleasant mood had lasted as long as the carousel ride. But she needs his permission if the idea is going to be anything more than vague thoughts in her head.

Today she waits for Sir Malcolm to collect the daily newspapers from the hallway. This is the best hour to catch him – any hangover should be subsiding, and it's too early for him to start drinking.

As Maisie has never asked Sir Malcolm for anything, he looks up from his newspaper with an expression of surprise when she stammers out the reason she wishes to talk to him. After an over-long silence, he scowls.

'I'm past bothering with that sort of thing, Maisie. And the noise would get on my nerves.'

But as she tries swallowing the lump in her throat, he speaks again.

'However, Hugo and I have a meeting in town with Mr Deveraux next Thursday. You may invite your people then. But only a small gathering, you hear?' he says. 'And Nancy must supervise. There needs to be a suitable adult present, and she's a whizz at hosting parties.'

★

There's no stopping Maisie after that. This is an opportunity to occupy her time with a meaningful task. She's often thought about Miss Catherine's ambition to write novels. Before Jesserton, Maisie was too busy surviving even to imagine the possibility of a career. Then, when she arrived in America, all her time was taken up with the governess. Now her whole life stretches out as an unpainted canvas. Sir Malcolm hasn't indicated that he expects anything of Maisie, but she feels a growing restlessness to achieve something for herself.

After pinning the carousel poster and a list of tasks to the inside of her wardrobe, she issues the invitations. She makes paper chains to string between trees. She gathers apples for the cook to turn into pies, orders extra cream from Mrs Papadopoulos and enlists the help of the servants.

It's just like Arnold to volunteer to tame a patch of the grounds, suggesting a picnic. There's no formal garden and no gardener at Fairweather House, so the vegetation has run wild. But he takes it in his stride, hacking away at undergrowth and pruning trees.

The enthusiasm must be infectious, because over the course of the next few days the ideas roll in thick and fast. Clara brings in a hoopla set. Maisie adds 'bobbing for apples' to the list, a game Aunty Mabel once described playing with her siblings in childhood. The cook decides to 'try something new'.

Maisie fully expects Nancy to turn up and take over the proceedings, but, after agreeing to Sir Malcolm's request to help out with a breezy *Leave it with me, Malcolm darling, I'll make sure the party lives up to the Randolph standards*, there's been no further sign of her, as though she was never really interested in such a small affair.

By the morning of the event, excitement has reached fever pitch. Maisie is woken early by a ball of nervous energy. She can barely eat breakfast, giving up when the staff join her in the kitchen. While the maid folds napkins, Maisie applauds the apple-meringue pie Peggy Mae parades in.

Rightly puffed up with pride, the cook beams. 'It was as if I was inspired by the Lord himself,' she explains, slapping away the hand of her youngest child, who is reaching for a piece.

Peggy Mae's older two children are racing around the table when Arnold struts into the room, dressed in orange breeches and a purple shirt with a sparkly green bowler hat atop his bald head.

'Roll up, roll up to have your ears rumbled and your eyes dazzled by the world's most splendiferous, most yoddle-wabble-naferous, spinning carousel!' he booms in a strange accent that sounds like a cross between the dock workers on Canvey Island and the Irish lilt of the station hand from a few weeks ago.

It's so unlike Arnold's usual, quiet voice that everyone giggles.

Clara is wide-eyed. 'Wherever did you get that outfit, Mr Arnold?'

He takes a bow. 'Swell, isn't it?' he answers. 'I always fancied myself as an actor. I've wanted to tread the boards since I was a boy, but my dad said going into service is a more reliable profession,' he explains. 'However, I still partake of amateur dramatics in my spare time. This here is the King of Bohemia's outfit from *The Winter's Tale*.'

He produces three yellow balls and starts to juggle.

'Aren't you a revelation, Arnold?' Maisie exclaims. 'You can be the Grand Ringmaster of the carousel.'

She has no idea if such a title even exists, and doesn't care, because there's an unusual feeling of warmth around her heart, a gratitude for how much effort they have made. The Jesserton staff were never this nice.

The only one who views the festivities with anything less than enthusiasm is Eric, the footman. 'Seems a lot of trouble for nothing,' he grumbles, sloping off for a cigarette.

The five Hutton-Bellamy children arrive first, wearing matching sailor suits, accompanied by their nanny. They are followed by the two youngest Janssens; and the offspring of the tailor, the coal man, the fish-seller and the grocer; and the Papadopoulos boys, all with a guardian and an offering of food. Nancy breezes in last, making a big show of having brought along a bottle of champagne.

The guests make a beeline for the carousel. Children race around the platform, while the adults stroll around the perimeter, nodding in approval. 'Isn't this grand?' the Hutton-Bellamy nanny remarks to the tailor's wife, and Maisie feels a surge of pride for this wonderful machine. She watches Peggy Mae's children make friends with the Papadopoulos boys beside the ginger stallion, and the Janssen daughters patting a little off-white pony with the Hutton-Bellamy clan. It's noticeable that the children have separated themselves into groups according to the wealth of their parents, and Maisie wonders if they will begin to mix over the course of the afternoon.

Eventually, everyone is encouraged off the platform with the promise of a ride later, and they swarm to an area of grass nearby, where the other entertainments are set up. Clara is in charge of the hoopla, and soon a cluster of giggling children are tossing rings made of rope in the general direction of tall wooden pegs. Even Eric has come around, and he organizes a game of hide-and-seek amongst the trees. As Maisie explains the rules of bobbing apples – as described to her by Aunty Mabel several years ago – to three of the fish-seller's children, she notices a familiar face approaching.

'You organize well,' Mrs Papadopoulos states, looking impressed. 'Everyone have fun.'

'I just did the spade-work,' Maisie answers modestly. 'Officially, this is Nancy's event.'

Mrs Papadopoulos looks over her shoulder, surprised. 'Then why she look so . . . grumpy?'

Maisie glances at Nancy standing alone near the house, her mouth downturned and her arms folded.

'Perhaps she's put out that the carousel is the centre of attention,' she can't resist saying.

As they laugh, Nancy looks at them and scowls at Maisie as though she can tell that she's the object of their amusement.

The next forty minutes pass quickly, and it's already approaching noon by the time the refreshments have been served. Maisie asks Arnold to start the ride. With a sense of purpose, he leaps on to the carousel's platform, twirls on the spot, waits for silence.

'Come, children, come, children, from far and near,' Arnold shouts in his stage voice. 'Come choose your steed, you galloping knights, to enjoy the fun of the carousel!'

70

There's a rush of children appearing from behind trees and along the shore, jostling for a horse. Maisie notices a little boy clinging to the skirts of Mrs Wadham, the tailor's wife. He's six years old at a guess, with the same serious, wide-eyed expression as Tommy at that age, the same thin little legs poking out from baggy shorts. Maisie approaches him and bends down.

'Don't you want a ride?' she asks him.

He shakes his head, sucks his thumb.

'It's fun,' she promises. 'Why don't you have a go, and you can tell me all about it when you get back?'

He gives a small nod, his grip loosening from his mother's skirt. Then he darts off, finds the last available horse, tucked away on the inner row, and hoists himself up on the golden saddle. Maisie can't wait to see his sombre little face light up in delight when the carousel begins.

'Thank you,' Mrs Wadham says with a grateful smile. 'Billy's a little shy and sometimes needs encouragement.'

'I used to know a little boy just like him,' Maisie replies.

When every last child is settled, giggling and squirming, Arnold races to the control panel.

'Are you ready?' he calls.

'Yes,' the children chorus.

Arnold lifts one hand to cup his ear. 'I didn't hear you! I said are you ready?'

'Yesssss,' the children scream, and the adults join in this time.

'In that case' – he pauses for dramatic effect – 'hold on tight.'

With that, he pulls down the lever just as Maisie had shown him; there's a dull hum followed by the first strains of music. Maisie can feel the children's excitement building with her own, and she claps as the carousel moves off.

Arnold begins tap-dancing between the horses, treating the plat-form like a revolving stage. He grips the poles to perform high kicks, glides across metal, spinning and bouncing on his feet as everyone cheers. Soon the carousel builds up speed, the images painted on the canopy blurring into streaks of colour.

As Billy's horse rushes past, Maisie waves, and he smiles. Tears prickle her eyes as she is taken back to the happy day at Clacton funfair. As the carousel moves around, the boy disappears from sight, then reappears a few seconds later, disappears, reappears, each time Maisie holding her breath until she spots him.

This time, though, his smile has vanished, and he's sobbing, barely clinging to the pole. Worried for him, Maisie looks at Mrs Wadham, whose face has turned pale. 'Can you tell your man to stop the ride?' she asks Maisie.

Maisie waves at Arnold, trying to attract his attention. There's a bright flash: it's the same lightshow that she and Sir Malcolm saw when they rode the carousel. As though a swarm of fireflies has descended, the underside of the canopy is alight, a kaleidoscope reflecting the patterns on the platform. A loud cheer follows. The glare is so strong that Maisie shields her eyes.

Seconds later, the ride ends, and a clamour of bright-eyed children spill down the steps like a giant wave. Rushing with Mrs Wadham to help Billy, Maisie runs past a line of horses. Seconds later they locate the horse with the golden saddle, but there is no sign of the boy. After circling the platform three more times, they still can't find him.

'Where is he?' Mrs Wadham asks Maisie, her forehead creased with worry. Without waiting for a response, she rushes from the carousel. 'Billy!' she shouts. 'Billy!'

Maisie stands at the edge of the platform, looking out. There are around thirty people here, including the children, and everyone has scattered in different directions. Some have already resumed playing hoopla; others are gathered on picnic rugs. Maisie can see the Papadopoulos boys heading for the shore with the fish-seller's sons. But Billy is nowhere.

Her heart races. Mrs Wadham is darting between the groups now, asking around about her little boy. With a growing sense of unease, Maisie joins her.

'How has no one seen him?' Mrs Wadham cries when they've questioned every person.

The woman is frantic.

'He must be here somewhere,' Maisie says, scared now too.

Mrs Wadham is close to tears. Her eyes dart between the lake and a poorly lit area of trees. 'I need to get my husband. He needs to be here.'

Surely Billy is hiding somewhere, waiting for his big moment to pounce out and scare everyone. Mrs Wadham ushers her three older children indoors so as to keep an eye on them while she uses the telephone, and Maisie sets off to find him. Several search parties are formed. Arnold leads the other servants to an overgrown area at the furthest corner of the grounds. Mrs Papadopoulos is in charge of the large group exploring the shoreline. Nancy looks distraught, her skin flushed and beaded in sweat. 'The poor little thing,' she murmurs, following Mrs Wadham to check inside the house.

'We'll find him. We will,' Maisie can hear people reassure each other.

She starts by crawling under the refreshments table. After finding no one there, or anywhere around the area where the games are set up, Maisie ends up back at the carousel. Perhaps Billy returned here. She stands peering at the structure, alert for any movement. The early-afternoon sun has dipped behind a bank of clouds and the space beneath the canopy is cast in gloom.

Goosebumps crawl along Maisie's skin. Sitting there with shadows playing on the metalwork, the carousel has lost its joyous sheen, and it now seems sinister. Perhaps it saw where Billy ran off to.

Don't be silly, she tells herself, the carousel isn't a person. She steps on to the platform and heads for the control cylinder, which is the only place left where no one has looked. Less than three feet in diameter, the small space is empty. Disappointed, Maisie emerges on to the platform again. A chill makes her shiver – it feels like she's being watched.

As she rubs her arms to warm up, there's a wail from the house. Groups emerge from different parts of the estate, and soon everyone is moving towards the direction of the sound, with Maisie hitching her dress off the ground and pelting at full speed. She imagines Billy having slid down the banisters and fallen off, or burned his hand on the gas stove. She tries to push the idea from her mind as she's the first to fly through the back door and into the kitchen.

Mrs Wadham is weeping on the shoulder of the worried-looking gentleman Maisie knows to be her husband, the tailor. He must have been visiting a client nearby to have arrived here so quickly. Billy's siblings are sitting quietly at the kitchen table, ashen-faced and holding hands. Maisie feels terrible for them all. Evidently, someone has telephoned the police because the room is filling up with men in blue uniform. One approaches Maisie, and the questions start: *How many guests were invited? Did you notice anything suspicious? Where were you when Billy disappeared?*

Just when Maisie thinks that the situation couldn't get any worse, Sir Malcolm bursts in, back from his meeting. She experiences a rush of dread. Her situation in this house is so precarious that the last thing she needs is his witnessing this chaos. It wouldn't surprise Maisie if he banished her from the household for bringing such trouble here.

'What in damnation is going on?' he demands, his voice like thunder.

Maisie is overcome by a sensation of light-headedness. An image appears, the frightened face of a little boy sobbing as he spins around on the carousel.

Soaring

9

November 1918

Maisie's face is lit red, white and blue as she takes a peek at Chicago's Armistice Day fireworks through a crack in the curtains. So many casualties, all that death marked by tubes of colourful gunpowder. The inadequacy of the gesture isn't so surprising, really, given that she alone still prays for Billy to be found safe. Though she will turn twenty-one in a couple of months, Maisie feels the ache of that terrible afternoon as acutely as she did at sixteen.

After less than a month, the police stopped searching, and rumours of what might have happened to the boy turned to dust. Even Billy's parents gave up on ever finding their youngest child dead or alive, sold the tailoring business and moved out east. But Maisie will never lose hope.

Perhaps he was taken by a childless couple wanting a family of their own, she tells herself, and is living a wonderful life somewhere safe. If she wills a happy outcome, it will be so. Occasionally, she slips up, catches herself assuming harm has come to him. *Dear Lord of the Water, please care for Billy's soul*, she murmurs, wondering why the charms failed to keep Billy safe. Did she lay too few pebbles? Were they in the wrong place? Then she retracts the prayer by throwing ten stones in the lake, the ripples disrupting the words.

He *will* be found.

Unable to shake the drama of that day, Maisie and Sir Malcolm have tacitly agreed to remain as inconspicuous as possible, closeting themselves at Fairweather in the years after the disappearance. To her relief, she wasn't thrown out of the house after Billy's disappearance, but she feels like she's been on very dangerous ground ever since. Fortunately, they keep to themselves, seldom crossing paths.

He resides mainly in the drawing room, almost never venturing to the city any longer for meetings, and barely sleeping, especially during the past few weeks. Meanwhile, her focus is directed towards household tasks like dusting and polishing and darning, spending any spare time reading or playing card games like Solitaire alone. The rooms they don't use are closed up, with the furniture covered in dust sheets, and a musty smell pervades the house, as though no fresh air ever enters.

Though she does make a point to go outdoors for a walk every day, her route never takes Maisie beyond the boundaries of the estate, and certainly nowhere near the carousel, which would only rekindle memories of the party. As far as she knows, the machine has lain undisturbed all these years.

This self-imposed solitude was made easier when America joined the war a couple of years ago. With so many men called up, and civilians encouraged to do their bit, socializing hasn't necessarily been expected. And now the Spanish flu looms as a threat. The infection has already claimed Eric's cousin, the Hutton-Bellamy nanny and Mrs Papadopoulos's two brothers-in-law over the past few months, all healthy adults between twenty and forty years old, and Maisie is playing it safe. It takes her straight back to the time at Jesserton when the scarlet fever wiped out a third of the household.

Trying to stem the rising tide in the city since September, Health Commissioner John Dill Robertson has also been cautious. Eric grumbles about smoking being banned on the streetcars; Clara can't understand why everything fun is closed – the movie house, the skating rink; and Peggy Mae alternately laughs and frowns as she reads aloud from the *Chicago Tribune*. 'Lord knows I don't have the prettiest face, but I'm not covering it with a mask in public,' she groans. Or she declares: 'It's like that too-big-for-his-boots commissioner thinks we're criminals – reporting when we're sick, telling the police to make sure we stick to his rules.'

Minutes after the fireworks reach their grand finale, Clara walks into the bedroom with a pile of fresh laundry. It's late for any staff to still be at the main house, and Maisie watches the maid move to the mahogany bureau, fumble with the bottom drawer, drop a stocking. Clara opens her mouth, snaps it shut, blushes and hurries to the door, without saying a word to her. This is strange, for usually the girl chatters away non-stop these days.

'Is everything all right, Clara?' Maisie asks.

Clara jumps as if stung by a wasp, and turns around.

'Well, ma'am, since you asked . . .' She clutches her apron. 'My mother is sick, and I need twenty cents to buy the special elixir from Madame Rose.'

Maisie tries to disguise her dislike of Madame Rose by offering a sympathetic smile. The one time they met, the woman was holding court in the kitchen, impressing the staff with a tale of how she foretold the downfall of the Russian royal family through the study of a clump of tea leaves. 'Darjeeling, mind you,' she'd claimed, waggling a bony finger. 'None of the cheap garbage.' Dressed top to toe in crimson silk with a yellow canary feather in her straw hat, she gave Maisie an uneasy feeling of pretending to know more than she actually did.

'I'm sorry about your mother,' Maisie says. 'But are you sure it will work?'

She stops short of saying that Madame Rose is probably peddling snake oil.

'Why, yes, ma'am, I am. Only I haven't received last week's wages. Or the wages from the week before.'

Maisie frowns. 'Are you saying you haven't been paid? For two whole weeks?'

Clara reddens, looks at her feet.

'I am, ma'am, and I wouldn't have troubled you except that Sir Malcolm suffers from a lot of migraines lately.'

She's correct of course. Sir Malcolm's alcohol intake has rendered his presence in the house ghostlike: the back of his head disappearing into the study, a shadowy figure hovering in the hallways late at night. Though she'd rather not have to deal with this problem, her ambiguous status as unofficial lady of Fairweather House leaves Maisie little choice.

'All right, leave it with me.'

Before she loses her nerve, Maisie hurries downstairs and heads to the drawing room. Aunty Mabel's favourite song, 'Kiss Me, My

Honey, Kiss Me' drifts along the dark hallway, the lights dimmed by habit to conserve electricity. 'May I have this dance please, madam?' she would ask whenever Maisie caught her humming the melody, and they would waltz around until the room spun.

She knocks softly. Her heart is pounding so loudly that she can hear it above the music. There's no answer. Perhaps he's fallen asleep. Perhaps another time would be more convenient.

Glad of the reprieve, she's about to return to her bedroom when the song fades to silence. It's now or never. Screwing up her face, screwing up her courage, she knocks again, louder.

Muffled swearing, then a bellow: 'Enter.'

Maisie forces her hands to rotate the door handle. 'I'm sorry to bother you, Sir Malcolm,' she says, stepping into the room.

He looks startled to see Maisie. Reclined on the couch in his pyjamas, he levers himself to half sit up.

'What do you want?' he asks.

Remember you're doing this for Clara, she thinks. 'There seems to be a little problem with the wages.'

Sir Malcolm shifts on the couch, looks away.

'Well, I can't give them what I haven't got.'

So it isn't just Clara who hasn't been paid. Maisie's heart sinks.

'What do you mean?' she blurts out.

The words hang between them, insolent.

Maisie shifts from foot to foot, wishing she could take them back, but also hoping that Sir Malcolm will explain. He reaches for his cigars and lighter, lights up and puffs. The darkened shadows under his eyes confirm his poor sleep lately. Loud noises from the drawing room wake Maisie in the middle of the night, and there have been fewer sightings of him in the daytime over the last few weeks, but she's been too preoccupied by her own thoughts to pay much attention.

Sir Malcolm gulps the remainder of his drink, leans back on the couch again and studies Maisie's face, still puffing.

'All my savings are gone,' he admits after a while. 'There was a nice little nest egg after selling up Jesserton. Then I decided to follow Hugo's investment portfolio.'

With Sir Malcolm preferring seclusion, Hugo rarely visits the house now, although the brothers speak frequently on the telephone. Voices travel, and, while Maisie tries not to listen in on the conversations, her ears prick up at any mention of Nancy. The week after the party, Nancy suffered a miscarriage, caused in part, perhaps, by the shock of Billy's disappearance. Maisie can still picture the woman's face soaked in perspiration the afternoon of the party, and how devastated she seemed. Despite some glimmer of hope over the years, the Randolphs are still childless, and, even though she and Maisie have never got along, Maisie is awash with sympathy for her.

Sir Malcolm puffs away on his cigar until finally he speaks again.

'It wasn't my brother's fault, of course. He had been telling me for a while about his successes with shares in ammunitions, so I thought to do the same,' he explains. 'But I hesitated and bought at the top of the market, instead of doing so when Hugo advised me to. Then the war looked like it was ending, and weapons manufacture was scaled down before I could move. I lost the lot last month.' He looks sheepish. 'Duke did warn me that I should spread my investments, but it seemed like I was on to a sure thing.'

Sir Malcolm exhales loudly as though relieved to have confessed his blunder, a plume of smoke rising to the ceiling. The situation must be serious because he never discusses money with Maisie. Or he's more inebriated than he appears, and has no idea what secrets he's divulging. It gives Maisie the confidence to press on.

'Is there nothing left?' she asks.

She still can't grasp how someone could let so much wealth slip through their fingers. Investing sounds an awful lot like gambling if a person's fortunes can turn so easily.

'All there is, is what you see. The house, the car, our possessions.'

It's somewhat reassuring that Sir Malcolm refers to '*our* possessions', because it hints at some affection towards Maisie. Her feelings for him are similar. While she's appreciative of everything he's done for her, there's more to it than that. Rubbing along together over the past eight years, she's grown used to his gruff manner, and is reassured by his gentle strength.

'Will you sell it all?' she asks, not daring to ask the question on her tongue, which is 'What will become of me?'

This concern, which has always lurked in the back of Maisie's mind, rises to the surface whenever there's trouble. Achieving some sort of security of her own might help. For a while now, she's been wondering how she will occupy her time once the world returns to a semblance of normality. The restlessness to do something meaningful has returned, but Maisie is lost as to what direction to take. Should she find a job? Take a leaf out of Mrs Papadopoulos's book and start a business?

Sir Malcolm shrugs, gives a hollow laugh. 'And go where?' He stubs the cigar out and stretches his right hand over to the gramophone on the side table. 'Hugo has been awfully decent and offered to help out, but a chap can't scrounge off his younger brother forever,' he says. 'No, Maisie, I shall have to continue trying to find a way to start from scratch. I've been looking into a few things – a mortgage, for example – but it's not easy, at my age.'

There's a *click, click, click* as the needle makes contact with vinyl, and the first bars of 'Kiss Me, My Honey, Kiss Me' sail into the smoky room. Sir Malcolm falls back, eyes closed, with his thumbs pressed to his temples as though the thought of it all is overwhelming.

Maisie departs from the room quietly. Her mind begins to spiral. She never wants to experience the poverty of Canvey Island again: the wrenching hunger, the constant cold with only rags for clothes, sleeping on bare earth in a leaking shack, and no firewood for heating. But how will Sir Malcolm make any money when he can't concentrate long enough to solve the problem of the servants' wages? If he doesn't muster the wherewithal to forge a way out of this situation, he leaves everyone – the staff, Maisie, himself – at risk of destitution.

No, she can't allow it.

Her monthly allowance sits unspent in a jar, saved up by Maisie as a safety-net against an uncertain future. This is the type of emergency it was meant for. For now, there are ample coins hoarded to cover the late wages, as well as another week paid in advance to make up for the delay.

Clara's eyes shine when she's handed the small envelope. Maisie wants to tell her not to waste it on Madame Rose's so-called remedies but stops herself. What business is it of hers how other people spend their money?

'We're picking apples today, Clara, so wrap up warm,' Maisie instructs her.

Realizing that if the servants' wages were neglected, the tradespeople are probably owed money too, Maisie has an idea to harvest their winter crop and offer it in trade to Mrs Papadopoulos. She can cancel the dress from the seamstress, use fallen branches instead of coal to light the fires, forage for sea creatures as she did on Canvey Island, but milk, cheese and eggs are staples that cannot be replaced. It won't solve their problems long term but will buy them some time. Enough time for Sir Malcolm to pull himself together, she hopes, and for Maisie to show him that she cares and will do everything in her power to help.

The wind skimming off the lake snaps at Maisie's face the next morning as she twists apples from their stalks, throwing them on to old sheets as Clara sorts them into large bundles. Working in tandem, they strip ten trees of their harvest within three hours. Arnold joins in at lunchtime, his strong arms tugging twice as fast as the women's, so that by the time Mrs Papadopoulos arrives mid-afternoon there are thirty-two bundles of fruit waiting by the front door.

'You not sleep well?' Mrs Papadopoulos asks as she approaches Maisie.

'Just tired after picking all these apples,' Maisie lies, hoping her voice is light enough to mask her desperation. 'I thought you could offer fresh apple juice to your customers. We could barter, if you like? Milk, cheese and eggs for apples.'

Mrs Papadopoulos examines her face with dark eyes. She's the kind of woman who doesn't miss a thing.

'Let's see fruit.'

Impressed by the quality of the produce, Mrs Papadopoulos cancels the Fairweather debt, offers a month's supply of whatever

Maisie wants and reserves the rest of the crop for further payment down the line. Maisie shakes on the deal, relieved that they won't starve for now at least. She couldn't bear to relive the twist of her stomach craving its next meal.

Picking apples day after day in the chill of winter is back-breaking work. She would have thought nothing of it on Canvey Island, but her body has become softened to outdoor labour, and she can continue only by ignoring the scream of her muscles, and the blisters on her feet. Tree by tree is relieved of its burden until the final row is left – the strip of orchard near the place where Billy disappeared. It's four years since Maisie has ventured to this part of the grounds.

She braves the view, taking stock of the landscape. There it is, strangled by bindweed, which creeps up the poles. The carousel, older, dirty, reclaimed by nature, sits waiting, a flash of bright colour against the slate winter sky. Two dozen horses frozen in time are poised to gallop to faraway places. Lapland. Camelot. Timbuktu. Up to the moon and back again. Even in this state, it takes Maisie's breath away.

Who wouldn't fall under its enchantment?

It doesn't feel nearly as bad to be here as Maisie's imagination had led her to believe. Her mind whirls into a wild plan; there might just be a way to keep them from ending up on the streets after all the fruit is picked.

Maisie finds Sir Malcolm in the study, poring over a newspaper, his hand poised over a china cup that appears to contain tea but is probably bourbon, because his expression is glazed as he glances up.

'Yes?'

She ignores his sullen tone. 'I was wondering if you have a moment to discuss a way to make money.'

He folds the newspaper, careful to smooth out the wrinkles. 'What are you proposing, Maisie?'

'It's the carousel,' she replies. 'That afternoon the local children came over was wonderful before . . .' Her voice tails off. *Before the tragedy.*

'Before the Wadham boy went missing,' Sir Malcolm finishes the sentence.

She feels tears stir at the corners of her eyes as the image of Billy's sad face in the moments before he vanished pops up. This was a terrible idea. She can't go through with it.

'Yes,' she whispers. She takes a deep breath. 'I was going to suggest we open up the carousel and charge for it, Sir Malcolm, add a few games like hoopla or hook-a-duck, but even talking about it brings back bad memories.'

Sir Malcolm's mouth pinches. They have never properly discussed that fateful afternoon.

'Life can be brutal, we both know that,' he says with a sigh. His sullenness is replaced by a softer look in his eyes than Maisie has ever seen there. 'Terrible things happen every day, and there's not a damned thing we can do about it.' He leans back in his chair. 'I had been half thinking to sell the carousel, to be honest – it's just been sitting there for all these years, and the proceeds would certainly be useful. But perhaps doing something positive with it might help offset the bad associations. Something good that other people will enjoy, like the time we had at the Clacton funfair.'

Maisie inwardly smiles at the thought of that happy day.

'But do you think people would want to come here?' she asks, now racked with doubt about her own idea. 'After what happened?'

Though it's been four years, with a war in between, news did filter through to the local press at the time. Sir Malcolm taps his fingers together, wearing his contemplation face.

'It's a fair question,' he replies. 'But it could have happened anywhere. Most people will understand that. And I don't believe lightning can strike twice.' He checks his pocket watch. 'I have a call with Duke in a couple of minutes, but let's pick up this discussion later. Over dinner, perhaps?'

'I'd like that,' she answers, meaning it.

As she turns to leave, Sir Malcolm speaks again.

'And, Maisie, I really do think you're on to something here.'

Maisie's heart is racing as fast as her thoughts. A lightness enters her mind, a glint of hope for the future. As soon as she leaves the study, she sets about opening the other rooms, drawing back curtains and removing dust sheets, throwing open windows to let cold air run through the house and chase away the ghosts of war and any remnants of the influenza.

10

Maisie dines with Sir Malcolm that evening, and every evening that week, weighing up the wisdom of the idea. The discussions circle around and around. Can they do this? Should they do this? By the end of the fifth dinner, a conclusion is reached: with careful planning, the scheme could work. It *has* to work, because neither has another idea up their sleeve.

Maisie soon learns that Sir Malcolm's information-gathering skills are impressive. By reading anything he can get his hands on and asking around, he soon discovers everything there is to know about carnivals.

Of most interest is the recent development of amusement parks – traditional travelling carnivals established at permanent bases, with an entrance fee to get in, and a set-up that isn't very different from Maisie's idea. And they're popular, apparently. Coney Island, for example, has several such places that are reportedly raking it in.

Inspired by this, Sir Malcolm draws up a business plan. Even from the parlour at the other end of the hallway, Maisie can hear him humming as he writes. She smiles to herself. What was originally a vague thought is forming into something tangible. Something constructive.

With an eye on the risk of starting a business from scratch, they've agreed that concessions are the way forward, an exclusive collection of stallholders who will pay rent. This gives Sir Malcolm an immediate income. They'd also like a dozen rides of their own to complement the carousel, but have decided to limit their ambitions to four, to start with: a helter-skelter – which the Americans call a lighthouse slip – a Ferris wheel, go-carts and a small steam train. Maisie has seen them advertised second-hand in the classifieds for a reasonable price. Given Sir Malcolm's financial predicament, however, all of this hinges on whether he can convince someone to invest.

Armed with a stack of paperwork, he approaches Hugo two mornings later. 'It's either that or he shores me up indefinitely,' he observes to Maisie with a wry smile as he heads out of the front door.

The meeting between the brothers is a success. They settle on a minority stake in the business for Hugo in return for a sizeable sum, and an opening date as the first day of spring, which is three months from now – timed for when the Health Commissioner is expected to lift the restrictions on gatherings in entertainment establishments after the harsh bite of winter.

With such a tight deadline, help is needed from the household staff. But convincing them is another matter. They are all worn out with the war, with sickness, the relentless bad news and trying to make the best of things. More importantly, every single one of the servants remembers that a child disappeared the last time the grounds were opened up to outsiders. When Maisie shares the news, Clara looks close to tears, Eric grumbles, and Arnold twitches. It leaves Maisie with a dilemma: to disclose that Sir Malcolm is on the brink of financial ruin and that they will all lose their jobs without some sort of change, or risk alienating the staff by ignoring their concerns.

Eventually, Peggy Mae breaks the stalemate. 'We can't mope forever. Life goes on,' she states.

Grateful for the support, Maisie squeezes Peggy Mae's arm. She's right. Life goes on.

'Well, don't say I didn't warn you,' Eric complains.

Despite his objections, the footman pitches in with everyone else. In the first week of 1919, they begin by clearing the area around the carousel and the machine itself of overgrown vegetation. Chopping down grass and tearing away ivy soon causes Maisie to break into a sweat, despite the frost hanging in the air.

Though neglect has aged the metal components and there are chips in places from where the weeds were cleared, its charm, the magic the carousel promises, still makes Maisie tingle with excitement. The staff too seem to fall under its spell again as they all buzz around, polishing and cleaning, amplifying the blues, reds, greens, purples of the horses. The task is engrossing. Maisie cleans the inside of the control cylinder, a section of the platform, half a dozen poles, working with such speed that she doesn't even notice the minute details of the intricate design being restored to their original beauty.

Sir Malcolm joins them during a break from his paperwork, rolling up his sleeves and helping to buff the metalwork until it gleams like jewels. He seems invigorated as he works, applauding when Arnold produces small tubes of oil paint to touch up the chipped paintwork.

Later that day, Arnold approaches Maisie. He looks nervous, wringing his hands together. She lays a hand on his shoulder.

'What is it?' she asks.

Arnold blushes. 'I was thinking I should very much like to continue operating the carousel.' He must notice Maisie's surprised face, because he rushes the next words. 'I could still work in the house in the mornings and evenings. Eric said he'd pick up the slack.'

Maisie considers the idea. 'I'll ask Sir Malcolm.'

When she broaches the subject, Sir Malcolm leaves it to her to decide. 'You might wish to take on some of the responsibility for the household from now on,' he suggests.

She relishes the idea, more than she expected she would, and runs off to inform Arnold of her decision. Hugging Maisie when she agrees to his request, he promises not to let her down.

Over the following weeks, Maisie and the staff continue to clear land before the lumberjacks arrive. To make space for all the attractions, a six-acre swathe of fruit trees needs to be cut down. Though reluctant to fell such glorious creations that so recently provided their only source of income, Maisie understands that it's a necessary risk if the business is to have any chance of success, and not one shred of wood is wasted at the sawmill, where huge trunks are sliced into planks that the carpenters use to construct a boundary fence. There's sufficient lumber remaining for the ticket booth and picnic tables, and a small pier, from which Mr Levander's pleasure boats will launch on their tours of the lake.

This is their first official concession holder, and a source of pride for Maisie. Someone putting faith in them boosts her confidence in this venture. Word gets out, and, four days after the agreement between Mr Levander and Sir Malcolm is signed, a line of hawkers forms at the back door.

It takes almost a week to sift through the 209 hopefuls. Turning away anything that resembles a freak show, Maisie ends up picking ten food vendors, twelve merchandise-sellers and twenty-five attraction owners, including a gentleman fresh from Vienna who possesses a dozen new-fangled pinball machines. She also takes on five hollow-cheeked general workers who drift in from a recently disbanded carnival in Peoria – not only for their experience but because it looks like they haven't eaten for a week.

Being granted a concession is such a prize that even Madame Rose enlists Clara to lobby Maisie on her behalf.

'Tell her she can set up a storytelling corner near the lake. She's good at inventing tall tales,' Maisie replies as she hurries off to oversee the sign being erected near the main entrance.

The evening before opening day, Maisie is a bundle of excitement. She checks herself. The last time she felt this way was returning from the funfair at Clacton. In second place is the morning of the party at Fairweather – and both times her happiness was snatched away soon after. She stays up late that night, arranging piles of pebbles near the carousel and around the grounds, enough to keep everyone safe.

The next morning glistens under a pale March sun. Everything looks new and shiny, and the enterprise promises to live up to its name: Silver Kingdom. 'Silver' on Maisie's suggestion, a nod to the sparkling surface of Lake Michigan, while Hugo came up with 'kingdom' as a tie to their homeland.

Leaning out of her bedroom window, Maisie admires the precision with which the amusement park is laid out in concentric circles: the concessions as an outer ring, the rides next, with the carousel as the centrepiece. She allows herself a tingle of anticipation. This place of pleasure is so needed after the many hardships of the last four years.

When the gates open, Maisie expects a mad rush of people. Instead, there's a small trickle of guests throughout the day. Disappointed, she stands by the entrance gate, willing arrivals to appear. What if the business doesn't work after all this time and money has been spent? Chewing her lower lip, she tries to calm the growing panic.

'Slow and steady wins the race,' Sir Malcolm says in a smooth, even voice, although Maisie can see that his jaw is clenched.

The following few days don't show much improvement. Small groups arrive in dribs and drabs, but there's no real growth. 'Slow and steady,' Maisie hears Sir Malcolm mutter again as he paces around the rides. He could lose everything if they've got this wrong. If Maisie has got this wrong.

Determined to see a return on his investment, Hugo takes matters into his own hands on the fourth day. He places advertisements in local newspapers and pays for billboards all along Michigan Boulevard. The marketing, and word of mouth, starts to build momentum. At the end of the first week, there are fifty visitors a day. One week later, and that number has quadrupled. Three weeks after opening, and there are one thousand people milling around the park.

Maisie is cautiously optimistic. She watches as, thirteen deep, a crowd clusters near the carousel, shoving one another for a place on a horse. Arnold waits until the commotion has died down to announce *The world's most super-duper marvellous, out-of-this-universe fabulous, breathtaking carousel!*

Pausing, he raises a silver-tipped cane above his head and begins to tap the central cylinder. *Tap, tap, tap*, like the ticking of a clock. The audience joins in, clapping. Then, with the hand that's holding the cane, Arnold tips his bowler hat, using the other hand to pull down the control lever, breaking into an extravagant tap dance as the music starts.

The spectators go wild. There's cheering, whistling, stamping feet, while the horses race around and around, and the canopy spins like a movie reel. At the end of the first ride, every person that is lucky enough to be seated on a saddle practically refuses to dismount. No one can get enough of the carousel, it appears.

As usual, Maisie is vigilant, her eyes constantly checking around the park for signs of anything suspicious. But, as each day passes without anyone disappearing, she feels herself growing increasingly relaxed.

One morning four weeks after opening, Sir Malcolm gives Maisie a clutch of dollar bills – her first pay packet, now they're doing well enough to afford it, with the arrears of her allowance also included. She holds the notes with reverence, flicks through them. Earning her own money tastes sweeter than accepting handouts. Maisie considers possible ways to spend it. A new pair of shoes. The silk nightdress she saw advertised in a magazine. A box of chocolates. These seem wasteful, unnecessary, when anything could happen in the years ahead. With that in mind, she puts most of the money aside as savings, stored in a box on top of her wardrobe, using only a little to buy a treat for the household.

The cook is crushing rosemary when Maisie enters the kitchen with the basket of sirloin steak that she ordered from the butcher.

'Seems we've come up in the world,' Peggy Mae remarks, as she notices how the redness of the meat stands out against its blanket of old newspaper.

'I thought we all deserved something nice since we're working so hard,' Maisie explains. 'There's enough for everyone,' she adds.

Maisie has continued to dine with Sir Malcolm every night.

'For dinner tonight, then.' Peggy Mae beams as she lays down the pestle and receives the basket. As she heads for the ice box, she pauses: 'There's a letter for Silver Kingdom on the table. Hand delivered.'

Most correspondence for the amusement park arrives by mail and usually consists of dull invoices. But Maisie's heart races as she reads the contents of this particular note. The niece of the movie star Mary Pickford visited the park earlier this week, it transpires, and has been raving about the carousel ever since. The upshot is that Miss Pickford's agent is requesting publicity shots for his client at Silver Kingdom, accompanied by the press.

Maisie can't believe their luck. This is a life-changing piece of news that will put them on the map.

11

Silver Kingdom is already alive when Maisie draws open her bedroom curtains. Her stomach flutters. After three weeks of preparations, liaising with agents and photographers, Mary Pickford and her entourage will be here today.

From this height, she can see two men hauling crates of flour to the corn-dog stand, and one of the ticket-sellers adjusting the angle of her hat before unlocking the office. Out by the lake, Mr Levander begins to clean the small yellow boats in which his customers plough across the water. Closer to the house, Mrs Papadopoulos is unloading huge vats of milk from her cart with Eric's help. Noticing her staring through the window, she waves and then breaks into a smile when Maisie puffs out her cheeks and mimics a Strongman.

Maisie now spends the first few minutes of every day like this, observing the inner workings of the amusement park from her bird's eye view. None of their visitors would ever guess the layers of hard grind that go into running Silver Kingdom. To them it's simply a land of dreams. One minute, you can imagine yourself as an eagle on the Ferris wheel, the next you're plunging on a floating toboggan on the Jules Verne ride, *Journey to the Centre of the Earth*, with the carousel casting a golden dome of light over everything.

Though nothing can beat gliding through the air on a wooden horse, Maisie has now sampled every other attraction, bar one. She would never be seen dead near Madame Rose's idea of a storytelling corner. A large red velvet tent decorated with golden stars has been erected in a quiet spot between the shore and a maple tree. Customers almost always leave in wide-eyed awe, shaking their heads and exclaiming 'How does she know?' Maisie considers her own belief in charms and rituals is a far cry from claiming to speak to the dead, and she would have put an end to the woman's supernatural nonsense long ago if *Madame Rose and Her Crystal Ball* wasn't the biggest draw at Silver Kingdom after the carousel.

She watches a broad-backed man carrying a toolbox step out of the path of Mr Parry – he of the *Popcorn Palace* – doffing his cap. A hierarchy has quickly established itself at Silver Kingdom. The five former carnival labourers – the *Crew*, led by Lucky Nate – are right at the bottom. Above them are the nine *Ride Jocks*: Arnold and a pair of operators for each of the four other rides owned by the Randolph brothers. And, above them, are the concession holders, or *Jointees*, almost fifty in number, who have their own internal pecking order. *Management* – Sir Malcolm, Hugo, Maisie – have needed to allot more time to them than they had expected. Slotted between the Jointees and Management are Silver Kingdom's royalty. The *Money Girls* sell tickets, count takings and hand out wages every Tuesday morning. Well turned out, Gloria, Betsy and Gayle command everyone's attention with their striking presence.

Tearing herself away from the window, Maisie dresses and hurries outside to muck in with the others. Every available pair of hands is needed to make sure the park is in tip-top condition today, and she spends the next few hours scrubbing stalls and setting up bunting, and fielding questions from the Crew about where to erect the pavilion for the park's special visitors.

Having decided to allow the actress thirty minutes of private time for the photo shoot before they open to the public, Sir Malcolm is pacing the entrance hall when Maisie arrives back inside to collect him a few minutes before 11.00 a.m. With the money they're now making, he's been able to resume business with their tradespeople, including the tailor. He is dressed in a new suit, with his hair slicked flat, smelling of cologne rather than alcohol for a change.

Thinking back to how withdrawn he was last year, Maisie finds that Sir Malcolm is like a different person, purposeful now, almost back to his former self from the days of Jesserton, as if he too is letting go of the past.

The crowd outside the gate roars. Maisie peers through the front door's glass pane and spies a tall graceful beauty with long curling hair waving with one hand, holding the hand of a little girl with the other. Hugo steps forward to greet the actress but is beaten to it by Nancy. It's a surprise to see her here. Years have passed since the two women have met in person. From the telephone conversations between the brothers, Maisie imagined that Nancy would seem diminished, but, adorned now in a sapphire dress and maroon lipstick, she is all smiles, embracing Miss Pickford as if the two are the best of friends.

'Ready?' Sir Malcolm asks.

Maisie tugs at her cuffs, smooths her hair, soothes her nerves. She *is* ready.

To a cheer from the crowd, Mary Pickford and her niece enter Silver Kingdom. The press swoop like locusts, gobbling information and snapping photos of the actress, as well as the Money Girls perched in a row on the carousel platform, their heads tilted playfully and wearing wide smiles. But, for all the glitz and glamour of these women, the sparkle of the carousel cannot be eclipsed. In the early May sunshine, paintwork shines and metal glints as if studded with tiny diamonds.

After fifteen minutes of posing, the actress declares that the photo shoot has been successfully completed, and that it is time to open the gates to everyone else. The thrum of music accompanies stallholders shouting out invitations to their entertainments. Arnold is standing on the carousel platform in his best attire, fidgeting with his green bow tie as Mary Pickford watches her niece choose a carousel horse. Catching his eye, Maisie gives him an encouraging thumbs-up.

The noon heat warms her skin. After all those years cooped up, it's good to be part of the world again. Sir Malcolm joins her, and she accepts a glass of champagne from him. They toast and watch the carousel move off, smiling as the speed of the ride picks up and colours flash past. On this perfect, bright day, Maisie's childlike rituals, the fear of curses and her belief that something bad always happens seem foolish.

'Which would you choose?' Sir Malcolm asks, indicating the horses.

Maisie watches oranges and browns, whites, reds and yellows, swirl by. Mary Pickford's niece circles into view, then is gone again.

'The horse with the caramel coat; there's something special about it,' she replies.

Sir Malcolm nods. 'Yes, I seem to remember you liked a pale brown pony at Clacton too.'

Maisie is astonished that Sir Malcolm recalls anything about her, let alone something that specific from so long ago. She feels a warmth around her heart as his eyes fill with affection for her.

'How about you, Sir Malcolm?' she asks.

He taps his champagne glass and nods as though he's taking the question very seriously. 'Any one of them that will support my weight,' he answers, his mouth twitching at the corners as he strokes one hand over his rotund stomach.

This sliver of humour is more like Hugo than the stern Sir Malcolm that Maisie knows, and she can't help smiling.

Nancy totters over. Up close, Maisie notices that the woman's appearance is less polished than it looked from afar: lipstick stains her front teeth; her hair looks unbrushed at the back; there's a tiny rip in the hem of her dress. As Nancy sways, Sir Malcolm steadies her just in time. Hugo comes running from nowhere, as though he's attuned to his wife's mishaps.

'You seem a little unsure on your feet, dear,' he says, his voice all forced cheer. 'I told you to take your tonic this morning,' he whispers to her, although not so quietly that Maisie can't hear.

'But Dr Carlton says we can't try for a baby while I'm on my tonic,' Nancy pouts. She leans into her husband and kisses his cheek. 'And trying for a baby is such fun, isn't it? You weren't complaining this morning.'

Hugo looks like he wants the ground to swallow him up. He removes Nancy's hands from around his neck and takes a step back. 'But you promised you wouldn't drink,' he hisses.

'Oh, but it's been ages since I've been able to have fun like this,' she giggles.

Maisie doesn't know where to look. It's been so long since she's seen Nancy in person that the concerned, caring woman who searched for Billy has been the enduring image in her head. This attention-seeking is more typical of the Nancy from Maisie's childhood.

Nancy must spot the tiny movement to her right because her gaze suddenly alights on Maisie, picking at fingernails.

'Be a good girl and fetch my shawl from Hugo's car, would you?' she orders. 'It's getting a little nippy.'

Glad of the excuse to remove herself from the situation, for once Maisie doesn't mind being spoken to like a child or a member of staff, and she agrees to the request.

As Maisie finds the shawl tucked under the passenger seat of Hugo's car, she notices a flash of red in her peripheral vision.

'Be careful,' someone says in a low voice. 'There's trouble coming from across the ocean.'

A hand alights on her arm. She turns to find Madame Rose staring straight at her with disproportionately large eyes for such a small face.

Maisie shrugs off the woman and hurries through the front door. None of Silver Kingdom's workers would dare follow her into the house. Leaning against the wall in the hallway, she takes a minute to compose herself. What on earth does it mean? What trouble? It makes no sense. Then Maisie catches herself. Madame Rose tells all sorts of silly tales in the hope of parting people from their money.

Feeling like a dark cloud has lifted, she heads outside and arrives back with the Randolphs at the exact moment Mary Pickford begins shouting. Maisie feels a prickle of dread.

'Has anyone seen my niece?' the actress calls.

12

Events spiralled so quickly that Maisie is still coming to terms with being named as the chief suspect in the disappearance of a young girl. The Crew sprang into action first, hunting through Silver Kingdom for Mary Pickford's missing niece, Clementine, ahead of anyone else, galvanizing the Ride Jocks and Jointees to help. It felt all too similar to the dreadful afternoon Billy had vanished. Fruitless searching turned hope into panic. The police arrived and a loop of questions followed.

One week later, Maisie was brought to this place, the lock-up, for a more extensive interrogation. It isn't prison, just somewhere to hold you until you've been properly questioned, it was explained. She was also given the choice of which visitors to receive. Ashamed of causing so much trouble, Maisie has point-blank refused to see any of the servants or Sir Malcolm or Mrs Papadopoulos, with the last arriving at the front desk every morning in the hope of being admitted, only to be turned away on Maisie's instructions. The sole person granted access from the outside world is the lawyer that Sir Malcolm engaged.

Mr Peabody has sat by her side in a mildew-scented interview room four times in the past three days, while two agents from the Bureau of Investigation have grilled her. Reopening Billy's case, they have questioned everyone who was known to be present when both he and Clementine went missing – the staff, Sir Malcolm, Nancy. While everyone else has an alibi for the little girl's disappearance, there are several crucial minutes between Madame Rose speaking to Maisie near the Randolphs' car and her return to the carousel when no one saw her.

The agents want to know Maisie's motives for pushing for the original party four years ago and the opening of Silver Kingdom.

They dissect second-by-second accounts of her movements around the time Billy vanished, and Clementine Pickford was last seen. Worryingly, no one knows where exactly the tailor and his family now live, which means Mrs Wadham is unable to verify Maisie's story that the two were speaking at the moment when the little boy disappeared into thin air. It feels like everything is stacked against her.

'Two children going missing under similar circumstances isn't normal, and all the signs point to you,' one of them said.

It *is* abnormal. And horrific, and presses the question – what *has* happened to those poor children?

For now, though, the racket of hundreds of women held here on suspicion of other crimes keeps her awake. They scream, laugh, fight. Curled up on the floor of a ten-by-ten-foot cell containing three narrow beds and eleven other inmates, she hears someone urinating into the bucket right next to her, smells the waste. This is a cage for animals, she thinks. She has no idea when she might be released, but it can't happen soon enough. The scuffle spreads, and someone's foot knocks over the bucket of effluent. The foul-smelling discharge spreads across the floor like a menacing shadow, engulfing Maisie's toes, the hem of her canvas shift. She will have to disinfect her skin at home. If she ever gets home.

A commotion in the cell makes Maisie tense. Three women have squared up to each other. 'Irish bitch,' one of them spits at a redhead with a scar on her neck. 'Black trash,' is the immediate response.

Keep still, keep quiet, she tells herself.

Without warning, the trio turn on Maisie. They drag her to the centre of the floor. The space erupts into cheers, and prisoners in other cells join in as the biggest inmate lands a punch on Maisie's face. And punches again. The shock numbs the pain for a moment. Then a throbbing sensation begins at her temples, radiating outwards. She can feel her pretty shoes being whisked off her feet. From the corner of her bruised eye, Maisie spots a guard saunter over. He stands watching for a moment before banging his baton on the bars until the attack stops.

Maisie crawls back to her usual corner, nursing her wounds.

This awful place has echoes of her time on Canvey Island, she soon discovered. The dirt and grime, rats lurking under the beds and nipping her toes at night, fighting for scraps of food, the wrench of an empty stomach. But surviving is in Maisie's bones, and she's determined to get through this ordeal.

Yet, by the fifth day, the hunger begins to eat away at her thoughts. Perhaps she really is guilty of some crime. Wasn't she talking with Billy before he disappeared? Is it possible she also spoke to Clementine without even remembering? She struggles to think that far back. If she confesses to something, they may release her for a time. Then again, she could be imprisoned here forever. No one questioned Maisie yesterday. Perhaps they've forgotten all about her. She's beginning to all but give up on ever tasting freedom when a rough-shaven guard comes for her.

'Interview time, Marlowe.'

She looks down at the filthy, prison-issue canvas shift, touches the knotted mass of her hair.

'No one gives a damn how you look . . . or smell,' the guard laughs as though her thoughts are transparent.

As he escorts Maisie down the corridor, dozens of hands stretch out through crowded enclosures. 'Pretty, pretty,' a voice cackles. 'She's mine,' a second voice barks. Flinching, Maisie keeps her distance.

Finally, he stops outside the usual interrogation room.

Expecting to greet the same agents, Maisie is surprised to find a completely different gentleman sitting there. He is fiddling with a piece of paper, deep in concentration. As she enters, he lays the paper on the table. Rather than lying flat, it stands upright, folded into the distinctive shape of a heron.

The gentleman rises to his feet, tall and angular.

'Thank you for seeing me, mademoiselle,' he says in an accent Maisie cannot place, his grey eyes searching in hers for an answer.

'Detective Laurent Bisset at your service.'

13

'Please take a seat,' Laurent says, as though they are sitting down to coffee at Café de Flore and not crammed into this dank room that smells of the effluent pumped into the Seine. This is worse than the cells at Notre-Dame, and they are notorious as the most dreadful in France.

As he watches the woman hesitate before sitting, Laurent is taken by surprise. When he left Paris, the American police were looking into a number of potential culprits. It was only when he reached Chicago yesterday that he became aware that the list has been whittled down to this individual, and he was expecting someone older; if this is, in fact, the person behind Clementine Pickford's going missing, it is obvious that she is too young to have had any direct involvement in Gilbert Cloutier's disappearance nineteen years ago, and, therefore, the later French cases.

Perhaps the Chief Inspector had been right. 'This did not happen in France, correct? So it is coincidence and our investigation remains closed,' he had declared when a stunned Laurent presented him with the afternoon edition of *Le Figaro*, which featured the photograph of a distressed actress sitting on the platform of a carousel that he would recognize anywhere, along with the story of a missing girl. And the boy vanishing four years ago mentioned in the second to last paragraph – those details had not reached France at the time, but both cases are all too familiar.

A part of Laurent had agreed with his boss. Fairgrounds are full of distracted people and therefore riddled with crime. But his gut told him there was more to it than that. Perhaps Victor had had an accomplice who evaded capture in France, and possibly tracked down the carousel. On the spot, he made the decision to take a full month's leave and journey to America. With a six-day voyage on the SS *La Savoie* to New York, and then a train to Chicago – and one week back – he is left with two weeks in which to explore whether there is a link between the cases.

It is ironic, really. When Laurent authorized the sale of the carousel to America, he was thinking of nothing more than where such a pretty folly would achieve the best price. If only he had chosen somewhere nearer – the Netherlands, perhaps. Or Sweden.

Packing in haste, he had promised a tearful Amélie that he would return soon. 'Do you have to go, Laurent?' Odette sighed as he kissed her goodbye. He did, yes, because this case has always had a strange hold over him.

The woman in front of him now plays with her fingers. Her clothing is rough and stained, her face covered in bruises and filth and goodness knows what else, her hair a knotted mess. Accustomed to the sorry condition of incarcerated suspects, Laurent quickly gets down to business. Since he is here, it is worth exploring every angle, and there is no telling what she might disclose.

'I am told that you are called Maisie. Pretty name. There is a flower called similar, non?'

His English is rusty, and he forgets the exact name. But the specific flower is not the point of his question. Over the years, Laurent has discovered that a calm demeanour and a compliment or two at the beginning of an interrogation soothes everyone. It is when suspects are most relaxed that they tend to slip up.

She fails to smile and sits quietly.

'This disappearance of the actress's niece is known everywhere. I myself am a detective from Paris with an interest in the case.'

As he watches Miss Marlowe shrug, he experiences a tinge of exasperation.

'Shouldn't we wait for my lawyer?' she asks.

Her voice is bold, but she works to avoid meeting his eye. If he dips to bring his face level with her own, her focus darts left. If he cranes his neck to match the direction of her gaze, she looks to the space behind him. It is the mark of a guilty person.

'If you wish. But I am not here in any official capacity. Consider me simply a visitor.'

It is very fortunate, indeed, that Laurent's colleague Constable Segal, has a second cousin working in a New Jersey police department who is owed a favour by a close associate of Agent O'Connell, one of the team from the Bureau assigned to the Pickford case. A jocular sort with a fondness for rum, the man has given him an 'in' with the American authorities, and a direct insight into the findings here.

'But I told the guards I wouldn't accept any visitors,' she replies with a frown. 'I thought I was brought here to be interviewed by the same agents as before.'

'So you are not interested in the fate of those children?'

She considers the question for several seconds. 'Well, I've already told them everything I know, and it didn't seem to help,' she says.

Shivering, she bites her lip. For the first time, Laurent notices that her feet are bare. He has an idea to lower her guard.

'You are cold?'

'Yes, a little,' she replies, her mouth twisting as if it takes great effort to admit this weakness.

Without hesitating, he removes his jacket and offers it to her. She looks so grateful for this small gesture that Laurent feels a glimmer of sympathy. He shifts on his seat. He must be careful this isn't fake emotion to manipulate him. Thinking back to the information shared by Agent O'Connell, Laurent remembers an interesting fact.

'You were born in England?'

She nods, huddling under the jacket.

'Does the name Victor Cloutier mean anything to you?'

'I don't know that name.'

'Perhaps a photograph will remind you,' he pushes. Digging into his briefcase, he produces a thick file and rifles through until he finds the newspaper article from five years ago. 'You will not understand the French, but news of the case may have travelled to England?'

She leans forward, studies the photograph of Victor flanked by four constables on his way to court and shakes her head. 'No.'

'The second photograph is of me and the Chief Inspector on the day of Victor's execution in 1914. Unfortunately, it is not the most flattering,' he explains, hearing himself justify his appearance. 'Victor Cloutier was tried and beheaded for murdering his uncle – the man in the second photograph – as well as other persons including a child.'

'I don't know who Victor Cloutier is. I was in America by 1914, so, even if word of his execution had reached England, I wouldn't have known. I don't keep in touch with anyone there, you see,' she says in a quiet voice.

'When did you arrive in this country?' he asks.

'1910. When I was twelve.'

Laurent makes a mental note to verify these claims in order to tie up any loose ends.

'And the carousel? How and when did you come across it?'

Her brow furrows in confusion.

'At Grand Central Station in the late summer of 1914. I saw it being unloaded from a freight train.' She pauses, tilting her head a fraction. 'But I don't see how that's relevant.'

So she must have been one of the first individuals to witness its arrival here. If there is an accomplice, it is not Miss Marlowe due to her age – but perhaps whoever it might be followed the carousel's journey, and was at the station at that time.

'And was there anyone you remember lurking around it? Anyone who seemed out of place?'

She gives him a strange look. 'Everyone seemed out of place, including me,' she responds. Pausing, she ponders for a few moments. 'No, no one I can think of. But I still don't see what this –'

He flips over the news article. The story about Victor runs to a second page, accompanied by a photograph of Gilbert Cloutier's carousel assembled in all its glory at the Paris Exposition. Crowds swarm around it. Perhaps there was an accomplice photographed there.

He hears a sharp intake of breath as Miss Marlowe's eyes widen. She looks at the image, up at Laurent, and then down to the image again.

'It's our carousel,' she gasps. 'Has it got something to do with what happened in France?'

Laurent considers his answer before replying. It would not do to reveal details that might jeopardize the Bureau's case, especially since he is relying on their goodwill for information.

'Victor owned it at the time of the disappearances,' he says carefully. 'Is there anyone in the photograph you recognize?' he presses.

Head bent over the newspaper, Miss Marlowe scrutinizes the photograph for several minutes. Eventually, she looks up.

'I'm sorry, no. I wish I did,' she answers.

Laurent has already been apprised by Agent O'Connell of her statements regarding the disappearances – she witnessed no suspicious-looking individuals in the vicinity. Hence, there is nothing else to be achieved here.

'Thank you for your help, mademoiselle. If anything occurs to you, please let me know. I shall leave my card at the front desk.'

As he begins to tidy away his papers, a delicate hand with the grip of the boa constrictor in the Ménagerie du Jardin circles his wrist. 'If you think it's connected, and you think I'm not involved in the French disappearances, please convince the American police to release me. Please.'

In his mind, Laurent has neither confirmed nor ruled out a link between the investigations in the two countries. He glances at Miss Marlowe. She is looking at him with a directness that makes the blood rush to his face. For a moment, he is caught off balance by a flicker of recognition. They have never met before today, but there is something about this waif of a woman that is strangely familiar.

He wills himself to keep his composure. 'I will see what can be done.'

14

'Up you get, mulatto.'

Maisie feels a hard tug of her arm, wakes to find a hairy-armed guard dragging her to her feet. It's still dark outside, pre-dawn, she thinks, and her eyes take a moment to blink themselves clear of sleep.

'She a high yellow?' one of the dark-skinned women shouts from a bed. 'No wonder she thinks herself better than us.'

'*Highfalutin' yellow skin/Black nor white has never been!*' a chorus of voices sing.

Though these terms are new to Maisie, the expressions of disgust are familiar. She saw them on the faces of Mrs Sixpence, the locals on Canvey Island, the Jesserton servants and the bullies at Clacton. It's another indication that she doesn't belong anywhere, with anyone. A reminder of her loneliness.

'Say your goodbyes, ladies. This one is out of here.'

Maisie could weep with relief. Thank you, Detective Bisset. Thank you. She doesn't know how he's done it, but an unfamiliar feeling of being truly seen by the detective told her that he would find a way to arrange her freedom.

The woman who punched Maisie jumps up and brings her face to within inches of her own. 'See you soon, mulatto.'

Not if Maisie can help it. She offers a smile through gritted teeth as the guard shoves her forwards, determined to do whatever it takes never to set foot in here again.

Out in the corridor, the box containing her belongings rattles as the guard slams it on the ground. Inside lies her pretty, navy dress along with a pair of prison-issue pumps. Noticing a small card tucked in the corner, she plucks it out and reads the front.

On the back is scribbled the name of a hotel in Chicago with a telephone number. She must thank him for showing her kindness at such a dark time.

The guard leads Maisie to a small tiled vestibule where a bucket of water, a quarter-bar of Sapolio soap and a ragged towel have been provided. Scouring off the stench feels as good as when she washed after her confinement with the scarlet fever. The water is brown, oozing along a groove in the floor and down the drain.

Once clean and dressed, she is led out of the building and to the front gate.

'And here's a dime for the journey. There's a streetcar stop down the street,' the guard explains.

Maisie has never taken public transport before, but she manages to find the stop, locate the nearest destination to Fairweather House on the small map stuck to the facing wall, and wait until the streetcar bearing the correct number finally appears. Worn out by her ordeal, she takes a seat at the back and leans on the window, eyes half closed.

Dawn is cracking over the horizon as she alights and makes her way on foot to the house. It looks spacious and welcoming this early, with the birds on the lake calling out their greetings.

The front door is flung open.

'Oh, ma'am, we just received word about you coming home!' Clara enthuses. 'You didn't need to walk – Arnold would have gone to fetch you.'

Clara throws her arms around Maisie. It feels strange to receive such tenderness after the brutality of the lock-up but comforting as well. Maisie falls into the embrace, grateful that Clara cares. From the hallway, she can see through to the drawing room and its floor-to-ceiling windows. The view of Silver Kingdom is eerie in the half-light of dawn, like a ghost town that sits at the edge of the lake.

'I'll be down later,' she tells the maid.

The rest of the day is surreal, as if Maisie is looking at her old life through a glass wall. Very little has changed other than that Silver Kingdom was shut down by the police on the day of Clementine's disappearance, and hasn't reopened. The silence of the grounds outside is striking, and she wonders how Sir Malcolm – and the rest of the workforce – is handling the financial implications of there being no paying customers.

He comes to find her in the parlour late morning and spends some minutes checking on her well-being before holing away in his study. The servants bustle about, as usual, and it feels to Maisie that her absence made no notable impact on the household. Readjusting to normal life is going to be more difficult than she had expected.

That night, Maisie awakes from nightmares of prison, and spinning around on a fast-moving carousel unable to get off. Drenched in sweat, she takes deep breaths.

How can such a wonderful ride – one that was a world away from the Sixpences, and filled Tommy and Maisie with hope – be associated with such ghastly crimes? The disclosure that there were victims in France on top of Clementine Pickford's disappearance changed everything. For the millionth time since that day, Maisie pictures Billy's frightened face as he clung to the pole of a carousel horse. That image makes more sense if whoever is taking the children loiters nearby. But it still doesn't explain what happened to him. Or any of them.

Without having a clear plan, she steals out of the house and across the grounds, accompanied by the screech of foxes. The light of the full moon is masked by a bank of clouds tonight, and walking through Silver Kingdom is eerie. Brash colours and the happy sound of children laughing are replaced by a menacing gloom as she heads down a path flanked by the hall of mirrors and the helter-skelter. Nearing the carousel, she pauses, her breath held. A scratching noise like claws dragging across stone is coming from behind the macabre poster for the ghost train. All at once, a shape emerges, looming above. Maisie is about to let out a cry when a tufted owl flaps past.

Her heart is still racing by the time she alights on the platform. Reaching out, she strokes a horse, then another, admiring the craftsmanship of each. There are scarlet manes and purple tails, elaborate patterns painted along the haunches. As she reaches the horse she saw Billy riding, she touches its golden saddle.

Her senses prickle. There's something different about this horse. An oddness. With a jolt, she realizes that this is the horse with the lifelike eyes that drew her in as it lay on the platform at Grand Central Station. Maisie isn't able to shake the feeling that this distinction is important somehow, though she can't pin down why.

Before anyone else is awake the next morning, Maisie is at the lake. A worry plays on her mind. Another child is missing and she herself was arrested, despite the pains she's taken to lay charms. Perhaps it wasn't enough. Clinging to the hope that everything will turn out all right, she prays over and over to the Lord of the Water, and lays more pebbles than ever around the carousel. She has to believe in these rituals. She has always relied on them to keep her safe, to ward off bad luck. Without their power, she's left exposed, vulnerable.

Back indoors again, Maisie is sitting in the parlour when Sir Malcolm walks in. She's surprised to see him already dressed in his best suit, as if he's planning a visit to downtown Chicago today. He fiddles with the cord of the Tiffany lamp, avoiding eye contact.

'We thought we'd let you rest yesterday,' he says, clearing his throat as if the words are stuck. 'But today we reopen Silver Kingdom. A celebration of your return, so to speak.'

Maisie feels her fear flare up. Opening Silver Kingdom is dangerous, not a celebration.

'With little Clementine Pickford still missing?'

Sir Malcolm sighs. 'Maisie, we simply cannot afford to keep the park closed any longer. We're still paying the employees, and will be lucky if anyone visits ever again with all this negative publicity. We've had to place advertisements in the local newspapers to reassure people that everything is back to normal. That certainly wasn't cheap, I can tell you.' He shakes his head. 'And, naturally, the concession holders are putting pressure on me. Their livelihoods are at stake as well, and the worry is that they will up and leave if we don't sort this out.'

Maisie understands his concerns. But what about her, and the safety of their visitors? No wonder he's so twitchy. He's probably been working up to tell Maisie of this decision ever since she returned. Fear gives way to anger that the two brothers are so irresponsible. Or perhaps they don't know that there might be a connection to the carousel.

'But the carousel is dangerous –'

He looks at Maisie like she's an overly tired child.

'I know lock-up can't have been easy on you, and I did try to arrange your release through Mr Peabody, but it seems he got rather distracted dealing with the problematic matter of unions, which Hugo and I asked him to look into.' He fixes his gaze on the floor. 'Perhaps I should have pushed him harder.'

Sir Malcolm flushes as though he knows that he's been shown up. While she's grateful for his assistance, this admission of carelessness revives Maisie's age-old fear of being abandoned by him.

'Look, the Bureau have gathered all the evidence they need,' he says in a soft, reassuring tone. 'They've scoured the grounds – including the area around the carousel, I might add – spent days here disturbing my peace, and they're happy for us to open.'

Maisie is stunned that he's so blasé. 'A little girl has been taken, Sir Malcolm,' she reiterates. 'A second child.'

'Which is terrible, yes, but has nothing to do with us. Someone has been picked up, a chap involved with the actress, apparently, so all is in hand.'

Caught by surprise, Maisie stares at Sir Malcolm. Perhaps this is why she was released. He moves to the drinks cabinet and pours himself a brandy. As this news sinks in, the tension in her shoulders loosens. She feels a glimmer of hope that the missing children are safe.

'So Clementine has been found?' she asks.

Clearly uncomfortable, Sir Malcolm bounces on the balls of his feet, his shoes leaving faint impressions on the oriental rug.

'I'm afraid not,' he admits. 'But it's still early days, so they are hopeful.'

She purses her mouth. Though the arrest of another suspect is good news for Maisie, she can't quite believe that Sir Malcolm has already forgotten the terrible events from before.

'But Billy went missing five years ago,' she retorts.

She prickles with a sense of injustice for the poor boy whose disappearance received far less attention because he wasn't related to a 'somebody'.

Sir Malcolm dismisses her concern with a casual wave of his hand.

'The Bureau are looking into that as well, no need to worry.'

It's obvious that his mind is made up and there's only so far that Maisie dare push it with him. And, deep down, she knows that he wouldn't want anything bad to happen to her. But what if this new suspect isn't the culprit? What if another child disappears? Fearful of being rearrested, she is torn – on the one hand, she hopes that everyone in Chicago has heard about the disappearances and is too scared to visit despite the latest advertisements. Then again, they need the money, and Maisie can see that reopening the park is really their only choice.

Running from the room, she rushes upstairs to her bathroom and switches on the shower. The water splutters before flowing like a waterfall. Maisie undresses and steps under the steady stream. Using soap and a scrubbing brush, she scours her skin in small circles, drawing blood. She cries out in pain, in anger, in frustration, hoping and praying that her worst fears don't materialize.

Far from putting people off, recent events seem to have flamed interest in Silver Kingdom. Ghoulish curiosity draws greater crowds than ever, as if half of Chicago wants to view the scene of the crime. Maisie's stomach churns as the gates open and visitors swarm to the carousel. She watches, vigilant, biting her lip when Arnold pulls down the control lever.

The horses are on the move, their colours streaming like ribbons in the wind. Her eyes keep track as she stands ten feet from the carousel, near enough to notice if anything should go wrong. Around her, people are laughing and joking. But Maisie feels sick.

The ride is almost over when there's a shriek from somewhere to the left. *No. Please, no.*

Frantic, she shouts at Arnold to stop the ride. But the music is so loud that her voice doesn't carry. Hitching up her dress, she leaps on to the slowing platform and weaves through the horses.

'Get off,' she screams at the riders. 'Arnold, get them off.'

The Crew must have heard Maisie shouting. She spots Lucky Nate diving through the crowd followed by the others. Pushing through spectators, they are already searching behind food stands and inside nearby rides for a missing child.

Maisie is close to sobbing as frightened parents run to save their bawling children. By the time she reaches Arnold, he looks like he's on the verge of fainting.

'Has another child gone missing?' he cries.

Maisie looks around. No one appears to have lost a child, and the crowd is melting away, grumbling. Another shriek pierces the air. With a mixture of relief and embarrassment, Maisie realizes that what sounded like a shout for help actually came from the nearby Ferris wheel, riders screaming with excitement.

Her own fear had created the panic.

'Move along, folks, the sideshow is over,' she hears Lucky Nate call as he directs curious bystanders to other attractions. 'Don't forget to tour the park on the mechanical train.'

It was a false alarm this time. But she can't go on like this. The worry will drive poor Arnold into an early grave and Maisie into insanity.

Rushing to the house, she retrieves the French detective's business card and dials the number on the back. Her hope is that the one other person who seems interested in the carousel's possible link to the disappearances is still in Chicago.

'Detective Bisset, I need your help.'

15

In Paris, it is a simple matter of notifying one of the constables to release a suspect, or bribing a fellow detective, perhaps with tickets to the Folies Bergères, to hasten the process. Chicago is not very different, it transpires. But without clout here, Laurent had to resort to the latter approach.

He had been informed within an hour of departing the interview room that suspicion had fallen on someone else. Still, there was some dragging of the feet on the part of the Bureau in releasing Miss Marlowe. Laurent cannot blame his American colleagues – sometimes it is simpler to detain a person than risk needing to rearrest them at a later date. But his instincts tell him that the woman he spoke to in lock-up was not capable of being caught up in the disappearances in either country. That, and the fact he offered her his reassurances compelled Laurent to slip a bottle of Merlot to Agent O'Connell on the understanding that Miss Marlowe would be freed within the day.

'It's not rum, but it'll do,' the man jested. 'I'll try a drop in my coffee later.'

It was unexpected, therefore, to receive her telephone call requesting assistance.

On the way to visit her, Laurent stops at the Chicago Public Library, keen to learn every detail about the latest suspect, Beau Armitage, specifically to find any links that he might have to France. A rich industrialist with influence and connections, the man has employed the services of a lawyer who is like a rabid dog, not only keeping Laurent at bay but ensuring that his client gives one-word answers to the interrogators at the Bureau. The lawyer has also blocked any attempt at a line-up on the grounds that Mr Armitage's face regularly appears in the gossip columns. All that is confirmed thus far is that he is the jilted ex-lover of Mary Pickford, involved in a furious argument with the actress in which he threatened her family, and several eyewitnesses have reported seeing a man matching his description at the amusement park that day.

Time flies as Laurent studies old newspapers with the assistance of the obliging librarian, a dark-haired woman with high cheekbones and a flair for sifting through information. Over the next few hours, it becomes apparent that Mr Armitage is a bad-tempered show-off who enjoys wild parties and flashy automobiles. Finding no mention of France, or Victor Cloutier, or carousels, Laurent calls it a day.

After so many hours of concentration, he is flagging by the time he arrives by cab at the amusement park.

Visitors are leaving at the end of the day. People stream past, weary but in high spirits, heading for the wrought-iron gates at the entrance to the estate. He tips his hat at a group of giggling young women, and returns the smile of a particularly pretty brunette.

The house is pleasantly large, set within spacious grounds that reek of money. No wonder the proceeds from the sale of the carousel were double what Laurent had expected.

He trudges up the driveway, past rows of verdant trees. This mansion is obviously not the home of the dishevelled individual that he encountered in the lock-up, but the address he was given was no more specific than this. As Laurent is deciding whether to wander around to the back and enquire at the servants' entrance or search for Miss Marlowe amongst the labourers in the amusement park, a round-faced young woman opens the front door.

'Who is that, Clara?' a man shouts from inside the house.

Clara steps aside and Laurent spots a stout gentleman with large eyebrows glaring at him from the hallway.

'I am looking for a Miss Marlowe,' he explains. The gentleman eyes Laurent with some suspicion. 'She sent for me. I am Detective Laurent Bisset.'

'Sir Malcolm Randolph, Maisie's guardian,' he bellows. 'And what exactly is it that you want with her?'

Laurent gives a small bow. 'Merely to help.'

Sir Malcolm grunts. 'Indeed.' After a long pause, he adds, 'She will be that way,' and points ahead before he disappears down a corridor to the left.

Astonished to be entering by the front entrance, Laurent follows Clara to a modest-sized room filled with antique couches. A young woman wearing a mauve dress, and with her dark brown hair arranged elegantly in a coiled bun, is pacing in front of a bank of windows. He hardly recognizes her as the same person from the lock-up, but this is indeed Miss Marlowe.

Without the filth of incarceration, she is surprisingly lovely, although her light brown eyes are wrought with worry.

'I appreciate you coming, Detective,' she says. 'Clara, that will be all.'

The maid exits the room, and Miss Marlowe takes a seat. She indicates the couch opposite and Laurent sits.

'And thank you. I don't know if it was your efforts or the police finding another suspect that led to my release, but I'm very grateful to be out. I couldn't have borne another second in that dreadful place,' she says.

Laurent acknowledges her gratitude with a smile.

'We can call it a little of both. It was an easier task once you were replaced as the chief suspect,' he explains, trying to sound modest.

Her eyes pinch at the corners. 'But are you sure it's him? Absolutely sure?'

He holds up his hands.

'I cannot say that, no. And it would not be my place to do so, since I am not from the Bureau.'

She looks to her lap, wringing her hands.

'But you *can* say that you're here because of the carousel. You think whoever did this followed it from France?'

So it is the photograph that disturbed her. Members of the public drawing their own conclusions is the exact reason that Laurent is usually so careful about the information he discloses.

'At this stage, we do not know if the American and French cases are connected. I am here to explore the possibility, that is all.'

She falls silent, staring out of the window. He follows her gaze to the view of the amusement park. It is bright and gaudy even in twilight, just as he would have expected from such a place.

As she turns her face back to the room, she straightens her spine.

'But, while there's still a possibility, don't you think the carousel should be closed to the public? Sir Malcolm won't hear of it, but I thought he might listen to a detective. You could tell him about your suspicions.'

He is put on the spot by this request. Perhaps if this was Paris, he might have ordered that the ride be halted until there was no doubt whatsoever that the perpetrator was caught. Without any jurisdiction on these shores, Laurent's hands are tied.

'Your upset is understandable, mademoiselle.' He makes sure to keep his voice calm and reassuring. 'It is not pleasant to become entangled in these matters. Perhaps it is best to push these thoughts from your mind, and let the American authorities do the worrying.'

Her hands flutter to her swanlike neck. 'I wish I could, Detective.' Her voice has dropped to a whisper. 'But sometimes when I close my eyes, I can picture Billy crying as he circled past. It was the last anyone ever saw of him.'

'Did you notice someone near him? Or see who or what he appeared to be frightened of?' he asks.

Miss Marlowe screws up her face, seeming to find thinking about the details an ordeal.

'The only other people around him were the other children on the ride. And I don't have any idea what might have frightened him, to be honest.'

'So you were not well acquainted with the boy, then,' he states.

Shaking her head, she slumps against the back of the couch like a collapsed soufflé.

'Not very, no. But I was the one who told him that riding the carousel would be fun. Every time I saw the flash of the golden saddle coming into view, I made sure to notice his reaction.'

A peculiar sensation thrums over Laurent's skin as he recalls a small detail from the witness statement provided by the fiancée of Gérard le Blanc, one of the victims in France.

'Show me which horse he rode, please,' he requests.

★

It is five years since Laurent has faced the magnificence of the carousel, and pride surges at this fine example of French craftsmanship. He had almost forgotten the intricacy of the carving and the vivid colours that made this ride like nothing else on earth. His eyes travel over the horses, each a magnificent beast in its own right. Miss Marlowe is already pointing to one on the inner row.

Laurent feels the hairs on the back of his neck stand up. The golden saddle is immediately obvious, as mentioned in the Le Blanc file, since the saddles of the other horses are varying shades of red, blue and green. But there are other identifying features that he is beginning to fit together: the caramel coat he now remembers Chloé Fourtou's grandmother describing; the *flaming auburn mane* that Nathalie Moulland's best friend spoke of. It was as if they were talking about different mounts. But it was, in fact, one and the same horse.

Strangely, it is also the horse with the raised blue diamond on its forehead that he rode himself that day in the evidence warehouse.

'That is the horse Billy was last seen on?' he asks, drawing closer with Miss Marlowe in tow.

'Yes. It's always given me a strange feeling. Perhaps it's because the eyes make it look alive,' she comments.

'Not just Billy,' he says in a quiet voice.

She looks at him with an expression that is as astounded as he feels. 'The French children too?'

'The eldest was a thirty-two-year-old male,' he corrects her, lost in thought.

What are the odds now that this is all down to chance? If only the prosecution team had thought to re-enact the last moments of every victim, however patchy the details, Laurent might have discovered sooner that this horse is a common thread.

'Did Clementine Pickford also ride this horse?' he asks Miss Marlowe.

'I actually wasn't paying attention,' she admits. 'For most of the ride, I was inside and at the front of the house.'

He makes a mental note to ask Agent O'Connell about Clementine's horse. Approaching the front, Laurent's fingers trace over the raised diamond on the forehead while examining the four letters – E O T H – spaced around the sides. For close to a minute, he turns his head from side to side, squinting while she also looks. Then he gets it.

'It is a name – Théo – the son of the carousel's creator, Gilbert, though it holds no relevance to the case, since the boy died years ago,' Laurent explains. 'If you remember from the interview, Victor, the nephew, was beheaded for his crimes. And now we must mete out the same punishment to his accomplice,' he adds, before realizing that he has voiced this last thought out loud.

Miss Marlowe's face contorts.

'But why would they do anything so . . . so . . .' She pauses, clearly struggling for the correct word. 'So appalling?'

It is a question he has asked himself many times over. An inheritance? Theft? Pure evil? Not one of these ideas explains why someone would take seemingly random persons from this ride. It feels like the answer is simultaneously in his sights and out of his grasp.

'We have not ascertained the reason,' he confesses, turning red. 'But this new discovery might bring us closer. It is like working on a puzzle – each piece put in the correct place gives us a better idea of the full picture.'

Miss Marlowe takes one step forward and reaches out to touch the horse. Her fingers freeze mid-air, suspended inches from the mane.

'Do you feel that?' she asks. 'The odd vibration?'

Laurent raises his hand in the air, holding it still. There is a faint breeze but nothing stranger. 'Perhaps it is just the wind.'

Shrugging, she lets her hand alight on the mane. 'Perhaps.'

Laurent begins to study the horse in detail, moving his hands from the shoulders to the haunches, tapping for hollows. Miss Marlowe follows his example on the left flank. While he kneels down to scrutinize the belly, she pulls the ears and the tail. She seems to share his conviction that they are on to something. But after several minutes, neither has found anything untoward.

He examines the control panel next. It is a mass of wires and incomprehensible connections. Back in France, even expert technicians were unable to fathom the workings of this ground-breaking machine. He steps inside the shadowy cylinder. As Laurent established in the evidence warehouse all those years ago, there is space in here for Victor and a victim. An accomplice could also fit, at a pinch, all hidden from both riders and audience. But it does not explain the link to the horse with the blue diamond: its position is not the nearest to the cylinder's entrance. In fact, the one in front would be more convenient for an abductor.

'Perhaps I should ride the horse,' Miss Marlowe shouts from the platform, as though she has heard his thoughts. 'One of us might notice something no one else has seen.'

Stepping from inside the cylinder, he sees that she is already mounted on the golden saddle and gripping a set of reins. His eyes check the vicinity – they are alone here with no would-be abductors lurking. If he maintains sight of her at all times, she will be safe.

After pulling down the control lever, Laurent races to be by her side. He notes her enjoyment as the ride gathers pace. A split-second later, however, she looks on the verge of tears.

He must stop the ride.

With one eye still on her, he leaps back to the lever. He pulls up. Nothing happens. He pulls down. Nothing. Up. Down. Up. Down. The momentum is impossible to stop. At this rate, the only option might be to haul her off the horse.

He looks over to check on Miss Marlowe and is horrified to discover that in the seconds his focus was elsewhere she has swung out of view. It takes only a moment for a person to vanish into thin air.

'Miss Marlowe! Maisie!' he shouts over the crescendo of fairground music.

His heart is pounding as he scrabbles across the platform again. The speed of the ride is picking up and the horses are now galloping fast. He dodges an orange stallion but is almost felled by a dappled pony. His head swings this way and that, searching. *Think, Laurent, think.* If he cannot catch up to the horse she is riding, maybe he should try to meet it head on. He starts running in the opposite direction from the horses, darting between them, and, eventually, spots an auburn mane. To his horror, there is no rider.

'Miss Marlowe!' he shouts again, diving aside in time to avoid another horse crashing into him. He looks inside the central cylinder in case an assailant has dragged her in there.

But she is nowhere.

It seems like forever before the ride finally stops. Lost, Laurent stands by the auburn-maned horse for several minutes in the hope that she will suddenly reappear.

A sound leads him around to a small nook on the other side of the controls, where he finds Miss Marlowe, hunched over and her entire body shaking.

'That horse. It's . . . it's' – she gasps between sobs – 'it's . . . cursed.'

Crouching next to her, he wears a look of sympathy. Curses and witchcraft are nonsense, of course.

'There, there,' he murmurs. 'Slow, steady breaths.'

He waits while her breathing settles and then hands her his handkerchief. Presently, she sits up and wipes away her tears.

'I saw something, Detective. Saw it like it was real. Something awful from childhood, as though I'd been taken back there.'

Talk of murder. Missing children. It is only natural that any person unaccustomed to hearing the grisly details of crime would become distressed, and believe they saw things that were not there. Witnessing Miss Marlowe erupt into tears again, Laurent is ever more determined to find the answer, to tie up every loose end before anyone else is entangled in this mystery.

16

Early the next morning, a compromise is reached. The carousel will remain open to visitors as usual with the exception of the one strange horse, which has been covered in blankets. Though Sir Malcolm was sceptical, he grudgingly agreed to this solution after Maisie returned to the house distraught, accompanied by the detective, who offered words of reassurance.

She would prefer for the horse to be completely removed from the carousel, but the Crew was defeated in achieving this, even with Detective Bisset translating the French instructions. 'Not had this before, but if you try to take off one horse, they all come off. Seems they're linked somehow,' Lucky Nate declared, scratching his head. Remembering the difficulty Mr Corbett's team faced when assembling the ride in the first place, Maisie believes him. What *is* normal about this carousel?

As the men gather their tools, Detective Bisset offers Maisie his arm, and she moves with him through the park, passing colourful amusements and food stalls setting up for the day. Mrs Ferretti and her adult son are up on ladders oiling the tracks that guide the dodgems. They chatter in Italian as they work. Maisie can't understand a word, but the detective greets the pair with a phrase that makes them laugh.

Mrs Ferretti takes the opportunity to ask Maisie about the possibility of having an awning erected to provide shade for the line of customers. 'I can't see why not,' she responds before walking on.

The air is crisp and dew clings to grass blades. On the lake, moorhens paddle amongst the reeds, dipping for pondweed beneath the rippling surface. It all looks so innocent that no one would have an inkling of Maisie's experience on the carousel yesterday.

'I am sorry you were frightened,' the detective says, as though he's looking into her thoughts. 'I should have known that the strain of incarceration, all this talk of mysterious vanishings, would be too much for you.'

Though he is being as kind as he was yesterday, Maisie must be careful. For all she knows, he may still believe she's involved in the disappearances and is waiting to catch her off guard to resume his questioning. Maisie doesn't believe that Madame Rose is a genuine fortune-teller, but her warning about trouble from across the ocean does seem strangely timed in the light of the detective's arrival from France so soon after.

It's obvious, as well, that he doesn't believe her claim that the horse is cursed. While part of Maisie worries that she might be losing her grip on reality, she feels a stab of irritation towards him. What she saw is clear in her mind: one second, she was enjoying the wild exhilaration of the carousel and the next everything turned black. There was a loud whoosh and then . . . and then – the memory is terrifying – she could swear an image appeared of the shack on Canvey Island. It was so lifelike, so real, with the smell of rotting fish and damp earth and the lumpy figure of Mrs Sixpence hissing *Just you wait until I get you, Maisie.* It makes no sense, but it really did seem that she was being sucked back in time.

She shudders, unable to shake the fear. She wanted to solve the mystery, but it was foolhardy in hindsight. Frowning, she thinks of Billy's terrified face moments before he disappeared. Poor Billy, whom she forced to ride the horse with the golden saddle.

'I feel sorrier for the people who disappeared,' she replies.

'And I am glad you are not one of them,' he replies quietly.

They have reached the Ferris wheel. Up ahead, Silver Kingdom's workers are gathered near *Fernando's Bakery*, waiting for fresh doughnuts and liquid refreshment before the park opens. They congregate here to exchange gossip and, Maisie suspects, watch the carousel, as the small booth sits a short distance away on a platform elevated two feet off the ground, providing the best vantage point. She has heard the workforce compare it with the carousels on Coney Island, and say that both its beauty and its speed are far superior. *Oh, boy, a rounding board that rotates like we're watching a movie!* is the comment most often uttered when the canopy spins, the general consensus being that no one, not even the most seasoned hands, has ever seen anything like it.

Noticing everyone staring at her walking arm in arm with a man, Maisie guides a route towards a quieter area, near the helter-skelter. She can tell by the nudging that they've got the wrong end of the stick. Most of them have known her for only a few short months, and they probably have no idea that she lacks romantic experience. Not that she's against the idea, but she's had very little opportunity, what with living in seclusion at Fairweather after Billy's disappearance, and then the war and the Spanish flu. The closest she's ever come is the unwanted kiss from James, and that doesn't count because she didn't even like him.

Clearly noticing the pained expression on her face, the detective interrupts Maisie's thoughts. 'If you are still worried about the carousel –'

'No, no,' she responds quickly, not wanting him to view her as a foolish girl. 'I was just thinking of someone in England.'

He studies her for a moment.

'Forgive me for saying, but you do not have the usual look of an English girl.'

Maisie stares down at her hands, hoping to hide the expression on her face. 'So I've been told.'

'I did not mean to offend,' he replies, picking up on it anyway.

'It's just not a subject I talk about because there's not much to say. My mother was very blonde apparently, and most likely pale like my aunt, which probably makes my father the opposite.' She shrugs, hoping to appear casual. 'That's really all I know. I think I must have been a baby when my parents died.'

All those wasted chances, Maisie thinks. All those times of letting Aunty Mabel avoid questions when she could have been discovering everything about her history.

'That must be difficult, not knowing where you come from.'

Maisie nods, grateful for his thoughtfulness. Not for the first time, she feels seen by this man. 'It's like being lost.'

She can feel herself blush. It's completely out of character for

Maisie to disclose anything so personal. But the way in which the detective is really listening, as though she's an adult and not the silly child that Nancy and – to a kinder extent – Sir Malcolm and Hugo view her as, convinces Maisie that it's safe to open up to him. An expression of understanding in his eyes makes her glance away before the buried sadness rises to the surface.

'How about you, Detective?' she continues, regaining her composure. 'Have you always lived in Paris?'

'I was born there, and I shall probably die there,' he muses, his mouth curling up at the corners.

'Then you must miss being away from your family and friends. I assume you came here alone.'

He offers a rueful smile. 'I did, but it is not so bad, and I am here for only another twelve days,' he explains. 'I have been catching up on reading, studying reports. My one complaint is that the cuisine here is not what I am accustomed to. The hotel insists that boiled liver is the pinnacle of American food.'

He states this with a tone of humour, but she feels sorry for him. An overwhelming desire to repay the kindness this man has shown her gives Maisie the push to suggest something she would never usually think to do.

'Why don't you come to dinner at Fairweather House tomorrow? Peggy Mae is a wonderful cook.'

Surprise flickers in his eyes.

'It will be my pleasure, of course,' he answers. He kisses the back of her hand. 'Until tomorrow,' he says. 'And now please excuse me, but I must depart. The discovery of the links to that one horse has blown everything open, and there is much to follow up on with the case.'

Maisie watches the detective amble out of the park, his long legs moving at quite a pace. As if pulled by an invisible force, she turns to gaze at the carousel in the mid-distance. What is it trying to say?

Maisie sets another pile of pebbles near the carousel to counteract the power of the cursed horse, then she goes in search of Sir Malcolm to inform him of tomorrow night's dinner. She hopes he won't be put out that she made this arrangement without asking him first. As she enters through the back of the house, she can hear voices at the front door. Eric is talking to a stranger who is demanding entry.

'Is everything all right?' Maisie calls.

Eric steps aside. A gentleman with light brown hair stands on the doorstep. Caught off guard, she can only stare, dumbfounded, at the sight of James.

17

While Sir Malcolm pours a round of drinks, his back turned to them, James smiles at Maisie. She frowns back. Her dislike of him hasn't mellowed over the past nine years. Wide shouldered and muscly, he dominates the drawing room with his overconfidence.

Accepting the tumbler of whisky from Sir Malcolm, James raises a toast. 'To reunions,' he says. 'And remembering those we've lost . . . especially dear Catherine.'

Sir Malcolm looks emotional. 'She was lucky to have a cousin like you to look up to.'

Remembering Miss Catherine's reaction to James at Clacton, Maisie silently questions Sir Malcolm's perception of the bond between the cousins. James has grown into a charmer, and Sir Malcolm is sentimental enough to lap it up.

He takes the armchair directly facing James, while she hovers in the doorway, fully intending to depart as soon as the opportunity presents itself. For a moment, Sir Malcolm stares at his drink, sombre-faced. Then he rouses himself and gives James a smile.

'And how's your family?' he asks. 'Your father, sisters – and especially your mother. Your aunt Lydia was always very fond of her sister.'

Maisie recalls the portrait of Lady Lydia, Sir Malcolm's dead wife, once in Jesserton's music room, and now hanging in his bedroom here.

'They're fine, Sir Malcolm, fine. The war was difficult for my mother, of course, with her son on the frontline. But I returned.'

James leans back in his armchair, clearly already at home at Fairweather House.

'You saw action, then?' Sir Malcolm asks, looking impressed.

'My regiment became known as a force to be reckoned with,' James boasts.

Sir Malcolm laughs. 'Good for you.'

Maisie watches James grin as Sir Malcolm leans forward and claps him on the knee. His hair is shorter than before, and he now sports a well-trimmed moustache.

'It was the war that made me realize you have to seize your chances. I'd been thinking about America for a while because it's a country with so much going for it,' he explains. 'So, when I saw a story about the vanished niece of an actress, together with a photograph of you, Sir Malcolm, it was a sign that perhaps I should scout out the place before making a decision either way.' He glances up at Maisie. 'It's funny, I didn't even know that Maisie was here with you, until I saw her name in the article. There it was, in a paragraph about the witnesses. It must have been an unpleasant experience all round.'

Sir Malcolm managed to keep the information about her arrest out of the newspapers, and James has no idea it was so much worse than unpleasant.

Maisie looks at the floor. She can feel James's eyes boring into her. Recalling her last day at Jesserton, her lie about possibly returning to Canvey Island. *I'll have you one day, Maisie*, he'd laughed.

'Aren't you going to sit down?' Sir Malcolm asks sharply, evidently noticing that she is backing out of the room.

'Actually, Sir Malcolm, I should really return to work. I only came in to tell you that I've invited Detective Bisset for dinner tomorrow.'

For a second, his eyebrows knit together, and Maisie thinks that he might grumble about the imposition. Then his eyes light up.

'Splendid idea. James you must come too. I'll ask Hugo and Nancy. My brother will want to catch up with you and hear all about your stories from the frontline.'

James wears a smile of triumph. Is he, rather than Laurent, the trouble from across the ocean that Madame Rose warned of?

By 7 a.m. the next morning, the household's preparations are in full swing: the best china has been removed from the storeroom and washed by Clara; Eric is cleaning the dining-room chairs with soap and water; Peggy Mae is shelling shrimp and slicing onions. Even Arnold has arrived to polish the cutlery before Silver Kingdom opens.

James's arrival has unsettled Maisie. Though they barely crossed paths in England, she knows enough about him to have reached the conclusion that he's full of himself, with eyes that seem to be on her every time she looks up. If a way to uninvite him had presented itself, she would have taken it.

Instead, she lays place names in strategic positions around the dining table. This is followed by a frenzy of flower arranging. Soon the scent of lilies mixes with the smell of garlic frying in butter, filling every room like a rich perfume. After a full day of preparations, she is heading to her bedroom to change for dinner when Sir Malcolm stops her in the upstairs hallway.

'Please do be polite to *all* our guests tonight, Maisie. Whatever possessed you to snub James like that yesterday? It's not like you.'

She takes a deep breath. 'I'm just concerned that his timing is a little off, Sir Malcolm. All this business with the missing children, and I've only just been released from the lock-up.'

Sir Malcolm raises an eyebrow.

'Well, it's not like he knew about your arrest,' he blusters. 'And he's Lydia's nephew, and one doesn't turn one's back on family.'

Clearly nostalgic, he's been taken in by James's smooth confidence, even charm, and doesn't seem in the mood to be reminded that not once has he mentioned James or any of the family since leaving England. She mutters an apology and hurries away, cursing James under her breath. One night, she tells herself, one night of having to endure him and then she will make sure to avoid him for the rest of his stay.

Taking her time, Maisie attends to her hair, twisting the thick coil into a knot, then adds an amber clip-hat. She dabs lavender oil on her wrists and neck next, working the excess into her hands. She slips on her velvet pumps, loops a pendant around her neck. As she reaches the bottom of the staircase, James appears.

'Looks like you can't get away from me,' he smirks.

Her revulsion flares.

'I wouldn't be so sure of that,' she retorts, sweeping past him.

18

Laurent walks briskly through Silver Kingdom. If he is quick, there is time for a detour before dinner. In the dark, with only the light streaming from the big house to guide him, he takes extra care not to stumble. Even so, he reaches the carousel in record time.

He is energized by the information Agent O'Connell shared this afternoon. That Clementine Pickford rode the horse *with the blue diamond on its forehead* leaves him in no doubt that all the disappearances are connected, which means there must be an unknown accomplice out there. Like his bosses, however, the American authorities have no interest in any crime that did not take place on their own soil.

'I can't see the relevance,' Agent O'Connell claimed as they sat side by side on their usual bench in Columbus Park, a spacious oasis of greenery in the city that reminds him of the Parc de Belleville.

Laurent suspects that his counterparts on this side of the Atlantic are too involved with their own recent breakthrough to consider any other leads. The news is not public knowledge yet, but the Bureau is about to pour all its resources into locating the Wadham family somewhere in the east of the country after discovering that Billy's father was Beau Armitage's previous tailor. It is hoped that Mr Wadham can shed some light on the dealings between the two men.

This leaves Laurent alone to unearth any link the industrialist might have to France. To Victor. Having had no luck looking through old newspapers, Laurent has begun tracing Beau Armitage's associates in the hope of ascertaining if and when the man might have travelled to France. Several ex-secretaries have already been questioned by Laurent. Miss Lewis was in the man's employment for *two months of hell*, as she put it, during which time she was forbidden from leaving work before midnight. Softly spoken Miss Archibald lasted three weeks, leaving in tears after he accused her of stealing a notepad. Mrs Gillespie, a buxom woman with flame-red hair, was fired for asking for a raise. All three women seemed perfectly amenable to Laurent, but were unable to recall any foreign travel that Mr Armitage might have undertaken. Miss Lewis mentioned the name of an ex-business partner who might know more details, however. Thus all he has gleaned so far is that there is someone else to interview, and the industrialist has a tendency to fall out with people.

Hoping now that another look at the carousel itself might prove fruitful, Laurent strides over the platform. Then he stops, peering closely. Something is different. The blanket is loose and fastened sloppily to one side. He spots this discrepancy because he wrapped the fabric himself and tied a specific double knot at the top in which the ends are tucked back under, as taught to him by his mother when they built make-believe castles under the dining table with sheets.

It means that someone has tampered with the protective covering. But who would do this? And why?

It is a surprise to see other guests assembled around the dining table, since Laurent believed he was the only person invited to dine at Fairweather House tonight. On the one hand, the timing of this party seems distasteful – Miss Marlowe has only recently been released from the lock-up and there is still a child missing, presumed dead. Then again, the well-to-do are never inclined to abstain from fun out of consideration for others.

'Here you are, Detective,' Miss Marlowe says, patting the empty dining chair beside her.

She is positioned at the head of the table with Sir Malcolm at the other end. Slipping into his seat, Laurent nods to the other three individuals – two men and a glamorous woman – who only briefly pause to acknowledge him before resuming their conversations. He observes Sir Malcolm whisper in the woman's ear, after which she cries *Oh, darling, stop it*, while throwing her head back and roaring with laughter.

'Apologies for my lateness,' Laurent says to Miss Marlowe. 'I thought Sir Malcolm said to arrive at 8.30 p.m.'

'You're not late. Everyone else is early. Clearly, they couldn't wait to enjoy our company.'

He notes there is a defensive edge to her tone. But, having spent some time with her, Laurent knows that it masks a vulnerable side.

'I would have been here sooner, but I stopped to look at the horse. Did you change the blankets or loosen the knot by any chance?'

For a moment, confusion crosses her face. Then her eyes grow round. 'No, I didn't. Are you saying –'

Sir Malcolm taps a dessert spoon against his champagne glass.

'Let me make the introductions,' he announces. 'Everyone, this is Detective Laurent Bisset. Laurent, this young chap is James Squires, my late wife's nephew. Next to him and opposite you sits my brother, Hugo, and to your right is his delightful wife, Nancy.'

'You're here about the grisly disappearances,' Nancy says, leaning towards Laurent. 'All the way from Paris. I've asked Hugo to take me there many times, but he's such a spoil-sport that he absolutely refuses.'

Nancy pouts, using the opportunity to finish her drink. Seconds later, a sombre-faced footman steps forward and quietly replenishes the glass.

'Yes, my dear, because we all know that were you to be let loose in Paris, I would be bankrupted within two days. It isn't known as the capital of fashion for nothing.'

Although Hugo laughs, there is a glint in the man's eyes. He turns to Laurent.

'I hear there's a new lead. Mr Armitage knew the tailor, apparently.'

From the corner of his eye, Laurent sees Maisie tense. Evidently, no one has apprised her of this development.

'Indeed. I was told just this afternoon,' he agrees, careful not to reveal anything more.

Nancy rolls her eyes. 'Yes, but that doesn't necessarily mean anything,' she chimes in. 'Everyone in Chicago is linked to someone else. Billy's father was the best tailor in the city – Hugo's suits haven't been the same since his family upped sticks – and Mr Wadham knew all of us, as well as the servants and Arnold, so that doesn't prove a thing.'

Laurent files this information in his head. From where he is sitting, the outline of the carousel is visible, shrouded in a darkness that lends it a greater air of mystery.

He notices that Hugo and Sir Malcolm share a look.

'Come, come, Nancy, no need to throw a spanner in the works,' Sir Malcolm replies in a jolly voice, although his creased brow suggests that he feels anything but. 'Let's leave it to the authorities to draw up theories. Police business is complicated. Isn't that right, Laurent?'

Laurent nods, although he has a distinct feeling that the appearance of a suspect – *any* suspect – suits the Randolph brothers if it means they can keep their business open.

'So if you're a French detective, what exactly are you doing in America?' James asks.

Stocky and tall, the man is built like a pugilist. Laurent has already noticed that throughout the conversation, James's eyes flick repeatedly to Miss Marlowe.

'There are unresolved questions from my investigation in Paris that are tied to the cases here.'

'Well, let's hope you get the answers you're looking for quickly. I'm sure you must be looking forward to returning home,' James replies smoothly.

Not entirely, would be Laurent's honest answer. The absence from his child is a sorrow, of course. But he has barely thought of his wife, the peaceful solitude of his bachelor days returning to bring a lightness to his existence.

'But of what importance are my wishes when there are children still missing?' he responds, having picked up on an undercurrent of unfriendliness from the young man. As a consequence, Laurent does not care to share that he is due to leave America in ten days.

Nancy studies her varnished nails. 'Oh, let's not spoil dinner with talk of dead children.'

As Sir Malcolm chokes on his drink, Hugo fixes his wife with a sharp look. It is enough to silence not just her but the entire room, which is plunged into awkwardness. Fortunately, a servant arrives with a platter of breaded shrimp on a bed of dressed lettuce and proceeds to serve the diners. Conversation between the brothers turns to the subject of old acquaintances in England, while Nancy ignores the shrimp and wanders over to the drinks cabinet to help herself to a tall glass of orange juice mixed with an equal part of vodka in place of the starter.

The marinade sauce is more fiery than Laurent is accustomed to, and his eyes water.

Miss Marlowe stabs a shrimp with her fork. He notices she lifts the food to her mouth, takes a small bite and returns the rest to her plate, uneaten.

'This is too spicy for you also, mademoiselle?' he asks her.

'I'm used to it,' she replies.

Perhaps she has lost her appetite because she is still troubled by the carousel. Her talk of curses has Laurent concerned. It is as non-sensical as Ouija boards, seances and the like. If she is not careful, Miss Marlowe is at risk of spiralling downwards. He saw this sort of sorry decline in his own mother.

With the other diners talking amongst themselves, it feels to Laurent like he and this woman are alone in the room.

'The accomplice will be found,' he assures her. 'The Bureau are convinced Mr Armitage is the culprit. If it is not him, I will continue the search.'

She looks at him. 'You think I imagined what I saw, don't you?'

Hesitating, he tries to find the correct words to talk her out of her illogical belief, without causing offence.

'I think that the mind is a powerful thing, and I would not wish your thoughts to cause you any distress,' he says gently. 'By chance, I rode that horse myself in Paris many years ago, and felt a yearning for a happy time with my mother. Perhaps nostalgia has played a part in your experience too.'

She fiddles with her napkin, silent for several seconds.

'Well, Detective, I can't say that I hold fond memories of that period in my life, but I appreciate your trying to make me feel better.'

'Please call me Laurent,' he requests. 'We are dining together, so we are friends now, non?'

Her face lights up. It is rare that a woman's beauty takes him by surprise. At his age, he thought he had seen it all. Striking redheads. Delicate blondes. Brunettes. Strong features. Soft curves. But in this split-second, it feels to Laurent as though he is watching a rainbow grace the skies after years of drizzle.

'So you must call me Maisie.'

'Maisie it is.'

She mirrors his smile. Over at the other end of the table, Laurent catches James staring at them, frowning.

'This party needs livening up,' Nancy states loudly, flouncing to her chair. 'It should really be the hostess's job, but I suppose it falls to me to step in,' she complains. 'Let's get the gramophone in here and start living a little.'

Immediately, Sir Malcolm signals to the footman that he should do as she bids. Perhaps music is a good idea. The room is a powder keg of emotions, and Laurent wonders who might explode first.

Well-versed in how to transform a woman's disposition, Laurent sees it as his duty to distract Nancy, if only for the sake of the others present. It is as easy to mould her into shape as the pieces of paper he crafts into birds. He asks questions about the latest fashions and talks about what she should see in Paris, if she were ever to visit. Soon she is giggling, singing along to one cheerful gramophone tune after another – although she fires daggers at Maisie if Laurent dares to try to bring her into their conversation. He has seen it before: mothers jealous of daughters, aunts of nieces, threatened by someone younger and prettier. But Maisie appears content enough to talk to Hugo while barely answering James whenever he asks her a direct question.

Laurent wonders what is going on between those two. He knows men of James's type – jocular and confident – and has never trusted them.

The main course of roast beef smothered in another hot sauce proceeds smoothly through to a dessert of syrupy lemon cake with vanilla ice cream. There is no rich Camembert to round off the meal, but Laurent's stomach is satisfied nonetheless.

'Good news, everyone,' Sir Malcolm announces, barely able to keep his inebriated body from tilting to the right. 'James is going to work at Silver Kingdom as groundsman until he finds more suitable employment. Personally, I think it's beneath the chap's capabilities, but he seems quite taken with the idea.'

Hugo speaks. 'So this is more than a fleeting visit? Malcolm told me that this trip was to size up the place.'

James looks smug, confirming Laurent's first impressions of him, while Maisie stiffens.

'I like what I see of Chicago, so I'm thinking of staying permanently. It's even more buoyant than I expected, and certainly livelier than England, which is still reeling after the war.' He takes a sip of his drink. 'I'm inspired by Sir Malcolm's story of success – yours as well, Hugo – and can see that opportunities abound for an ambitious fella. I've even managed to secure a three-month lease on a small apartment downtown.'

There is the sound of Maisie scraping back her chair.

'If you could excuse me a moment, please,' she says, standing up.

Laurent watches her disappear from the room.

'There she goes. Always making everything about herself,' Nancy says in a voice loud enough to carry through the house.

'I'm sorry dinner was so eventful. I invited you hoping to give you some nice company. Instead, I dragged you into this circus.'

Laurent is standing with Maisie in the hallway. He is surprised to see Arnold wheeling the drinks trolley from the dining room, since he knows from his time at Silver Kingdom yesterday that this is the person who operates the carousel. Although he would like to speak with him about the disturbed blankets, the man looks run ragged, and Laurent decides to wait until tomorrow.

The other gentlemen guests are retiring to the drawing room for another round of drinks, while Laurent excuses himself on the pretext of the punishing time difference between Chicago and Paris. In truth, Laurent suspects that further drama is inevitable, given the amount of alcohol consumed, and despite the fact that he helped Nancy into a cab home, leaving Hugo at the party fuming.

Maisie chews her bottom lip, worry lines creasing her forehead. Having spent dinner with the people closest to her, he now understands why she protects her vulnerability inside a hard casing like a walnut shell. Wondering if she is thinking of James, he wants to ask what connection they share. But he refrains. If she wished to tell him, she would.

'Circuses are my second favourite leisure activity after amusement parks,' he jests.

As she breaks into a smile, it feels like a beam of sunshine cracking through dark clouds. He smiles back, meeting her gaze for what feels like an eternity and a brief moment at the same time.

He has a sudden urge to do something for her. He thinks back to what she said about never having known her parents. It would not be difficult for a detective to dig up the past. More than anything, he wants to tell her: *Look, you are found.*

19

The following day, Laurent sends a telegram to Constable Segal in Paris before departing for Silver Kingdom. Arriving at the amusement park a few minutes after opening time, he struggles to make his way through the crowd. There are so many more people here than he has ever seen in any French fairground, and with a vaster array of amusements. Trust the Americans to want things bigger and better than anywhere else in the world.

Turning north-eastwards, he heads for the carousel to talk to Arnold and watch the ride on a normal working day. The disturbed blankets unsettle Laurent. If it is a relevant discovery, the chances that Beau Armitage is Victor's accomplice are greatly diminished, since the man is in custody. Before flagging the matter with Agent O'Connell, however, he must rule out other possibilities. Perhaps Arnold had reason to rearrange the knot, or he saw someone else doing so. Perhaps in the hurly-burly to get on and off the platform, the crowd accidentally loosened the covering.

Some might say that he is making too much of this matter, but in Laurent's experience it is little details like this that often solve a crime. Possibly the accomplice unwittingly left behind a crucial piece of evidence and returned to retrieve it. Yesterday evening it was too dark to notice anything of value, but whatever it is could still be there.

He passes *Wild Bill's Rootin' Tootin' Shootin' the Bad Guys*, where metal cut-outs of famous bandits are taken down with rifles, then *Quacks-a-Daisy*, which appears to be an entertainment involving hooking wooden ducks on a long pole, run by a trio of Armenian sisters. Approaching the coconut shy, he is taken back to the summer day more than thirty years ago with the sun glinting off the metal struts of the merry-go-round and the lapping water of the nearby

Seine and the shiny bruises like purple bracelets on his mother's wrists.

'I'll wager you two dollars that I can knock more coconuts off than you,' Sir Malcolm barks.

He has appeared beside Laurent, his large eyebrows arched. Given the state of the man last night, Laurent is staggered to see him up and about with an almost normal visage. The only giveaway is the unmistakable pungent smell of liquor that surrounds him.

'It is an irresistible bet,' Laurent replies, rolling up his shirtsleeves.

Sir Malcolm grunts. 'As all good bets should be.'

With a steady hand, Laurent aims and throws. The ball glances the middle coconut, which holds firm in its place. He tries and fails with the second ball, then the third. After the fourth, he gives up.

Fingers trembling, Sir Malcolm drops the first ball at his feet.

'That doesn't count as a throw,' Laurent offers generously.

'As you wish.'

Sir Malcolm picks up the ball, hurls it through the air and slices a coconut free with a loud crack. There is a cheer from onlookers as another two coconuts tumble to the ground with the next three balls.

'Years of cricket, old chap,' Sir Malcolm explains, patting Laurent on the back.

'And there I thought I would have you with my pétanque skills,' Laurent replies while he fishes in his jacket for his wallet.

'No, no,' Sir Malcolm insists. 'It was an imaginary bet.' He removes two cigars from his pocket and offers one to Laurent, who declines. 'So what brings you to Silver Kingdom? Didn't you get enough of us last night?'

Lighting up, Sir Malcolm puffs clouds of fragrant smoke into the air.

'How could anyone tire of the beauty of this place?' Laurent says, sweeping his hands in the general direction of the lake.

'True, true,' the older man agrees. 'But really? Why are you here?'

He looks at Laurent, his gaze probing. Laurent keeps his own eyes cool and steady. Under normal circumstances, he would simply shrug and claim that this is private police business and there is nothing further that he is able to disclose. But this is not France.

'I know for a fact that the blankets around the horse have been disturbed. The knot I used to secure it is unusual. It is something that needs looking into.'

Sir Malcolm pauses puffing. He motions for Laurent to follow him to a quiet nook at the rear of the popcorn stand.

'And why is that?'

'Because it might eliminate a suspect. As was discussed last night, the tailor was known by many people, not just Mr Armitage.'

Sir Malcolm's eyebrows knit into a frown. 'Look here, Laurent, you were invited to dinner in a friendly capacity, not to snoop. One of the agents at the Bureau has told me that *you* closed the case in France. Let me remind you that *they* are in charge in America.' His jaw twitches in what Laurent takes to be a warning signal. 'Wouldn't you prefer to go back to your family, rather than bother yourself with a couple of children who have likely been abducted by some local lunatic?'

Laurent feels heat rush to the back of his neck. Does the man really care more about his business than the fate of the missing persons?

'If you are not concerned about the victims, you have only to say so.'

Sir Malcolm looks like he might explode.

'Of course I'm damn well concerned,' he bristles. 'Of course.' His mouth is drawn into a thin line. Laurent can tell that the man is trying to rein in his emotions. 'But if you're going to be hanging around here, I must insist that you dress less like a detective; it's off-putting to the customers.' He stabs his finger towards Laurent's formal three-piece suit. 'Immediately.'

Sir Malcolm stomps off. Rejoining the masses, Laurent is now acutely aware that he is conspicuous amongst the parade of light coloured, casual attire. As he heads to the exit, his attention is caught by the sight of Maisie and James standing by the base of the helter-skelter. It is easy to see that the pair are embroiled in a heated discussion of their own.

As Laurent watches Maisie attempt to get away from James, he feels an unexpected surge of annoyance that the man has been pestering her.

20

Maisie turns on her heel and strides away from James. It was bad enough having to endure him staring across the table at last night's dinner, but he's been following her around the park ever since he started working here this morning. Mindful of Sir Malcom's request for her to be pleasant to James, Maisie did try hard to ignore him, her patience snapping only when he started bragging about how lucky Chicago is to have him here.

She meets Laurent coming the other way.

'I thought you might need assistance,' he tells her.

They watch James heading towards a cluster of sour-cherry trees, a pair of shears in hand.

'I think I've got through to him now,' she replies, hoping she's right. She notices Laurent's briefcase. 'Are you here to do some investigating?'

He looks self-conscious. 'I was, but first I need more casual clothing in order to blend in. Since I packed in a rush, nothing I brought with me is suitable.' He indicates the black suit, black tie and black fedora that he's wearing. 'Could you please tell me where I might purchase such items?'

Maisie has a better idea. At Silver Kingdom she can never escape from the reminders that those two small children could have met with a nasty end. Maisie hears the workforce share their opinions, is regularly asked for updates by the visitors – and she's desperate to get away.

'Why don't I accompany you? The maid tells me there's a wonderful department store in the city.'

He breaks into a smile, and Maisie is struck by how perfectly straight his teeth are.

★

With no friends to speak of, Maisie has only ever accompanied Sir Malcolm on visits to the city, and those occasions have been few and far between. She also isn't brave enough to venture there alone, nor does she need to when all their tradespeople, from Mrs Papadopoulos to the fish-seller to the coalman to the seamstress, come to the house. She is, therefore, tingling with a mixture of nerves and excitement as Laurent holds open the door of the department store just a short while later.

Marshall Field's is every bit as wonderful as Maisie has heard from Clara. The great hall is a marvel of layered columns surrounding an atrium that rises to a domed ceiling, filled with exotic perfume as if a royal palace has been constructed in the centre of the city. The glamorous Money Girls were sales assistants here before they were lured to Silver Kingdom, and Maisie can imagine them fitting right in. Though she tries not to stare in wonder like a newcomer to Chicago, even someone who isn't a detective would guess she is captivated.

'It reminds me of the Galeries Lafayette in Paris,' Laurent comments. 'You have heard of it?'

Maisie laughs. 'No! I've heard of nothing in Paris except the Eiffel Tower. Perhaps if I'd stayed in England, I might know more, since it's so close to France. But I've been in America since I was a child.'

She stops for a second to examine a pair of brown leather gloves.

'Was it not disconcerting to find yourself in a strange country? I am quite astonished by the differences between America and Europe.'

She considers the question. 'Less disconcerting than what I left behind in Essex.'

'Then I am glad you are here.'

He sounds like he means it, and it leaves Maisie with the impression that the detective is genuinely caring. As she is drawn to an assortment of colourful silk scarves next, he stands near the display without complaint.

'It looks like you're quite used to waiting around for a woman,' she remarks. Deciding against buying anything for herself today, she moves on with Laurent by her side. He looks surprised by the comment, then his face falls serious.

'My mother always insisted that it was rude to keep a lady waiting, and even ruder for a gentleman to chivvy her along.'

They have arrived at the sweeping staircase, and he ushers Maisie upstairs to the second floor.

There is an overwhelming choice of garments in the men's department, more than Maisie could ever have imagined any gentleman would need – morning suits, evening suits, cravats, handkerchiefs, belts and suspenders, sweaters, bowler hats and bow ties, formal shoes, walking boots, blazers, flannel pants. She runs her fingers over a cashmere cardigan, then a row of neatly folded shirts while Laurent follows, his hands behind his back as though he intends to defer to her opinion.

'How about this?'

She pulls a button-down shirt in light yellow from the stack, and holds it up. The collar is floppy and round, not stiff and starchy and crisp white like Laurent's. He looks so dubious that she can't help laughing. 'Or that's even better . . .'

She points to a wax mannequin adorned in a soft-silhouetted, light grey lounge jacket and coordinating pants without a vest, complemented by a pale blue button-down shirt, and navy-and-red-striped tie. 'That's how you need to dress if you want to fit in with our other gentlemen visitors.'

'It will do no harm to try it on, I suppose,' he acquiesces.

Before he changes his mind, Maisie calls over the sales assistant and instructs him to find the entire ensemble in Laurent's size. When the detective emerges from the dressing room, he stands on the spot, fidgeting with the limp collar. The grey jacket brings out the colour of his eyes, the cut of cloth accentuates his athletic torso.

'It feels not quite right,' he comments.

'Well, it all looks perfect.'

His cheeks redden. 'I know little of American fashion, so perhaps it would be as well to listen to you and buy the entire outfit.'

On the way to the cash register, she grabs a straw boater from a table display. 'And a new hat to complete the look.'

As they breeze past the perfumes on their way out, Maisie catches the stares of every woman in the store directed at them. After getting to know him a little better last night, she feels a rush of pleasure at being seen with this attractive man.

Returning home in a taxi with him, Maisie glows. The unusual turn of events this afternoon has chased away the awful experience of the lock-up, her frightening ride on the strange horse, James's unexpected arrival – and opened her eyes to a dazzling world of possibilities.

21

The Grand Ringmaster of the carousel is a natural suspect, but it quickly becomes evident to Laurent the reason why the Bureau discounted Arnold. Numerous witness statements backed up his claim that at no time was he out of sight. Laurent has been observing the ride ever since returning from the department store thirty minutes ago, and can see this for himself. Either the man is dancing around the platform, or announcing the next ride, or talking to the visitors.

Laurent has also learnt that Arnold does not enter the central cylinder to start the ride. Instead, he stands at the narrow opening with his back turned to the interior. In theory, someone could lurk inside without his noticing.

He watches Arnold shoo away a young man from the vicinity of the horse covered in blankets. From his observations, he has discerned that no one is allowed near enough to disturb the covering accidentally. And he is more convinced than ever that the commotion of the fairground provides a useful distraction for an abductor to slip in and out unnoticed.

He waits for Arnold to take a break. Keen to speak to the man at last, Laurent pushes through the throng around the platform. He reflects that Maisie was right about his outfit. Laurent now looks like all the other gentlemen here. His pulse races as he thinks of the pleasant hours that they spent together earlier.

Visibly shaking when Laurent explains his concern, Arnold follows him across the platform. The blankets are in place with the retied knot, just as Laurent left it yesterday evening.

'Are you absolutely certain that you did not rearrange the protective covering? Or that you did not see anyone else doing so?'

Arnold shakes his head. 'Not a soul, Detective. And I make sure no one rides that horse.'

Laurent notes the information. 'Could you please delay the next ride until I've checked something?' he requests. Seeing Arnold's concerned expression, he adds, 'It won't take long.'

As Arnold sits on the edge of the platform, Laurent uncovers the horse. The bright colours shine. He is not certain what he is looking for – a strand of hair, an item that a would-be accomplice might have dropped – but his fingers move over the paintwork, examining the stirrups and the grooves of the mane. Finding nothing after several minutes, he secures the blankets as usual and descends the platform.

Next, he asks the neighbouring stallholders whether they unfastened the knot or witnessed anyone doing so, but his enquiries are met with a succession of head shakes and shrugs.

Why is nothing ever straightforward with this case?

Convincing Beau Armitage's ex-business partner to grant him an interview was no mean feat. 'As I explained to the Bureau, I want to put all that behind me,' Mr Jeremiah Swain had initially told Laurent before slamming down the telephone. Frustrated by the case after speaking to Arnold yesterday, Laurent had made a follow-up call, employing his most persuasive tactics before the man could get a word in edgeways. Wouldn't Mr Swain wish to see the industrialist brought to justice if the pair had parted on unfriendly terms?

And now here Laurent is in the lobby of his hotel with Mr Armitage's ex-business partner sitting opposite him.

'When I first met Beau, I was dazzled by his promises to make me a very rich man,' Mr Swain admits, rubbing the back of his neck. 'It was only after he stole my idea for an electronic television and claimed it as his own that I realized it was the other way around. It was me who was going to make him even richer.'

Laurent tuts in sympathy. 'I think you are not the only person to have crossed swords with the man. I have spoken to three ex-secretaries, but none of them was able to tell me if Mr Armitage has ever visited France.'

Mr Swain squints. He has a habit of screwing up his eyes just before he speaks, Laurent has perceived.

'He never mentioned visiting France to me. Then again, Beau is the kind of man who tells you only what he wants you to know about him,' he says. 'He once suggested a business trip to Frankfurt, though, some sort of trade fair to drum up interest in my inventions. I was all packed and ready to go when I discovered his betrayal,' he explains. 'I pulled out, naturally.'

Laurent's interest is sparked. Once in Europe, it would have been simple enough for Mr Armitage to travel between countries.

'Did he still go?'

Mr Swain shakes his head. 'No. There was no point without me. He couldn't explain the technicalities to potential investors on his own, you see.'

As he thanks Mr Swain for his assistance, Laurent attempts to quell a rising sense of despondency that he is approaching the half-way point of his time in America, and he has drawn another blank.

He is no closer to understanding the significance of the horse, or finding any connection that Beau Armitage might have to Victor Cloutier. Meanwhile the Bureau has made yet another step forward: Billy Wadham's family has been found living in Philadelphia – minus Mrs Wadham, who having never recovered from the loss of her son, passed away last year. Agent O'Connell has rushed off to question them. Up until now, Laurent has been ambivalent about the industrialist being the accomplice, but, as the Bureau potentially close in, Laurent is left with an uncomfortable feeling that he is lagging behind.

He looks at his watch. His next meeting with another of Beau Armitage's associates is not until late this afternoon, which gives him ample hours to recheck the caramel horse. Once more, he finds himself drawn back to Silver Kingdom.

There are no further leads at the carousel, however. After studying the horse and speaking to Arnold again, Laurent leaves behind the crowds and wanders to the shore.

'No wonder you failed,' he can imagine his father bellowing. As an only son – an only child – Laurent had been expected to follow in his father's footsteps and enter politics. The clergy would have been an acceptable alternative, he was told. Laurent shakes his head at the idea of himself as a priest. He would have found it difficult to maintain the chastity vow. Not only that, but he cannot contemplate ever being satisfied with any employment that does not involve detective work. Logic and clues, solving mysteries, give him a solid foundation, a sense of purpose.

His hands behind his back, he stares at the lake. This is a quiet spot away from the commotion of the entertainments. In a place like this, he can hear himself think in a way he is unable to in the chaos of a police precinct or the manic streets of Paris. His mind drifts towards the vast body of water, stirring distant memories of splashing and a blood-curdling scream.

'Perhaps you're looking in all the wrong places.'

Laurent turns around. A woman of around his own age is watching him. Large eyes sit in a ruddy face, unblinking. Her attire is eye-catching. Scarlet fabric is wrapped around her hair like a turban and she wears a long, flowing scarlet robe.

'And where should I be looking?' he asks.

She smiles, and with a flourish indicates a red tent perched all alone in a prominent position forty feet away. 'I know the perfect place.'

As though he is helpless to refuse, Laurent follows the woman inside the tent. The small interior is a deep ruby, womblike, and it takes his eyes several moments to adjust sufficiently to perceive that a glass sphere the size of a football sits on a table, surrounded on both sides by a mismatched assortment of wicker chairs.

'Sit,' she says, and he obeys.

She lights a thin stick balanced on a small dish, then pours him a cup of tea. Soon the exotic pungency of cinnamon dances with the smell of stewed water.

'Drink up,' she tells him.

Gingerly, he takes a sip, and is pleasantly surprised by the refreshing taste. He finishes the drink, and she takes the cup from him. Her eyes dart between its contents and the crystal globe.

The things he does in the pursuit of a case. Once, Laurent found himself on the nasty end of a magic guillotine trick while investigating the Great Magician Ronaldo, Pierre Rochet to his friends, who claimed he had played no part in the malfunction of the mechanism that caused the gruesome death of his business manager.

Presently, she holds out her palm. 'Madame Rose has learnt over these many, many years that a pure message can come only after an adequate exchange.'

Naturally. Digging in his pockets, Laurent hands over a collection of American currency without understanding its value. Seemingly satisfied, Madame Rose tucks the bills in her turban and places her small hands on the ball. Her already huge eyes widen, her nostrils flare.

'Yes, yes . . .' She breathes heavily. 'Yes, there are answers you seek. Many, many answers.'

Laurent fidgets in his seat. He should have known as much. This will be a vague amble through a predetermined list of statements in the hope of stumbling on to something relevant to his personal life or work. Vowing to give nothing away, he stays quiet.

'I see great turmoil for those you love. And hidden clues.'

He perks up at the mention of clues, then he remembers that, by now, probably half of the employees of Silver Kingdom are aware that he is a detective from France. And a person who makes a living from noticing things will be especially observant.

'Anything else?' he asks pleasantly.

She strokes her fingers across the sphere, her eyes staring into its depths. For close to three minutes, Laurent watches Madame Rose muttering under her breath. With eight days remaining, he has no time for this. He has paid up, and he has learnt his lesson. Her gaze is so focused on the glass ball that she doesn't even notice Laurent scraping back his chair and making for the exit.

'And the young woman who creeps into your thoughts of late . . .' a voice behind him whispers.

He freezes. He is caught between turning back to hear more and avoiding any more flimsy pronouncements. Through the tent flap, he can see life at Silver Kingdom continuing as normal: the Ferris wheel is in full rotation; customers are lined up to ride the carousel;

and the popcorn stand is doing a roaring trade; and, finally, there is Maisie. She is laughing as she talks to an older woman by the burger stall. As he watches, a breeze lifts from the lake, tousling her hair. Laurent is transfixed. It is the first time he has seen a tendril of hair move in slow motion, its dance calling to something inside him.

'What young woman?' he asks quietly, rooted to the spot.

The breeze ripples through the tent.

Laurent cannot tell if it is Madame Rose's voice, his own voice, his imagination or the wind itself, that answers: *There is a reckoning ahead if you do not take more care with this one.*

22

Maisie is helping Mrs Papadopoulos unload bottles of double cream for Mr Cornelius to make into the milkshakes for his burger bar when she spots Laurent bolting from Madame Rose's tent. He strides with considerable speed towards the open-air *Smugglers' Saloon*, where young men dressed as pirates serve cold beer while slapping their thighs and declaring, *Shiver me timbers*. He orders a pint and downs it in one. Surprised to see him looking anything less than composed, Maisie stares.

'You like him,' Mrs Papadopoulos observes.

Maisie flushes. 'Mr Cornelius?' she asks, feigning innocence. 'I'm meant to like all the Jointees. It's my job.'

Mrs Papadopoulos smiles. 'You play that game. But I know what I know.'

'Maybe all you know is that I'm taking an active interest in the case,' Maisie replies, trying to keep a straight face.

She is less on edge since the shopping expedition, with a lightness to her thoughts that she hasn't felt in a long time.

'There is no shame to want a man,' Mrs Papadopoulos says. She winks. 'And he has good looks. If not for my Nico, you and I would fight for the detective.'

Maisie laughs. She watches Laurent order a second pint, noting how his new shirt fits nicely over the contours of his chest. Mrs Papadopoulos shoos Maisie in his direction, clearly knowing exactly what's running through her mind.

Laurent seems to sense Maisie before seeing her, because he looks around and nods to the seat next to him. His face is serious and pale. Maisie guesses that he's been unsettled by the fortune-teller.

'You look like you've seen a ghost,' she remarks. 'If it's any consolation, some people leave Rose's tent looking an awful lot worse.

We even had to call for a doctor once after a man collapsed. She doesn't usually work on Fridays, so you must be a special case.'

It seems like he's trying to force a smile but gives up. 'It is peculiar what she seems to intuit.'

Assessing his face, Maisie softens her voice.

'Laurent, I really wouldn't take much notice of what she says. Before she worked here, Rose had the servants buying all sorts of nonsensical quack remedies.'

Maisie deliberately omits mentioning the warning about trouble arriving from across the ocean. It wouldn't help Laurent to know that she herself has become uneasy.

Laurent fiddles with his collar, silent. He can barely look at her. An awful sensation floods through Maisie that perhaps his obvious upset is caused by bad news concerning the case. Has Clementine Pickford been found?

'Is there a development with the investigation?' she forces herself to ask.

'*Shiver me timbers*,' a waiter says, returning with the second beer. Laurent glugs this one down as well.

'Only that the Wadham family have been located,' he explains, and Maisie inwardly relaxes. 'The Bureau can now question the tailor. It may or may not produce any useful information.' He rests his head in his hands. 'Trying to prove the connection between Mr Armitage and Victor Cloutier is proving difficult,' he says with a sigh. 'It has always been a troubling case. And now I cannot fathom the discrepancy with the blankets, although I sense it is important. Yesterday I questioned Arnold and any stallholder in the vicinity of the carousel, and they all deny untying the knot, and they saw no one doing so.'

The ride still half terrifies Maisie, but she's been somewhat reassured that the protective blankets seem to keep people off the cursed horse. It's unsettling to think that someone might be meddling with the only thing that stands between the general public and a disastrous fate.

'I'll ask everyone to keep a look-out and to let me know if they see anyone hanging about that horse.'

He looks up, his eyes a little brighter. 'I would appreciate that.'

'It's in my interests, remember?' As his face falls, Maisie has a compulsion to lift his spirits. 'Why don't we take a walk and clear away the cobwebs?'

He agrees, refusing the offer of a third beer from the server. The idea is to blend in with the crowd, but, before they have even exited the Smugglers' Saloon, Maisie has been approached by two of the Ride Jocks about how to handle *rubes* – the term used by the workforce for visitors – who flout the safety measures for the rides. 'Later,' she promises.

'The place would collapse without you,' Laurent comments.

This is a fresh perspective on Maisie's position here, and she mulls it over as they circle the park.

Maisie is struck by the level of excitement. There are squeals of pleasure everywhere. 'I never thought in my wildest imagination that I'd fly one day,' she hears an elderly woman tell a small child as they disembark from the Ferris wheel. Maisie remembers the thrill of the Clacton funfair, now so many years ago, and despite everything she can't help but feel a warm glow that she's created a similar experience here. They are giving people what they want: delights, freedom, their dreams come to life.

She is strolling with Laurent along a row of food concessions when a commotion up ahead stops the crowd's forward momentum. There's wolf whistling followed by sustained cheers. It could only mean one thing. Sure enough, Gloria, Betsy and Gayle appear like sirens with million-dollar smiles, their hair sleek, hips rolling as they stride confidently in high heels. A path clears in front of the ticket-sellers like the parting of the waves. Men bow and doff their hats; women scowl at their husbands. Catcalling follows.

Fully expecting Laurent to be equally blown away, Maisie is surprised to notice that he's staring at her expectantly, completely oblivious to the fact that the women of most men's fantasies are no more than four feet away. Gloria gives him the side eye and appears just as baffled as Maisie that he fails to respond with anything more than a blank face.

He leans in closer to Maisie, so close that she can smell his cologne.

'I was asking, do you like Jules Verne?' he says.

For a moment, she is confused. Then she realizes that he's pointing to the poster announcing their imminent arrival at a large wooden structure, inside of which a procession of small boats travels through a series of dark, meandering tunnels: the Journey to the Centre of the Earth.

'I've never read anything by him, but the ride is fun.'

Laurent stares at the poster, a soft smile on his face. The crowd has melted away, most probably following the trail of the Money Girls like dogs on heat, and she is standing alone with him under the shade of an apple tree. Dappled, golden light plays on the detective's face, accenting the sculpted line of his jaw.

'I was not aware this ride was here.'

Maisie laughs. 'Don't let Mr Partridge hear you. He's always complaining that we've given him the worst spot in Silver Kingdom.'

Laurent's eyes are glazed as though he has woken from a dream.

'The story holds a special significance. My mother read the book to me at bedtime when I was a boy.' He looks wistful.

A warm sensation in Maisie's heart radiates throughout her body. Everything is glistening – the sky, the leaves, Laurent's eyes. There is a light touch on her arms, a sensation of being pulled as he steps forward. Then he stops, looking past her shoulder with a frown.

Maisie turns around and notices James watching in the distance.

A fraction of a second later, he has disappeared.

23

Laurent is awash with irritation. It is patently obvious that James is making Maisie feel uncomfortable with his attentions. After depositing her back in her office, he goes looking. Soon he is meant to interview Beau Armitage's former accountant. But he does not care. His single-minded focus is on finding that man.

Laurent marches between the labyrinth of stalls. He looks at the rear of the catering units and behind rides, coming face to face with the innards of Silver Kingdom. At the Smugglers' Saloon, an airless side room is filled with servers changing shift. 'Who's gonna join me for a card game at Barnie's?' the pirate who served Laurent calls in a thick American drawl, removing an eye patch.

Nothing is what it seems here. Staff in costume. Fabric ghosts. The mountainous backdrop of *Billy Goats Gruff Land* made of painted papier mâché. Clever lighting disguising the rigging that operates the puppet dragon in the *Oriental Paradise* ride. A carousel at the centre of a great mystery.

'Illusion is all distraction.' Laurent recalls the words of the Great Magician Ronaldo, said with a cryptic air, during their final interview about his business manager's untimely death by guillotine. After being released the next day on bail, he was never seen again. This is what Silver Kingdom is, Laurent decides. One giant magic trick.

Near the dodgems, he asks a group of workers whether they have seen the new groundsman. These are the silent wheels of Silver Kingdom, Laurent has observed. With gnarled hands and shoulders as powerful as dray horses, they heave sacks on their shoulders and scale the rides to check the parts. The men exchange glances.

'The cherry orchard,' the oldest man answers in a gruff voice, pointing north.

Stealthy as a fox, Laurent cuts a zigzag past row after row of trees.

Soon the sound of whistling draws him to a deserted spot beside the lake. He spots James reaching for a handful of sour-cherries with his back turned. Too late, the younger man senses someone approaching, and turns around.

Laurent advances with speed. Taken by surprise, James backs against the gnarly tree trunk. Mutual dislike hangs in the air.

'I'm Sir Malcolm's family, so you better step away,' James warns, his face red.

Laurent fixes James with a stare.

'I know exactly who you are,' he responds in a firm voice. 'The sort to cause a young woman discomfort. It is clear that she wishes you to leave her alone.'

A shadow crosses James's face. 'And I know *your* sort, which is why I have my eye on you,' he says. 'I saw it in the army. Officers swanning in and sweeping the local girls off their feet, then leaving them heartbroken when it was time to deploy elsewhere.'

Laurent is momentarily thrown. 'There is no need to concern yourself with me,' he says, attempting to hide his uneasiness. 'Simply leave Maisie in peace.'

With a final cold look, he steps back. James strides off, scowling.

'Fuck you, Detective,' he calls over his shoulder, disappearing behind a line of trees. 'Fuck you!'

Laurent experiences a bloom of shame. It does not take away from the fact that he senses the younger man is a pest to Maisie, but James makes the same point as Madame Rose. He thought he was doing so well in heeding the fortune-teller's warning. He took care not to look at Maisie earlier, merely to engage in pleasant conversation.

Now a troubling comprehension creeps upon him. Before, when they came upon the Jules Verne ride, he was near enough to feel her body heat, bringing his face close to hers. This was not to make himself better heard, nor to bring her attention to the figure lurking in the distance, he admits to himself. No, he had been on the point of kissing Maisie. Only the sight of James had stopped him.

Laurent resolves to do better. Whatever his own desires, he must tread softly when it comes to Maisie's feelings.

24

A car screeches up the driveway, spitting gravel. Maisie watches from the parlour window as Hugo leaps from the driver's side, runs around to help his wife out and disappears indoors, calling for Sir Malcolm. She wasn't aware that the Randolphs were visiting today, but since Silver Kingdom reopened Hugo has become a regular visitor again, sometimes dropping in unannounced. Occasionally, he's accompanied by Nancy, but only if she isn't busy shopping or lunching with friends.

Perhaps Hugo is here to talk to Sir Malcolm about the business once more. Their only topic of conversation is how to recoup the money from the short time that Silver Kingdom was forced to close. Maisie can tell that the matter causes Sir Malcolm considerable anxiety, because for the past few nights he's been back to barely sleeping, banging about downstairs until the early hours. With the visitors reaching ever greater numbers, day on day, Maisie hopes that soon they won't have to worry so much.

She waits for Nancy to enter the house and start bossing everyone about, more wary than ever after the woman's overbearing behaviour at the dinner party.

It comes as a shock, then, to observe that Nancy is the polar opposite today. She stands silent in the driveway, staring at the sky, dressed in a lacy cream shift that could pass as a nightdress. She appears altogether less colourful, as though she's been wrung out. What has happened to her?

'Would you like a drink, Nancy?' Maisie asks, going outside.

As though she hasn't heard the question, Nancy looks around and gives the trace of a smile, but her eyes hold a vacant look. Pity tugs at Maisie's heart.

'Perhaps a lemonade on the patio?' Maisie continues. 'It'll be nice to talk.'

Nancy lets Maisie take her by the arm and lead her slowly, first to the kitchen to collect refreshments, and then to a bench outside the drawing-room windows overlooking the shore. It's clear that she's under the influence of some sort of medication. This must be the tonic Hugo was referring to on the day Clementine Pickford disappeared. Maisie has seen the full-page advertisements for barbital in newspapers.

The lake gleams like a pearl in the early-morning sun, lapping gently. Maisie sits sipping pink lemonade, watching the dance of light form patterns on the surface while Nancy gazes into space.

'Dr Carlton thinks I should stop trying for a child because the next miscarriage might kill me.'

Nancy's voice makes Maisie jump. Croaky and soft, it sounds like it's been lying dormant for years. Maisie doesn't like to point out that the doctor could be right. She's heard countless stories of women bleeding to death in childbirth – from the servants muttering amongst themselves, to obituaries in the *Chicago Tribune*.

'And what do you think?'

Nancy looks taken aback, as if no one has ever sought her opinion about her own body.

'I think . . .' she says, her voice a little stronger. 'I think I don't care about dying if there's even the smallest chance of having a baby. I would see it as a good thing to bring another life into the world.'

It's Maisie's turn to look surprised, because she hasn't given much thought to having children of her own. Even marriage doesn't hold a particular interest for her, and Sir Malcolm has never mentioned the subject. She supposes it will not only be expected of her one day, but it might be necessary if something happens to him. The question she has repeatedly asked herself over the years pops up again: what would become of her without a male protector?

Unintentionally, her mind wanders to Laurent. His kindness makes Maisie feel safe, and being treated like an adult by him is making her start to feel like one. She feels a stirring inside. His grey eyes are hypnotic: the colour of storm clouds, with the same power behind them. The way they gaze without guile makes Maisie believe that their sole purpose is to absorb everything about her – and, truthfully, she likes it.

No, she can't get her hopes up. They haven't even kissed, and he is leaving in less than a week.

'It's not something I ever really think about,' Maisie admits quietly.

Nancy's glazed expression focuses on Maisie for a moment before drifting towards the lake.

'But having children is why we're here, as women. What else are we, what's our point, if we aren't mothers?'

Nancy asks this question as though she's never considered anything else.

'We could have jobs, fulfilling lives anyway, couldn't we?' Maisie asks.

She thinks back to her own restlessness to do something with her life, and Laurent's belief that Silver Kingdom is dependent on her. After the lock-up, Maisie believed she might never again find joy in helping to run the park, but that's beginning to change.

A long silence follows before Nancy speaks again.

'Do you think Hugo will be very upset if he never has an heir? He hasn't really said.'

It occurs to Maisie that Hugo becomes less easy-going and more uptight every time she sees him. On the fateful day Mary Pickford visited Silver Kingdom, he had kept a watchful eye on his wife, and then, at last week's dinner party, Maisie noticed his jaw flexing at some of Nancy's comments. She casts her mind back to the telephone conversations she overheard, when Sir Malcolm consoled his brother, reassuring him that everything would be fine.

'I'm sure he's more worried about you,' she replies.

'Yes, sometimes I worry about me too.'

It's a strange thing to hear from someone who is usually so sparky.

'What I wouldn't give to at least hold one of them,' Nancy continues, as though she hasn't registered Maisie's lack of response. 'It's not asking for a lot.'

It makes Maisie think of her own mother, denied the chance of seeing her daughter grow up. In this moment, she understands

Nancy's pain with all her heart, shares her loneliness. For all her wealth, this glamorous woman ultimately lives as small a life as Maisie.

Nancy reaches out and takes Maisie's hand.

As the two women sit side by side, Maisie's thoughts circle around to the mothers of the missing children. Billy's mother. Clementine's mother. What suffering they must have endured. If only she could make everything better by bringing their children back one day.

25

It is often this way with investigations. A lull, a sense of despair, precedes a major advancement. Then an unstoppable momentum takes hold.

The last few days have been a mistral of meetings: Mr Armitage's previous accountant, five ex-employees, two barbers and, finally, a fourth ex-secretary.

Although Laurent was almost twenty minutes late to his appointment this morning, courtesy of a telegram from Constable Segal that needed a response, Miss McFarlane was still waiting for him in the hotel foyer. Her eyes teared up when Laurent introduced himself. Holding the record for Mr Armitage's longest serving secretary, she had been shocked at his sudden announcement after a year of service that her perfume was too overpowering for an office environment. As a result, she couldn't wait to spill the beans on her former employer. 'He never even gave me the chance to wash it off,' she sniffed, burying her reddening nose in a lace handkerchief.

Producing copies that she had made of entries in the industrialist's diaries from 1913, the woman glowed when Laurent complimented her administrative skills. Together, they pored over the details. And what details they were. Scrawled in delicate handwriting was the itinerary of a European business trip the man had taken that year. There was more – he was in Paris on the very date of Chloé Fourtou's disappearance.

It is a staggering piece of information, and could not be better timed, since Laurent has only three days left in America.

Now he watches Agent O'Connell cross the park to their usual bench. Laurent can tell from his jaunty walk that the man is returning from Philadelphia in triumph. He discloses his own good news first, earns a pat on the back from the agent, and then sits back, all ears, as O'Connell shares the lengthy story of Mr Wadham.

Apparently the tailor had crafted a suit from the finest silk for Mr Armitage, only to be accused of using inferior material when the bill was presented. Refusing to pay, Armitage had threatened harm to the entire Wadham family if the tailor pursued litigation. Not believing anyone could be so petty, Mr Wadham filed a complaint in court anyway. This was two days before the children's party at Fairweather House that he had mentioned in passing while the suit in question was being measured up.

'With this and the information you've just given me about his links to France, I think we can have another crack at interviewing Armitage tomorrow. Possibly, his lawyer will advise him to give a proper account of himself. We might even get a confession. And an understanding of where . . .'

The agent's voice tails off, and Laurent understands. The two men shake hands warmly before parting ways.

Laurent is filled with a sense of satisfaction. It was not so long ago that O'Connell seemed disinterested in the link to the French investigations. Now they are integral to the Bureau's own case.

That evening Laurent stands near the carousel, sketching its likeness. The park's visitors have drifted home, and the place is quiet save for the distant sound of Silver Kingdom's Crew playing card games after work. He can hear raucous laughter, see a glint of a campfire, but they are too far away for him to discern much else.

Laurent has already used a tape measure to note the exact proportions of the machine, and examined the mechanical instructions with the aim of having a diagram for reference when he is back in France.

'Did you go to art school?' Maisie asks, peering over his shoulder.

He half turns his head. She is standing so close that he can smell the faint aroma of her skin – lavender, he believes – and see the soft down on her cheeks. His whole body is electrified. Laurent feels his fingers tremble and he almost drops the pencil.

'I . . .' He swallows hard. 'I did not. My father would not have permitted anything so frivolous.'

He can tell she is thinking this statement through, because she chews on her pretty mouth.

'Didn't your mother have a say?'

He is silent. How can Laurent express the truth that his mother's voice always counted for nothing?

'Childhood is very frightening,' she continues almost as if she were in the room with him at the worst times. 'Before I went to Jesserton, I can't remember a moment when I wasn't terrified. Sometimes I worry that if I let myself get too happy, it'll be taken away and I'll go back to those days.'

A feeling of sadness overwhelms Laurent that this precious, kind-hearted woman could fear anything.

'My mother taught me to draw. She taught me everything good about myself,' he is able to say.

Maisie moves around to face him.

'Then she must be very proud.'

Laurent hesitates. He has never discussed details of this topic with anyone, not even Odette, who would like nothing more than to feel a closeness to him but is kept at arm's length, just as Laurent has always done with every woman.

His breathing quickens as he thinks of his mother's lovely face, and those dark grey eyes tainted with worry.

'Be a good boy, Laurent,' she said to him one day while he was preparing his toy soldiers for a fierce battle on her dressing table. 'Don't come in, don't run for help, whatever you hear. Will you do that for Maman?'

Of course, he agreed; he would have agreed to anything she asked of him. To make sure, she studied his eyes with a haunted look. Then, with a kiss on his forehead, she stood up and disappeared into the bathroom.

From the corner of his eye, he can see that Maisie is scrutinizing him with a worried expression. Without pressing for an answer, she lays her hands over his, barely touching, as if she understands everything that Laurent has experienced without words.

'Perhaps she would be proud,' he replies quietly. 'It is just that . . .' He struggles to continue. 'My mother drowned herself in the bath when I was a boy.'

Maisie's eyes are misty. 'Laurent . . .' she whispers.

She slides her arms around his waist and pulls him into a hug. Laurent lets his eyelids close as he drops the sketchpad and clings to this woman as though he might break into pieces if he lets go. They stand together like this for many minutes. He can feel Maisie's fingers stroke his back, such soft, soothing movements that his breathing begins to settle.

He loses track of time. After a long while, he loosens his grip and opens his eyes. Sunset has morphed into dusk, and a light display of stars has come out. Maisie leads him by the hand to the carousel and they sit on the edge of the platform.

Here, he talks about his mother spending most days weeping in bed and describes his futile attempts to make her feel better; then he moves on to the emptiness of a childhood without her, the cane his father used to whip him while shouting that he was ashamed to have Laurent as a son. When he is finished, Maisie begins to speak. She seems hesitant to share much until he pulls her close to him, his arms shielding her from the wind starting up on the lake. Then the words flow. He learns that she used to go to bed cold and hungry, her only comfort a little boy called Tommy whom she had to leave behind, that she lost a cherished aunt, and still suffers from the loneliness of feeling that she doesn't belong. 'I've never told anyone all this,' she admits, her head resting on his shoulder.

'Nor I,' he replies.

She looks up at him. Behind Maisie, the moon glows – almost forming a halo around her head. As they lock eyes, Laurent cups her face and kisses her lips.

26

Laurent scours Silver Kingdom until he finds Maisie helping to unload flour at the corndog booth.

'I wanted you to hear the news from me,' he says, breathless.

He has been hovering around the police station for the past thirty-six hours, awaiting the outcome of the Bureau's interrogation of Beau Armitage, and has not seen Maisie since their kiss. She turns, her eyes brightening when she realizes it is him. Around them is a swirl of people, and noise from the nearby helter-skelter. But it is like they are held in a bubble of their own.

The strength of his emotions has taken Laurent by surprise. Naturally, he is attracted to Maisie, how could he not be? She is enchanting, with skin the colour of almonds, and graceful curves. But this is not the animal lust he experiences with his secretary, or the serving girls in the pâtisserie, or any of the others. Maisie is not someone he would wish to bed casually. He has become aware that whenever he is in her presence, it feels like she is reaching inside the most closed part of his soul and gently prising him open.

'What's the matter?' she asks, looking anxious.

He leads her to a quiet area behind the helter-skelter. Placing his hands on her shoulders, Laurent gently explains what Agent O'Connell shared with him an hour ago. Her eyes become round, and she shakes her head in disbelief.

'So, it's over,' she says. 'Really over. Mr Armitage has confessed to being Victor's accomplice, and no one else will be taken.'

She repeats his words verbatim, as though she is letting everything permeate her awareness. He notices that her eyes dart nervously to the carousel before returning to him.

'You appear troubled,' he remarks.

Maisie gives a small shrug. 'A confession is strong evidence, I know that, and I should feel relieved, but . . .' Her voice is shaky. 'I'm more bewildered, to be honest. None of it makes sense.'

Laurent can only agree. This case has always been riddled with mystery.

'Perhaps I can help soothe some of your worries,' he offers.

From the way in which she straightens her spine, he can tell that she is steeling herself to ask the most logical question first.

'Billy and Clementine. Are they –'

Even eighteen hours of continuous interrogation – with methods that Laurent guesses were similar to those employed against Victor in France – have not prised from the industrialist an explanation of what has happened to the victims.

'The Bureau are still searching for them.'

She bites her lip. 'Has he told the Bureau how he snatched them away? I saw his photograph in the newspaper and I don't remember seeing his face at the party four years ago.'

Laurent recalls the re-enactment of Chloé Fourtou's disappearance for the benefit of the court at Victor's trial, and the fact that no one saw the moment of the abduction nor the seconds afterwards.

'Not specifically. Agent O'Connell believes that he may have been hiding behind a rock near the shore. My own theory is that it is possible for an abductor to lurk within the carousel's central cylinder, unseen. Both suggestions were put to Mr Armitage but he refused to answer.'

Maisie looks unconvinced. 'What about the horse? The strange one? Has he said anything about why it's important?'

Thus far, the agents have been unable to elicit any details on this link, nor motives either.

'That also is an ongoing line of enquiry.' He notes Maisie's small frown. 'But there is nothing to be concerned about,' he adds, hoping to soothe any fear she still holds of the horse being cursed.

Given her worry, Laurent refrains from mentioning that the Bureau was also unable to ascertain from Mr Armitage how he managed to ensure that the victims all chose to sit on the same horse. Since it is increasingly clear that they were targeted, he had hoped to have at least this loose end tied up.

'I see.' She gazes into the distance at the carousel's gold-and-indigo flag, which is just visible above the other rides. 'But what about the blankets? Isn't that a worry?' she probes. 'Mr Armitage was in custody when they were meddled with, wasn't he? So it couldn't have been him.'

This had been Laurent's concern in the first place. But he considers the fact that there has been no further sign of tampering.

'On balance, I believe it is probably not relevant. This is often the case – we find and then we discount discoveries.'

They are both silent for a moment, aware what this confession means. Although not all questions are answered, Laurent has learnt enough to continue the information-gathering in France – pursuing revenge as a motive, following up on when and how Victor and Beau met in Paris, the significance of that particular horse – and he has no excuse to extend his stay.

'So you leave tomorrow,' she says.

Laurent feels a sting in his heart. 'We could write to one another, if you wish?' he offers.

He notices Maisie pinch her fingers before giving him a faint smile.

'I would like that very much,' she agrees. 'And, in the meantime, you must come to dinner tonight. If you arrive early, we can have cocktails on the patio beforehand.'

'It sounds wonderful, and provides the perfect opportunity to present you with a gift.'

Laurent swirls his Martini, staring out at a flock of noisy, mid-sized birds dotted along the lake's shore. The surface gleams like polished silver at this time of evening. Quite beautiful. As the drink slips down his throat, Laurent feels the tension in his shoulders dissolve.

He leans back. From this distance, Silver Kingdom looks tiny, the rides like children's toys. But the beauty of the carousel stands out nonetheless. Little did Laurent know when he signed the paperwork for its sale that he would be travelling halfway across the world to follow it. But here he is, sitting on a bench next to the loveliest woman he has ever met.

'Interesting birds,' he comments.

'Don't you have sandpipers in France?' Maisie asks.

Sandpipers. The name is unfamiliar and he cannot think of the French translation.

'I have never seen them along the Seine, although curlews are similar.'

'But you know of herons,' she says. 'The first time we met, in the interview room when I was in lock-up, you made a heron out of paper. I saw it on the table.'

He is surprised that she noticed. 'I started making shapes from paper as a boy. My mother loved them.' He turns his head a fraction to look at Maisie. 'And your own mother,' he asks. 'You really remember nothing?'

She shakes her head, flushing.

'No. It's going to sound silly, but I used to imagine she was a queen or a princess or something. I understand now that it isn't true,' she admits. 'But I still like to think of her as doing something special. My father too. Something noble and brave that made sense of their deaths. It makes me feel better.'

Laurent has been hesitating all day about whether to go through with his idea for Maisie's gift. With the assistance of Constable Segal as the man on the ground in Europe, he has researched Maisie's background and discovered a good deal about her history. Just this morning, a flurry of information arrived by telegram. In this moment, however, he realizes that disturbing the past has a time and a place.

Searching through the inner pockets of his jacket, he is careful to avoid the report he has spent all those hours on, and instead he pulls out the flyer for Silver Kingdom he picked up at the ticket office. It was intended as a souvenir to show Amélie the great American amusement parks, but he can collect a replacement just as easily.

'It sounds perfectly reasonable,' he says. 'And now for your gift. What is your favourite bird?'

Her face lights up. Looking amused, Maisie watches Laurent struggle with bends and folds, turning and manoeuvring the paper, until he is finally able to present her with a wonky cockatoo, resplendent with a fanlike crest.

Soon it is time for dinner. The seconds seem to be travelling at triple the normal speed; the starter and main course are swiftly followed by dessert, with the bare minimum of conversation exchanged between the three diners. Everyone seems distracted this evening: Sir Malcolm is vacant, Maisie looks downcast, and Laurent has become trapped by a muddle of thoughts. He imagines that he and Maisie are the owners of Fairweather House, dining like this every evening before retiring to their bedroom and making love through the night. Then he thinks of Amélie, excited about his return home, and his vow of loyalty to Odette.

'Come to my study,' Sir Malcolm mutters to Laurent as the cheese board is removed by the footman.

Maisie chimes in. 'And then find me in the parlour before you go. I have a gift for you in return for yours.'

Laurent follows Sir Malcolm into a well-proportioned room with a large desk and comfortable leather armchairs. He accepts a crystal glass filled to the brim with brandy.

'To the conclusion of the case,' Sir Malcolm toasts. 'Despite our earlier differences, I appreciate that you didn't impede the investigation, thus ensuring the matter progressed' – Sir Malcolm appears to be groping for the right words – 'in the right direction for everyone.' He lays down his glass. 'Here's a little something for you.'

Laurent watches with interest as Sir Malcolm fumbles in his cigar box and pulls out a small brown envelope.

'There is no need,' Laurent says quickly, not wishing to know what it is that Sir Malcolm is offering. He hesitates. 'I would ask two favours of you, however.'

Fishing out the report, he lays it on the desk. Sir Malcolm eyes it with suspicion.

'I looked into Maisie's parents,' Laurent explains. 'But I decided not to show her the findings. I did not think it would benefit her to add to all the distress she has experienced recently.'

'Ahh.'

Sir Malcolm reopens the cigar box, but this time he pulls out a cigar and offers one to Laurent, who again declines. Lighting up, he takes a puff and sighs.

'Her aunt never really talked about the circumstances. She said there was no point looking back and I didn't like to press. But it was obvious there was something unpleasant,' he explains with a pained expression. 'Many years ago, Maisie did ask me if I knew anything about them, and she seemed upset when I couldn't give her an answer.'

'So, you think she would wish to know?'

Sir Malcolm nods his head from side to side. 'One day, perhaps. But you are correct – not now.'

Laurent considers the options, then he pushes the report across the desk.

'So we agree. With something like this, timing is everything,' he says. 'I shall trust you to decide when the moment has come.' He removes a smaller envelope from his jacket pocket. 'And would you be kind enough to give Maisie this letter tomorrow morning? After I am gone.'

The word *gone* is like a lead weight on Laurent's tongue.

'Of course, old chap. Leave them both with me,' Sir Malcolm replies. 'I care very much about Maisie, you know.'

Laurent is relieved. But there is still the problem of James. His own warning from before is insufficient, as he will not be here to follow it up.

'It is good to hear, because my second favour is about your nephew.' Laurent pauses in order to choose his next words with care. 'Your nephew's interest in Maisie, to be precise. I believe that he has become an annoyance to her.'

Sir Malcolm settles his cigar on the ashtray.

'No need to fret about James. He has always been a friendly fellow. I'm sure he and Maisie get along fine.'

Sir Malcolm gives a reassuring smile, but Laurent is not so easily brushed off.

'In any event, it is worth your keeping an eye on the situation, is it not?' he persists.

Sir Malcolm nods. 'Anything you ask,' he replies, staring into space. 'James is Lydia's nephew, you know. I was very fond of my wife. I was fond of them all. Mabel, Catherine, Lydia. Still am . . .'

His voice fades, and his eyes fall closed now, as if he is drifting off to sleep.

It occurs to Laurent that, for all the privileges that come with Sir Malcolm's status, he enjoys no immunity from tragedy. Leaving the man to his thoughts, Laurent locates Maisie in a cosy room at the front of the house decorated in pale blues. She is sitting on a small couch, reading. He lingers in the doorway, trying to preserve the image of her in his head. Before they met, Laurent really did believe that fondness was the deepest emotion he could feel for a woman.

'That didn't take long,' she says, looking up.

She leaps to her feet and thrusts an object in front of his face. It is a brown-and-white-speckled feather and must once have adorned a sandpiper.

'Now you won't forget me.'

She studies him with a look of admiration that Laurent knows he does not deserve. He thinks of Madame Rose's words. *Take more care with this one.*

They are like ice down his back, like an accusation following him from his past: the other women harmed by his selfishness; the casual lovers who always wanted more from him; his mother, whom he could have saved if he had plucked up the courage to run for help.

Maisie is better off without him.

'It would not be possible to do so,' he says truthfully.

Laurent bends to kiss the back of her hand. For a brief second, she runs the fingers of her other hand through his hair. He waits until she has finished to straighten up, and finds her eyes are filled with tears. Stroking her cheek, he memorizes the beauty of her face.

With every ounce of effort he can assemble, Laurent walks away. From Maisie. From the carousel.

'Au revoir, old friend,' he catches himself thinking.

27

'You land-stealing son-of-a-bitch. You've no right to encroach on my side.'

Mr Melville of the *Botanical Soap Company* is poking his index finger dangerously close to the face of Mr Parry from the Popcorn Palace. The men are squared up to one another on either side of the imaginary line separating their concession stalls.

'No need to holler, Eustace. All my faculties are intact including my eyesight and I can see that *my* joint is on *my* land. So put that in your pipe and smoke it, you cantankerous old goat.'

Mr Melville turns to Maisie, his face pinched. 'Are you just gonna stand there and let him take liberties? Anyone can see he's moved the marker stakes.' He points to the iron pegs at the corner of his pitch. 'And you know my needs take priority.'

For no reason that Maisie can discern, food stands are considered less important than stores selling non-perishable goods, which in turn sit below the independent rides.

'But I pay good money for my spot,' Mr Parry complains. 'If you can't deal with this fairly, we need Sir Malcolm here.'

Maisie doesn't miss the questioning of her competence, but she really isn't in the mood to handle a dispute today. Her head hurts, her eyes are bloodshot, and she feels nauseous. After Laurent left last night, she sobbed alone in her bedroom for hours, wanting to crawl into a hole and never come out.

'Fine. Perhaps he can knock some sense into you both,' she snaps.

Both concession holders are surprised into silence by her uncharacteristic sharpness.

Maisie goes looking for Sir Malcolm. But he's in none of his usual haunts at Silver Kingdom, neither by the ticket booth nor near the carousel. He doesn't appear to be indoors either.

'If you're after the master, he's poorly today and is upstairs in bed,' Eric says, passing by the parlour, where Maisie has ended up.

Maisie wonders what's wrong with him. She had noticed that he was off during last night's dinner; he barely ate or spoke, but neither did she, so she didn't think much of it. There were no empty bottles in the drawing room this morning, so alcohol hasn't caused this mysterious illness.

'Oh, and he says there's a letter for you from the detective,' Eric adds. 'I'll fetch it.'

Maisie feels like her senses have been set on fire. Eric seems to take an eternity to return, though he's back within a couple of minutes. 'In actual fact, I found two for you,' he says, handing her both.

Maisie's fingers are trembling so violently that she can barely tear open the first envelope, the smaller of the two.

Dearest Maisie,

A courageous man would have declared his true feelings earlier. I am not such a man, but I couldn't leave without confessing that I have fallen in love with you. It has been an unexpected joy to find myself captivated by your kindness and beauty.

I have not always behaved decently, but this is my attempt to do so. It pains me to admit that I am not a free man, Maisie. If only I was, everything would be different, please believe me. But I am married, and you deserve better.

You are always in my heart,
Laurent

Maisie is winded by the shock. Married! All this time she was allowing herself to open up to him, and he was secretly committed to another woman. It can't be true. She could feel their connection, as tangible as a silver thread stretching between their hearts. And what about the kiss that they shared? It was like melting into a pool of liquid love.

But it meant nothing, and she was naive.

She screws the letter into a ball and throws it into the trash can. The room swirls. Maisie can hear Clara humming from the dining room, organizing the crystal, and in the kitchen Peggy Mae is bust-ling about with large pans. It's like listening in to a life that isn't her own. Maisie doesn't really belong here. For a while, she thought she belonged with Laurent, but, now that hope is extinguished, she has never felt lonelier.

Maisie has no idea how long she sits staring at nothing. As she rouses herself to open the second letter, she feels as weary as someone who has been trudging through a snowstorm for days.

She pulls out two pieces of paper entitled 'Report on the Parents of Miss Maisie Marlowe by Detective Laurent Bisset'.

She can hardly believe it. This document must contain some of the details that Aunty Mabel never had the chance to tell Maisie. With a growing sense of excitement, her eyes roam over the sen-tences on the pages. There's a brief introduction explaining that the following information has been gleaned from birth certificates, marriage certificates, death certificates and official reports. And then comes the real substance, the knowledge that Maisie had long given up ever learning.

It appears that her mother, Eliza Marlowe, was born in Chelmsford, Essex, to George, a haberdasher, and Margaret. Both passed away within months of each other from consumption twelve years ago. Maisie pauses to pray for her grandparents before moving on.

There's a jump in the timeline, and the next two events are the birth of a baby – Miss Maisie Marlowe – and the marriage of this child's parents one month later, at twenty years of age, in Pimlico, London. *Eliza Marlowe and Mr Yousuf Choudary from India became husband and wife in February 1898*, the report reads.

Her father was Indian. Maisie's mind latches on to the one thing she knows about the country, the story of the Maharaja of Lahore riding bareback on an elephant, as told by Nancy at Grand Central Station five years ago. It all sounds so exotic.

Maisie's excitement flounders on the second page.

Several police reports indicate that the couple turned to crime. A pair of gold candlesticks were stolen from a church in Islington . . . to evade the

*law fled England for France, where further police reports have been un-
covered. Last such reports for the pair were from the Cour des miracles area
of Paris in January and February of 1919.*

February 1919 was only five months ago. Maisie's emotions veer
from shock to joy to distress at the realization that her parents had
been alive all this time and never tried to make contact. There is a
roar in her ears as she reaches the final sentence. *Local law enforce-
ment believe that the pair still operate in this area – Yousuf as a pickpocket
and Eliza as a prostitute known as Belle.*

Maisie retches. It feels like everything she thought she knew
about herself was contained within a glass ball that has shattered into
a million pieces, and she is wading through shards that cut her to
the core. The Sixpences were better parents than her own, which
is saying something.

The voice inside her head begins to scream. How dare Laurent
go poking into her past and stirring everything up? As if he hasn't
already done enough damage. Her fingers are shaking, and a tremble
starts that travels up her arms and through her body. With a violent
sweep of her hands, she sends the objects arranged carefully on the
surface of Sir Malcolm's desk crashing to the floor. Clara runs into
the room, quickly followed by Eric and Arnold.

'Get out!' Maisie screams. 'Get out!'

Knowing better than to interfere, they scurry away.

Maisie rounds on the desk drawers next, tossing everything on to
the floor. Leaving Tommy; believing her parents were dead; Aunty
Mabel and Miss Catherine dying; the worry for the missing children – they are now like wild animals escaped from a cage.

She glimpses a decanter of a dark brown beverage on the windowsill. If it works for Sir Malcolm, there's no reason why it can't work
for Maisie. She removes the stopper and sniffs. The sharp smell
makes her nose wrinkle. She takes a swig. The whisky is bitter,
repulsive, and Maisie has an urge to spit it out, but she makes herself swallow every drop. The second mouthful is easier; she holds
her nose and forces in the liquid. As she takes a third, Maisie spots
the carousel in the distance, silent and mysterious, as though it's
mocking her. She wants to take an axe and smash it to pieces.

Falling

28

It is a relief to be back on dry land. The return voyage across the ocean was worse than the journey there. This time a storm midway across the Atlantic tossed the boat for an entire night and extended the crossing time from the expected six days to eight and one quarter. Laurent was counting.

He had almost gone back. As he sat on the hotel bed with his suitcase packed and his head between his hands, Laurent's impulse told him to return to Fairweather House and beg Maisie to be his. Even when he reached New York, he dithered. It was not too late to catch the 4 p.m. train and arrive in Chicago the next day. But Sir Malcolm would have given her the letter by then, and she would quite rightly be too angry to contemplate running off with him. Instigating the kiss without first explaining his marital status was a mistake. Yet in that moment he had not been able to help it.

Weary, he winds through the disembarking passengers. It is strange to be surrounded by his mother tongue again. A mad scramble for the station and Laurent catches the next train from Le Havre to Paris. The familiar sights of the French countryside stream past – endless fields of lavender, peasants tending crops, lines of laundry pegged between lime trees. By the time he arrives in the city, Laurent has feasted on liver pâté and Camembert washed down by a fine Bordeaux in the buffet carriage.

Hailing a carriage from the station, he watches Paris clatter past. The majesty of the Eiffel Tower. Montmartre like a giant molehill. When they reach the Jardin du Luxembourg, he knows that it is only a matter of minutes until they enter the street that he has called home for the last thirteen years.

The apartment building is just as he left it four weeks ago. Painted a graceful mint green with vermillion shutters and turquoise wrought-iron balconies, the place would have the appearance of a bohemian duchess if it were a person. Trudging up the stairs, Laurent passes the familiar smell of bœuf bourguignon mingled with lemon meringue emanating from Madame Gauthier's first-floor apartment, and continues on to the second floor.

He stills himself for several seconds. His state of upset is not the fault of his family. He will make an effort. He will be a better husband and a better father.

Before he can find his keys, the front door is flung open.

'Papa!'

Amélie throws her small arms around his legs. It is then that he remembers that he was so caught up with saying goodbye to Maisie that he entirely forgot to acquire a replacement Silver Kingdom flyer for his daughter. Shuffling into the apartment with Amélie still clinging, Laurent deposits his suitcase by the umbrella stand.

'How I've missed you,' he says, patting the crown of her curly brown hair.

Odette enters the hallway, looking gladder to see him than he had expected. Perhaps this could hail a fresh start for the marriage? Before they have a chance to greet one another, Amélie pulls both parents into the living room. A chocolate-and-cherry gâteau – his favourite – sits triumphantly on the coffee table.

'Absolutely wonderful!' he exclaims, touched by the thoughtfulness.

'I chose it, Papa,' Amélie says, bouncing with excitement. 'The best gâteau in the world for the best papa.'

'From the best daughter,' he responds and tickles her until she squeals for him to stop.

Odette cuts the cake, with the largest slice reserved for Laurent. As she passes him the plate, her fingers linger on his hand. Without thinking, he pulls back from her touch. A quizzical expression appears in her eyes. Concern mixed with scrutiny. He looks away and reaches for a napkin. Remembering his decision to make an effort, he squeezes her hand, then drops it. 'Later,' he promises her quietly.

★

That next morning, the usual noises accompany Laurent along the corridors of the 6th Arrondissement precinct: typewriters clacking, screams from the interrogation rooms, ribald laughter in the constables' mess.

Constable Segal is lounging in Laurent's office, eating a pain aux raisins with his feet up on the desk.

'I see you've made yourself comfortable in my absence,' Laurent comments.

The constable splutters and jumps up.

'And an absence that was all for nothing.' He points to a postcard-sized piece of paper on the desk. 'A telegram came yesterday from that agent I put you in touch with. The actress's ex-lover has retracted his statement.'

Laurent scans the brief message with a sinking feeling – it appears that Beau Armitage has a new lawyer who is accusing the Bureau of roughing up their suspect. Not just that: the man has found an alibi for his client. Forcing a false confession is always a risk if the heavy-handed techniques that Laurent suspects were employed are too heavy.

Perhaps the Bureau were pressured into concluding the case. After his conversations with Sir Malcolm – in particular the one on his last night in Chicago, in which he was offered a brown envelope *for ensuring the matter progressed in the right direction for everyone* – it would not surprise Laurent if the Randolph brothers had bribed the American authorities in order to save their business.

In any event, Laurent considers that his trip was not wasted. The discovery of a link between the victims and the fudge-coloured horse has thrown up the existence of an accomplice who, by the looks of it, is still out there somewhere. Quietly and without the knowledge of his superiors, he intends to reinvestigate by digging through Victor's history and identifying his associates in France.

'On the contrary, Segal,' he says eventually. 'It has given me much to follow up on.'

'If you say so, sir,' the constable replies. He looks his superior up and down, and up and down again, and bursts into uncontrolled laughter. 'What on earth are you wearing?'

Laurent examines his attire. He had completely forgotten that he is dressed in the casual suit he acquired from the American department store. He takes a deep breath, his hand moving to rest on the breast pocket, where the sandpiper feather is stored. While he knows he should try to forget about Maisie both for her sake and in fairness to his wife, Laurent feels a need to make up for his behaviour first. If he can find the current location of Maisie's parents and broker a reconciliation, perhaps she will forgive him. Perhaps he will forgive himself.

29

Nursing a glass of wine, Maisie tries to block out the joyful sounds of the amusement park. In the ten days since Laurent has been gone, she's steered clear of Silver Kingdom during opening hours. Being confronted by the sight of lovers strolling arm in arm, or mothers holding the hands of their children, would be too much to bear. Instead, Maisie inspects the park late in the evening. She has decided to do the paperwork in the parlour for the time being, and has transferred the necessary business files from the office near the ticket booth to the house. The workforce know either to see her in the parlour or, better yet, to speak to the Randolph brothers if they need help. So far, there's been nothing more taxing than organizing another print run of entrance tickets, ordering a gallon of oil for Mrs Ferretti's dodgems and looking over the accounts, which is just as well, because it's been difficult to concentrate. Consuming thoughts repeat in Maisie's mind like a stuck gramophone record. *Will I always be angry? Why did my parents leave? Why did Laurent kiss me?*

That moment felt as if she were dancing with him on the edge of the universe, gliding past stars. It clearly meant less to Laurent, at least not enough for him even to have told Maisie that he had a wife.

A restless ache makes Maisie want to scream, tear her hair out, rage. But she holds herself in check to avoid alarming the staff. Ever since her outburst after reading Laurent's letters, all the servants have been keeping an eye on her: Peggy Mae bakes cookies for her; Clara brings in magazines; Eric tidies her papers; and Arnold visits every night to reassure Maisie that he's still keeping Silver Kingdom's customers away from the caramel-coloured horse.

It felt like a wound was being ripped open when she learnt from Hugo one week ago about Beau Armitage's release. Bumping into him outside the parlour, he'd explained that the Bureau didn't believe the alibi provided by some married woman, who had claimed she was with him that day and late into the night, so they wouldn't be looking for anyone else. Still, Maisie was horrified: an abductor remains out there, whether it's Beau or not. Or there's more to the disappearances than meets the eye. Maisie is no nearer to explaining her strange experience on the ride.

Hugo must have noticed her expression, because he'd added, 'It's fine, Maisie. Mr Armitage is moving to Los Angeles to get away from it all. And the authorities there will keep an eye on him, let the Bureau know if he returns to Chicago, so he's prevented from coming back to the park.'

Sir Malcolm was equally relaxed about the news when Maisie had questioned him over dinner later, brushing away her concerns with a wave of his hand. That night, Maisie spent thirty minutes laying stones near the carousel to ward off another disappearance.

Draining her glass, she glances at the drinks ranged on the chest of drawers: that was the last of the white wine and red makes Maisie feel worse. Careful to keep on the right side of tipsy during working hours, she saves the bourbon, gin and brandy for the evening to fully anaesthetize the pain.

She heads for the drawing room, where she hopes to procure a bottle of Chablis.

'Nice to see you, Maisie.'

The voice makes her jump. Turning around, she's taken aback to see James standing in the doorway of the study, dressed in a full set of tails, complete with a white bow tie.

'Aren't you a little overdressed for gardening?' she asks.

He looks amused. 'Didn't you hear? I've found a permanent job. Arnold's cousin works at a jazz club and they had an opening there. Gus, the owner, couldn't wait to snap me up once he'd read my résumé,' he claims, not even trying to disguise the pride in his voice. He holds out a small package. 'I'm on my way there now. I only stopped by to bring Sir Malcolm a thank-you gift for helping me out when I first arrived, but I can't find him.'

She's astonished that no one thought to mention it. Then again, the focus of her discussions with Arnold has been the carousel, and Sir Malcolm hasn't been himself lately. Thinking back to her nightly dinners with him since Laurent left, Maisie now realizes that they've spoken less and less each night, both lost in their own thoughts. It makes James's news a pleasant surprise – at least he won't be hovering around Silver Kingdom any more.

'Sir Malcolm is probably dealing with a problem in the park. Just leave the gift on the console table, and he'll see it when he comes in.'

From her position near the staircase, Maisie spies a bottle of champagne through the open door of the drawing room. A couple of glasses should prove sufficiently strong to blur her thoughts for the next few hours.

'You look like you need cheering up,' James says, as though he can see into her mind. 'And I know just the thing. Come along to the jazz club. It's my night off tomorrow, and I can show you around the place.'

Maisie frowns. 'No, thank you, I'm busy,' she lies.

'Oh, come on, it'll do you good,' he insists. 'Don't you fancy a few hours of fun with a friend?'

She hesitates. James is pushy and arrogant and she doesn't consider him as anything more than a vague acquaintance. But, with Laurent gone, Maisie feels so desperately alone that she finds herself tempted by any chance of companionship. Although she is on good terms with the servants, ultimately, they are still staff and, therefore, duty-bound to be courteous to her. As a result, she doesn't feel it's fair to burden them with her confidences.

'All right,' she agrees, hoping to flush the detective from her mind.

30

Maisie follows James through a series of grimy corridors, twisting first left, then right, and right again; then they descend a staircase and arrive at another long corridor, at the end of which is a set of double doors guarded by a huge man in a dark fur coat and green trilby.

'Evening, Bernard. It's quiet tonight,' James remarks, handing over a dollar.

Bernard shrugs. 'Wednesdays never see much action.'

He bangs twice on the double doors, pauses and bangs three times in quick succession. A few seconds later, the doors swing open from the other side to reveal a sight Maisie could never have imagined.

A cavernous space bedecked in red-and-silver swags of silk reveals a stage where a smiling man in a tuxedo is singing an upbeat tune Maisie doesn't recognize, surrounded by an orchestra. Milling about, lounging at the bar, dancing, are people of every colour, dressed like exotic creatures of the night. Fascinated, Maisie can't take her eyes off them. A tall man sporting a live snake around his neck like a scarf parades past, followed by an assortment of bejewelled young women. Most surprising are the gaming tables set up in a dark corner, crowded with excited patrons throwing in their bets. Gambling is illegal, so it's no wonder Bernard is careful about who he lets in the club. As she watches the roulette wheel spin, Maisie is reminded of the carousel.

'Let's find a table,' James shouts over the buzz.

He shepherds Maisie through the room, greeting faces in the crowd with shouts of 'How's business, Nigel?' or 'Good to see you, Johnny.' Maisie can tell that he's at home in this hurly-burly, and she's surprised at how quickly he's adapted.

As they settle in a booth near the back with a view of the stage, a bald waiter appears.

'A gin sling for me, Curly.' James turns to Maisie. 'What'll you have, Maisie?'

Something stronger will take the edge off.

'A vodka. Make it a double, please,' she says, having been inspired by Nancy to try it for the first time. He looks at her, surprised, but makes no comment. The volume of the saxophone rises, and it becomes too noisy to talk. Sitting back to enjoy the music, Maisie tries to assimilate into these strange new surroundings. She's out of place here, prim in her buttoned-up, floor-length gown and tense seated next to James. The other women are dazzlers, carefree and laughing, in slinky dresses that show their legs, their cleavage. Confident, they dance with abandon, flirt with men, smoke. Women her age. Women her colour. Women darker and lighter than Maisie. It makes her wonder what she's been missing out on all these years.

The wine she consumed this evening before leaving is beginning to wear off and she wills the waiter to appear with her drink. Melancholy is threatening to creep in. She wishes, despite herself, that it was Laurent here with her. But Laurent is back in France with his wife.

The waiter glides back to the table, deposits the drinks and glides away. Maisie gulps down the vodka, slams the glass on the table. Good riddance to Laurent.

James grins. 'Atta girl, Maisie.' He lifts his glass. 'To the great nation of America, where women can come to clubs like this and do whatever they please.'

There's a lull in the music and conversation breaks out on the surrounding tables.

'It seems like you're really embracing America,' Maisie comments.

'And it's embracing me. I like it here. I like the opportunities, the people . . . and I like the women . . .'

James sips his drink, eyes Maisie over the glass. Emboldened by the heady atmosphere in here, she holds his gaze. He finishes his drink and wipes his mouth with a napkin from a pile on the table.

'Don't you miss England?' she asks.

'Do you?' he counters.

It's been nine years since she left the country of her birth, but Maisie still remembers the sunrise colours of the flowerbeds on her last day at Jesserton.

'I have some fond memories,' she admits.

His eyebrows shoot up. 'Well, I hate to break it to you, but the war changed a lot of things. There are strikes, riots, food shortages.' He looks more thoughtful than Maisie has ever seen him. 'It wasn't easy returning from the frontline and finding there were no jobs for those of us that had put our lives on the line,' he admits. 'But in America they can see what I'm made of. Working in the club is a first step.'

The double vodka must have hit Maisie's system, because the room is beginning to spin. She takes in the scene of performers on stage, the croupiers, the waiters and bar staff and can't decide how James fits in.

'What do you do in the club?' she asks.

He leans back in the seat as though he's trying to appear casual. 'If there's trouble amongst the patrons, I help out.'

It seems an unnecessarily vague answer. He signals to the waiter to bring more drinks, then refocuses on Maisie.

'Why didn't you tell me you were going to America with Sir Malcolm when we spoke at Jesserton? You made it seem like you were returning to your previous home on Canvey Island.'

His directness takes Maisie by surprise. She thinks back to that morning beneath the weeping willow tree, his overbearing presence, the snatched kiss.

'Because we hardly knew each other, and you were full of yourself,' she answers, any tact drowned by the vodka.

'Fair enough,' he laughs. 'Though I'd prefer to call it driven. I know what I want, Maisie, and I go all out to get it.'

More drinks appear as the singer bows and disappears behind a gold curtain. Maisie notices James's eyes are now roaming the room, moving from the stage, where a curvy woman in red is getting ready to perform, to the entrance, where a party of ten are streaming in, and finally to a group of ladies in garish dresses who are gathered in the far corner.

'Excuse me for one moment,' he says.

James slides from the booth and dives through the crowd. Maisie watches him head towards a short man in a multicoloured vest. They talk for a moment before James hands him something.

'Such a beautiful woman cannot possibly be James's love interest.' A wiry, middle-aged man sporting a twirly moustache and a velvet smoking jacket addresses Maisie. He sits down next to her. 'Frederick Fortescue but call me Freddie.'

'Maisie Marlowe. But I'm definitely not his love interest. We've known each other since childhood,' she slurs.

His eyes glint as though he's won the jackpot tonight, and he twiddles his moustache.

'So what secrets from James's youth can you share with me? Is his uncle really a duke, as he's been telling everyone?'

Maisie flinches as Freddie arches his eyebrows playfully. She knocks back her second drink before answering.

'If you tell me what you know about James, then I'll tell you,' she responds, deciding not to reveal to this total stranger that James has, of course, been exaggerating.

Freddie calls to the barman. Another round of drinks appears immediately, this time bright green shots. Absinthe.

'Do you really want to know?' he asks, his face falling serious.

The question catches her out. Before she can decide how to respond, James himself returns, his face an incandescent red.

'Get out of here, Freddie. I'll —'

Freddie jumps up as though he's been struck by lightning before James can finish his sentence and escapes to the roulette table on the other side of the room. James sits down again. Maisie says nothing, downs her drink. The bitter taste of aniseed makes her involuntarily shudder.

The singer in the red dress begins to croon a haunting melody, a slow rhythm gradually ramping up until, with the blast of a trumpet, a dancing troupe parade on to the stage. Half a dozen beautiful girls clad in thigh-length dresses kick their legs in perfect synchronicity.

Maisie is mesmerized. As their hips sway, they move as one, the colours of their barely there outfits swirling, the spotlights focused on bare flesh. Breasts. Midriffs. When the girls turn around, bend over and wriggle their frilly knickers, the audience erupts, whooping and clapping.

Maisie is overcome with a sense of freedom. In this place, women hold the power. They gyrate against each other, tease men with their bodies. She thinks of her mother. Perhaps the desire to run wild courses through Maisie's own blood. She could do anything here, and no one would tell her not to.

Suddenly Maisie is up on her feet. James cheers. She's in the midst of a tangle of bodies. Drums beat. *Boom-ba-ba-boom-ba-ba-boom*. Trumpets blow. *Eee-waaa*. She copies the women to her left, rotating her hips and flapping her arms. Then she doesn't need to copy anyone, because the music swims into her senses and tells Maisie what to do. Shimmy to the left, roll her limbs like a snake. As she spins around and around, flashes of the room appear. The blackjack table. Gleaming brass cocktail shakers on the bar. Silver confetti falling from the ceiling. James watching intently.

Sweat pours down her neck. As Maisie undoes the top button of her dress, a hand slides on to her back. A man has appeared behind her. A stranger in white tails and a yellow vest. He pushes his body close, one arm around Maisie's waist as he sways gently from side to side. She imagines that the fingers stroking her neck belong to Laurent and she arches her back. Maisie is sinking, eyes closed, willing him to kiss her mouth.

Someone grabs her hand. James has appeared. He twirls her on the spot as he breaks into a theatrical show of footwork. Laughing in surprise, Maisie is guided sideways and forwards by him, trotting in step. They move like this for several minutes. When the song changes, James begins pulling her to the exit.

'We've got to leave. Sabrina's cousins are here, and they're on the warpath,' he explains.

He glances at the dancer in the centre of the troupe on stage: a pretty black-haired girl with long legs has her eyes fixed on him. She's out of step with the other dancers and her neighbours on each side begin to wobble. The knock-on effect is a clumsy stumble by all six and a loud cheer from the audience.

Evidently, Sabrina is the dancer, and her cousins must be the five huge men striding towards them. Following James from the room, she races past Bernard, taking the staircase at speed, pushing past groups heading downstairs and out into the night. There's shouting and the sound of many pairs of feet stampeding as she enters a narrow passageway that James has dived into.

He holds his index finger to his mouth, warning Maisie to keep quiet. When he signals it's safe to come out, his face is sheepish.

'Sorry to cut things short. Sabrina can't get it into her head that it was a one-time thing,' he explains. 'Come to the jazz club again sometime once she's calmed down.'

Maisie makes no comment as she hails a taxi and slips into the backseat. She has no interest in James's love life. In the cool, clear air, she is dizzy, the blessed numbness of alcohol is quickly fading, and her head is throbbing.

Overtired by the time she gets home, Maisie thinks she hears jingly carousel music, though it must be past midnight. She peers into the distance. There's no movement, and all is quiet now.

31

In the cold light of the next day, it scares Maisie to think how easy it is to lose control. She had been on the point of kissing a complete stranger. Wanting it. Wanting more. Anything could have happened last night if James hadn't pulled her away. Despite a pounding headache, there's a clarity to her thoughts, a dawning awareness that numbing her pain with alcohol, as she's been trying to do for the past twelve days, might bring greater problems. A proper return to work could prove a safer way to take her mind off things.

Before she has second thoughts, Maisie rouses herself from bed, consumes close to a full pot of sweet tea and heads outside with a box of paperwork that she intends to take back to the office.

The sky is overcast as though a storm is gathering on the horizon. As Maisie cuts a route from the back of the house to Silver Kingdom, she notices the Crew throwing up tarpaulins to protect the food stands from becoming drenched in the event of a downpour. Before, she would have felt a ripple of pleasure at seeing the rides and stalls burst into life like unfolding flowers, but now there's only an all-encompassing flatness.

The problems begin immediately, as though they've been waiting for Maisie: the supply truck bringing sugar and flour to the food vendors fails to turn up; another quarrel breaks out between Mr Parry and Mr Melville over the boundary of their pitches; one of the Money Girls sends notice that she's sick.

With a hangover, Maisie can't face this stress alone and she goes looking for Sir Malcolm. A long search ends in the dining room. Hunched over in a chair, he's wrapped in a blanket.

Sober now, Maisie is struck by how thin and pale he looks. Since reading the report on her parents, she's been toying with the idea of asking him if Aunty Mabel ever told him why they had abandoned her, or anything at all about them. Though he claimed ignorance many years ago, there might be something he can confide to her. Recently, however, they have crossed paths only at dinner, which isn't an appropriate time for such a serious topic – and today he doesn't look up to any sort of discussion at all.

'Sir Malcolm?' she says quietly.

He stares into space. His skin is clammy and Maisie now notices that his hands are trembling. She's never seen him looking this wretched. Was he only pretending to be relaxed about Beau Armitage's release? Is he back to worrying about money?

'Is everything all right with the business?' she asks.

Sir Malcolm doesn't appear to have registered her presence, but he eventually speaks. 'The business is back on track,' he answers in a soft voice. 'Money rolling in.'

Though relieved to hear this, Maisie is concerned that, if this isn't work-related, something might be wrong with Sir Malcolm's health.

'Should I call the doctor?' she asks him.

His eyes fall closed. 'No doctor. I'm simply tired, Maisie.'

While Maisie has a sneaking suspicion that there's more to it than that, she also knows that Sir Malcolm doesn't take kindly to being told what to do.

'There are a few matters that I need help with in the park. Perhaps Hugo –'

'No, don't bother Hugo,' he interrupts with a sigh. 'My brother is dealing with domestic issues of his own,' he says, the meaning of which Maisie can guess. 'You can handle Silver Kingdom, can't you?'

It appears she has no choice.

Maisie spends the rest of the morning sorting out the issues. She negotiates a truce between Mr Parry and Mr Melville, arranges for Clara to cover Gloria's absence, and is in the middle of contacting alternative flour suppliers when Arnold discovers an issue with the carousel ten minutes before the park is due to open.

'It won't play music,' he says, frowning. 'It spins around as normal but there's no sound.'

Maisie feels like going back to bed. She curses the day she ever set eyes on the carousel.

'Do you think the riders will notice? It's not like we're short of music from the other attractions.'

Arnold looks at Maisie as if she's taken leave of her senses. 'We can't have a silent carousel. It's . . . it's a desecration.'

Suppressing the urge to roll her eyes, Maisie agrees to summon Lucky Nate and his men.

All five labourers cluster around the controls. There is conferring, clicking of tongues, shaking heads. Maisie feels jumpy as she spots the gates opening and a swarm of people heading in their direction. Without their star attraction operational, Silver Kingdom – more precisely, Maisie – will be on the receiving end of complaints, certainly demands for a refund.

'Gotcha!' Lucky Nate declares. He holds a small matchbox-sized piece of metal. 'The music box was outta place but simple enough to fix. Strange, mind, because it doesn't move easily by itself.'

He shows her how to lever the piece back in with a chisel in case of repeat issues, but, in this precise moment, Maisie is too preoccupied with sourcing raw ingredients for the food stalls to care about the whys or hows. Dashing off, she eventually finds one willing to deliver all they need at short notice.

Like a runaway train, the difficulties build momentum into the next week. A young man breaks his wrist on the dodgems on Thursday and threatens litigation; on Friday, both the Oriental Paradise ride and the mechanical train break down. By the following Tuesday, official word comes that another bout of Spanish flu is sweeping across Chicago and the other two Money Girls also call in sick.

It's enough to start a near riot.

Tuesday is pay day. At 8.00 a.m., the Money Girls usually start handing out small packets – the wages for the Crew and the Ride Jocks, and any share of profits minus rental fees owed to the Jointees. Their absence was unexpected, and by 8.05 on *this* morning Maisie is sitting in the office, splitting the cash just as she's seen them do. She works quickly, consulting the wages ledger for the correct amount due to each person and placing the appropriate dollar bills and coins in envelopes. But this is a job for three.

'Where's our money? I've got two kids to support.'

'We're not working without another cent coming our way.'

With no sign of being paid on time, the line in front of the nearby ticket booth is turning ugly. Maisie can hear people hammering on its shutters. This panic is similar to the bank runs she's heard about.

Grabbing the megaphone Arnold uses to announce the carousel ride, Maisie runs outside.

'Let's get a union formed,' someone shouts.

'Let's go on strike!'

There is cheering. Maisie could swear the last voice belonged to the owner of the Oriental Paradise ride who is usually so softly spoken that she has to lean in to hear a word he says. Her face floods with heat. The last thing she needs on top of everything else is any hint of workers' rights. Having experienced poverty in childhood, Maisie would gladly raise everyone's pay, but it isn't her decision to make.

She stands on the steps of the nearby helter-skelter. Mr Levander spots her immediately and points.

'If there isn't enough for everyone, you should start with the Jointees and work your way down,' he booms at Maisie.

Mr Levander would think that, since, as owner of the leisure boats, his position is secured at the summit of the pyramid of workers. Maisie can see Lucky Nate flex his fists, silently signalling to his crew that they should barge a path to the front of the line. The workers surge forward. There's a wail as Mrs Gonzales of the ghost train is squashed against the boundary fence. Her husband tries forcing his way to her side and is shoved back by a mass of hands.

'Us whites should get paid first,' another person yells.

There's an angry roar from the dark-skinned Jointees, and rough jostling. From her experience in the lock-up, Maisie knows that the situation could very rapidly descend into violence. This is far more serious than squabbles about pitch sizes. If she doesn't take control, Silver Kingdom will implode.

'There's enough money for everyone,' she shouts. Her promise seems to carry because the noise of the crowd dies down and is replaced by nudging and muttering. 'And you'll have your share by lunchtime. You have my word.'

'Why should we take the word of a woman?'

Maisie is staggered at how quickly they seem to have forgotten all the hard work she's put into Silver Kingdom.

'I've been given special authority from Sir Malcolm,' she explains, experiencing a wave of annoyance at having to use his name to get taken seriously.

A grudging agreement settles over the disgruntled workforce. As Lucky Nate nods, his men drift away, and then everyone else does the same as if the real power holders at Silver Kingdom are the Crew. Maisie hurries off to get on with the task before the rabble decide to hold her accountable for the delay.

'If I could have a word with you, ma'am.'

Madame Rose has cornered Maisie near the office. She's wearing a lilac dress instead of the usual scarlet and Maisie almost doesn't recognize her at first.

Maisie sighs. 'I've promised everyone they'll get paid and I mean it.'

She shoves past, determined to maintain her focus, and enters the office. Sitting at her desk, she stares as Madame Rose follows her in uninvited, and takes a seat.

'You've never come to me for a reading,' Madame Rose states, smiling. 'Everyone else at Silver Kingdom has, including Sir Malcolm. He got a lot out of it.'

Maisie is taken aback. Sir Malcolm is usually so sensible. On the other hand, steady, logical Laurent also visited the fortune-teller. Maisie finds her mind drifting to that day, strolling through the park with him. It feels like a lifetime ago that she felt carefree and so light-hearted. She bites her lip, forcing the memories down.

'If you'll excuse me, Rose, I really must get on with sorting out the money.'

Making a big play of staring at the wages ledger, Maisie begins to tick off entries.

'What is it that you want to learn, my dear?'

Maisie's pulse quickens. *Will I always be angry? Why did my parents leave? Why did Laurent kiss me?*

She glances up. As she catches Madame Rose's eye, it feels as though her deepest worry, the one that haunts her thoughts night and day, is being siphoned from her mind.

'Where are the missing children?' she asks.

The question escapes before Maisie can contain it. Holding her breath, she hears her own heartbeat. *Boom, boom, boom.* Seconds pass like water from a dripping tap.

'With the answer comes great peril to yourself,' Madame Rose replies in a slow, steady beat. 'A peril for which you are not yet prepared.'

Six weeks later, and the sheen has come off Silver Kingdom. There are enough quarrels, enough problems, enough work to fill every moment of Maisie's day, and then some. Invoices to pay, books to balance, staff rosters, supplies to order. If she isn't playing referee between the Jointees, or scratching her head over the constant cycle of machine breakdowns, there are complaints from the visitors to take in – 'The benches are uncomfortable', 'There's not enough salt on the popcorn', 'The lines for the rides are too long'.

By the time Maisie returns to the house after finishing the paperwork, the staff have retired to their own quarters, and it's up to her to warm a plate of food left by Peggy Mae.

If she could only talk these difficulties through with someone, it might all feel easier. But who? She doesn't even see Sir Malcolm any more. Holed away in his bedroom all day, he's stopped making an appearance at dinner. The only hint that he still lives at Fairweather House is the odd noise downstairs in the middle of the night, as though he's rearranging furniture. It leaves Maisie with no choice but to keep her thoughts to herself and muddle on silently.

Whenever she wonders whether to tell Hugo about his brother's vague state, she remembers Sir Malcolm's clear instruction that Hugo wasn't to be disturbed. Besides, when he does occasionally turn up at Silver Kingdom, Nancy is glued to his side. Either she arrives in a white dress – serene and medicated, in which case Maisie takes time out of even the busiest of days to sit quietly with her on the patio bench – or she appears in brash colours, loud and obnoxious, and is best avoided. There's nothing in between, and her mood is unpredictable. It's better to keep Hugo out of it.

On a warm evening falling in the last week of summer, Maisie is heading indoors for another evening alone. She has decided to reread the report on her parents. The shock is wearing off and there are still questions she would like answered. Why did her parents leave her behind? And where are they now? Deep down, part of her also wants to feel some sort of connection to the detective. He touched the paper, created the structure of the sentences with his entire focus on Maisie.

She hears someone calling her name. Arnold is racing across the grounds. As their paths converge by the helter-skelter, he pauses to catch his breath.

'I've just received a telephone call about my father,' he pants. 'He's gravely unwell and I need to return to St Louis to be by his side. There's a train leaving first thing in the morning.'

Maisie wonders what it's like to have a father you care about, who cares about you. While of course she can't refuse his request, it brings with it the biggest hurdle she's yet faced. Though the special horse is still covered in blankets, Arnold is a second line of defence. The old fear flares up as Maisie realizes that without him someone else might vanish into thin air. Though Beau Armitage is out of the picture, all the way in Los Angeles, what if he never was the abductor? Or what happens if he returns? She can play it down all she likes, but Madame Rose's warning about a future peril has Maisie spooked, and she can't take the risk of another disappearance.

Now that she is running the business, she understands why the Randolph brothers were so reluctant to close the carousel. It's Silver Kingdom's glorious centrepiece, attracting visitors from as far away as Peoria. Without it, they might as well shut the entire park. Though half tempted to go down this route, Maisie knows that the workforce would stage an all-out revolt.

Sending Arnold off to pack, Maisie wanders over to the carousel, its majestic outline silhouetted against twilight. What is it about this chunk of metal and wood that everyone finds so compelling?

She spends the next few hours trying to find a replacement for the Grand Ringmaster of the carousel. Every single one of Silver Kingdom's workers flat out refuses, unwilling to take on the responsibility of keeping people away from the caramel-coloured horse, and still smarting after their wages were late. 'Your problem is that it led to bad whispers about working at this place, so you won't find anyone further afield that's willing to chance it,' Lucky Nate explains with a shrug. 'Especially at this short notice.'

She fares no better asking the household staff: Eric grumbles that he's busy doing the job of both butler and footman; Clara is too shy; Peggy Mae is focused on cooking and bringing up three children alone. Maisie would do it herself but she is run off her feet as it is.

Brooding, she retreats to the parlour. Her mind turns over an idea, then discounts it. Maisie already knows that it's impossible to detach that one horse without detaching them all, and she isn't confident that she won't face the same problem if she asks Lucky Nate to hack it off at its pole.

James suddenly materializes in the doorway. What with being so occupied, she hasn't seen him since the evening at the jazz club. Or given him a second thought.

'It's my night off and I popped by because I haven't heard from Sir Malcolm for a while, and was worried,' he explains.

Relieved that someone else has noticed that something is off, Maisie asks him to take a seat. She explains her concerns about Sir Malcolm's health, and the strain of finding herself in charge of a business. When James promises to come by more often to check in on Sir Malcolm, she feels like a weight is lifted.

'Leave it to me,' he says, brimming with efficiency. 'And what are you doing to let off steam? You can't just work, work, work, Maisie, it isn't good for you. Come to the jazz club again. You liked it, didn't you?'

Maisie loved the jazz club, maybe too much.

'I don't have time, James, and I need to keep my focus on this place.'

James looks thoughtful. 'I suppose Arnold taking off doesn't help. His cousin Jacob, from the club, told me about his father.'

Maisie feels totally defeated. 'I can't find anyone to take his place,' she admits. 'Let alone someone I trust to keep people away from that one horse.'

'The one the French detective in particular was interested in?'

James has obviously paid more attention to the goings-on here than Maisie realized. As she nods, he leans back in his chair, tapping the armrests, his face inscrutable.

'I'll do it,' he replies.

Maisie hesitates. On the one hand, she isn't confident that James is up to the job. Then again, she's reached the point of desperation, and no one else has volunteered.

'Thank you,' she agrees with some reluctance.

32

The Cour des miracles slums are vile by day: rats coexist with feral dogs; the stench of open sewers mingles with putrefied chicken droppings; pickpockets and paupers scramble for loose change. Night-time is even worse. It feels like every undesirable in Paris slithers from the gutters when darkness falls. But, with his workload tripled since his return from Chicago three months ago, Laurent has little choice but to enter this unsavoury area after twilight if he is to pursue the extracurricular puzzles in his life.

His home life suffers as a result. Before going to America, he made every effort to arrive home before Amélie's bedtime. But these days he is late more often than not – either drawn to the police archives after hours in his search for the names of Victor Cloutier's criminal associates or to this place: the slum featured in the police reports discovered by Constable Segal.

For three months, Laurent has returned again and again to the taverns and whorehouses here, the crooked streets, anywhere that might be frequented by a pickpocket or a prostitute. He has questioned thieves and paupers, drunkards and pimps. But no one has any knowledge of Eliza and Yousuf, it appears. Sometimes Laurent believes that he will be forever caught in this wild goose chase. But he cannot give up, for Maisie's sake.

Weary, he pushes through the crowd. Sly eyes follow him. He is well known in these parts as a high-ranking detective, and it is not always guaranteed that the authorities will look the other way if a crime is discovered.

A young lad darts in front of him and sticks out a filthy palm.

'Just a centime, monsieur,' the child begs. 'For my sisters.'

The boy points to a group of youngsters with dirty faces between the ages of approximately seven down to babyhood, all wearing rags. Probably they have been left here by parents, who are off drinking or cavorting or God knows what else. If they have parents. Laurent reaches into his pocket for a franc as he fixes the boy with a stern look.

'It's for food, do you hear? Not chartreuse or cigarettes . . . or anything else.'

The boy salutes and grins before running away to show off his prize.

Where the slum widens, three taverns compete with two brothels and an opium den. This is the rowdiest area in Paris. Depending on which establishment a patron has frequented, people are stumbling around and shouting drunkenly, or high on satiated lust, or passed out comatose on the street.

A burly man with black teeth guards a doorway, his arms folded. He looks Laurent up and down.

'You again?'

Laurent stares him straight in the eye. This is his fifteenth visit, always with the same purpose.

'I'm not here for pleasure.'

The man juts out his jaw and tilts forward, menacingly.

'Our women not good enough for you?'

'Official police business,' Laurent claims.

He taps the fourth finger of his left hand. Although he does not wear a ring, it is an unspoken and universal sign of marriage. In truth, he cannot bear to touch another woman these days, can barely bring himself to pretend with Odette. It has developed into a source of friction between them. 'I don't feel very wanted, Laurent,' she often complains. The fresh start is quickly souring. Even when he devotes extra energy to being attentive by bringing her cherry bonbons or complimenting her hair, there is a tension behind her smile.

Laurent waits. Eventually, the man draws aside a tatty curtain as he smirks. 'They all say that.'

The fragrance of cheap perfume is overpowering. Dimly lit for privacy, the vestibule splits into four equally gloomy passageways, off of which are a series of tiny, partitioned rooms. Noises guide

Laurent's way – giggling, grunting, a squeal. Fruitlessly, he peers into one sordid space after another. Just as he is about to give up, Laurent notices a glint of long golden hair at the very end of the final corridor. From Maisie's limited description of her mother, he is searching for a blonde.

A woman with her back turned to the passageway sits on a stool near a bed that is constructed of planks of wood and what looks like old curtains. She is well covered for a prostitute, in a corset and long skirt.

'Belle?' he calls.

As the woman turns around, Laurent's disappointment is immediate. From the brown fringe peeking out, it is obvious that she is wearing a wig. 'Sorry,' he mumbles, turning away.

'Eliza, you mean?' she asks.

Laurent stops in his tracks. These women safeguard their real identities and step away from their noms de plume only for rare friends.

'She doesn't work here any more,' the woman continues. 'Thought she could get more clients elsewhere. She said that man of hers wasn't earning enough, he put pressure on her to make more, and they left a couple of weeks back.'

Laurent presumes the man must be Maisie's father, and he removes his notebook from his jacket.

'Do you happen to know where this elsewhere is?'

She shrugs. 'Sometimes she hangs about in the industrial area. Reckons workers on their way home with a day's wages are easy prey.'

Tilting her head, she hitches up her skirt. Once Laurent might have been tempted. Now he is saddened by the disgusting conditions she endures in order to eke out a living.

As she starts to unbutton her corset, Laurent stops her with a shake of his head and scribbles in his notebook. A solid lead, at last.

33

With the arrival of autumn, there is a softening. As the trees shed their leaves, Maisie begins to experience a wistfulness for her parents. There could be a hundred reasons for their actions – and shouldn't she feel glad that they're alive? Excitement tingles that one day she might even meet them. She could try to find them. Or they might come for her. She stores the idea in her heart: they might still want Maisie.

Her resentment towards Laurent is also released. It was a brief moment in time when two lonely souls were thrown together, she tells herself, and is best left in the past. Four months on, and the ache in her heart is manageable if she doesn't let herself dwell on him.

While Maisie's hopes of romance have been crushed, Clara's prospects have been boosted by the changes in the household. Unable to keep away from the new footman, Robert, she giggles in the hallways, distracting everyone else. For once, Maisie is grateful for Eric's dourness.

'Clara Higgins, get back to work,' she can hear his shout echo as he catches the maid neglecting her duties for the third time in an hour.

Eric is now the official butler. Returned the week after his father made a miraculous recovery, Arnold had asked Maisie to release him from household duties.

'My dad's illness showed me that we have to make the most of our lives, and working two jobs was getting too much,' he'd admitted with a regretful expression. 'I would've said something sooner, but I didn't like to let you down. I think my place is at the carousel.'

Wishing him nothing but happiness, Maisie had agreed. She was glad to see him back at the carousel, although – and she would never share this thought with Arnold – James was admirable in his absence. Maybe even a better guardian. Swooping in, his large fists clenched, not a single person dared approach the strange horse.

James has also kept his promise to keep an eye on Sir Malcolm. He visits three mornings a week and spends his evenings off at Fairweather House. He even summoned a doctor, despite Sir Malcolm's objections. 'There's nothing physically wrong with him,' Dr Carlton diagnosed. 'Just overtiredness. Make sure he gets plenty of bed rest.'

One evening, James appears as usual, but with a square package in one hand and a bottle of vodka in the other.

'If you're too busy for the jazz club, I'm bringing the jazz club to you,' he explains.

Astonished, Maisie follows him to the drawing room where he begins to nudge the couches against the walls. Next, he rolls up the rug with Maisie's help, and then shows her the contents of the package. To her excitement, he has brought along five new gramophone records, black and slick like the eels she used to catch with Tommy on Canvey Island. She turns one over in her hands and sets it on the gramophone. The insistent notes of a trumpet burst into the air.

'These are the latest tunes,' James explains. 'You get the cocktails mixed while I pop up to see Sir Malcolm. I'll be back in a jiffy.'

Ensuring there's only the tiniest drop of vodka in her own glass, Maisie adds orange juice. By the time James returns, Maisie is already swinging her arms as she circles the room on tiptoe. James joins in for a time before he changes the record and breaks into the moves that she recognizes from the jazz club. 'This is called the Fox Trot,' he tells her, his eyes gleaming.

Maisie mimics him, managing to keep up until the rhythm is so fast that she can hardly catch her breath. With an over-exuberant twirl, she loses her balance and her ankle is turned askew. Falling back on the couch, she winces. Immediately, James switches off the music and crouches on the floor to examine her foot. He looks serious, tilting his head.

'Luckily, it's not broken. And it's nothing too serious – you can still rotate your ankle. You'll only get a small bruise.'

'Are you sure?' she asks. 'It feels like I've been stomped on by an elephant.'

James laughs. 'I'm very sure. My mother trained as a nurse, and I picked up a thing or two. She met my father when treating him after he returned injured from a military expedition to Burma, as it happens,' he explains. 'At around the same time, Aunty Lydia met Sir Malcolm at the garden fête that the Randolphs threw every June.'

Maisie removes her shoes, and lies back on the couch with her feet elevated on the armrest. The throbbing subsides.

'Sir Malcolm has never talked about your family,' she discloses.

James remains on the floor, crossing his legs.

'I'm not that surprised. My mother blamed him for Aunty Lydia's death. It was Sir Malcolm who bought the stallion she fell from. It was wild and untrained,' he says. 'There was a big falling-out afterwards, with all my extended family taking my mother's side, and even my grandmother, who usually wants everyone to get along, won't hear his name mentioned.'

Maisie has never experienced the closeness of a big family or grandparents growing up. By abandoning her like this, her parents denied Maisie more than themselves, and it feels like she's been cast adrift from herself.

'Don't they mind that you're here?'

He shrugs. 'As long as they don't have to see him, I have their blessing,' he explains. 'I'm the only one of my family who was ever close to him in any way, mainly because Sir Malcolm was decent enough to pay my school fees.'

She absorbs this information

'I didn't realize your family isn't rich.'

James's blue eyes study Maisie with interest. 'I *am* going to make it in America, Maisie. Nothing will stop me.'

For the first time, Maisie thinks that she might believe him.

After that, they settle into a new routine of dancing together on his evenings off. Each time, James teaches her the new steps that he's learnt from the patrons at the club. The Texas Tommy. The Black Bottom. It doesn't take long for Maisie to guess that he's trying to woo her. Even so, she is taken by surprise when, at the end of one such evening, James gets down on one knee.

'Marry me,' he says, with an urgency in his voice.

Maisie is speechless. In all their times together, she hasn't once thought of him in a romantic sense. James must pick up on her hesitation because he stands and finishes his drink.

'Please just think about it,' he says, and departs.

Maisie turns the idea over in her head for a full week. As she walks towards the patio at the end of a long day at Silver Kingdom, she takes a seat on the bench. Late autumn has brought a gentle glow to the Fairweather Estate. Against a backdrop of pale yellows and browns, the carousel stands out, its vibrant colours brightening the landscape.

Over the last few months, James has shot up in her estimation, but shouldn't she be feeling more *something* – excitement? passion? – at a marriage proposal? If Laurent had asked for her hand in marriage, Maisie wouldn't feel like this, she knows that.

But where is Laurent? Back in France with his wife.

She digs her fingernails into her palms to stop the images of the man she loves with another woman. Is she going to resign herself to the life of an old maid for the sake of a man who doesn't want her? Secretly, she craves romance, needs companionship.

When James arrives at Fairweather on his next evening off, Maisie opens the door for him. Both fear and hope appear in his eyes.

'I've thought about it,' she says. 'And the answer is yes.'

34

1920

Swishing down the sweeping staircase with Clara holding the train of her dress, Maisie catches sight of the carousel through the drawing-room windows. It's the middle of winter, and icicles hang from the canopy. A sheen of ice covers the horses, making them appear ghostly. Luckily the park is closed until the weather improves in early spring, or every morning would be spent defrosting the mechanics of the rides.

Silver Kingdom is eerily quiet without the Crew, the Ride Jocks and the Jointees. They are all wintering in Florida, Mr Levander told Maisie before he left. Most of the rides have gone with them, since side gigs have been organized down there for the season. It's surprising how much Maisie misses the hurly-burly and even the bickering, and she can't wait for their return at the end of February.

She takes stock of the drawing room. Devoid of the usual furniture this morning, it is filled with five tables and forty chairs borrowed from the food stalls. It makes the day seem real, and a tingle of anxiety sends a shiver up her spine. She woke up thinking of her mother this morning, wondering if all those years ago she had also been a jittery bride. Was there any sign at all of what married life would hold for her? Running from the law. Abandoning her child. Mrs Papadopoulos has reassured Maisie that nerves are normal on one's wedding day, and she holds on tightly to this thought.

As she walks along the hallway, Maisie spots a letter addressed to her on the console table. No one usually writes to her. As she picks up the envelope, she almost gasps in surprise. The slanted, loopy handwriting belongs to Laurent. On the back, he has included his details: *Detective L. Bisset, Police Precinct of the 6th Arrondissement, Paris.*

Maisie feels burning hot, as if she's suffering from scarlet fever. Then a chill travels along her limbs. Why has he written after all these months? Before Clara gets wind of this development, she sends the maid to fetch a shawl.

Her hands tremble as she makes a small tear in the paper. Then she pauses, debating whether to open it.

Arnold hurries from the direction of the kitchen, resplendent in a purple velvet suit.

'Off you go, Miss Maisie. Sir Malcolm is already in the Daimler.'

He places his hands on Maisie's shoulders to guide her to the front door. Alarmed, she swivels around; she can't arrive at the church with Laurent's letter in her possession. And she can't leave the envelope sitting in the hallway for anyone to notice.

'Arnold, stop.' She brandishes the envelope under his nose. 'I need you to put this somewhere for safekeeping.'

His eyes widen as he reads the sender's details. More than anyone, Arnold might have guessed that something was afoot between Maisie and Laurent. But she trusts him.

'Leave it with me,' he whispers. 'I shall store it in Sir Malcolm's usual place.'

In the study, he means, in the top drawer, under lock and key.

Satisfied with this arrangement, Maisie allows Arnold to lead her to the car and accepts a cream shawl from Clara.

'Wait here, I almost forgot,' Arnold gasps.

He runs into the house and returns with a navy ribbon embroidered in gold lettering – MAISIE AND JAMES, JANUARY 3RD, 1920 – attached to which is a small diamond made of paste and a sprig of winter jasmine. With Clara lifting the trailing sleeve of the wedding dress, Arnold ties the ribbon around Maisie's wrist.

Not having even thought about a corsage, Maisie is almost moved to tears by this gesture. As she kisses his cheek, Arnold turns scarlet.

Inside the Daimler, Sir Malcolm's chin is resting on his chest, his eyes closed. With a start, he wakes up as Maisie slides in next to him on the back seat. He is smart for a change, probably courtesy of Arnold, in a set of tails and his hair brushed flat to his head. The look is marred only by his crooked tie, which Maisie begins to straighten without thinking.

Sir Malcolm attempts a smile, his mouth slanted up at one side.

'Your aunt used to do the same thing for me,' he says. His voice is so quiet that Maisie has difficulty hearing him. 'I would have married her like a shot, you know, but we had to wait until her divorce came through. Until then, I didn't want the servants gossiping, tarnishing her reputation,' he continues as though he's unaware that it's Maisie he's speaking to. 'So we had to keep it quiet. Mabel said we should just run off and leave it all behind.'

This is the first time that Sir Malcolm has owned up to Maisie about his relationship with her aunt, and it sounds like they were in love.

'Catherine used to try before that,' he adds. 'But her fingers were too little to be of much help. They were made for writing. She would have made a splendid author, don't you think?'

Hearing Sir Malcolm talk about Aunty Mabel and his daughter with such fondness stirs an understanding in Maisie. Through the pain of losing his loved ones, he took in a stray girl and treated her with kindness, even though he owed her nothing. He isn't blood, but Sir Malcolm is the only proper father Maisie has known.

She places her hand in his, feeling protective towards him.

'She certainly would. I told her as much at Clacton funfair.'

Maisie gazes out of the window, watching Fairweather House disappear as Eric steers the car past leafless tress arching under the weight of snow.

When she spots James at the end of the aisle, Maisie feels like her stomach has bottomed out. She remembers Laurent's letter waiting at home. His grey, questioning eyes. The passion of that kiss. James turns around, his face shining with excitement.

It's too late to change her mind now.

There's a ruckus in one corner of the drawing room. This afternoon, Nancy is in one of her spiky moods and is causing a scene at the reception luncheon. She has risen from her seat and is stabbing her finger at Clara, accusing the maid of spilling red wine on her new silk dress.

All eyes turn as the volume rises, with the exception of Sir Malcolm, who remains staring, blank-eyed, at a watercolour of an English landscape above the fireplace. While the maid runs off, Hugo tries restraining Nancy. Even some way off, Maisie can tell that he's having considerable trouble managing his wife's temperament.

Maisie spots James beckoning her back to her seat. She breaks off her conversation with Mrs Papadopoulos's eldest son, who is now a burly young man of fifteen, to sit down next to her new husband.

James leans into Maisie. 'My money's on Arnold getting walloped by Nancy's handbag next.'

They watch as Nancy runs from the room, while Hugo jumps from his seat and strides towards them.

'I'm taking Nancy home,' he announces abruptly. 'Sorry for the fuss.' He runs his fingers through his hair. 'I shouldn't have insisted she come. I understand it's unacceptable behaviour, but she had another miscarriage last week, and she's finding things difficult.'

'We understand, old chap,' James replies. 'No hard feelings.'

Hugo looks relieved. He hands James an envelope. 'Your wedding gift,' he explains, and departs to deal with Nancy.

Hugo is so wrapped up in his wife that he didn't even mention his brother's state of mind today, probably didn't notice that Sir Malcolm is now leaning against the mantelpiece with his head buried in his hands.

'There's a hundred dollars in here,' James exclaims, awestruck. 'We should place this somewhere safe.'

'All right, but hurry back. It looks like there's going to be dancing,' Maisie says. 'We can show everyone how to do the Fox Trot.'

James laughs and pulls Maisie to her feet.

'You're coming with me, Mrs Squires. I still don't know my way around this big old house.'

Having both agreed that Sir Malcolm shouldn't be left living alone at Fairweather, James has given up his apartment in the city and moves in today.

Maisie follows him to the hallway, fielding offers of congratulations on the way. The sensible place to put anything is in the top drawer of Sir Malcolm's desk, out of action, but, with Laurent's unopened letter in there, she needs to find an alternative. Careful not to trip on her train, she ascends the stairs and heads to her bedroom – their bedroom now – with James trailing behind.

Clapping from downstairs probably means the dancing is about to begin.

Maisie switches on the lamp. Though it's only mid-afternoon, dusk has suddenly appeared. Goosebumps creep along her arms despite the long sleeves of her dress. The room is chilly and she's left her wrap on the back of a chair. The fire hasn't been lit in the hearthside and she makes a mental note to ask Clara to fetch some logs up later. Eager to find a suitable location to store the money and return to the guests, Maisie scans the room. It still looks like a young girl's bedroom, with its pink wallpaper and frilly bedcovers. Perhaps they can redecorate.

On the top of her bureau sits an ivory jewellery box. Stashing the money amongst the few worthless trinkets, she's about to turn around when James comes up from behind and circles her waist with his arms.

'Dance for me,' he whispers in her ear and begins softly swaying from side to side.

Maisie freezes. She realizes that this is what James has wanted, to engineer them away from the party. He nuzzles into her while she lets him undo the buttons at the back of her dress, feeling no stirring of desire herself.

She returns downstairs a few minutes after James, and is about to rejoin the others when she spots him seated with a group of his friends, grinning as ribald laughter breaks out. Avoiding them, she sits alone in the hallway on the bottom stair. Mrs Papadopoulos appears and, taking one look at Maisie, brings her a glass of whisky.

'Here. Drink,' she orders, a look of concern on her face. '*Moro mou*, what is wrong?'

Maisie shakes her head. What happens between a man and his wife is private. 'Nothing,' she replies.

Mrs Papadopoulos strokes Maisie's tousled hair.

'If you need anything, you come to me. Understand?'

Maisie sips the bitter drink, then hands back the glass. She's experienced worse than pretending to enjoy the touch of her own husband.

35

Unaccustomed to sharing a bed with another person, Maisie is awake that night, listening to the hoot of barn owls. Careful not to wake James, she removes his arm from across her chest, gets out of bed and tiptoes down the stairs and into the study.

Laurent's letter lies unopened in the top drawer of the desk. Maisie wavers. It seems disloyal to read a communication from another man on her wedding night. But it could be an urgent matter of police business, she reasons.

Retrieving the key from beneath Sir Malcolm's cigar case, she easily finds the envelope, which she opens with shaky hands. Inside is a single piece of paper in the shape of a swan. Laurent's trademark. She unfolds it slowly to reveal a letter. Her eyes scan the page. It isn't much, but, at the same time, it is everything.

Dearest Maisie,

I arrived safely in France some months ago, but was uncertain whether you would wish to hear from me again. Please forgive me for any hurt I have caused you. It was never my intention.

I think often of our time together. It is not an exaggeration to say that those memories are amongst the fondest I have. Thank you for showing a hapless Frenchman around your wonderful city. My colleagues in the police department are most fascinated by the cut of American couture. It is quite unlike anything seen in Paris.

Yours,
Laurent

Placing her hand on the paper where his hand must have lain, Maisie remembers the greyness of his eyes, how they drew her in with their questions. How they gazed at her, while all the time he was married. Heat rushes to her head as anger simmers up. In what way does an apology fix the rip in her heart?

Maisie is deciding how to dispose of the letter when she notices a flash of movement outside. Peering from the window, she spots the distinctive shape of the carousel in motion.

36

Who on earth is riding the carousel at this time of night?

With a sense of trepidation, Maisie replaces the letter in the drawer, throws on a coat and boots, and runs outside.

The moon is a stitch in the sky and barely illuminates her way. Hurrying as fast as the icy ground will allow, she moves across the park and past the closed-up concession stands. The colours of the carousel are spinning with abandon, pirouetting like a ballerina. As it circles again, Maisie gets the fright of her life. She sees blankets strewn on the platform. Then she registers the absence of music, the same problem Arnold flagged up months ago. Has someone been tampering with the mechanics again?

Out of breath now, she pushes on. The carousel is slowing by the time she gets there, and Maisie leaps on, striding across the platform. There's no sign of anyone or anything out of place except – and it takes Maisie a moment to notice in the dark – an object on the platform. A small cry escapes from her mouth as she recognizes Sir Malcolm's trilby lying beside the hooves of the caramel-coloured horse. Its unsettling eyes watch Maisie scour the vicinity for the man himself. But he's nowhere to be seen. Has Sir Malcolm vanished like all the others?

Calm down, she tells herself, calm down. He could still be in the house. Hastening back, she soon discovers that there's no sign of him there either. Not in his bedroom or any of the downstairs rooms. Driven by desperation, she returns to the carousel, clinging to the hope that her worst fears are unfounded. Sir Malcolm must be around somewhere.

Huddled in the blankets usually wrapped around the wooden animal, she sits on the platform and prays, just as hard as she used to when Tommy was by her side all those years ago. Her breath is like mist as she murmurs, *Dear Lord of the Water, please let Sir Malcolm appear.* She hears waves lapping in answer, the screech of a fox, the breeze rushing off the lake, followed by the swings squeaking as though the ghosts of children are playing. A silver streamer from her wedding dances past. For hours she waits, shivering, hoping that Sir Malcolm will suddenly turn up with the simple explanation of having taken a midnight walk to clear his head and lost all track of time. The sensation that she isn't alone makes Maisie want to run away, but she stays, compelled by an overwhelming need to see him. It's only when dawn is a purple line on the horizon that hope turns to panic.

She wants to scream, shout for help. But she suppresses the urge long enough to think through her situation. Maisie was the chief suspect until Beau Armitage came to the attention of the Bureau. Then he found an alibi, and by all accounts he's currently in Los Angeles – while right now, Maisie is here. It doesn't look good for her. She imagines a quick arrest, a trial and probable conviction. Incarceration. Possibly the same fate as Victor Cloutier. There's no Laurent to shield her from the American authorities, no master of Fairweather House to wield his influence. No father figure to protect her.

It won't be long until the servants arrive at the big house for the day, and the next fifteen minutes pass in a frenzy. First, it needs to look like no one was at the carousel tonight. She swaddles the wooden horse in blankets, then she locates the matchbox-sized music box jutting out of a recess under the control lever and presses it back into place with the chisel, as she saw Lucky Nate do all those months ago.

Maisie runs inside. Sir Malcolm's bedroom is dark, but she doesn't dare switch on the light. Grabbing a handful of his clothes, she proceeds to the shore and leaves them, along with the trilby, in a pile near a rock.

Back indoors again, Maisie hurries to the study and removes the typewriter from its case, pausing while she decides on the exact wording to use. *Clack, clack, clack.* Thinking back to the cheques Sir Malcolm signed for Silver Kingdom, Maisie attempts a similar scrawl as she signs the letters in his name. She leaves three – one for Hugo, one for Eric and one for herself – on the desk in brown envelopes.

Creeping quietly, she is back in bed on the dot of sunrise.

James stirs but stays asleep. Pulling the covers up to her chin, Maisie shivers, stunned. Only now can she allow herself fully to absorb the terrible fate of Sir Malcolm.

Minutes pass slowly. There's a clatter downstairs. Thumping and swishing as furniture is moved back to its normal place after yesterday's party, curtains drawn open. Still James snores on. Her breath held, she hears Eric's voice, urgent, shouting. He must have discovered Sir Malcolm's suicide notes.

37

'I can't believe dear Malcolm is gone. Such a terrible business,' Nancy says, dabbing her eyes with a handkerchief. 'It seems so out of character for him to have ended it all.'

They are sitting in the cramped offices of Sir Malcolm's lawyer in downtown Chicago, the odour of garlic from the restaurant downstairs sticking to their clothes. Nancy looks every inch the sister-in-law in mourning in a black silk dress covered in black feathers, and a pillbox hat with a veil. For a change, she seems both sober and unmedicated, her stormy mood at the reception party a fortnight ago blown away. Probably recalling all those times that the pair of them have spent sitting together quietly on the patio bench at Fairweather House, she gives Maisie a compassionate look.

In return, Maisie attempts a small smile, struggling to keep her face from giving away the truth about Sir Malcolm. The letters and pile of his clothes by the lake were enough evidence for a presumptive death certificate, and convinced the police to buy the suicide story – drowning after wading into the icy waters of Lake Michigan. But it appears that Nancy isn't as easy to convince.

'It is indeed a terrible business,' Mr Peabody of Peabody & Laine Associates agrees from the other side of his oak desk, as if there were a standard response to a person killing themselves.

He sits like a king on a throne, a framed certificate hanging behind him. If the aim is to impress clients, the effect is ruined by the peeling paintwork.

Hugo gives a polite smile. 'It came completely out of the blue.'

James leans forward and looks along the row at Hugo. The men sit at either end with their wives in the centre.

'Except you have to admit that he's been looking miserable for a long while,' James says.

Hugo's head turns sharply to regard James, as though this is shocking news. As Maisie had suspected, he never did register his brother's decline.

'I fear Mr Squires is correct. It seems that the matter has played upon Sir Malcolm's mind for some time, because a couple of months ago he came to me about inserting a clause in his will that his assets should be bequeathed to his heirs with or without a body,' Mr Peabody explains. 'I told him there might be legal complications. In this instance, a death certificate was issued, but it isn't always the case. So we settled on drawing up a written deed gifting his assets, which would come into effect at my discretion. A power of attorney of sorts.'

Maisie picks at her fingernails. It sounds like his disappearance was planned. She casts her mind back to the music box being dislodged, to the rearranged blankets, to Sir Malcolm's increasing vagueness. Are they all connected? If so, could he have been secretly riding the horse for a while, knowing the risks? Does it mean that he willingly abandoned Maisie? Like her parents and Laurent. All she has left is her husband.

As if he can read her thoughts, James reaches for her hand.

'I won't beat about the bush,' Mr Peabody continues, looking up from his paperwork with small, mouselike eyes. 'Your brother has bequeathed the house to you, Hugo. As well as the contents.'

Maisie was expecting as much, but departing from Fairweather House will be a wrench. Where will she and James live? While he still works at the club, being based downtown would suit him, but Maisie needs somewhere close to Silver Kingdom. That is, if she still has a job there.

Nancy claps in delight. Mr Peabody frowns with the authoritative air of a man who is unused to interruptions. She mouths 'sorry' and places her hands in her lap.

'There is a clause, however, stipulating that Maisie and her spouse and her issue – that means children – will be permitted to live there for as long as she chooses.'

Nancy audibly gasps. Before she can speak, Mr Peabody throws another warning look and continues. 'This clause does not prevent you and Mr Randolph from moving in, of course.'

Hugo mutters something Maisie can't catch. She looks at James, trying to gauge his feelings. Sharing their living accommodation with the Randolphs – especially mercurial Nancy – would be an adjustment, to say the least. He shrugs his shoulders and squeezes her hand.

Mr Peabody ignores the frosty atmosphere to list a number of small gifts to a chosen few: Arnold is to receive the gold watch; Eric will get a pair of cufflinks; Clara the silver sugar bowl; Peggy Mae a set of Wedgwood china for herself and ten dollars for each of her three children; and even Robert the new footman is remembered with an engraved silver tankard.

'Moving on to Silver Kingdom,' Mr Peabody says.

Maisie tenses. Silently, she prays that there's a condition stating she should be kept on.

'Of Sir Malcolm's portion, five per cent is awarded to Hugo with the remaining ninety-five per cent going to Maisie, which gives her a seventy per cent controlling interest in the business.'

The room sits in stunned silence. No one is more surprised than Maisie. Here she is, little Maisie Marlowe from Canvey Island, now a person of substantial means. Sir Malcolm has given her the gift of financial security. It feels just like the magical moment when Aunty Mabel appeared on the footpath leading to the Sixpences' shack.

James's grip of her hand intensifies. To her right, the undercurrent of hostility emanating from the Randolphs makes Maisie nervous. Sir Malcolm's death looks doubly suspicious now she's gained so much from it. Anyone who knows where Maisie came from – the squalor, the filth of the shack, the history of her parents – would want to examine the circumstances of this sudden inheritance.

It's Nancy who speaks first.

'Suicide is a mortal sin and Malcolm will burn in hell for what he's done.'

She waits, expecting an admonishment, but when not so much as a squeak comes from Hugo, Maisie decides to step in.

'Thank you, Mr Peabody.' She leans across the desk to shake his hand. 'It makes sense for me to stay at Fairweather House so I'm close to work.'

Maisie throws Nancy a smile, enjoying the look of fury on the woman's face, any closeness they might once have shared snuffed out like a candle. She turns to James for back-up, but he is silent, his mouth drawn into a thin line.

James's silence persists on the way home. At Fairweather House, he helps Maisie from the cab without making eye contact, pays the driver and strides inside.

'James, don't you think we should stay?' she asks as soon as they're alone.

He swings around, his eyes taking her in.

'In actual fact, I do. Nancy shouldn't have said what she did about Sir Malcolm and I'm glad you stuck up for him.' He frowns. 'But, Maisie, we're a team now and you should have talked it through with me before announcing it to the whole world.'

Maisie can see his point. She was so upset by Nancy's spite about Sir Malcolm that she didn't consider her husband's feelings, and he's the only person she now has in the world. His face relaxes and he holds out his arms. Leaning into him, Maisie hears the steady rhythm of his heart, smells his musky aftershave. They stand in the hallway, the only sound the gentle patter of light raindrops falling on the driveway. Minutes pass. In these arms, Maisie is wanted.

A funeral is held that same week. Though Sir Malcolm long ago stopped attending church, and there's no body, the minister was amenable to a service without the burial. 'We became used to families of soldiers lost on the battlefield asking for similar in the war,' he'd explained, believing Hugo's story that his brother had drowned by accident.

Maisie is riddled with guilt. The consequences of her actions on her wedding night are beginning to sink in. Thanks to her, everyone else thinks Sir Malcolm killed himself, and no one is out looking for him.

Two days later, Maisie learns that her decision to stay at Fairweather House hasn't deterred the Randolphs from moving in.

As Hugo's car rolls up the driveway, followed by two large trucks, she has a hard-to-shake feeling of impending doom.

'Place the personal goods in the hallway and the furniture in the garage for now,' Nancy orders the men in an overly loud voice, as though she's putting on a performance especially for Maisie. 'We'll clear each room of the old junk in due course.'

Soon the entire contents of the Randolphs' narrow townhouse begin to emerge. Maisie searches out Peggy Mae to talk about making extra for dinner tonight, passing Nancy's maid, who is burdened with an armful of dresses. There's no cook in the kitchen, but she finds Hugo struggling to find space for a box of groceries in the pantry.

'Let me help,' she tells him.

Hugo moves aside and watches Maisie reorganize the shelving.

'I would have stayed at Albany Avenue,' he says with a defeated smile. 'But I didn't exactly get any say in the matter. It's going to feel awfully crowded with all of us living under one roof.'

Fairweather House is large enough for them all, in Maisie's eyes.

'Not if we respect each other's space,' she replies.

This proves easier said than done. Hugo and James get along, reminiscing about the good old days of England, sharing bottle after bottle of Sir Malcolm's best wine, and toasting Cuthbert and Mr Lionel and every other mutual acquaintance. But the tension between Maisie and Nancy intensifies. It's as if the lawyer's office marked a shift back to their relationship of old, although Maisie holds greater power now than she did previously.

The women tussle over who has priority over the servants, can't agree on dinner menus, glare at one another across the dining table on the evenings that the Randolphs aren't either out or hosting their huge circle of friends. There are the Prestons and the Hurleys, the Galvestons and the McBrides, and around a dozen other couples that Maisie has forgotten the names of, all of whom love parties and fashion and sharing their loud opinions. Sometimes she catches the women staring at her and whispering amongst themselves, and she can only guess what Nancy has told them.

Worse than anything, living in close quarters with another married couple removes any chance of privacy.

'The sound of that woman's voice really is grating,' James remarks over breakfast one morning.

The pitch of Nancy's voice rises from the Randolphs' bedroom, once Sir Malcolm's. Though they're located at the furthest end of the hallway, all the way upstairs, their voices are sufficiently audible for Maisie to glean that Nancy is upset about the cut of beef from the previous night's dinner. If arguing with one's spouse was a competitive sport, Maisie decides, Nancy would win first prize.

'I don't know how Hugo puts up with it,' Maisie agrees.

James sets down his cutlery and places one hand on hers.

'Well, I was hoping for a quiet moment to discuss something with you, but it seems there are no longer any quiet moments here.' He smiles ruefully. 'There's been an interesting offer for the carousel from Mr Ingersoll, who owns a dozen Lunar Parks around the country,' he explains. 'If it was sold, Silver Kingdom could afford five or six new rides with the money he's willing to pay. Or we could invest the proceeds in something else – there are several interesting business opportunities I've heard about.'

Maisie is taken by surprise. Getting married and Sir Malcolm's death have preoccupied so much of her time that she wasn't aware of other amusement parks taking an interest.

'You don't seem too enthusiastic,' James intuits.

Maisie gathers her thoughts. 'It just seems to have come out of the blue. I didn't even realize Mr Ingersoll had approached us.'

James leans forward, excitement written on his face.

'He didn't exactly. I've been putting out feelers, thought it wouldn't do any harm in seeing where improvements could be made. It's an idea worth considering, isn't it?'

Maisie doesn't know what to think. On the one hand, not too long ago she wanted to take an axe to the carousel for all the heartache it's brought to her life. But of all the rides at Silver Kingdom, it's the number one attraction. Though it's peculiar to expend any emotion on an inanimate object, she also feels an attachment to the machine. Nostalgia, perhaps? On top of that, while it's in her safekeeping, Maisie can do everything in her power to ensure that no one else vanishes.

'But I'm not sure we need to do anything so drastic.'

James is quiet for several moments, his head nodding almost imperceptibly as though he is deep in contemplation.

'Then I'll tell Mr Ingersoll you're not selling. Even though I might not agree, it's your decision at the end of the day.' He scrapes back his chair and pecks Maisie on the cheek. 'Right, to the club with me. The opportunities won't wait all day.'

As soon as he's gone, a second round of Randolph bickering starts up, although this time the subject pivots to a baby. 'I don't want to wait!' Nancy screams.

How Hugo could ever find himself in the right frame of mind for baby-making is beyond Maisie. But soon the voices drop and are replaced by rhythmic moaning. A few minutes later, there is laughter and the sound of footfall along the upstairs hallway. Maisie escapes to the study. Besides this being the quietest room in the house, this morning she is packing up the contents before Nancy implements her threat to replace Sir Malcolm's desk and bookcase. Resigned to the fact that the inner workings of Fairweather House are out of her hands, safeguarding Sir Malcolm's possessions is the best Maisie can do.

She can smell his presence in the room: the scent of cigars lingers. Though Sir Malcolm had been slowly disappearing, bit by bit, for years, she imagines him whole again, sitting in his chair, puffing away while staring absent-mindedly. She peers out of the window. The snow has melted, revealing a carpet of emerald. In this watery winter light, the carousel is so luminous that it's hard to believe it could be involved in anyone's disappearance.

She turns away, unable to bear thinking about that night again: the desperate wait for hours, then the horror of realizing that Sir Malcolm wasn't returning. And now the terrible guilt at covering up what might have happened to him.

The front door closing means Hugo has left for the city, as is his usual habit on a Monday. Maisie can hear Nancy singing a lullaby, a sign she'll be in a pleasant mood for the next three hours. It's strange how quickly one can learn the peculiarities of people who a month ago were practically strangers.

Focusing on the job in hand, Maisie deals with the books first. Her eyes alight on the *Collins' Graphic Atlas*, which she sets aside for later, deciding to take a look at the geography of her parents' lives to feel a little closer to them. Since her own wedding, Maisie's curiosity about her history has been roused.

Once the bookcase is emptied, she turns her attention to the items laid out on Sir Malcolm's desk. She finishes packing and calls for Robert and Clara to help her transport the boxes to the parlour, where they will be safe, since Nancy considers the room too small to waste her efforts on. Next, she clears the desk drawers, sorting through paperwork. At last, she is ready for the final task, finding a safe place for the confidential contents of the top drawer. Locating the key beneath the cigar box, she finds the title deeds to the house, to be passed to Hugo, along with the original business agreement between the two brothers.

The letter from Laurent is tucked at the bottom, every word, every nuance, committed to Maisie's memory. Now the shock has receded, she considers replying, but can't think what to write. He asked no questions, and she prefers that he never learns of her marriage, never sees her as anything but the Maisie she once was. And what would happen if she informed the detective that Sir Malcolm is gone? Returning to pursue the case is a possible outcome, and that wouldn't be fair on anyone.

To be safe, she should destroy the letter, but it would be like losing Laurent all over again. Instead, she runs upstairs to hide it. Opening her wardrobe, she slips the envelope behind the poster that is still pinned there from the time she invited the neighbourhood children to enjoy the carousel. The awful day Billy disappeared.

On her way out of the bedroom, Maisie notices that her jewellery box is open, even though she knows the lid was closed earlier. Rifling through, it's immediately obvious that the wedding money from Hugo is missing. She rummages a fourth and fifth time, removing everything. When double- and triple-checking still produce nothing, she slams the box shut and sits on the bed, picking nervously at the sleeves of her blouse. James must have taken it.

38

The industrial quarter stretches beyond the eastern limits of the city, following the twists of the Seine. Although Laurent was aware that Paris is a hive of manufacturing, it was not until he began looking for the possible location of Maisie's parents here that he realized the difficulty of this quest.

The area is vast, crowded with warehouses stocked with boxes of who knows what and workshops for cutting and sawing, and weavers and rug-makers and tanneries. Since Laurent's time after work is limited, it has taken close to five months to explore three quarters of this district, trudging across the landscape in all weathers.

He is driven by renewed guilt. Sending Maisie a second letter was a desperate attempt to fill the void of loneliness. Gone are the quiet evenings when he would read and Odette would embroider in tolerable companionship. Instead, they have begun to quarrel over trivial things like where to store the butter and whether to buy new curtains, although this is no excuse for selfishness and Laurent knows it.

Poking into abandoned buildings and quiet alleyways, he has searched for any sign that Maisie's parents might have set up home here. He asks around, and everyone from foremen to runners shakes their head and claims never to have seen the unusual sight of a white woman with an Indian man.

By chance, the vicious throat slitting of one of the four brothers of the Boucher gang has brought him near enough to the area that he can slip in an hour without being missed at the prefecture. Perhaps a mid-morning snoop will be more beneficial.

He climbs a steep hill flanked by dilapidated shed-like buildings and peeps into open doorways. There is activity everywhere he looks. Pounding and hammering and lugging. Stray dogs howl to the noise of clanking. Laurent wrinkles his nose. Is that the stench of a glue factory? Covering the lower half of his face with a hand-kerchief, he peers under bushes and behind barrels, anywhere he thinks a pickpocket and a prostitute might have set up camp.

Presently, he reaches an area of scrubland. Apart from grass and a smattering of bare trees, there is nothing. He turns back, taking care not to slip on the way down. Gravel and a steep incline are a dangerous combination.

He is passing a toy workshop on his left when he spots it. Swinging in the late winter breeze is a faded sign: CLOUTIER CAROUSEL FACTORY.

His senses tingle. Of all places in his search for Maisie's parents, he is here. Fate has dealt a cunning hand.

A set of huge double doors is ajar. They squeak as Laurent squeezes through. Inside is a bustle of activity. Whirring and grinding drown the cry of howling dogs. There is sawdust everywhere – on the floor, in the air, the smell floating up his nostrils.

This is his first time here. As the most junior of constables when the disappearance of Gilbert Cloutier was reported, Laurent was never permitted to visit the premises since his superiors considered enough time had been wasted on the case by other officers.

Laurent hovers in the doorway until a middle-aged man with large brown boots and a big smile strides towards him.

'Are you Frau Hoffman from the Düsseldorf Fair?' he shouts to make himself heard above the din.

Laurent holds out his hand to shake. 'Detective Bisset. I'm searching for an Indian man travelling with a blonde woman. I was informed they might be in the area.'

The man scratches his chin. 'Not seen anyone like that recently. There was once – they slept rough near the tavern at the foot of the hill close to here, and I would see them as I walked to work. I remember because they had a baby with them, and it's uncommon, isn't it? This was before the turn of the century, though, and I can't remember anything else.'

Laurent's heart races. Was the baby Maisie?

'So before Gilbert Cloutier disappeared,' Laurent says. The man looks surprised. 'I was on the investigation into Victor Cloutier.'

The man's face drops and Laurent sees him wipe away a tear.

'Ah, yes, sad business. Gilbert was my friend, you know, as well as my boss. I still miss him after twenty years.' He shakes his head. 'When we workers clubbed together to buy the workshop, we kept the name out of respect. Not that most of them remember Monsieur Cloutier. The original set-up were conscripted and never came back – Jules, Olivier, Jean-Luc . . .'

Along with the one million other French soldiers, Laurent thinks. A thought occurs to him.

'Since you were a friend of Gilbert, you may have known Victor, the nephew, and whether he had any particular acquaintances?'

Laurent holds back from mentioning the word *accomplice* in case he is later accused of leading a witness. His search thus far has brought him to one dead end after another. Trawling through the police archives, he has discovered that Victor moved in very shady circles indeed, and most of his associates have either suffered an unnaturally early, gruesome death, or they have been languishing in prison for years.

The man wrinkles his nose. 'I never did like Victor, and I doubt he had any friends –'

'Perhaps someone called Beau Armitage?' Laurent asks.

Agent O'Connell surprised him with a telegram last week. Despite being unable to poke holes in the alibi, the Bureau is still convinced that Beau is their man. Deciding to keep an open mind, Laurent has agreed to ask around in the course of his other enquiries.

'Unusual name, not one I've heard, but there's someone here who might know about Victor's acquaintances. This way,' the man says. 'I'm Antoine, by the way.'

Antoine leads Laurent past a series of long work benches and a small dingy room without furniture or a ceiling of its own. 'That's Gilbert's old office,' Antoine explains. They sidestep a drilling machine and then exit by a back door. Laurent can make out the harbour, the freight ships appearing like paper boats from here.

'It's a shame that Gilbert disappeared just before the Paris Exposition and never did see what a success it was,' Antoine continues, as they stroll past an outhouse and across an area of bare soil.

'The world had never seen a bigger, better, finer carousel. Probably never will again. None of us could understand his design, you know.'

Laurent is inclined to agree. The carousel is magnificent.

They arrive at a large wooden building clustered with two other grand buildings. As they step inside, Laurent is bombarded by clanging. Half a dozen men are using hammers and tongs to strike anvils. This must be where the carousel's metal components were made. A large iron furnace dwarfs the huge space. Antoine signals to a tall, raven-haired man who slopes over with a blow torch still in his hand.

'Since you are the only other person who was here at the time, I thought you might know if Gilbert's nephew, Victor, ever brought any friends here,' Antoine says.

The man shrugs and shakes his head as he avoids Laurent's piercing gaze. In his head, Laurent is calculating whether this person would have been old enough to have been involved in Gilbert Cloutier's disappearance.

Antoine claps the young man on the back. 'This man here, Detective, is our most precise metal worker. We could have done with his help back then. The details on that platform were a devil to get right. But he was only an apprentice in those days. Isn't that right, Emmanuel?'

The young man nods. He seems reluctant to speak.

Laurent is following Antoine out of the building when a hand lands on his shoulder. He swings around to find Emmanuel staring with intense eyes.

Emmanuel takes a big breath and hesitates. 'I used to watch Mr Cloutier when he thought no one was looking.' He takes another deep breath. 'He would weep as he made that horse. And speak to it. The one named after his son.' A sigh. 'It's like he thought it *was* his son.'

The words leave Laurent with an uncomfortable sensation, as if a spider is crawling across his skin.

Emmanuel turns on his heels, returning to the men at the furnace, to the heat, the noise of pounding, the sweaty work, as the stench of burning metal and sawdust and glue envelops them.

39

The Silver Kingdom workers return with a bang after winter. Lucky Nate and his men arrive first, having hitched a ride all the way from Florida in a truck hauling peanuts between states. The Jointees and Ride Jocks are next, and finally the Money Girls, who saunter in to wolf whistles three days later. Rides are re-erected, stalls scrubbed and stocked. The noise and the flurry of activity are a breath of life after the hibernation of winter.

The happy reunion is dampened by Sir Malcolm's absence. News of his death had reached them months ago but naturally everyone is still saddened. The Crew even organize a memorial of sorts, with the workforce standing on the shore in their most sombre outfits. As the mourners disperse, Maisie notices James and Hugo engrossed in conversation.

When she questioned her husband about the missing money, he was quite open – some might say shameless – about needing it to buy a batch of discount perfume to sell on for a hefty profit. 'It was too good an opportunity to miss, darling, and there was a deadline,' he explained breezily. 'I thought you wouldn't mind, then I forgot to tell you.' After a few firm words from Maisie about teamwork working both ways, the dust soon settled.

Watching the eighty-strong workforce go about their tasks, Maisie's stomach flips over. The enormity of her new role is beginning to dawn on her. Although she was the stand-in manager for months, being the boss feels very different, since the livelihood of everyone working here is now her responsibility. The carousel is her responsibility.

She heads in the direction of the lake to talk to Mr Levander about the possibility of extending the pier. Spotting Madame Rose hovering nearby, she diverts past the helter-skelter and runs into Nancy instead.

'Just the person I wanted to catch alone,' Nancy declares.

Maisie immediately raises her guard. 'Oh, yes?' she asks without slowing.

Nancy walks alongside Maisie, matching her pace as they step over a pile of lumber and around two of the Crew, who are hoisting a pirate flag outside the Smugglers' Saloon.

'Hugo and I were reminiscing about Sir Malcolm yesterday. It's the first I'd heard of it, but apparently their nanny left them unattended near the Jesserton pond when they were very young. Sir Malcolm almost drowned,' she says glancing at Maisie. 'And he detested water after that. Hugo doesn't agree, but it's obvious that if he'd chosen to die, he'd never have done it that way. It's odd, isn't it?' Nancy frames this as a question, although it's clearly a statement.

Like Nancy, Maisie had never heard this anecdote before. She could kick herself for choosing self-inflicted drowning as a cover story.

'Poor Sir Malcolm,' she says. 'But he did leave letters. Mine said he was sad.'

Nancy stops in her tracks and grabs Maisie by the arm, bringing her to a halt as well. They are standing by the carousel now. It takes all the willpower Maisie can muster to keep her eyes from straying to the horse that's been re-covered in blankets.

'You got one too? I shall need to see it. Hugo gave me his, but it didn't say anything about his state of mind.' Nancy frowns. 'The police won't listen to my concerns; they're being quite useless, in fact, and told me I was being hysterical. So I intend to get to the bottom of it myself.'

Maisie's throat constricts as if a noose is tightening around her neck. What an almighty mess she has created for herself.

Unable to erase images of the police turning up to arrest her, Maisie tosses and turns that night. The idea doesn't seem that far-fetched when Nancy uses the following dinner time as an occasion to share the titbits of information she's gleaned, as though Sir Malcolm's death has given her a fresh sense of purpose.

'Eric says that a set of Sir Malcolm's clothes are missing, like he was wearing two layers that night,' she announces during the main course.

Maisie's grip on the cutlery tightens. Fortunately, the men are out – James left early for the club, and Hugo is meeting Mr Deveraux in the city – and no one else can see her face redden.

Nancy takes a delicate bite of salmon.

'It was bitterly cold that night, so perhaps he wanted to wrap up warm,' Maisie replies, aware that she is clutching at straws.

Nancy looks askance. 'Why would he care that much about being cold in the circumstances? Besides, if that was the case, where is his coat?'

Maisie's appetite withers. Realizing that Sir Malcolm must have been wearing his coat when he was taken, she opens her mouth to say that he probably forgot to remove it before plunging into the lake, closes her mouth because this sounds implausible and forces down the rest of the meal to avoid drawing Nancy's suspicions.

What else has she overlooked?

By opening day, Maisie is so worn out by nervous energy that it feels like she's trudging through the sludge-sand on Canvey Island after a day of cockle picking, her clothes laden with seawater. As she stands at the front gate with Hugo, she greets the excited visitors, who swarm towards the carousel as usual. The buzz, the cheering, the smell of fresh doughnuts, begin to act as a pick-me-up. It takes Maisie back to a year ago, when Silver Kingdom was opening for the very first time. How much has happened since then.

Mr Lee from the Oriental Paradise approaches. He tips his hat at Hugo.

'Mr Randolph, sir, I would like to discuss the rate I pay for my concession,' he says in his usual nervy voice. 'I hear that Mr Parry is charged two per cent less for a fifteen per cent larger pitch.'

Maisie is quietly rankled by Mr Lee's assumption that Hugo, who usually makes himself scarce, is now in charge.

'You'll have to speak to Maisie; she's the owner now,' Hugo responds curtly, striding off.

Mr Lee makes a valiant attempt to mask his surprise, but it's evident that he, along with everyone else at Silver Kingdom, Maisie suspects, believes that she was little more than Sir Malcolm's mouth-piece for all those months. She spends the next twenty minutes talking through the figures with him, and is concluding their conversation when she spots a diminutive gentleman dressed in green tweed and a brown bowler hat.

Despite his lack of physical stature, the man pulses a certain presence. So much so that a ring of space has formed around him, as though the crowds sense danger.

Maisie approaches him with a tight smile. 'Welcome to Silver Kingdom, Mr Fortescue.'

She recognizes the twirly moustache and mischievous smile of the man whom she spoke with at the jazz club before he was warned off by James. Away from the dark, smoky atmosphere of that night, a yellowish tinge to his teeth is obvious.

'Nice set-up you have here,' Freddie Fortescue remarks. 'Very, very nice.'

His eyes roam around Silver Kingdom like those of a ravenous lion.

'I didn't know you were a fan of amusement parks. I can't remember seeing you here before,' she says, keeping up the pleasant tone.

'I like anything that makes money,' he answers bluntly. 'Speaking of which, I'm looking for your husband. We're in the middle of a rather delicate business transaction.'

Considering their less than friendly interaction at the club that night, Maisie is surprised that the two men are even on speaking terms.

'More perfume?' she asks, trying to appear knowledgeable.

Freddie snorts. 'Is that what he told you it is?'

40

'Moonshine? You're mixed up in moonshine?'

Maisie is a ball of outrage, pacing in front of the run of windows in the drawing room. She had masked her growing unease long enough to lead Freddie to the Smugglers' Saloon, where James was enjoying a pot of coffee, waited for them to conduct whatever affairs needed attention and then summoned her husband indoors.

He sits leaning back in what has become his favourite armchair with his legs outstretched, nonchalant.

'It isn't moonshine, Maisie, it's whatever alcohol was knocking about after Prohibition set in a few months ago. Stored in bars, warehouses, in the basements of clubs, and the whatnot. We're lucky to have got our hands on it,' he claims, sounding pleased with himself. 'Once those supplies dry up, we might have to turn to moonshine, yes.'

Maisie stops pacing to stare at him open-mouthed.

'It won't be very lucky if you get caught, will it? Bootlegging means a prison sentence, James.'

Maisie has read about the raids conducted by the police at various establishments, and, even if she wasn't worried about her husband being incarcerated, she certainly doesn't want the authorities sniffing around here. Not with Nancy stirring up the circumstances of Sir Malcolm's disappearance.

'It's one of the risks of doing business. Demand for alcohol hasn't dropped just because a load of interfering busybodies say it should.' He thinks for a moment, tapping his fingers together. 'Freddie and I are simply making the best of the situation. Do you think Mr Rockefeller made his millions by letting opportunities slip through his fingers? A bit of chancy dealing is quite normal.'

Maisie feels her annoyance rising in direct proportion to James's calm, condescending approach.

'If it's so normal, why did you lie about how you invested the money?'

He shrugs. 'Because I knew you'd react like this,' he admits without missing a beat. 'I did try to keep it away from you,' he adds in a softer voice.

James reaches out to take her hand, but Maisie shakes him off.

'Then do a better job of keeping it away from me, from Silver Kingdom. I don't want Freddie coming here again.'

Mrs Papadopoulos is never late. The next morning, Maisie waits at the end of the driveway for thirty-five minutes. Usually by 7 a.m. the milk crates have been unloaded by Stavros and Georgios, and there's time for a quick chat before Maisie is waving off the older woman. But there's no sign of the cart today.

Maisie shields her eyes with one hand and peers down the long avenue again. James is still in bed, but probably not for long, and this is the best opportunity Maisie has to ask advice from someone she trusts about relationships. James's duplicity bothers Maisie, and she's seeking wisdom from another married woman on whether this is normal behaviour for a husband.

'Sofia won't be coming today.'

Maisie turns around to see Madame Rose holding a basket of herbs in one hand. The scent of thyme eddies on the early-spring air.

'Mrs Papadopoulos,' Madame Rose clarifies. 'Nor tomorrow, or any time.'

Fear rushes in. Is this one of those awful insights? 'Are you saying she's had an accident?'

For a second, Madame Rose looks confused. Then she laughs.

'Nothing like that. Mr Randolph told Gloria, who told Mr Levander, who told me that they've landed a big contract and can't keep up with demand. Apparently, Sofia has arranged for the O'Reilly Milk Company to supply Silver Kingdom instead.' Madame Rose can't contain her mirth and holds her sides. 'And you thought it was the power coming upon me.'

It isn't funny, Maisie thinks. After their last encounter, in which Maisie felt that Madame Rose was probing into the deepest recesses of her mind, she's even more uncomfortable around the fortune-teller. Rose's face falls serious and her eyes glaze over. Maisie has seen that look before. She strides away, but not before the woman begins to speak.

'About the great peril you will face . . .'

Maisie quickens her pace. She doesn't need to hear about perils. She doesn't need to hear that if anyone else vanishes, Silver Kingdom might come crashing down and her own neck will be on the line.

She heads for the parlour. Kneeling on the floor, she begins searching through the boxes from the study for an invoice from Mrs Papadopoulos. The overpowering smell of eau de parfum wafts into the room. Maisie pretends she hasn't noticed Nancy and continues rifling through the cartons. If she can find a current address for the Papadopoulos family, she will try to visit. She is hurt that the woman she considered more than an acquaintance would have left without saying a word. Have they really only ever shared a business connection?

Nancy sinks into an armchair. Maisie debates whether to leave or to stand her ground. The two women have coexisted thus far by making a point of avoiding one another, apart from at dinner times. The unspoken rule is that the last one into a room makes a swift exit.

Maisie stands up and looks out of the side window, dithering. From this position, she can see Silver Kingdom as well as the curve of the lake disappearing into the distance, though not for long. Insisting on privacy, Nancy has persuaded Hugo to pay for a boundary fence separating the house from the amusement park, and work has already started. So many changes in such a short time to the life Maisie and Sir Malcolm established.

'Someone was spotted creeping around Silver Kingdom on the night Sir Malcolm allegedly drowned,' Nancy pipes up. 'I've just asked James and he says he was asleep and has no idea who it could have been.'

Beads of sweat gather at the back of Maisie's neck. The grandfather clock that used to live in the hallway at Jesserton now stands in the corner of this room, and it marks out the seconds of silence. She wills herself to stay put so it doesn't look like she's trying to evade Nancy's questions.

'Who was it that saw the person?' she asks.

In her mind, Maisie has already eliminated Silver Kingdom's workforce, who were away for the winter. This leaves the Fairweather staff – unless there was someone else lurking in the shadows. She always has a sense that she isn't alone near the carousel anyway, but what if she really wasn't that night? The idea that she was being spied on makes Maisie's pulse jump in panic.

'Obviously, I can't disclose confidential information until all the evidence is in,' Nancy replies. 'Anyway, did you see anything?'

Everything, and nothing. Maisie still doesn't actually know what happened to Sir Malcolm, and can't bear to dwell on it. Every time Nancy brings up the subject, Maisie relives the fear of that awful night and is overcome by guilt.

'It was my wedding night, remember?' Maisie answers, careful at every turn. 'So I was sleeping too. But, if I think of something, I'll let you know.'

As the week drags on, Maisie's stamina plummets. Silver Kingdom's new dairy supplier is causing a stir. According to Mr Cornelius, the milk is of a lower quality than before, and arrives late more often than not. When Maisie explains to him that the decision made by the Papadopoulos family is out of her hands, she could swear he mutters something along the lines of 'That's what happens when you put a woman in charge.'

In the household, Nancy is like a ferret down a rabbit hole, talking nonstop about Sir Malcolm over dinner each evening. Her new focus is the suicide notes, more specifically the one to Eric, the existence of which she discovered only when he commented yesterday that he was touched that Sir Malcolm had thought to thank him for his dutiful service.

Having found nothing of significance in Maisie's letter a few weeks ago, Nancy had pounced on this new piece of evidence. It turns out that there are a couple of spelling mistakes Sir Malcom would never have made, turns of phrase that he would never have used. Panicking inside, Maisie wills her expression neutral, and pretends to be absorbed in her meal as Nancy grills the men on their analysis of the situation. James mouths, '*Dear Lord, save me*,' when Nancy turns around to ask Robert to bring more drinks.

By Sunday evening, Maisie is too tired to eat, and she skips the hour-long ordeal in the dining room, which will be especially taxing tonight as the McBrides are expected. James promises to bring her a plate of food before he leaves for the club. It's clear that he's trying to make up for their quarrel, and Maisie likes the feeling of being wanted. But she also can't throw off the fear that James is introducing danger into their lives.

She sits on the edge of the bed, feeling light-headed, hearing Cassandra McBride's raucous laugh drift up from downstairs. Tomorrow is Monday, the day Silver Kingdom is closed to the public, and she intends to put her feet up. Leaning down to remove her stockings, she is hit by a wave of nausea. With a jolt like an electric shock, Maisie realizes that her last monthly bleed was nine weeks ago. Or is it ten? It's been so busy, she never registered how late it is.

She falls back on to the pillow, stunned, and places her hands on her stomach. Her fingers press gently. Her belly is no rounder than usual, but, now that she thinks of it, her breasts have grown tender.

The magnitude of what might be happening inside her body starts to sink in. Could there really be a tiny human growing – a real person? If there is, will it take after Maisie or be more like James? Will it be anything like her own parents?

Maisie grips the blanket, her knuckles turning white, as she relives the moment that she learnt they are alive. The punch in the gut that spiralled into weeks of pain.

She makes a silent vow not to be the kind of parent that her own were – a promise to protect any children she ever has.

41

There are occasions when Laurent is on the point of admitting defeat in the search for Maisie's parents; usually when he is overwhelmed by his workload, or another lead dries up. After a day or two of rest, however, he rallies himself by recalling his pledge to make amends to Maisie.

Failing to discover any sign of her mother or father near the tavern, or anywhere in the industrial district, he decides to change tack at the beginning of April. It is ten months since Laurent embarked on the search. Perhaps digging deeper into their history will unearth a lead on their current whereabouts. Habits, preferences, pastimes – all are useful clues.

The British Embassy in the 8th Arrondissement seems the most logical place to start, since not only does it offer a connection to England but also to the British Raj. There, he meets Mr Chisolm, an attaché to the Liaison Officer. A quiet man with a warm smile, he listens to Laurent's explanation over a pot of tea, nodding along. 'I'll contact my colleagues and ask them to dig through their records,' he says at the end of the meeting.

One month later, the attaché comes up trumps. While there is no further information on Maisie's mother, some details have been uncovered about her father. Yousuf was born in the Punjab area of India, the eldest son of a rich landowner sent by his father to study political economy at University College, London. A concerned letter from Mr Choudary senior to a chief secretary in the Indian Civil Service about his son's antics in England – particularly his involvement with a white woman – suggests that the young man was about to be disinherited in 1896.

By the time May glows into the heat of June, Laurent is still deciding how to proceed with his discoveries. After his last letter to Maisie, he has discounted the idea of writing to her again, but should he contact Sir Malcolm? Get in touch with the university for further information on their former student?

The weather is muggy this month, a cloying heat that sticks to his clothes. Laurent believes he has never felt so suffocated. With tall ceilings and generous room proportions, it is not the fault of the apartment. But compared with the spaciousness of the Fairweather House, Laurent feels confined.

To compensate, every morning he slides up the windows to allow air to circulate. As soon as she notices, Odette closes each one, complaining of dust from the street. When she leaves, Laurent reopens them. Open, close, open, close. It has become their daily marriage dance. The only one they do.

Everything about their relationship is summed up in this one act. The squabbles ceased some while ago, and they barely speak now or spend time together alone. Laurent works. Odette cares for Amélie and the household. They are civil to one another as a tension pulses beneath the surface. Although Laurent has considered putting them both out of their misery, duty, honour, sacrifice, have been drummed into him since childhood and further ingrained by his stint in French intelligence during the war. More importantly, a fear of appearing a failure in his father's eyes compels him to stay. Separate lives while remaining married. Isn't this the fate of so many?

For the fourth time this evening, Laurent pulls on the window cord and returns to the dining table. His papers are laid out as usual, and he digs through until he finds the sketch of the carousel. In the year since he drew it, that evening has never left his thoughts.

Laurent studies the design. It is certainly on a bigger scale than any of the carousels dotted around Paris. *It's like he thought it was his son.* Emmanuel's statement is eerie and has played on his mind ever since. But no stranger than Maisie's claim that it is cursed.

There is a rustling sound. Laurent looks up and is surprised to find that Amélie is on the dining chair beside his, scribbling on a piece of paper. Engrossed in his work, Laurent did not notice his child enter the room.

Automatically, he looks around for Odette. The apartment is too small for an assigned study and so the dining room doubles. It has been established for some time that no one enters when Laurent sits here after supper.

He is about to shoo away the child when he catches sight of the picture. A circle in the centre of the page is covered in small oblongs with sticks poking out. Horses on a carousel. It is crude but it is not a bad likeness for a seven-year-old. He watches as she draws a wobbly canopy next. Her tongue poked out, she glances at Laurent's sketch and then scribbles a crooked rectangle that he presumes is the flag.

She must notice him watching because she suddenly looks up with a shy smile. With a sense of regret, it dawns on Laurent that at one time his daughter would never have acted this reserved around him. She used to giggle and prance about and put on shows for his benefit. The trip to Chicago, Laurent now realizes, stirred up so many emotions about his mother that he has withdrawn from Amélie since returning, not wanting her to know the same loss he has.

His mother's death shattered him. As a six-year-old, Laurent couldn't even begin to pick up the broken pieces and retreated into himself. As an adult, he has developed no other way to cope, and hurts those caught up in his suffering. A wife who sees through the fakeness of their marriage. Maisie, the woman he loves, deceived by his actions. It has created a shockwave of pain radiating out-wards, with Laurent at its core. This is not a life he would wish for his child. He loves Amélie with all his heart, as much as he loved his mother.

An understanding sparks in his deepest consciousness like a crack of lightning. More than anything, Laurent now realizes, he is ter-rified of losing his daughter as well.

As though she can perceive his sorrow, Amélie sets down her crayon and strokes Laurent's face. Her eyes gleam as he smiles. She looks so like his mother on one of her 'good days', when she would climb out of bed and get dressed, then sweep off the eiderdown with a flourish to make soldiers' camps or the sail of a pirate's ship. *Ahoy!* she would call, standing on the dining table while looking through a rolled-up newspaper as the maid brought in afternoon tea. 'Is that treasure I spy?'

What he would give to relive one of those times again, despite the pain of losing her. Even a 'bad day' would do. He would grasp every second, absorb each emotion.

He takes Amélie's hand in his and leans over to study her artwork.

'A masterpiece,' he declares with an appreciative nod. 'I think tomorrow we should visit the Louvre.'

42

Steam lifts from the lake, and the petunias in the flowerbeds are wilting. The end of June this year is scorching. Even the back kitchen, where the freezing units hum like a colony of bees, is too hot for someone six months pregnant. Maisie wipes sweat from her neck with a dishcloth and resumes positioning ice-cream tubs on a tray.

'I'll take these out, Peggy Mae,' she calls to the cook, who is measuring vanilla essence. 'I'm heading that way, anyway.'

She notes Peggy Mae's small smile. Maisie still doesn't know who spotted her running around Silver Kingdom that night, but she's become vigilant around the servants and Arnold, always searching their faces for any sign, always looking over her shoulder. Was Eric remembering something when he gave Maisie a puzzled look last week? Did Clara mean anything by her comment that Maisie appears anxious these days?

Maisie takes the long route through the front of the house, avoiding the garden, where preparations for next week's 4th of July celebrations are under way. A party wasn't her idea. It's too much work on top of everything else, but Nancy insisted it could double up as a proper memorial to Sir Malcolm.

'She needs her spirits lifted,' Hugo explained when Maisie tried to veto the plan.

What he meant was that Maisie's pregnancy is affecting his wife. It would be hard to miss the sideways glances, the surreptitious looks at Maisie's growing belly. There have been louder attempts at baby-making, and episodes when Nancy is quiet and vacant, staring towards the lake while mumbling under her breath.

Maisie wanders through Silver Kingdom. The thrill of the funfair has never left her, not since her first experience at Clacton, and within a few years she will be seeing it all through her child's eyes.

She imagines the joy of the first ride – the carousel, of course – the clapping and beaming with pleasure. For a moment, Billy's sad face comes to mind, but Maisie bats away the image. She will never let her child come to harm. More alert than ever, she has been laying stones around the carousel again.

After depositing the ice cream and conferring with Mrs Ferretti and Lucky Nate about a problem with squeaking dodgems, Maisie is heading back to the house when someone calls her name. Looking around, she spots James standing on a ladder near the patio, helping to set up the bunting, with Nancy issuing instructions from below. He beckons to Maisie. The last place she wants to be is anywhere near that woman with her persistent suspicions about Sir Malcolm's death, but lately it's become obvious that Nancy is trying equally hard to avoid close proximity. Sure enough, as Nancy notices Maisie approaching, she steps away from the ladder and drifts inside the house.

James clambers down and lays his hand on Maisie's belly. The baby kicks, and he grins. Ever since learning that he's to be a father, James has strutted about as though he's a prize stallion.

'Strong like a true Squires male,' he says proudly. 'And he'll want for nothing. I'll make sure of it.'

Maisie bites her lip. Any talk of his money reminds her of where it comes from.

'You're worrying for nothing, you know,' James says, able to read her thoughts. 'Freddie and I have set it all up so that if anything goes wrong – which it won't – there will be no comeback on us.'

'So no one else knows what you're doing?'

James pulls a face. 'Not exactly no one, but we know who to trust.'

Maisie's heart hammers an alert. The fact that other people are involved increases the risks.

'I don't like it, James. I think you should find another business. There's something threatening about Mr Fortescue,' she remarks.

They've had this conversation a thousand times, and can never agree. True, James has kept Freddie away from Silver Kingdom, and he seems very comfortable managing the danger, but Maisie fears for the life she's creating with him. Until this pregnancy, she hadn't grasped how important having her own family is to her.

'He's a pussycat, really. All menace on the surface, but underneath it all harmless enough.'

Maisie cradles her stomach. 'And are we the mice?'

James sets his hands on her shoulders.

'I'm in control of the situation, Maisie. Nothing bad is going to happen.'

It's impossible not to get swept away by the atmosphere of excitement. Two days until the party and the house is crowded. There are caterers and photographers, the seamstress and the tailor. Three florists and a team of handymen scurry about the place. Peggy Mae orders the pastry chefs from Hugo's favourite bakery out of *her* kitchen, so they're loitering by the new dance floor, smoking. Eric runs about the house carrying piles of silver servers. Robert does any task asked of him.

The pyrotechnics crew arrives to set up on the lake, and chaos ensues when one of Mr Levander's tiny boats capsizes with three boxes of fireworks aboard. Maisie watches the men use oars to salvage as much as they can. She is sitting on the bench with Clara while a large marble sculpture of a mermaid is being manoeuvred beside the patio, from which oyster cocktails will be served at the party. Maisie takes every opportunity to rest her feet these days, and this is easy work. They are sewing gold sequins on to a large indigo cloth for the area above the stage in the centre of the garden.

James has arranged for the entire jazz club to come here for the night. He stands laughing with Hugo as they watch the gambling tables being positioned near the shore. Another group of men approach him and they all shake hands warmly. Maisie wishes she was half as popular as her husband – Mrs Papadopoulos hasn't been in touch and no amount of searching has uncovered any old invoices with an address for her. Missing paperwork. Missing people. The curse of Silver Kingdom.

Nearby a man is practising dance moves between the rose beds, warbling scales at the top of his voice. Maisie recognizes him as the singer from the jazz club, though today he's in a drab pair of slacks and grubby vest.

Minutes pass with the sun bearing down on the back of her head. Moisture collects on her fingertips, and she almost drops the needle.

'You all right, ma'am? You look a bit hot,' Clara calls over.

She checks whether Clara's face shows any signs of being suspicious of her, any hint that the maid is Nancy's witness, then looks at her watch. She should really be doing the accounts at this time of the morning. The business continues with or without a party.

'I think I'll go inside for a while,' Maisie replies.

After the glare of outdoors, it takes Maisie's eyes a while to acclimatize. She heads for the study. Someone has closed all the doors and the hallway is unusually dark, so she doesn't see the figure approaching from the opposite direction until it's almost too late.

Automatically, she presses her back to the wall. Nancy looks straight ahead, confident, swinging her hips, her body slinky in a calf-length, dropped-waist shift dress. As she is about to pass Maisie, she stops.

The two women are alone for the first time in months. Outside, there is laughter and loud voices. But in here, the air is still and quiet. Maisie holds her breath as Nancy's gaze lingers on her stomach. She squirms, tries to hold steady under the scrutiny.

All of a sudden, Nancy's eyes flick up. They are hazel with amber flecks, and quite beautiful. She regards Maisie with an ambiguous expression, a mix of disinterest and victory.

'This morning, I decided to retrace Sir Malcolm's possible movements on the night he supposedly drowned himself,' Nancy says coolly. 'And I found this caught inside a crevice of the rock where his clothes were left.'

Extending her hand, Nancy uncurls her fist. The world slows down. Glinting in the gloom is a small diamond made of paste attached to a navy ribbon embroidered with gold thread, surrounded by brown withered foliage. Maisie's wedding corsage.

43

Maisie fastens the buttons of her mauve cocktail dress. She really isn't in the right frame of mind for a party, but, if she bails out now, Nancy will take it as a sign of guilt.

The corsage is incriminating. 'I needed some fresh air that afternoon, after . . . you know . . . James and I had . . . and looking at water always relaxes me,' she had claimed, trying to explain it away by appealing to Nancy's sensibilities as a married woman.

Nancy's eyes had gleamed as Maisie blushed.

'Another oddness,' Nancy had commented. 'I was half thinking anyway to question everyone at the wedding to see if they could throw light on Sir Malcolm's state of mind that day, but this has decided me.' She was almost crowing. 'I'll arrange a series of meetings for next week, after the party, and we can verify who was where and when . . . then we can take it from there.'

It feels like Nancy has been waiting for this moment for months. Maisie's blood runs cold thinking about it. While everyone saw the bride and groom leave the reception together, and return separately, she knows that, by speaking to the staff and guests at the reception, Nancy will discover that no one saw her by the lake, and she was alone for only a couple of minutes, which isn't enough time to have wandered down to the shore and back again. Piecing together what must really have happened isn't that difficult: tied to her wrist all day, and hidden by the trailing sleeves of her dress, the corsage was easily forgotten when Maisie undressed for the evening – and just as easily fell off in the mad scrabble of covering her tracks later that night.

Maisie feels as though she's being hunted by a pack of circling wolves. She wonders if this was how her own parents felt when they made the decision to flee England, and set in motion the events that led to her abandonment.

The fear that the same fate might await her own child has jolted Maisie into a decision. If the law catches up with her, it leaves James as the only meaningful parent. Tomorrow morning, after the party, she's going to have another talk with him about finding legitimate work, but this time she'll make him understand, even if it means telling him the whole story.

From the corner of her eye, she can see him straightening his bow tie while he peers from the window. He catches her looking and saunters over with a self-satisfied smile. Reaching inside his jacket, he produces an object that he loops carefully around her neck. Her fingers flutter to a long gold chain studded with tiny rubies.

It's gorgeous and elegant and must have been bought with dirty money.

'Thank you, you shouldn't have,' she says.

He gives her mouth a prolonged kiss. The bristles of his moustache poke her upper lip.

'Nothing more than you deserve, darling,' he says, moving to the doorway. 'See you later. I told Walter and Neville they could meet my beautiful wife, so please do come and find me.'

With reluctance, she applies make-up, slips on a pair of gold pumps and heads out a few minutes after him.

The party is in full force. From the top of the staircase, Maisie has a panoramic view of the downstairs hallway. Here are the Prestons, and the Hurleys, the Galvestons and the McBrides, as well as the rest of Nancy and Hugo's many friends; James's friends from the jazz club; a smattering of Sir Malcolm's friends, friends of friends, business associates – an eclectic mix all flitting between the rooms, dressed in bright silks – cerise, buttercup yellow, ruby, emerald, electric blue – like beautiful birds of paradise. Gliding in zigzags, waiters carry shiny silver platters piled with bite-sized creations of lobster and smoked salmon and foie gras. Near the front door, an earnest-faced young man plucks away at a harp, the notes indistinguishable from the tinkle of laughter and the clink of glasses.

The headiness is a hundred times more intoxicating than the jazz club, but any excitement is tempered by the sight of Nancy standing beneath the chandelier in her silver ballgown. Surrounded by a group of fawning young men, she is dazzling.

While Nancy is distracted by a particularly handsome gentleman handing her a drink, Maisie hurries downstairs and dives into the kitchen. Eric is slicing cucumber, while Clara and Robert are helping Peggy Mae crush ice, the three puffing with the effort. The cook stops what she's doing to bustle over.

'Out of my kitchen, Miss Maisie. You're to have fun tonight,' she orders.

With considerable force, she pushes Maisie out of the back door and into the garden. It seems like the entire population of Chicago has spilt on to the lawn. Hundreds upon hundreds of people are gathered, mostly congregated around the gaming tables or in front of the stage, where the singer in the blue tuxedo is duetting with a woman wearing a yellow tutu.

Peering over the tops of heads, she can see no hint of James anywhere, and no one she recognizes. She heads to the dance floor, shoving away a greasy-haired gentleman who plants a kiss on her forehead, then a thin woman who juggles five balls in her face.

Maisie stops in a quiet place under a crab-apple tree, circling on the spot. To the left is the bar where champagne and cocktails flow freely. Her concerns about the blatant serving of alcohol in public were shrugged off by James. 'Not to worry, darling, Hugo has invited the Chief of Police, who says he's looking forward to a decent Martini.'

She notices Arnold to the right, dressed in a flashy gold suit, and is on the point of heading towards him to ask if he would mind keeping her company when he joins a large crowd around Madame Rose, gathered at her feet like she's a prophet. Sitting in an armchair within a circle of candles the fortune-teller looks over at Maisie, her eyes dreamy. Maisie turns on her heel and hurries towards the patio, where she finds herself near the marble mermaid. A group of men are cheering as two drunken women smear foie gras over each other's bare breasts. The sight appals her. She wants her unborn child nowhere near this debauchery.

Leaning one hand on the bench, she catches her breath. It's too noisy here, too raucous. She looks back at the house. Partygoers are streaming in and out, laughing and shouting. It won't be much better inside. Keeping to the shadows, she walks across the garden and opens the gate to Silver Kingdom.

Immediately she feels better. Heading in the direction of the lake, she stops at the carousel and with some difficulty clambers on to a horse. Pregnancy has made Maisie less supple and it takes a few minutes to get comfortable. She stares out. At night, it's magical here. The sky and lake merge with the darkness, so it appears as if the carousel is floating amongst the stars. Maisie holds tightly to the pole. What if the carousel could transport her to any place she wishes? She imagines galloping across the lake, across the ocean, across to the other side of the world and to France. To her parents.

To Laurent. The thought escapes before Maisie can stuff it back down.

There is a clinking sound and footsteps. To her amazement, Mrs Papadopoulos appears, holding two glasses of champagne. For a moment, Maisie forgets all about her troubles and spreads out her arms for a hug, almost crying with stunned happiness.

'You're here!' She accepts a drink and watches Mrs Papadopoulos mount the neighbouring horse, a dark grey beauty. 'Here's to a long-awaited reunion.' She raises her glass. 'But I can only do a small toast.'

She taps her round belly, and Mrs Papadopoulos beams.

'I am happy for you, so happy,' she replies, and it seems like she means this. 'You will be good mother, I know.'

Maisie attempts a small smile. It means a lot that Mrs Papadopoulos has such faith in her. At the same time, the knowledge that she might not be around for this child is like an arrow in her heart.

'*Moro mou*, what is wrong? There is problem with baby?'

Mrs Papadopoulos looks so worried that Maisie experiences a sensation of being held warm and safe in a thick, fluffy blanket. It's been a long time since she's felt properly cared for like this. James usually dismisses her fears with a self-assured laugh. She's already anticipating an uphill struggle to be taken seriously, if and when she shares her current concerns with him.

'The baby is fine; it's me who isn't,' she replies. Backed into a corner by Nancy, she has nothing to lose by pressing on. 'There's a little problem with where I was around the time Sir Malcolm . . . drowned.'

Mrs Papadopoulos looks confused and Maisie clears her throat.

'Nancy found my wedding corsage under the rock where his clothes were found, and she thinks it means something that it doesn't.'

Maisie feels her body grow hot as Mrs Papadopoulos allows herself a few moments to think this through.

'You were at lake in reception?' she says, her eyes probing.

Maisie looks away, stares at the pattern of swirls on the horse's pole. 'No, but later I was,' she admits in a whisper.

'I mean you were at lake in day. In reception. I look out of window and see you.'

Maisie's head jerks up. The older woman is staring at her with a knowing look.

'I see you,' Mrs Papadopoulos repeats.

The timeline would work – the pair sat alone in the hallway at the reception for a good ten minutes, enough time for Maisie to have walked to the shore and back again. Months of feeling hounded by Nancy, of watching every step and guarding every word, wash away like debris on a wave. Exhausted and relieved in equal measure, Maisie collapses against the horse. Seconds later, she finds Mrs Papadopoulos's strong arms around her.

'I'm so glad you're here,' Maisie says. 'I was beginning to think I might never see you again.'

Mrs Papadopoulos strokes Maisie's hair.

'If you just ask me to come, I come. There are no hard feelings. You choose different company for milk, it is fine.'

Maisie straightens up. 'You mean *we* have no hard feelings that *you* got a better offer elsewhere,' she corrects. Mrs Papadopoulos wears a quizzical expression, and the penny drops. 'Are you saying that Hugo switched tradespeople without telling me?'

Maisie can't believe she needs to clarify the situation. Sir Malcolm's will made it very clear that she holds the controlling interest in Silver Kingdom. Is this some sort of coup?

Mrs Papadopoulos looks uncomfortable.

'No. Your husband. He say you find better price elsewhere. But he will give you my telephone number to talk. Then you never call.'

There's a loud cheer from the direction of the shore. Maisie can see a flash of yellow as the flotilla of pleasure boats drifts away from the pier. The fireworks are about to start.

'But I didn't find a better price . . . I never got your number . . . that's not what happened . . .' Maisie stumbles over the words, confused. There's only one way to clear this up. 'Save me a place near the water; I'll join you soon,' she says to Mrs Papadopoulos. 'I need to find James.'

There must have been a miscommunication. Why would James go behind her back like this – what would be the reason to? As Mrs Papadopoulos heads off, Maisie holds the pole and manoeuvres herself off the horse.

A loud bang makes her jump. A fountain of blue light streams through the air, illuminating Silver Kingdom in a sparkling dome. Shadowy areas are now lit up, and she can see a pair of partygoers heading this way, deep in earnest conversation. A prickling unease takes hold as Maisie recognizes her husband with Freddie.

The men advance towards the carousel. For a fraction of a second, a look of surprise crosses James's face when he spots Maisie standing on the platform, looking down. Then he smiles broadly.

'I thought you were enjoying the party,' he says. 'Freddie wanted a personal tour of the park. Isn't that right, Freddie?'

James shoots Freddie a quick glance. Maisie's unease magnifies. Her husband has broken his promise to keep that man away.

'As I told your wife before, this is a very nice set-up.' He looks at Maisie. 'And it's even more impressive at night, Mrs Squires. Have you ever considered extending your opening hours? Your takings would probably grow by twenty-two per cent, at a guess.'

Maisie plays her fingers through the necklace. There's detail to this idea that suggests it hasn't just been plucked from thin air.

'I'll certainly think about it,' she replies through gritted teeth.

An awkward silence persists. Maisie looks between the men. James focuses on adjusting his cufflinks, while Freddie's eyes shine with mischief.

'On that note, I shall leave you two sweethearts to it. I just wanted to check in on my collateral,' he says, strolling off.

Maisie's mind swirls. Collateral?

There are a series of explosions as more fireworks soar through the night sky. Maisie feels sick to her stomach. Placing her hands on her hips, she surveys her husband through narrowed eyes.

'Well?' she demands. 'What's Freddie doing here? And what does he mean by collateral?'

She can feel anger bubble up.

'Darling, let's talk this through calmly. I see it as a loan from Silver Kingdom that I intend to pay once this latest deal goes through.' His voice is as silky as ever, steady and strong. 'I needed as much money as I could get my hands on to invest. It's why I accepted Freddie's offer of a loan. All he asked in return was the carousel as security in case anything goes wrong,' he explains. 'Which it won't, of course,' he adds quickly.

Maisie is reeling. Though she has no idea if James can legally use her property against a loan, Mr Fortescue doesn't seem the type to concern himself with the law – and her gut tells her that he isn't a man to cross.

'Then how could you afford this necklace?' she asks.

James smiles smugly. 'I thought it would be nice to use a little of the loan to treat my wonderful wife.'

So it was paid for with Freddie's money.

The park is spinning, juddering. James has brought the menace of that man to their door. He's put the carousel at risk, Silver Kingdom at risk, and threatened the livelihood of their family.

'How much is the loan?' she asks, collecting her thoughts.

'You're making too much of something minor, darling,' he responds glibly.

Maisie stares at him. James still hasn't grasped the gravity of the situation. 'How much?' she repeats.

'Two thousand dollars,' he admits, his confidence faltering for the first time.

Maisie mutters under her breath. Wrenching the necklace from around her neck, she flings it at him.

'There's part of your loan paid back to Freddie.'

She strides down the platform steps and past the closed hotdog stand. James follows hot on her heels. He tries to talk to her, but Maisie isn't listening. They're approaching the gate to the house when she spots Mrs Papadopoulos loitering near the office. She must have heard the fracas and hung back to check on her friend.

As Maisie remembers why she wanted to speak to James in the first place, she becomes aware that his hand is settled on her back, apparently steering her away from crossing paths with Mrs Papadopoulos. She glances at him.

'What are you . . .' she begins.

Blushing, James looks away. An awful realization hits Maisie that he looks guilty. The discovery that he's desperate for any money he can lay his hands on. Inferior products from their new tradespeople. Keeping Maisie and Mrs Papadopoulos apart. It's obvious now that James must have switched Silver Kingdom to cheaper tradespeople, faking invoices with higher prices so he could cream off the profits.

Maisie keeps steady on her path, giving Mrs Papadopoulos a small head shake to signal that she doesn't need help.

Ignoring James's ever louder excuses, ignoring the maelstrom of partygoers, Maisie crosses the gardens and sweeps into the house. Upstairs, she stretches up and removes a box of money – her secret stash of the profits and salary she has saved – from above her wardrobe. She hands the lot to James.

'And that's the remainder of the loan paid off.' She gives him a cold stare. 'This is so the carousel isn't used as collateral. I shall check that Freddie gets it.'

James looks awestruck.

'Darling,' he says breathlessly. 'Darling, that's very generous of you. You'll get it back soon, I promise.'

Maisie can't stand the sight of him. Being wanted isn't enough, she realizes. She has to want James back.

'And you're going to pack your things and move out of the house,' she says in a firm voice. 'Tonight.'

Slowing

44

Maromme, France, October 1923

To begin with, Laurent had perceived a minor blur at the edges of his vision. Then it had grown increasingly difficult to study the newspaper without holding the pages at arm's length. Now all but the largest script is lost to him, and he struggles to write his crime reports. It is a most irksome by-product of the descent into middle age, but there it is. He will need to visit an ophthalmologist for reading glasses.

He checks the clock on the mantelpiece. If he hurries, there is time for an eye test.

'Odette!' he calls.

There is no sound save for his voice echoing off the long, stone walls in the hallway.

He finds her in the garden. 'There you are,' he says with a faint smile. 'I was looking for you all over the house.'

Odette is crouched on the ground, trowel in hand, planting bulbs for the spring. The country life is good for her and puts a little colour into her plain face. It is good for them both, in fact. With three times the space of the Parisian apartment, Laurent has requisitioned the quietest room downstairs as his own study. He has his own bedroom too. And bathroom.

'The child needs fresh air, as do you,' he had announced two years ago, when he could no longer bear the suffocating feeling of the apartment in summer.

He had also hoped a change of scene might revive the marriage. Since Laurent has kept his job in Paris, they have maintained the apartment there as his pied-à-terre. Even with spending less time in close quarters, it didn't take long to discover that they had taken their problems with them. Things were brought to a head when Laurent realized how much he dreaded the return commute to Maromme on a Friday evening. Duty, sacrifice, honour, are all very well, but he has come to understand that his mother had stayed in an unhappy marriage, and Laurent is tormented by what happened to her.

Earlier this year, Laurent broached the subject of a separation. Odette appeared relieved. By mutual agreement, it was decided that the current arrangement of Laurent weekending in Maromme would continue in order to enable Amélie to spend time with her father while giving Odette some leisure time. It suits Laurent well, and for a while they rubbed along fine without the pressure of having to get on. But lately she has seemed irritated by the interruptions to her life that his presence brings. 'It's difficult to move on with you staying here so much,' she has complained on more than one occasion.

It is a valid point, but Laurent fears what any further change would mean for Amélie and his relationship with her. At ten years old, his daughter is an interesting companion and has become quite the chatterbox. They discuss ballet and doll's houses, and draw together, and visit museums and tea rooms, and take little tours on steam trains. It reminds him of the good times with his mother, and takes the edge off his loneliness.

Predictably, his father was appalled by Laurent's change in marital status. 'I don't know why I expected more of you,' he had bellowed before Laurent strode off. The relief was immediate. It felt like an ugly, festering weight of judgement had been lifted from him. Days turned to weeks and then months without any contact between the two men. Half expecting to experience some form of grief from this estrangement, Laurent was surprised that the feeling of lightness only increased over time. They have still not spoken, and Laurent is uncertain whether they ever will again. But he takes it as a blessing not being viewed as a disappointment all the time. It makes him kinder to himself, more understanding of his own flaws.

Odette wipes her face with the back of her hand, leaving a smear of soil on her forehead, and stands.

'I did tell you I was going to be outside, Laurent,' she replies, unable to restrain her annoyance.

'You did,' he admits, now remembering. 'I just came to tell you that I need to go into town, but I shall be back in time for the teddy bears' picnic with Amélie.'

There is a pinch around Odette's mouth. 'Since you're going, could you buy a baguette while you're out, please. It will save me a trip later.'

'Of course.'

Maromme is a pretty little town near Rouen, with quaint residences, and it is only a leisurely, twenty-minute stroll from the house along a dirt track that winds through lush, Normandy forest turned orange at this time of year. He is rather a celebrity here. The Great Parisian Detective, he is known as by the locals, solving the country's worst crimes.

The priest waves from the church steps. 'Bonjour,' Laurent calls back. He tips his hat at the elderly women gossiping on the corner, smiles at a group of small boys playing marbles in the street and passes the bakery, the scent of sweet pastries reminding him of Odette's request. What is it that she wanted? No matter, it will come to him before the return journey.

The premises of the ophthalmologist sit just beyond the main square. The receptionist looks up from her paperwork. Were it not for the expression of boredom on her face, she might be quite attractive in a wholesome, red-cheeked country sort of way.

'I would like to see your eye doctor, please.'

She doesn't even try to stifle a yawn.

'Monsieur Duval is busy, so you'll have to wait a while,' she replies.

'That is fine,' Laurent says and takes a seat.

His mind drifts to Maisie, as usual. In the hope of winning her back, he has written again, several times, in fact, with the news of his separation from Odette. He also added other details: his emotions, everything he feels for Maisie decanted into several short paragraphs describing the weather or the view from the train window. Receiving no response, Laurent is unaware whether he is forgiven, or if his missives even reach their destination. As a way to feel a connection to Maisie, he pours his efforts into continuing the search for her parents instead. Deciding against writing to Sir Malcolm until he had something more substantial to share, Laurent contacted Yousuf Choudary's old university. Information supplied from a professor and two former friends has led him to believe the couple are still alive, but that they left Paris for rural France three years ago. It has seen Laurent travel to Provence, where he had a particularly illuminating talk with a Madame Florian.

After thirty minutes of waiting to be seen, impatience takes over. Scanning the room, his eyes alight on a pile of dusty books in one corner. All are thick, scientific manuals written in French apart from one – *The American Journal of Ophthalmology 1921* – slimmer than the others and in English. It looks as dry a read as the sawdust in the carousel factory, but it is better than tapping his foot on the floor with nothing to do.

Holding the publication two feet from his face, he begins reading a series of articles written by eminent clinicians specializing in the health of the human eye. There are complex technical terms, and tedious hypotheses on retinas and irises. By page eight, his eyelids are fighting to stay open. But then he reaches a report by Dr William Wilmer on the curious story of one of his patients, known only as Mrs H. Laurent's interest perks up. Because of the difficult English phrases, it takes him fifteen minutes to reach the conclusion, but he is engrossed.

If what he has read is true, it could change everything. Buried in the pages is a clue, an answer, possibly *the* answer, to the mystery that had begun with Gilbert Cloutier twenty-three years ago. His pulse races as he rereads one paragraph in particular.

With some force, he slams the book shut and jumps up. The receptionist jumps too, dropping her pen.

'I would very much like to see Monsieur Duval now, if possible,' he requests. 'And to take this journal with me.'

Without waiting for a response, he bursts open the door at the back and enters a small space where a well-built man with a long beard is snoring in a chair.

'Monsieur Duval, I must have a pair of reading glasses immediately. And the use of this journal. Here's twenty francs for your trouble.'

The ophthalmologist wakes with a loud snort. There is something about the man's manner that reminds Laurent of Constable Segal.

'But it takes three weeks to make the correct lenses. I have only Madame Leroy's replacement spectacles, which she is to collect later,' Monsieur Duval replies, indicating a small box on his desk.

'Then I shall take those. It is a matter of life and death.'

Ignoring the ophthalmologist's objections about tailor-made prescriptions, Laurent marches from the premises – the journal under one arm, the reading glasses stored safely in his jacket pocket – and heads home, sailing past the shops, including the pâtisserie. He needs to get to America. And urgently. Maromme is not too far from Le Havre, and he will catch the first passage to New York. If no tickets are available, he will charter a ship. In truth, he will cross the Atlantic in a hot-air balloon if necessary.

45

1923

'Mama, look.'

Milo is ankle deep in water, his chubby, little legs splashing up and down, his big, blue eyes shining with excitement, as though it's a diamond necklace and not a long, wriggling creature that he's dangling. At three years old, he reminds Maisie of herself at that age, paddling in the shallows, fascinated by the beings living in the sea.

'Well done, Milo, let's put it in the jar.'

With the lamprey settled in its new abode, Milo holds Maisie's hand as they cut past the westward side of Silver Kingdom. Maisie can feel his grip tighten as they spot a figure in the distance, waving. Madame Rose. It's early for any park workers to have arrived, and this confirms Maisie's suspicions that the woman is living in her red tent.

'It's all right, she won't hurt you.'

Milo whimpers. He has always been terrified of the fortune-teller. Perhaps it's the way Madame Rose's eyes stare as though she knows things about you that you wouldn't want revealed, or maybe Milo has picked up on his mother's dislike.

Maisie hurries along the path to Essex Cottage, which lies in a quiet spot on the northern fringes of the park. A single-storey, timber-framed building centred around a large brick fireplace, it isn't grand like Jesserton or Fairweather, consisting only of a kitchen, bathroom, living room and two bedrooms, but for the first time ever in her life Maisie owns her own home, with every colour, every minute detail, chosen by her.

Milo places the jar on the oak kitchen table, his eyes glued to the lamprey's dance, while Maisie serves up porridge.

'Breakfast. Put the lamprey on the counter, please.'

'He's called Mr Arnie,' he corrects Maisie.

Milo is obsessed with Arnold. He follows his godfather around Silver Kingdom, giggling at the dramatic introductions to the carousel. 'Roll up, roll up,' were amongst the first words to spring from Milo's mouth.

'Then put Mr Arnie on the counter, please.'

Pouting, Milo shakes his head.

'Milo Malcolm Squires, if you aren't good, we won't play tiddly-winks this evening.'

It never fails to amaze Maisie that she has to coax her son to eat when she herself spent a good part of her childhood grateful for tiny portions of gruel and stale bread. Milo frowns, but does as he's told. Ruffling his hair, Maisie is overcome by her emotions for this small person. Sometimes the force takes her breath away. As she first cradled her son, admiring his little fingernails and tiny toes, Maisie had sworn always to protect him. No matter what, she could never, ever leave him.

A knock on the door sends Milo scurrying to the hallway. There's laughter and squealing, and he bounds back into the kitchen followed by James.

'And how's my boy today?' he asks Milo, ignoring Maisie.

Not that she wants acknowledgement. After the abrupt end of her marriage, she struggles to be around the man. Like a sea fog evaporating, she can now see James for what he really is. But she tolerates him for Milo's sake. Of everything she desires in life, her child feeling wanted in the way she wasn't by her own parents is at the top of Maisie's list. It's why she hasn't got around to an official divorce. They don't need to – James repaid her the two thousand dollars within a year, and both he and Maisie support themselves financially, with an unspoken agreement to share any costs relating to their son.

Of course, bringing up a child alone is challenging. There's no one else to share the big milestones with: sitting up alone, tottering around without help, his first ride on the carousel, held on Maisie's lap while he bounced up and down in excitement. No one to worry with when he's sick or sad. She does all this and more, gladly. And the staff at both the house and Silver Kingdom help out whenever they can: Clara babysits; Eric is teaching Milo how to ride a bicycle; Peggy Mae brings pies; doughnuts, pizza, hotdogs and clam chowder arrive from the food concessions; the Crew do repairs on the cottage. As long as she doesn't have to live with James, who rents an apartment near the club, it will be fine.

The absence of grandparents for her son tugs at her heart sometimes, but what can Maisie do about that? James's parents live on the other side of the Atlantic, and she long ago gave up on the idea of searching for her own, because how could she possibly find them when they were last seen thousands of miles away? Her desire to feel wanted has lingered, however, and she still holds out hope that they will come looking for her one day.

She kisses the top of Milo's head. 'Mama is going now. Will you be good for Papa, please?'

He nods, his face solemn, then pulls his father to admire the lamprey in the jar.

Outside, the Jointees are now setting up for the day; restaurants fire up ovens, staff pile in, shuttered stalls open, chalk boards are positioned, awnings unfurl in a domino effect. Workers tip their hats as Maisie passes, so many of them now that she can't always remember their names.

Business is booming. Joining the original set-up are twenty-three new rides, sixty-five further concessions, an acrobatics show and an upscale restaurant. There's even a streetcar stop, an extension of the original Clark-Wentworth route running into downtown Chicago. Negotiated between Maisie and the Chicago Railway Company, it loops over reclaimed marshland, bringing customers straight to the park's door without disturbing the neighbours. Taking note of Freddie Fortescue's idea, she's extended their opening hours at weekends, and once or twice she even considered following the example of Mr Ingersoll's Luna Parks by introducing Silver Kingdoms in other locations.

The past couple of years have been busy, with Maisie's eyes fixed on one goal: escape.

Strolling across the park, she spots her pebbles still dotted around the carousel. It's been more than three years since Maisie has felt the need to lay any more, ever since she came up with an ingenious idea to keep everyone safe from disappearing, once and for all.

A little older, a little more worn from all those eager riders patting and stroking horses, wriggling on the saddles, the ride is still magnificent. And now the strange horse is enclosed in a glass cabinet, inaccessible, giving it a fairytale quality. It's their very own Snow White. Their very own version of a freak show, attracting spectators from far and near. Maisie has even set aside one hour at the end of each day for visitors to have their photographs taken beside the horse.

The unresolved mystery of what happened to the people who vanished attracts a long line. Would-be sleuths swap theories: kidnappings gone wrong; coincidence; a publicity stunt; communist spies. 'It was Martians from outer space, you mark my words,' one man claimed, pointing to the sky.

Maisie keeps her thoughts to herself. She knows for certain now that Beau Armitage wasn't involved, having discovered a couple of years ago through the gossip pages that he was attending a movie premiere in Hollywood on the night Sir Malcolm disappeared. The little voice in her head had begun asking questions again. What was the relevance of her own experience of riding the strange horse? Why were the police forces in two countries still stumped? Then, last month, she visited a bookstore in the city with Milo. As usual, everyone took stock of Maisie holding her son's hand, eyeing her with the same quizzical expression as the parents visiting Silver Kingdom, and the sales assistants in the toy department at Marshall Field's. Asking themselves, *Who is this pale-skinned, blue-eyed child to you?*

Ignoring the stares, Maisie had helped Milo choose a book for himself, then spent a few moments browsing the adult fiction section – and there, with its golden spine, had sat *The Time Machine* by H. G. Wells. Open-mouthed, she had read enough to know that she had to buy this book. After absorbing every word, she got a wild idea – could the horse be a device for snatching people away to the past, where they become trapped?

She pulls up the collar of her coat against the autumn wind. The majestic outline of Fairweather House looms into view with the usual sight of Nancy staring from her bedroom window in a white nightgown. Though she might have felt some victory at reclaiming Fairweather House for herself, something seemed to break in Nancy when Milo was born. Maisie had tried to continue their quiet moments sitting together on the patio bench when Nancy was in one of her vague states, but the woman withdrew completely. She barely talks or eats or sleeps now and stays in her room, alone, according to the servants, who are Maisie's eyes and ears in the big house. To Maisie's secret relief, Nancy even lost interest in Sir Malcolm's death, appearing to believe the alibi Mrs Papadopoulos provided a few days after the party. It seems she is safe, for now – though the guilt at covering up his disappearance persists.

Arriving at the office near the ticket booth, she is immediately met by a letter lying on the desk. She recognizes the slanted handwriting, knows the sender without having to check. Laurent has written again.

She wonders if his wife knows that he writes to another woman on the other side of the world. What does Maisie care anyway, since she's sworn off romantic love? She's doing fine by herself, and James involving Freddie Fortescue in their lives taught Maisie that a husband doesn't necessarily offer protection. With that, she places the envelope with the other nine, all unopened, in the top drawer.

As Maisie settles down to work, her nerves are frayed. She tries focusing on the accounts, but can't sit still. Her palms sweat, and she feels hot. This is it. This is the big day.

Hugo arrives an hour later. To no one's surprise, he has tried to play peacemaker between Maisie and James, staying friends with both. He often invites James over for dinner or a game of tennis on the new court by the lake, or drinks on the patio. Her estranged husband usually arrives with a much younger woman in tow. They are always very pretty, very giggly and never last longer than a couple of weeks. James makes a big display of zooming up the driveway in a zippy sports car, talking loudly enough for the sound to carry over the fence to Silver Kingdom. If this is for Maisie's benefit, it's a waste of effort, because she couldn't care less as long as these temporary love interests are kept away from her son.

It does mean that Maisie now refuses to step inside Fairweather House. On her insistence, James left that night of the party just over three years ago, protesting. When it became clear that he was a welcome visitor to the house, courtesy of Hugo and Nancy, she took refuge with Mrs Papadopoulos briefly until Essex Cottage was built.

'You sent for me,' Hugo says, settling in the brown leather armchair.

Maisie hands him a cup of steaming Darjeeling, hoping that he doesn't notice the tremble in her hands. He sips, his mouth curling around the rim as if he's sucking a lollipop. Hugo looks bored, distracted, staring out of the small window at the ticket office.

'There's something I want to tell you.' Maisie's stomach flips over. Leaning back to appear relaxed, she places her hands on the desk that was once Sir Malcolm's. 'I'm selling my share of the amusement park.'

Her heart beats extra fast. Maisie has practised this line many times over, but it still sounds strange spoken out loud, with a finality like a death knell. She has wrangled with this decision, back and forth, back and forth, since the moment three years ago that she decided to wipe the slate clean after her failed marriage. Even this morning she woke up undecided yet again. Silver Kingdom has been interlaced with Maisie's fate for half a decade. She remembers the first spark of an idea, the excitement of setting up a business with Sir Malcolm. It was their creation, and saying goodbye will be like leaving behind an old friend.

On the other hand, the memories at Silver Kingdom are ghosts that haunt her day and night. Now Maisie has her own child, the horror of what might have happened to the missing children is amplified – and their fate was also Sir Malcolm's fate. The night she waited in vain for him to return, frightened and alone in the dark, is a constant, replayed in her mind and tangled in a messy web with the heartache of losing Laurent. It all came back after she ended things with James, as though her marriage had been plugging a hole in a dam. Strolling past the dodgems, or standing near the carousel at sunset, or arriving at the Journey to the Centre of the Earth ride, trick her mind into imagining 'what could have been'. No, the way to silence these thoughts is to create a new future.

With the proceeds from the sale, she is moving to Joliet, a pretty city fifty miles south-west of downtown Chicago, with a river and train station and elegant residences. It creates a distance from James, but is near enough that he can still spend time with his son. Having secured the rental of a two-storey building consisting of an apartment on the top floor and a dried-goods store below, which she will run herself, she hopes to live a simpler life there, without the responsibility of hundreds of workers. It wasn't intentional, but her future living arrangement reminds Maisie of her mother and Aunty Mabel growing up above their parents' haberdashery shop. Perhaps life is like that, Maisie thinks, perhaps life is like a carousel – it has ups and downs but it eventually comes full circle.

Hugo splutters. He sets down the cup, wipes a dribble of tea from his chin, dabs his collar.

'Bloody Indians with their bloody tea, making a chap ruin his best shirt,' he mumbles.

It's funny how people like Hugo – civilized, polite people who believe they act better than the women in the lock-up – forget or aren't aware of Maisie's true origins, say things to her face that they would never dream of saying otherwise.

'Bloody Indians like me, you mean?'

He looks up, his eyes widening as he realizes his faux pas.

'No, no, I didn't mean you, Maisie, you're not like . . .' he stutters. His voice trails off and he sits, squirming.

'We're good at business, though, from what I've heard. So, for the sake of business, I'm giving you first refusal.'

Hugo takes a moment to compose himself. As he runs his fingers through his hair, Maisie can see that it's thinning.

'I don't know, Maisie. I would need to liquidate all of my other assets and mortgage the house, so it may take some time.'

Hugo must have realized this day might come. Maisie is certain that someone with his experience has a built-in contingency. She likes him, but this is business.

'Time isn't something I'm willing to offer,' she counters.

'Have you told James?'

Maisie purses her lips. Talking to James is her next step, but she's been waiting for everything to be finalized because she doesn't want his overconfidence undermining her decision.

'You let me worry about him.'

Hugo studies his fingernails. 'Are you absolutely certain it's over between you two? You know he still adores you and would take you back in a shot. He never shuts up about you.'

Maisie taps the desk, unable to hide her impatience. Hugo's interference, albeit well meaning, is another reason she needs to leave this place.

'You have forty-eight hours, Hugo, then I'm putting my share on the open market.'

46

Waiting for Hugo to make his decision turns each torturous second into days. Thirty hours after the meeting, and Maisie has heard nothing. She prays for him to find the funds to buy her out, because if he can't . . . no, she won't think like that. The plan needs to work.

Finishing her paperwork, she locks the office door and heads into the magenta twilight as the sun sets over Lake Michigan. The moments after work are delicious, filled with the promise of an entire evening cosied up with Milo at the cottage. Dropped off minutes ago by James, who is heading to the jazz club, he's already found Arnold, and Maisie can see the pair running around the new rollercoaster in the distance.

As Maisie rounds the corner between the hall of mirrors and the carousel, the hairs on the back of her neck stand up. There's the familiar sensation of being watched, but this time she's absolutely certain that a presence is lurking in the shadows. With her breath held, Maisie's eyes dart from the Smugglers' Saloon to the dodgems, from the popcorn stand to the chocolate emporium, and back to the carousel.

A small movement to the right makes her jump out of her skin. Turning around slowly, she notices a figure crouched behind the doughnut stand – it's Nancy, who hasn't been seen anywhere except at her bedroom window for years.

'What are you doing here?' Maisie asks, approaching her.

There's no answer. Maisie bends down and lays one hand on Nancy's arm. Her skin is cold to the touch, and she is so still and so pale that she could be mistaken for an ice sculpture. No wonder, because she's dressed only in a thin nightdress. Automatically, Maisie removes her coat and places it over Nancy's shoulders. Nancy doesn't seem to notice that anyone has joined her. She is mumbling words Maisie can't catch while her fingers move near her neck, as though she's touching an invisible rosary. Silver streaks her once chestnut hair, and she's as thin as Sir Malcolm was at his worst.

'Nancy, are you all right?'

Nancy lifts her eyes. They are bloodshot and rimmed with grey circles. 'Just peachy,' she answers with a trace of sarcasm, getting slowly to her feet.

For once, Maisie is glad to see the spark return. She watches as Nancy looks around nervously.

'Is Hugo here?'

'No, but I can get him if you wish,' Maisie offers.

Nancy grips Maisie's arm.

'No, don't. He doesn't know I'm out of the house, and I don't want to go back just yet.'

Nancy makes it sound like she's frightened. Noticing that Nancy's legs are beginning to give way, Maisie leads the woman to the bench situated directly opposite the carousel. When Silver Kingdom is open, this is the most crowded spot, with everyone vying for the best position to watch the ride spin around.

'Sometimes I think I'm just like that horse. Trapped in a prison with invisible walls.'

Maisie follows Nancy's gaze. The caramel-coloured horse looks more mysterious than ever in this light, other-worldly. Reflecting off the glass are the colours of the setting sun, casting an ethereal glow.

'Then why don't you venture out more often?'

Nancy raises her eyebrows.

'You've always been a funny little thing. Hugo wouldn't hear of it. He worries I might harm myself. Being barren has made me lose my mind, apparently.'

Being sad isn't a madness, Maisie thinks. She takes Nancy's hand in hers and strokes the skin softly. Nancy closes her eyes as if it's been a long time since anyone has touched her in this way.

'I'm sure he doesn't see it like that. Hugo loves you. You're his wife.'

Nancy's eyes snap open and she snorts. 'For someone who walked out on her husband, you have a quaintly romantic view of marriage.'

Blushing, Maisie looks away. Even in her weakened state, Nancy knows how to make Maisie feel small.

'Sorry, that was harsh, and you've always been very good at tolerating my horrid moments.' She gives Maisie's hand a squeeze. 'I'm just not used to company any more, being in my room most of the time. I don't know how to behave. I think that's why Hugo has asked for a divorce.' Nancy leans in and drops her voice to a whisper. 'Poor man hasn't had the best run with wives, has he? First, Charlotte dying of appendicitis at twenty-five, and now me.'

She sits up straight and smooths her hair, as though she's about to be presented to fine company. 'We haven't told anyone. It's all very hush-hush. I'm leaving for Assumption next week and will stay there while everything is arranged.'

Maisie is floored. No wonder Hugo has seemed so distracted. How has he been coping with it all?

'But why Assumption?'

Nancy looks closely at Maisie, noting the surprise on her face. Then she shakes her head in disbelief.

'You really don't know, do you? I'm going back home, Maisie. To the farm in Illinois where I grew up. It won't be very exciting, just cows and lots of grass, but the change of scene might do me good. And my mother is looking forward to our praying together.' She looks amused at Maisie's wide-eyed expression. 'I met Hugo by chance when I slipped away from my church group's tour of New York and stumbled into the Met,' she explains. 'I'd never seen anywhere more wonderful. I decided on the spot that I always wanted to be surrounded by such beauty.'

Maisie struggles to reconcile the picture she has of Nancy as a New York socialite with this new information.

'But you're so' – Maisie tries to identify the right word – 'sophisticated.'

'Which just goes to show that things aren't always as they seem.'

There's shouting in the distance. Maisie looks over her shoulder and sees Hugo pelting across Silver Kingdom followed by the servants.

'Well, goodbye,' Nancy says wearily. She pushes herself upright and strokes the top of Maisie's head. 'Think kindly of me sometimes. And take care of your little boy. He is a darling. I watch him playing around Silver Kingdom. He's got your spirit.'

Maisie feels suddenly bereft. She has known this woman since she was twelve years old. They have been through so much together, and it feels right to leave things between them on a kind note.

'Sir Malcolm always said you were a breath of good luck for his brother.'

Nancy looks down at Maisie with a sparkle in her eyes.

'Ah, yes, I think he thought it was good for Hugo to come out of his shell a bit; he was shy when we first met,' she explains. 'Sir Malcolm was always wonderful to me. We became particularly close at the end. He used to talk about all sorts when we got drunk together.' As if she's remembering a treasured memory, Nancy's mouth curls up at the corners. 'You know, he once told me he rode that peculiar horse and found out something interesting. It's how I've always known the carousel had something to do with his death.' She gives Maisie a meaningful look. 'There never was a witness, of course, and I found your corsage tucked behind the potted palm in the drawing room. But playing amateur sleuth gave me a distraction from . . .' Her voice fades.

As Maisie realizes she was duped, Nancy leans down to plant a kiss on her forehead. 'And don't feel too sorry for me. I intend to leave in a fanfare of glory.'

Hugo pounds across the ground. His face is red and he's breathless. Behind him, Eric and Robert appear with Clara, and Nancy's maid, Lucy, bringing up the rear. Both women are red-eyed as if they've been crying.

'There you are, my dear. I thought something terrible might have happened to you,' Hugo pants, addressing his wife as though he's speaking to a child. 'It appears you forgot to take your tonic today.'

He passes Nancy, still wearing Maisie's coat, into the servants' care. She doesn't look back as she's led slowly through the park.

Hugo gives Maisie a tired smile. 'Thank you for taking care of her,' he says, and turns to follow the others along the path.

Maisie watches the group leave through the gate to Fairweather House, then she faces the carousel. 'What did you discover about the horse, Sir Malcolm?' she asks out loud.

47

Eric returns Maisie's coat and holds out an envelope.

'From Master Hugo.'

It's after 9 p.m., and his shoulders droop as though it's been an especially tiring day. Maisie can only imagine the disarray at the big house after Nancy's escape. There's probably been an enquiry about how a woman kept in a locked room could have got out.

She eyes the envelope with suspicion. 'What is it?'

Eric shrugs.

'What you wanted, apparently. Master Hugo has made an appointment with that lawyer for Monday to get it signed if the terms are acceptable.' Eric drops his voice. 'I don't know what it all means, don't need to know, but I wish you the best of luck.'

Trying to contain her excitement, Maisie curls up in an armchair in the living room, looking through the contents as soon as Eric is gone. There's no note, simply a contract to buy Maisie's share of Silver Kingdom in exchange for a fair price.

It can't be coincidence that Hugo's decision has come hours after Maisie spoke to Nancy. In any event, it's a relief to know that soon she will be free. After all these years of careful planning, she's really doing this.

Though the fire crackles in the hearth, Maisie is gripped by the cold, so she retreats to Milo's bedroom, burrowing under the patchwork eiderdown with him in his little wooden bed. He smells of wax crayons and sleep. It reminds Maisie of snuggling up to Tommy on freezing winter nights at the shack, their arms around each other and their breath like mist as they whispered secrets about their parents. *My mum's a ballerina*, he would claim, his huge eyes shining. *Well, my mum's a duchess and she takes tea with a talking dolphin every day*, Maisie would reply, and they'd both try not to wake up the Sixpences by giggling.

Maisie feels a tear slip out and she hugs Milo tighter. Did her mother ever lie with her like this? Did she ever gaze at her child in adoration, watching her sleep? Or show any affection? Probably not. The only adult Maisie remembers as being tender was Aunty Mabel. It felt how Maisie imagines it would feel to bathe in angel kisses when her aunt brushed her hair every morning.

There's a gentle tap on the front door. If this is Eric with another missive from Hugo, he will need to wait until morning. Maisie is too cosy to get up for anything. Snuggling closer to Milo, she ignores the second knock as well.

Until there is a third. 'I know you're in there,' someone whispers through the letter box.

With a groan, she gives up. She knows exactly who it is.

She opens the door to James, who is leaning on the doorpost. The familiar irritation at seeing him flares up. They have fallen into a strict arrangement whereby their only interactions take place when care of Milo is being passed between them. James shouldn't be here. She moves to close the door, but his foot is lodged in the doorway.

'There's something I need to talk to you about,' he says. 'It involves Milo. And it's urgent.'

Maisie's eyes narrow. She would sooner brave the wild dogs on Canvey Island than let James in, but Milo is her soft spot and she reluctantly relents. Docile as a lamb, James follows Maisie to the kitchen and sits at the table while she remains standing, her arms folded. He is twitching, one foot jigging up and down on the spot. For someone usually brimming with confidence, he's displaying signs of anxiety that spread to Maisie. She can't imagine what's brought him here at this time of night.

'So?' she says, wanting James to say his piece and leave.

He removes a bottle from the inside pocket of his jacket, unscrews the lid and takes a swig. Maisie can't believe what she's seeing – and smelling. Moonshine? After everything?

'Sorry,' he says, reading the expression on her face. He replaces the lid and puts away the bottle. 'It's been . . .' His hands are trembling. 'There's been some trouble.' His forehead breaks out in a cold sweat. 'My chum, Maurice, says I can stay with him for a few days but then I need to leave. Permanently.' He looks Maisie directly in the eye. 'I want you and Milo to come with me. A fresh start for us.'

Blindsided, Maisie stares at James. Has he lost touch with reality? While she thinks on what to say, she pours a glass of water for him.

'I'm sure it's not that bad,' she replies, deliberately ignoring the statement about leaving with him.

It feels like she's talking to Milo after he's cut his knee or can't find his favourite toy. James produces a cigarette, tapping it on the table and making no attempt to light up. Maisie wonders when he took up smoking.

He sips the water. 'It's worse than bad. A shipment of moonshine Freddie and I were transporting from Tennessee got intercepted by the police, and he's blaming me.'

Getting involved with Freddie Fortescue and his dodgy dealings was always going to lead to trouble, but this isn't the time for 'I told you so'.

'You can't honestly expect us to go on the run with you,' she says instead. 'It wouldn't be safe for Milo.'

Maisie can see the expression on James's face harden. He scrapes back the chair and stands up. She's never seen him like this, and can't wait for him to leave.

'Then all I need is my share of Silver Kingdom.'

Maisie is overtaken by a fear that everything she's worked so hard for is melting away. Does James know she's selling up? Did Hugo spill the beans?

'*Your* share?' she replies, trying to keep her voice down in case Milo hears through the wall. 'Silver Kingdom has nothing to do with you.'

His face turns scarlet. 'But, darling, we're still married, so what's yours is mine,' he says. 'I'll settle for half of whatever savings you have lying about.' His eyes roam the room. 'Where do you keep your cash these days?'

Safe in a bank, since that night she handed the box of money to him, Maisie refrains from saying.

'No, James, that's not how it works, by law. Sir Malcolm gave

Silver Kingdom to me, and I've built its success. Even if we divorced, I get to keep my inheritance.'

He looks like he's been slapped. Clearly, this was James back to his old trick of trying to part Maisie from her money, not knowing that she had consulted Mr Peabody on her marital rights within days of the separation. As he absorbs this information, James scowls.

'And he should have given it to *me*,' he hisses. '*I* was his family. *I* should have gone to America with him, not you. A court might say you stole that inheritance.'

Maisie's mouth dries. Has James secretly resented her all these years?

'Then take me to that court if you think you'll see one cent of what you believe is yours.'

She has no idea what would happen if he did, but the overwhelming need to safeguard her child's best interests has imbued Maisie with an impulsive ferocity.

Before she can react, James has made up the distance between them. He grabs her wrists and is pulling her out of the kitchen and along the hallway. She represses the instinct to scream, more terrified by the possibility that her son might wake up than by what might happen to her. As James reaches the front door, Maisie tries to break free, but his bulk is too strong, and she finds herself bundled outside.

Shadows dance across the little garden surrounding the cottage, and out on the lake the surface is shiny black, as though a shoal of mackerel have risen from the depths. Maisie looks back helplessly as James grips her arms and pushes her through the picket gate and out into Silver Kingdom. All she can think about is that Milo is alone inside.

'James, our son needs us,' she says in a quiet voice, wanting him to release his grip and let her return to the cottage.

She hopes that appearing calm and talking about Milo will soothe James sufficiently for him to come to his senses. He shoves Maisie forward, passing the rollercoaster and several food stalls. Rides that offer so much enjoyment in the day are silent witnesses to James's roughness now. When he reaches the heart of Silver Kingdom, he manhandles Maisie up the steps to the carousel platform.

'Why are we here?' she asks, feeling increasingly fearful.

James snakes between watchful horses until they arrive at the central cylinder.

'This bloody machine,' he hisses. 'You've always cared more about it than you ever have about me. We'd still be together if it didn't exist.'

While Maisie admits to feeling a strong connection to the carousel, James is talking about this collection of metal and painted wood as if it were her lover. If she wasn't so frightened, she would laugh at his jealousy of it.

With one hand keeping her held still, he uses the other to open a flap and begin pulling at wires. Orange sparks fly and there's clunking. As Maisie struggles to push him away from the mechanism, he pins her against the cylinder, his full weight crushing the air from her lungs. She can't breathe, can't focus. Without thinking, she wrenches an arm free and reaches inside the cylinder for the chisel she once used to lever the music box into place. James must feel a sharp blade against his neck because his eyes widen and he jumps back.

'You'd really hurt me for this machine?' he spits.

Maisie doesn't know what she'd do if it came to it, but she daren't lower the chisel now in case he lunges at her.

'To protect myself,' she says, advancing another step.

They half circle the platform like this, Maisie taking one step forward for every step James takes back. His eyes are wild, and she is beginning to panic about how they will resolve this stalemate, when there are pounding footsteps, a vibration across metal. Lucky Nate approaches followed by the rest of the Crew, the huge hulk of their figures stopping only feet away. They must have heard noises of a struggle.

'Fine evening for a stroll, ma'am,' he says, tipping his hat at Maisie.

Both James and Maisie are silent, caught in the act. The men look between each other before forming a circle, their arms folded. Lucky Nate is nearest to Maisie.

'You're safe now,' he says softly in her ear.

He places one hand on her shoulder and takes the chisel. James takes his chance to scrabble down the carousel steps. He kicks the platform, then runs off into the darkness.

'Goodbye, James,' Maisie shouts, trying to sound brave.

Shaking, she collapses against Lucky Nate. *It will be all right. It will be all right.* She is leaving soon.

48

Hugo acknowledges Maisie with a handshake as she enters the office, while Mr Peabody's smile stretches across his face.

'My grandchildren love Silver Kingdom,' he discloses. 'Adore the rollercoaster. But it's the carousel we're always drawn to. I have to say, I'm particularly fascinated by that horse in the glass case. Have there really been no further developments in the investigation?'

Maisie must have been asked this question a thousand times – by the park's visitors, reporters, by anyone she encounters in her day-to-day life who knows about her link to the carousel. She wishes there were. Settling in the same seat transports her back almost four years, to the time just after Sir Malcom's disappearance, when she was unaware of the turbulence she would soon face: taking over Silver Kingdom, motherhood, her marriage ending. Through all those changes, there's been one constant – the mystery has never been solved.

Hugo waves his hand, dismissively. 'The carousel is nothing. I'm thinking of commissioning a special ride. Something that blows everything else out of the water.'

It pains Maisie to admit, even to herself, that the nature of amusement parks is changing rapidly. Once a groundbreaking wonder, the carousel is now a quaint, outdated relic. To Maisie, herself, it will never lose its magic. Their fates have been interconnected since she first spotted the coloured piece of paper floating on the seas off the coast of Canvey Island, and leaving it behind will be a bigger wrench than she'd expected. For a second, she considers changing her mind. But, no, it's too late to back down.

'We better get on with it, then,' she says.

Hugo sits up straight.

'I spoke to my accountant, and he believes I should drop my offer.'

Maisie was half expecting him to try renegotiating at the last minute, like any half-competent business person. Though desperate for the deal to go through, she fixes Hugo with an unblinking stare.

'That's fine. I'm happy to find another buyer.'

Maisie is banking on the fact that Hugo won't want anyone else owning an amusement park that borders his house. He twitches nervously. Then he nods to Mr Peabody, who produces a thick document.

'The terms are exactly as requested, with midday today the time and date when control passes from you, Mrs Squires, to you, Mr Randolph,' Mr Peabody explains.

Quickly, Hugo signs the last page. Without hesitating, Maisie scrawls her signature next. There, it's done. A huge sense of relief washes over her, but also something else. Apprehension, she thinks, the knowledge that she's about to step into the big unknown. This time there's no Aunty Mabel as her guide, no Sir Malcolm.

Mr Peabody hands over a banker's cheque with a bigger number written upon it than Maisie has ever seen before. Her hands are shaking. To think, once eight pennies had impressed her, and now she's the possessor of an infinitely larger sum. The formalities over, she bids farewell to everyone and collects Milo, who has been kept occupied by the secretary. Stopping by the bank, a large stone build-ing with a brass door and echoing floors, she deposits the cheque, then heads for Lincoln Park Zoo.

The morning merges all too quickly into afternoon. Ever since James paid his recent visit, a sense of dread has followed Maisie everywhere. The Crew managed to fix the carousel so there was no long-lasting damage, but she can't dispel the worry that this isn't the end of it. While Milo is entertained by waddling penguins and sharp-fanged tigers, and especially by the creatures in the new aquarium, Maisie is on tenterhooks, convinced that trouble is brew-ing. When it's time to leave, he's predictably reluctant.

'Come on, I've invited Mrs Papadopoulos for supper this evening,' she reminds him.

In a hurry to spend the evening with the woman who has been so supportive over the years – someone she might see only sporadically after tonight – Maisie persuades Milo into a taxi, which drops them at the large iron gates to Fairweather House.

This will probably be the last time she will ever approach the amusement park from this direction, the last time the strong outline of the carousel with its waving flag will guide her way home.

Maisie's sense of unease heightens: flocks of birds are flying away from the direction of the estate like a parade of colourful clouds, casting the driveway into shadow. She picks up her pace, chivvying Milo. As the house appears from behind the line of trees, Maisie is hit with a shocking sight: tall flames reach up like the legs of stretching chorus girls towards the late-afternoon sky.

The carousel is burning to the ground.

49

The fire crackles. Paralysed by helplessness, Maisie is rooted to the spot. Arnold appears moments later with the servants and a couple of the Ride Jocks returning from their day off. Then Mrs Papadopoulos arrives in her cart. There's a collective gasp followed by stunned silence. No one knows what to do.

We can't just stand here. Picking up Milo, Maisie races to the entrance of Silver Kingdom with the others in tow. Her heart is pounding, but there's no time to let fear get the better of her, because someone needs to do something. Flames as tall as a man encircle the carousel, pitching black smoke upwards.

'Find the Randolphs,' she orders Clara, Lucy and Peggy Mae. 'And Eric, call for the fire trucks.' She spots Arnold, Robert and the two Ride Jocks immobilized nearby. 'You lot, fetch some buckets from the shed and start throwing water on the fire.'

While the servants scatter in different directions, Maisie takes Milo by the hand and, closely followed by Mrs Papadopoulos, enters the big house. It's gloomier than she remembers, as if everything is shrouded in sadness. The familiar smell of cigar smoke tinged with rosemary is replaced by the bitter odour of boiled cabbage; a pile of torn newspapers nests under the console table; and a bundle of Nancy's pretty clothes has been heaped at the bottom of the stairs, as though someone hurled the contents of her wardrobe from the second floor.

Maisie leads Milo and Mrs Papadopoulos upstairs into Maisie's old bedroom. It's disconcerting to find the room preserved like a museum, everything exactly as she left it. Her hairbrush sits on the dressing table; a stocking is draped over the chair as if she was always expected to return. There's the lipstick she usually wore and a copy of *Vogue* next to it; a large vase containing brown stalks that were once lilies; and a snow globe of Chicago, which she gives her son to play with as she sits him on the bed. Milo sucks his thumb, calmer now, as he watches his mother join Mrs Papadopoulos at the window.

From this height, she can tell that the fire has been raging for some time – the canopy is alight, the flag is gone, and the metal platform is the only thing separating the wooden horses from the ring of flames that surround the carousel. Maisie can't bear to watch it burn.

'Can you stay with Milo, please?' she begs of Mrs Papadopoulos, who agrees, seeming to take everything in her stride.

Maisie races back downstairs, finds two buckets in the back kitchen and runs across the garden and down to the lake's shore. Filling the buckets with water, Maisie grimaces as she struggles to clamber up the slope. With a determined push, she makes it. Didn't she drag cockles across Canvey Island when she was just a child?

She meets Eric running the other way.

'The fire trucks won't be here for another thirty minutes,' he gasps as they pass.

Thirty minutes will be too late. Her muscles fighting, Maisie keeps up her pace. She almost feels sorry for the carousel: damaged by James a few days ago, and now this.

Arnold and Robert push past on their way back to the lake to fill up their containers. As Maisie weaves through the other attractions, she begins to cough. Smoke, rising in columns in every direction, is filling her lungs.

As Maisie reaches the doughnut stand, she is almost forced back by the heat. Stronger than a furnace, it forms a dome around the carousel. This close, the flames are fiercer than she first realized, licking like the tongues of hungry wolves, and Maisie would run from them if she couldn't now see that the horses are in danger.

A chunk of the burning canopy has crashed on to the platform, spitting sparks outwards. Two horses are already charred, and flames are eating away at the hooves of the three in the row behind. There's a loud groan as the platform begins to buckle. Over by the controls, metal is melting, returning to its molten state.

Maisie's eyes are drawn to the caramel-coloured horse inside its casing. Flames reflecting off its coat ripple as if the horse is in motion. She catches its eye. The gold flecks glitter. It seems to be looking back at her, but she cannot decipher its expression.

As another chunk of canopy breaks off, events seem to move in slow motion. The vibration sends a shockwave outwards, and Maisie is propelled backwards. With a roar, a wall of flames barrels towards the cabinet. The glass cracks. A jagged pattern spreads and then shards of glass are slicing the air. The horse is free.

Maisie stumbles forward again, as though pulled by some sort of magnetic force. She needs to get to the horse, to ride it, the feeling as vital as breathing. Only a rough shove startles her from her daze.

'Get out of here,' a voice shouts, barely audible above the fury of the inferno.

It takes a second to recognize the sooty face as belonging to Madame Rose. Without acknowledging the fortune-teller, Maisie's eyes are pulled back to the horse: flames ravage the tail and haunches. A leg snaps off. Golds and blues and reds turn black and disintegrate into ash. The eyes are last. Watching its own destruction, the creature is finally gone.

'Out,' Madame Rose screams and this time Maisie obeys.

She looks back over her shoulder as she runs, bewitched by the remnants of the carousel silhouetted against the orange sky. Flames are spreading foot by foot, like a wine spill to engulf anything in their way. Small fires have popped up everywhere now. The helter-skelter is ablaze. The pier. Even the roof of Essex Cottage.

Maisie is pushing her legs faster, gasping, desperate to get to Milo and evacuate Fairweather House when she lets out a cry as an apparition emerges. It took almost half a decade for her prayers to be answered, but appearing from within the smoke, through the ash that falls upon everything like black snow, is Laurent.

50

Without wasting a second, Laurent grabs Maisie's hand and pulls, following Arnold and the others through a gate and to a sheltered spot near the big house. There are only moments to spare. The carousel groans, followed by a rumble and a creak.

'Get down,' he barks.

An almighty explosion rocks the air. Flying upwards are splinters of wood accompanied by chunks of metal glinting like shooting stars. If what has happened is what Laurent suspects, he will need to warn Maisie. Sir Malcolm should be present as well.

'Is Sir Malcolm in the house?' he asks her.

Her eyes widen and tears spring up.

'No.' She is gasping, struggling for air.

Gently, he lays a hand on her arm. 'Slow and steady breaths.'

She exhales deeply. 'He rode the carousel and never came back one night.'

A wail of loud sirens approaches as a procession of emergency vehicles screams up the driveway. Dozens of heavy-booted men jump from four fire trucks. Reluctantly, he tears himself from Maisie's side, leaving her in Arnold's care, and seeks out their leader.

'Detective Bisset from Paris,' he says in introduction to a burly man as they reach the edge of Silver Kingdom. 'There's something else you need to know before your men go in.'

Laurent waits on the sidelines for the firefighters to extinguish the cluster of fires. They battle against a furious wind barrelling in from the lake that pushes the flames to ever greater heights.

His gaze keeps straying to Maisie, sitting on a bench and surrounded by staff. He now notices that her hair is shorter than before, styled sleekly in a way that is fashionable these days, and her dress shows the lower part of her legs – the 'flapper' style, he thinks. She has blossomed into herself. Her face is older and wiser, and there is a newfound strength beneath the vulnerability in her eyes, as though the years have given her beauty infinite layers of depth.

Eventually, water vanquishes fire as the sun goes down for the evening, leaving a scarred mess of decimated stalls and rides. Stepping through the debris with care, Laurent cuts a jagged route to the carousel. The firefighters have made a discovery. Now to see it for himself.

'What brings you to America, Detective?'

He swings around to find Maisie has followed him. She regards him with the same weariness that he has felt himself during the years of their separation. He still cannot tell if he is forgiven, nor whether she has read his latest letter. Laurent thinks of the countless other letters he has sent in the past four years. All those words of restrained passion poured into the missives that perhaps she chose not to see.

He hesitates to inflict further anxiety. But she is not a child; she deserves the truth, no matter how unpleasant. And she will find out soon enough anyway.

'I believed you could be in danger.'

A look of surprise dances across her face. 'You knew there was going to be a fire?'

He takes a deep breath.

'Not from a fire, no, but the carousel. The horse, to be precise. I believed you might disappear.'

Maisie is silent as she looks towards the heap of charred wood piled around the metal platform, torn open by the force of the explosion. Without warning, she steps past him and ascends the partially melted step. He follows close behind.

Peering into the chasm, the sight is more gruesome than Laurent could have imagined. This is where the murder victims have lain hidden the entire time.

51

Maisie sits on the patio bench, huddled in a blanket and sipping sweet tea. There is a flurry of activity around her: Mrs Papadopoulos has taken Milo to her house; Hugo is near the lake, looking distraught, talking to the Crew, who heard the news from the Ride Jocks; the police have arrived. The wooden horses and the canopy are completely destroyed, but three quarters of the metal structure is left and a group of officers are combing through the remains of the carousel with Laurent.

He looks older than before, and more serious. There is silver in his hair, but this only adds a debonair edge to his appearance. In truth, Maisie had forgotten quite how attractive he is. Tall with long legs, and grey eyes that speak without words, Laurent still makes her senses tingle, despite everything.

Maisie watches as he becomes involved in a discussion with the officers, pointing at various areas of the carousel. After a very long while, he leaves the police to their business, and returns to sit next to her. They are side by side, exactly as they were on his last evening here, as though he had popped away for only a few minutes. Her heart both sings and weeps because those days are long ago. Maisie is a different person. Laurent is probably a different person. When she first saw him appearing through the smoke, it felt like her heart was bursting open. Daring to believe that he had crossed the ocean to see her again, her buried emotions had risen to the surface. Now Maisie is terrified of the pain his leaving will cause. He is here on business, as he explained. The carousel brought him to America.

She sips the tea, fighting to keep her feelings in check.

'I did not wish you to see what you saw. It was a terrible sight,' he consoles her.

Maisie realizes her hands are trembling and she sets down the cup.

'I honestly . . .' She can hardly speak. This is all so much. 'I really did think there was something other-worldly going on because I saw something so peculiar when I rode it.'

Laurent regards Maisie.

'It is understandable,' he replies with a softness in his voice. 'I have always remembered what you said about the carousel being cursed. It is that statement of yours that gave me a vital lead in the case. It simply took me all these years to realize it.'

But it wasn't cursed, she admits to herself. *There are no curses. And no time machines. And no need for good-luck pebbles.*

'You believed there were strange forces present because you were hallucinating,' Laurent explains. Sensing her confusion, he continues. 'You are aware that this is a special carousel?' She nods. 'Your other rides are powered by steam and clockwork, as is normal. The carousel, however, is so advanced that gasoline is used as fuel. It gives a certain power to the mechanics.' Laurent pauses, looks to the scene of devastation. 'But it also brings risk because the substance is flammable, which alerted me to the fact that the carousel could explode. It is also how I discovered the method of death.' He lets out a deep sigh as though he is as exhausted as she feels. 'The by-product of gasoline is carbon monoxide, which is, of course, toxic.'

She tries to grasp his meaning. 'They were poisoned?' she asks after a pause.

'As were you. In small doses, it can produce strange imaginings. I chanced upon an interesting journal article at my ophthalmologist's office in which a number of supposed hauntings were chronicled; in reality, these visions were induced by faulty gas lights.' Laurent frowns. 'I was not sure how it was administered and to only the person riding the one horse until I checked the carousel earlier.'

He waves his hand in the general direction of Silver Kingdom.

'In addition to the main exhaust pipe that pokes out from the top of the control cylinder, there is a narrow pipe running from the engine into the pole of that particular horse, with a set of tiny holes at face height disguised by the engraving. The pipe is hidden within the jumble of other components, and the holes are noticeable only if one is looking for them,' he continues. 'This releases a spray of invisible fumes into the rider's face.' He ponders a moment. 'When you rode that horse, Maisie, you were exposed to just enough carbon monoxide to alter your perception of reality for a few seconds. It would not cause death, and the gas dissipates before reaching the riders of other horses.'

Maisie's mind wasn't unravelling. She thinks of Sir Malcolm's deteriorating mental health towards the end. It all makes so much sense if he was regularly riding the horse.

'So that's not what killed the victims?' she asks.

'No, it is not. That level of exposure, outdoors and in a small quantity, simply makes the rider groggy, so they do not call out for help. There is also a second, larger pipe that I discovered only because the carousel is now blown open. This runs from the engine to the hollow area inside the platform. In an enclosed space, and with the volume of fumes such a large engine produces, the dose is lethal within a couple of minutes. Even with the exhaust pipe, enough toxic gas would have pooled in there.'

Maisie's thoughts are spinning. She has a scramble of questions inside her head.

'But how would they get inside the platform? And without anyone seeing?'

Laurent strokes his chin and hesitates as if he's considering his next words.

'This, Maisie, is where the centre of the mystery lies. How would the bodies reach the place where we found them? Unnoticed? So quickly? One minute they are here, and the next they are there. Like a magic trick. And, like any good magic trick, there needs to be a mechanism and a distraction.'

Maisie gasps. 'The lightshow, and the rotating canopy –' She can hardly get out the words. But it's finally all so clear. Then she reflects for a moment. 'But would no one really not have noticed?'

Laurent acknowledges her doubt with a small nod.

'When the members of the court were shown a reconstruction of the last few minutes before the disappearance of one victim, they did not even notice a large man snatching someone out of the room,' he states. 'The actual mechanism used needed two or three seconds of distraction, at most.'

He waits for Maisie to ask the obvious question. She isn't sure she wants to know, however, and, after an overlong silence, Laurent continues. 'There is a trapdoor that opens in the platform at the same time as the horse tilts on its pole, tipping the riders to their fate. The vibration you felt when you were close to the horse was you stepping on to the exact spot where one of the large springs was located, I believe.'

Maisie's head hurts. This is why the horses needed placing on the carousel in a particular order. It also explains the intricate etchings on the platform – the squiggles and hexagonal shapes camouflaging the outline of a door that she had failed to notice while she was cleaning up the carousel for Silver Kingdom's opening. Would she have spotted it – or the holes in the pole, for that matter – if she hadn't been so engrossed in the task? Possibly not, because no one else was ever any the wiser.

'Then why didn't everyone who rode that horse disappear? And who opens the trapdoor?'

Laurent shifts his position so he half faces Maisie with one arm slung on the back of the bench.

'It is not a person, but a catch attached to a lever and spring that opens the trapdoor, automatically,' he says. 'It took a while to find, but behind the remains of the music box is a clockwork device – set at midday and midnight – that is wired to activate this lever. It means that these are the only two times it is possible to vanish.' His face floods with embarrassment. 'Perhaps if I had discovered the pattern, I might have considered that the carousel itself, rather than an abductor, was behind the disappearances. As it is, I was convinced there was an accomplice. The Bureau focused on Mr Armitage. And you . . .' He pauses, and Maisie's face flushes now, anticipating that his next words will be about her belief in the curse. 'You were the only one to think that the fudge-coloured horse was directly responsible.'

Even so, she still never worked it out. It saddens Maisie to think of all the victims who could have been saved had this been discovered sooner. How many times did the police in two countries examine the carousel?

'I'm struggling to grasp the fact that, in almost twenty-five years, no one found the bodies.'

She holds back from explicitly mentioning that Laurent was himself in charge of the French investigation, but he looks rueful anyway.

'The platform is in one piece. The bodies would not have been obvious, even when the carousel was moved. In addition, the exhaust pipe directed away any smell of . . .' He pauses. 'Of decay.'

Thinking back to when the ride first arrived at Fairweather House, Maisie realizes that he is correct. She now remembers the rattling noise when the platform was lowered into place, and shudders.

'And perhaps we all only look for evidence that confirms our own beliefs,' he adds. 'Especially if certain officers felt the pressure of solving a high-profile case and, at the same time, were persuaded by certain businessmen to look elsewhere.' He coughs. 'None of which is helped if the mechanics of the machine are so ground-breaking that not even the men building the carousel understand how it is put together. In my opinion, this complexity is why no one guessed the true purpose of the carbon monoxide pipes when the machine was being assembled or dismantled.'

She thinks of the detailed instructions, and the recent conversation with Nancy. *He once told me he rode that peculiar horse and found out something interesting.* It's becoming ever clearer that Sir Malcolm did, in fact, plan his disappearance.

'Sir Malcolm,' she whispers.

Laurent gives her a sympathetic look. 'It would have been a painless death, like drifting to sleep,' he says reassuringly.

Dusk is falling rapidly. A fox shrieks from somewhere in the trees. Weary, Maisie lets her mind absorb the terrible, gory details. It's difficult to accept the idea that such an enchanting object was used for something so horrific. As an awful truth dawns on her, she looks at Laurent.

'It was Gilbert who was behind it all,' she exclaims. 'Not Victor.'

Laurent stares at his feet. Maisie notices that his shoes are shiny and new, and she wonders if his wife accompanies him on shopping expeditions, like the one that they spent together at Marshall Field's. Pinching her thumbs, she pushes down the ache.

'It was, in fact, Gilbert. The mechanisms, the construction, suggest that the carousel was designed this way by its creator . . . leaving Victor blameless.' He swallows hard. 'It is something I shall have to live with for the rest of my life.'

An innocent man was executed. Maisie is hit with the horror of the injustice meted out to him. She watches Laurent clench his teeth, shaking his head as though he would take it all back if he could. What a sorry mess it is.

'But why would Gilbert do something so terrible?' she asks. 'And will you be able to find and arrest him after all this time?'

Laurent's jaw flexes.

'Unfortunately, an arrest is not possible. We believe we have found his remains down there, amongst those of the others. Gilbert's voting card was tucked into the trouser pocket of one of the bodies. His son's birth and death certificates were also there: these indicate that the boy was born at midday and died at midnight, a month after his ninth birthday, and account for why the trapdoor was set to activate at those times,' he explains, shaking his head. 'Grief is a peculiar creature.'

For several seconds, Laurent looks lost in thought, exhaling deeply before continuing. 'There is also a tiny inscription on the inner wall of the platform which means *You too shall fly* in English. Gilbert was thrown into a kind of insanity, as described by his employees. If his wife and son could not live, no one would, including himself. It was a revenge on the world, I believe.'

The phrase sounds beautiful, not vengeful. Retribution as a motive wouldn't even occur to Maisie. If, God forbid, something unthinkable befell Milo, she would never want anyone else to suffer the same heartache. And how does it all tie in with always feeling as if she were being watched, and the strange urge she had to ride the burning horse? It was a compulsion, a need, more than just her imagination. Wasn't it? Or perhaps every carousel is magnetic in a way, pulling a person in with the promise of enchantment and escape.

Laurent looks up at her again, a gaze that makes her heart leap. Maisie fights the urge to touch his hand, which lies only inches from her own. No good will come of it, she reminds herself. He is a married man.

She forces her eyes to shift to the lake, to the calm surface covered in particles of ash that look like tiny bobbing boats from here. *Please, dear Lord of the Water, let me get through this.*

'I did not know if you were still living at Fairweather House,' Laurent says quietly.

Considering that she hasn't responded to any of his letters, this isn't surprising.

'In actual fact, I won't be from tomorrow. Sir Malcolm bequeathed most of his share of Silver Kingdom to me, but I've sold it to Hugo and am moving to Joliet,' she discloses. Beside her, Laurent visibly tenses. 'Tonight, I'll stay with Mrs Papadopoulos before catching the afternoon train,' she says. 'My son, Milo, as well.'

Laurent looks at Maisie with an expression that says he is only just comprehending that she's a mother.

'The little boy who went off with Mrs Papadopoulos?' he asks, as observant as ever. 'I should have known that he was yours from his mischievous laugh.'

Maisie smiles to herself. 'He looks more like James, though. I'm always told that.'

Laurent studies his hands. They are both quiet for some time, sitting next to one another while gazing at the sun dropping behind the horizon. A group of police personnel trudge up the shore.

Laurent clears his throat.

'My American colleagues tell me the fire that triggered the explosion was no accident. They have found evidence of lighter fuel around the carousel and are collecting a list of potential suspects. Is there anyone you can think of who might have had cause to destroy Silver Kingdom?'

'No one springs to mind,' she replies, avoiding meeting his eye.

★

Washed out, Maisie collapses beside Milo on the Papadopoulos' couch, shifting to find a comfortable position. Their train to Joliet is booked for 3 p.m. tomorrow. This leaves her having to make another decision, like all those that went before. To journey to America. To marry. To separate. Some choices weren't even conscious, and so weren't really choices at all – having a baby is the biggest one she can think of. Several were drastic; others so minuscule that blink and they were gone. But together they form the tapestry of her life. She wonders if she would unpick some of the stitches, given the chance, or if she could, use different threads. Or will she weave a new story now?

52

'Milo say he wants to help with my rounds this morning. He hard working Greek like his mother.'

Mrs Papadopoulos perches on the edge of the couch where Maisie is still lying, drained of energy after very little sleep. She can hear Milo giggling with Georgios in the room next door.

'I know you always say I'm Greek because of how I look, and I like you thinking that, because it makes me feel like I belong somewhere. But my mother is English and my father is from India,' Maisie admits. 'I'm sorry I didn't own up sooner.'

Mrs Papadopoulos laughs. 'Oh, *moro mou*, Greek not where you come from. Greek is your heart. Strong. With passion. You strong with big heart, huh?'

They hug, then Mrs Papadopoulos hurries to get the rest of her family, as well as Milo, into the cart on time.

When, finally, everyone is gone, Maisie gets up and wanders to the kitchen for a glass of orange juice. Taking small sips, she admires the shininess of everything in this brand-new house. The Papadopoulos family business is obviously thriving because theirs is the first residence constructed in this exclusive cul-de-sac of five residences near the Chicago suburbs, bordered by acres of greenery. As Maisie stares at the mesmerizing dance of grass swishing in the semi-light, she notices a figure near the house. She almost drops the glass in shock. James is creeping across the lawn, keeping low to the ground. How does he know she's staying here? Has he been following her?

Driven by indignation, Maisie grabs a saucepan and hurtles out of the back door. James jumps back, caught unawares.

'I'm not here to hurt you,' he says quickly, holding up his hands to prove he isn't armed. 'So please put the pan down.'

James is unshaven and unwashed, and he hasn't changed his clothes since she last saw him a few evenings ago. Once her heart might have gone out to him but not now. Not after he tried to extract money from her again. Not after he dragged her out of the house and to the carousel. She lowers the pan but keeps it firmly in her grip.

'If you're here to see Milo, he's gone out.'

His eyes soften. 'I came for you. It's always been about you ever since we met at Clacton funfair.' He bites his lip. 'I shouldn't have asked you for money again. I'm not even that bothered about it. I wasn't myself that night.'

Maisie is flabbergasted. Does he really not understand that it's over between them? She's still trying to fathom the answer when Lucky Nate's weatherbeaten face emerges from the shadows. He looks between James and Maisie, taking in the scene with his shrewd eyes. Before she can ask him what on earth he's doing here, he beckons to a figure.

Maisie lets out a gasp as a wiry man with a twirly moustache steps forward flanked by half a dozen brutish-looking companions. Freddie Fortescue. She hears the clink of coins as a flash of silver is dropped into Lucky Nate's palm. He pockets the money and walks over to Maisie, standing quietly by her side.

'Don't react,' he says in a low voice.

James is dragged to the edge of the pasture and forced to his knees, held in place by two of the henchmen, his head down. Freddie looks around the neighbourhood, at the partially built houses overlooked only by rolling grass and herds of disinterested cattle.

He turns his thin-lipped smile to Maisie.

'I thought you might like to witness this since James could never stop bragging about how you'd unwittingly bankrolled his entire investment in our business. Gullible, is the word he used.'

Maisie opens her mouth to explain to Freddie that, while it was a horrible way for a husband to behave, she really doesn't care about any of that now. But Lucky Nate's hand applies pressure to her shoulder.

The next few seconds pass both slowly and so quickly that Maisie thinks it can't be real. She hears her breathing become fast and laboured. James looks up, meets Maisie's eye. He is mouthing words to her. *Sorry, so sorry.* She tries to move, to get to him, but a pair of hands hold her back. A pillow is produced, then a revolver. There is no sound but suddenly James is slumped on the grass and blood-soaked feathers are flying everywhere.

53

The body of a Caucasian male is discovered mid-morning. Three fishermen trawling through marshland chance upon a large beer barrel turned on its side with a leg sticking out.

Laurent is at the precinct when the body is wheeled in, speaking to a group of detectives about the persons responsible for the fire at Silver Kingdom. All three have agreed on a theory, and the suspect will be brought in for questioning within the hour.

'Anyone know whose body this is?' an American detective shouts loudly enough to be heard above the hum in the room.

It is a large desk-filled space with an assortment of police personnel. Laurent has to admit that the ambience here is more appealing than the shabby rooms at his own place of work. Almost pleasant, in fact. There is no stench of open drains from the street, no screams from nearby cells, and the walls are freshly painted.

A man with a nose the colour and shape of a radish raises his hand.

'A wallet in his pocket indicates that he's Mr James Squires, originally from England. His wife is arriving to identify him.'

Although Laurent always believed the man would come to a sticky end, it is a surprise to hear the name nonetheless. Yesterday, when Maisie had disclosed the identity of Milo's father, it felt like a dagger had been plunged into Laurent's heart. Of course, he did not expect her life to exist in suspension. But to marry that brute?

Discussion turns to bootleg whisky, and Laurent feels justified in taking a break downstairs. He is tired after barely sleeping a wink last night. All he could think about, all he ever thinks about whether he is aware of it or not, is Maisie. His emotions are all over the place. After finding her again at the fire, he had been building up to ask her a question. Discovering her married put a brake on that idea.

Now his senses are electrified again. While he is worried that the timing might be inappropriate, this might be his final chance, since she leaves to catch her train this afternoon.

On returning from the café across the street, Laurent spots her instantly. He would spot her anywhere. But here, in the reception area, she is a dazzling light amongst the rabble. Her head is turning in different directions as though she is lost. His heart quickens as he shoves his way through the crowd.

Maisie looks shaken; she is trembling.

Laurent needs to share some other news with her. As it is a delicate matter to explain, he places a hand on her shoulder. She does not flinch or shrug him off and he is glad.

'We have found evidence that Mrs Randolph is the person responsible for burning down the carousel, and Silver Kingdom with it.'

Maisie looks fatigued. Her face is washed out, and he notices that she is struggling not to cry.

'There are numerous witness statements placing Mrs Randolph alone in the house yesterday,' he adds gently. 'And an almost empty bottle of fuel was found hidden behind a pile of shoeboxes in one of her wardrobes. The same type of fuel that was splashed around the carousel and enabled the fire to take hold.'

Her eyes widen. 'Poor Nancy. She has a miserable life.'

She stares sadly along the corridor. Laurent studies the profile of her face. Even in the harsh glare of a police precinct and tainted with melancholy, she still radiates beauty.

'Do you think you could help me find the room where I'm meant to identify James?' she continues, fiddling nervously with her purse.

Composing himself, Laurent agrees and finds an available sergeant to escort them to the morgue in the basement. Maisie baulks at the sight of her husband, his lips blue and his features frozen. He is as white as a marble statue, with a hole the size of a one-centime piece in the centre of his forehead.

Maisie produces a handkerchief from her purse and dabs her eyes.

'Can you confirm that this is James Squires?' the sergeant asks.

Maisie covers her eyes and nods.

'You need to speak,' he says.

'Yes,' she whispers.

Thankfully, the sergeant affirms that the identification is complete. Once Maisie has signed a form, he hands over a small bag of James's possessions. She follows Laurent back to the entrance.

As Maisie turns to say goodbye, their eyes connect. Laurent is transported back to the moments before their kiss when they bared their souls to one another.

Only one other person has ever laid themselves open like this. His mother – who had packed her suitcases but was too frightened to leave – showed him everything she could have been. *Promise me, Laurent*, she had urged, her face soaked with tears. *Promise you'll never let your chances slip away.*

He cannot understand how he could have left Maisie all those years ago. Although he had justified it to himself at the time as being for her own good, perhaps deep down a part of him was not ready. But now he is.

'Why don't we go to my hotel? It is quiet there, and we can talk.'

54

The Sissy Miller Hotel sits ten blocks from the precinct, a leisurely stroll through downtown Chicago. Pale yellow brick on the outside, it has an elegant mix of cream furniture and veined orange marble inside. The desk at the furthest end of a square vestibule is a polished mahogany piece that looms large, as if it were constructed on the spot and everything else built around it. A candle next to the red leather guest book releases the scent of expensive patchouli. Clearly, Laurent enjoys a certain luxury in life.

The grey-haired receptionist has a liking for him, it seems; she simpers about how happy she is to provide home-made cake without extra charge, and makes no objection to his announcement that they will take their refreshments upstairs, despite the NO VISITORS ALLOWED IN GUESTS' ROOMS notice. Next comes the ceremony of pouring and sugaring and adding milk, and sipping from delicate china cups while they engage in small talk about the Illinois weather at this time of year compared with Paris.

'And is the climate in Joliet very different from Chicago?' Laurent asks.

Maisie smiles because it's evident that he's unaware of the local geography.

'Joliet is only an hour from here. James and I have been separated for some time, but I chose somewhere near especially so that he could still visit Milo . . .' Her voice dies down as it occurs to Maisie that she's now free to move wherever she pleases. 'He's the one good thing to come from my marriage.' She stares at the creamy tea. 'I think I only married James because I needed to feel wanted by someone. It wasn't fair on him or me.'

Realizing that she's slipped into sharing her innermost thoughts with Laurent, Maisie raises her guard. She was on the verge of revealing that she's always clung to her feelings for him.

He sets down his teacup. They are sitting in armchairs facing one another, and he leans forward.

'This is what I wished to talk to you about,' he says, as though he's been waiting for his cue. 'I am sorry, Maisie, that I behaved in the way I did. It is understandable that you were deeply hurt.' He takes a moment to think. 'My mother's death affected me deeply, and I was never able to fully love a woman, even my wife, Odette.'

Maisie presses her lips together. So his feelings never matched her own. 'I see.'

Laurent must have understood the thoughts invading her mind, because he looks abashed.

'Apologies, I am not explaining myself properly. It was all pre-pared in my mind, but now, seeing you . . .' He takes a deep breath. 'What I am trying to say is that I was never in love with my wife, and we are now separated, and I am ready to change. Because I love you, Maisie, and I wish you to come to Paris with me.'

A tornado of emotions renders Maisie short of breath. The excitement of Christmas morning and unwrapping birthday pres-ents and the first snowfall of winter, all rolled into a ball with hope and wonder and a trace of nerves.

'I . . . I love you too,' she whispers, almost too stunned to speak.

It feels surreal to allow these words their freedom. This is the moment Maisie has secretly prayed for ever since their kiss. She should be shouting from the rooftops and dancing with joy. And yet a crushing fear rears its head. France is thousands of miles away, a country with different customs and language, where she knows no one apart from Laurent. Would it be foolhardy to risk everything for love? Or is embracing the unknown in her blood? She thinks of standing in the Jesserton study as a twelve-year-old, agreeing to accompany a near-stranger all the way to America. That brave adventurer still lives inside Maisie.

'And you'd be fine with Milo coming with me?' she asks.

Laurent takes her hand, stroking it in small circles.

'More than fine. I would very much like to meet and spend some time with him. And he will like my daughter, I am certain.'

Laurent is a father. It seems ridiculous that Maisie has never considered the possibility, even after learning that he had a wife. She thinks of standing at the lookout spot, her eyes searching across Canvey Estuary. She thinks of whispering to Tommy as they lay on the Sixpences' dirty floor, dreaming of ways to escape. She thinks of a little girl in Paris, imagines her face pressed against a window, waiting for her father to return.

'What's her name?' she asks.

'Amélie, and she is ten years old. I believe she will be the artist I never was when she grows up. Already she is able to sketch portraits that are a striking likeness. It is quite extraordinary.'

The life Maisie imagined in Joliet is already fragmenting like the tiny pieces of a broken mirror. Images of strolling alongside the river and the little apartment above the store are replaced by staring at the Eiffel Tower, sipping coffee at cosy cafes nestled in the shadow of Montmartre, spending every day and every night with the man she loves. Before she floats away with this idea, Maisie brings herself back to reality.

'She sounds as talented as her father, and I can't wait to get to know her,' she says. 'And I would love to come to France, Laurent, and I will, but there's something I must do first.' He looks both relieved and slightly wary. 'Though I sold my stake in Silver Kingdom, I feel a need to help the workforce with the aftermath of the fire.' She bites her lip. The thought of how upset they must be causes Maisie anguish. 'Hugo is distracted with his own problems, and I'm not certain he'll be able to deal with it all.' She hesitates. 'It might be a few months. Can you wait that long?'

She already knows the answer, because he breaks into a smile. 'I will wait as long as it takes,' he replies.

Minutes pass quickly as they enjoy each other's company. A discussion about parenthood is followed by talk of moving dates. Maisie feels like she's living in a fairytale.

'I have spent four years wishing for this moment,' Laurent says with a wonderstruck timbre to his voice.

'Me too,' she admits.

He sits forward in his armchair and places one hand on her thigh. It is electrifying, an unexpected jolt of pleasure from such light pressure. As she looks at him, the question in his eyes asks whether she would like him to continue. Understanding her silent agreement, he stands and pulls her gently to her feet while his gaze holds her steady.

Watching every reaction, he strokes down to her waist with soft, slow caresses. Her body responds to the tenderness, her back arching, and there's a gasp of surprise at revelling in an experience that was barely tolerable with her husband. Laurent undresses her slowly, undoing the buttons of her blouse first, in no hurry, savouring every moment. Then the skirt and stockings, his fingers tracing up her thighs. Her undergarments are last. By the time he's naked himself, she has opened herself completely.

Every emotion Maisie has suppressed for this beautiful man is released, every second of heartache and prayer for his return are expressed as desire. She welcomes him inside, pulls at him as carnal instinct takes over. Laurent is an experienced lover, she can tell, as he lets her explore his body with her hands while never looking away, matching the pace of her moans, her waves of pleasure.

They cling to one another, neither wanting to let go.

Afterwards, she lies with her head resting on his chest, tracing figure-of-eight patterns on his skin. If only she could bottle this feeling of being fully alive.

'Thank you,' she whispers.

He shifts position so their heads rest on the pillows, facing one another, an expression of amusement on his face.

'You are thanking me for our enjoyment?' he asks.

'For *my* enjoyment.'

As though he suddenly understands her gratitude, a shadow of sadness enters those beautiful grey eyes. 'I am sorry it was not always this way for you.'

He strokes her face and kisses her forehead, pulls her closer. With his hand stroking along her hip, Maisie drifts to sleep, entwined in both body and mind with the man she loves.

She wakes to find Laurent watching her, his eyes lost in thought. Reaching out, she strokes his mouth with her finger, tracing the outline. He smiles, kisses her hand. Knowing she is truly safe here gives Maisie the courage to voice what she's wanted to say for four years.

'I never read your letters after the first couple you sent me. I was angry with you. It wasn't just because you were married.' She can see him flinch, and wills herself to carry on. 'I was devastated about my parents. The truth came completely out of the blue . . . I was still upset about the disappearances, and you'd only left the day before. But I still shouldn't have taken it out on you.'

His eyes open wide. 'You read the report the day after I left?'

As Maisie nods, he strokes her cheek, wipes away a tear.

'You were not meant to see it so soon. Naturally, you were upset about your parents. Sir Malcolm and I had agreed that he would break the news gently when the time was right. It was the only reason I left my findings behind.' He looks thoughtful. 'I do not know why that did not happen.'

There is a strain at the edges of his eyes like he's holding back.

'You know something else, don't you?' she asks.

He is silent but his reddening cheeks give it away. Maisie doesn't blame him for being reluctant to share any knowledge. She lays her palm on his chest. His heart is pounding. Maisie is breathless, almost too frightened to ask after having long given up on ever finding her parents.

'Did you meet them?'

He shakes his head. There is a wave of disappointment. But she believes he knows something. She remains calm, hoping to reassure him.

Eventually he speaks.

'It seems they have spent two decades moving from place to place. I have a map in my study pinpointing their exact whereabouts, year by year,' he admits.

Maisie looks up at this confession, surprised.

'You spent your earliest years in Paris with them, in actual fact. Strangely, I suspect near the industrial area where Gilbert Cloutier owned his carousel premises and from where he disappeared.'

Perhaps this explains why Maisie has always felt a connection to carousels. Despite the warmth of lying naked against Laurent, a chill wraps around her skin.

'Did you ever get close to finding them?' she asks.

'I thought at one point I had them in my sights, but by the time I arrived they had been gone for five months, according to their landlady, Madame Florian,' he explains. 'But the women became friends, and your mother shared some useful information. She talked about you quite often, it appears.'

There is raucous shouting in the hallway and Laurent waits until the noise dies down. Maisie holds her breath.

'Her travelling companion was, indeed, your father. And she had a daughter living in England whom she sent there for her own safety.'

Maisie imagines herself as Moses, placed in a basket and pushed across the English Channel.

'Why wasn't I safe with her?' she asks

Laurent's eyebrows knot together.

'Because of your father's violent tempers. If your mother didn't do exactly as he ordered, it was like a storm cloud was passing through the place, according to Madame Florian. She said the whole house shook when he shouted. If she wasn't so fond of your mother, she would have thrown them out.'

'It wasn't bad enough for her to leave with me,' Maisie whispers.

Laurent thinks for a moment.

'Maybe your father threatened to find and punish you both if she escaped. I do not know. What I am aware of is that she told Madame Florian that you were living with her childless sister and thought you very happy.'

It jogs a memory of the day she talked with Aunty Mabel in the linen room at Jesserton, but with a difference in perception. *I'm sorry it took me so long to collect you. It's not that I didn't want you because I did. But my Bertie thought different.* With a sharp pain, she suddenly understands that Mabel was responsible for her ending up in the Sixpences' care; her husband must have been paying for Maisie's upkeep there. The woman that had led Maisie to believe she was kind and caring, who gave her treats, planned their happily-ever-after future, was the same person who had thrown away a little girl like a pair of mouldy socks. Maisie would have done anything for her aunt back then. This was a betrayal, an underhand trick.

Defensive, she brushes Laurent's fingers away. No one can hurt her ever again, if she doesn't allow them to get close.

Undeterred, he finds her hand hiding beneath the sheets and brings it to his mouth. With a gentle kiss, he looks her in the eye.

'I will not leave you as they did, if that is your fear. I swear upon all that is precious to me.'

He studies her face with infinite tenderness, and Maisie believes him.

55

As Maisie catches the streetcar from Laurent's hotel, she feels giddy. For a change, she lets herself revel in the excitement. Over the next few days, they will discuss solid plans for her move to Paris, and Laurent will spend some time with Milo. She considers how to tell her son about his father's death. It's all so tragic. If James wasn't so desperately driven to be something more, if he hadn't delayed escaping to come for Maisie, he would still be alive. *Sorry, so sorry.* Despite everything, Maisie experiences a sorrow that James's dreams were cut short at the age of twenty-eight, while she has the rest of her life to enjoy.

With the park closed to visitors, Maisie is the solo passenger by the time the streetcar stops at Silver Kingdom. Her main purpose in being here is to sift through the wreckage for any surviving possessions; even before she reaches the gates, the stench of smoke is a clue that the task will prove fruitless. Nevertheless, she treads carefully through the ruins, heading for the cottage's red-brick chimney, which rises as the only surviving structure like a beacon. The cottage itself has been razed to the ground, as has the amusement park, with the rides little more than black mounds sitting amongst a landscape of utter devastation. Ash piled upon ash hides further layers of ash. After twenty minutes of digging through and recovering only a melted fork, three partial chair legs and a cracked earthenware pot, Maisie gives up and wanders towards the shore.

Removing her shoes, she embarks on her second reason for coming here. She takes an empty jar from her purse and wades into the shallows. It's bitterly cold, but she pushes deeper for her son's sake. Sticking her hand in the mud and rummaging around, she finds a plump lamprey. She places it into the jar with water before returning to the bank. There, Milo will never know the difference from the first Mr Arnie.

A lone figure has appeared, her long, scarlet dress flapping in the breeze scuttling across the lake. Before, Maisie would have made her excuses and left, but she owes this woman her life.

'Thank you for bringing me to my senses,' she says to Madame Rose, as she replaces her shoes. 'It was lucky for me that you came along when you did.'

The fortune-teller cocks her head slightly as if she's considering a curious question. 'Luck? Or destiny?'

Maisie gives a weary smile. She doesn't know why she was expecting anything more than a cryptic answer.

'I'm not sure I really believe in either,' she admits.

'Oh, I don't know about that. Those little stones you lay around Silver Kingdom would say otherwise.'

Maisie blushes. She had no idea anyone else even noticed. 'People would think I'd lost my mind if they knew.'

Madame Rose laughs as if she's quite accustomed to the feeling. She links arms with Maisie as though the two of them are close friends. They head towards the tennis court, where a large group is gathering. The workers have arrived, most probably to demand answers from Hugo about the future. Feeling terrible for them, Maisie wants to start helping out immediately.

It's slow progress through the debris. Passing the remnants of the helter-skelter, and a lump of wood where the doughnut stall once stood, Maisie can't help remembering all the happy times here. Madame Rose stops by a circle of warped metal, staring into space. Maisie looks away. This is the wreckage of the carousel.

'Did you ever sense what happened?' Maisie asks. 'Is that why you told me that I wasn't ready for the answer?'

Madame Rose smiles kindly at Maisie. 'I believed *you* knew what happened. You see things, sense things not everyone does, but you hold yourself back.'

Maisie's eyes flick briefly to the carousel, and back again to Madame Rose's smiling face, her thoughts focused on what possessed her even to think about mounting a burning horse.

'Trust it,' she tells Maisie. 'That's what makes you different.'

Maisie thinks of all the people she's ever known in her life.

'Isn't everyone different? Which really makes us all the same.'

Madame Rose grins in answer, her teeth gleaming.

They reach the tennis court. The clamour from the workforce is deafening, and Maisie can barely hear as Madame Rose whispers in her ear, 'Best of luck with your new life.'

Maisie wants to ask more questions, glean as much information as she can from this all-knowing woman, but Madame Rose has already drifted into the crowd, like flotsam taken away by the tide.

It quickly becomes apparent that no one has seen Hugo since yesterday evening. People are panicking, and there are worried faces. She can hear Mrs Ferretti wailing. Betsy the Money Girl is sobbing on the shoulder of one of the pirates from the Smugglers' Saloon. 'I've lost everything,' someone says, and there's a chorus of agreement. Their distress is distressing to Maisie.

The noise dies down to a murmur as Maisie is noticed. Mr Parry nudges Mr Melville. Arnold and Mr Levander exchange thankful looks. There's now a little hope in the eyes of the workforce. Evidently, they all trust Maisie to get this right. Hesitating, she catches Lucky Nate's eye. He nods.

'All right, listen up, everyone. Here's what we're going to do.'

Full Circle

56

Paris, France, February 1926

Laurent has promised Amélie a special gift for her thirteenth birthday. How the time has flown. He vaguely remembers her baby years as a blur of sleepless nights and the Cloutier case, but not much else. The main benefit of the mystery finally being solved is that Laurent can focus his attention on the people who are most dear to him.

The toy department in the Galeries Lafayette is abuzz with small children weaving through displays of teddy bears and gadgets, and harassed mothers chasing them. He spots the object immediately. It has been on display for six weeks and Laurent has been dithering. Now he sees it again, he realizes that nothing could be more perfect.

The size of a tennis ball, a small silver disc supports a dozen tiny carved and painted wooden horses beneath an indigo canopy. Best of all, when a small handle is wound, a tinkling tune plays as the disc rotates. A beautiful, magical, miniature carousel.

'Can I help you, sir?' a voice asks.

Laurent swings around. A young man of around seventeen has appeared behind him. He is long and lean and his suit hangs off him as if it was borrowed from someone much broader.

'I will take this item, please,' he says.

Laurent strides to the sales till with the assistant following behind. He has a busy day ahead and cannot dally. After this, he is taking Maisie and Milo to Juliette's Pâtisserie to choose a cake for Amélie's birthday party this Sunday, and then he will send them home in a taxi while he conducts a secret mission of his own. Having heard that a detective is searching for the whereabouts of a blonde woman who is associated with an Indian man, Maisie's mother has left something with her old friend with the yellow wig from the slums – word came yesterday via a constable working the beat in the Cour des miracles area. There have been other false alarms and disappointments, but Laurent maintains a degree of optimism. It is his deepest hope that in due course he might be able to engineer a meeting between Maisie and her mother.

As though his thoughts have called to her, Maisie turns around and waves at him. She is at the furthest end of the department with Milo, amongst the model aeroplanes. Even after more than two years, he cannot get enough of the simple pleasure of looking at this woman. Rubbing her round belly, she refocuses on the toys. Three months. In three months from now, their baby will arrive. Laurent is beside himself with anticipation.

'Here you go, sir. It's a good choice,' the assistant says with a smile as he hands Laurent the wrapped-up carousel. 'Hope to see you again soon.'

Laurent pulls his gaze from Maisie and returns the assistant's smile.

'Thank you, Henri, I hope so too.'

He indicates the name badge as though this is how he has identified the young man when, in actual fact, Laurent has followed Henri Cloutier's progress for years, silently opening doors for him. Arranging for Mr Fraser, the owner of the auction house, to skim a portion of the proceeds from the carousel sale all those years ago was the first step. This money was sent to Laurent. With the help of his secretary, Suzette, a number of cash-filled envelopes were left with the local priest to pass on to Henri's mother. It will never make up for the young man losing his father, and Laurent will never absolve himself of having sent a blameless man to the guillotine. But he feels glad that he has played even a small part in keeping the boy from a life of destitution.

The rest of the day passes in a mad rush. Returning home from the slums, Laurent is exhausted but also puffed up with jubilation. The prostitute has given him something of note for Maisie. Hurrying to his study, he closes the door. From the window, he can see Maisie teaching Milo how to skim stones across the large pond in the garden. The boy is giggling, as usual. Sometimes he is wilful, Laurent has discovered, but on the whole he is a joyful little chap who tags behind Amélie on the weekends that she stays with them in Paris. Laurent smiles as Milo tries to copy his mother's technique. Engrossed in their game, neither has realized that he is home. Good, there is time to make everything perfect.

He sits at his desk and wraps layers of pink tissue paper around the item, then scribbles a small card addressed to Maisie. Leaning back in his chair, he half closes his eyes. He is not quite recovered from the influenza he picked up from the slums last month, and the weariness has taken hold again. Perhaps it would have been wiser to return home with the others after the pâtisserie, but he could not deny Maisie this surprise for any longer than necessary. It is the way his mother taught him.

'No, Laurent, it isn't polite to keep a lady waiting,' she would say when he arrived downstairs five minutes after afternoon tea was served, having got distracted once again by his toy soldiers.

After allowing himself some minutes to regain his strength, Laurent is in the midst of standing up when a sharp pain shooting down his left arm throws his body off balance. He stumbles and ends up on the floor.

As he lies sprawled, Laurent thinks of Maisie as he always thinks of her – when he wakes, when he dreams, when he eats and sleeps and prays. He thinks of her face upturned and ready to kiss him, a tendril of hair falling, the sparkle in her eyes, the joy of her smile when she presented the sandpiper feather that he has kept close to his heart to this day. He thinks of her beauty, her glorious love for him, imagines all the other moments they could have shared if this wasn't his very last breath.

57

New York City, September 1981

As she leaves the glass skyscraper housing the offices of Silver Kingdom Inc., Maisie smiles at the pretty receptionist whose name always deserts her. 'See you Monday,' she says. She hails a cab, which is quite the achievement along Fifth Avenue on a Friday afternoon, and lets her head rest against worn leather. Once she might have walked, but these days her joints would complain too much.

'Greenwich Village, please.'

The driver eyes Maisie through the rearview mirror. 'Where are you from, lady?'

Always the same question. To Maisie, at least, never to Milo or to Joanna or to the grandchildren with their pale skin, as though they've always belonged here. It amazes Maisie that, after all this time, her colour still sets her apart.

'Illinois.'

'I mean before America.'

'England.'

He looks dubious, but Maisie stopped justifying herself to anyone, particularly strangers, long ago, so she doesn't elaborate. He doesn't need to know that her roots are firmly anchored in the ancient soil of England, that she's been blown by the winds of America and France, and blood from another continent runs through her veins – a continent with languages, cultural traditions and points of reference so unlike her own that, when finally people from India were permitted to settle here, she discovered they were as much strangers to her as if they'd grown up on the moon. Maisie recalls what Mrs Papadopoulos once told her: *Where you come from isn't a place, it's your heart.* And that's all anyone needs in common, isn't it?

'Have you ever been back?' he asks.

'Of course – in fact I enjoyed tea at Buckingham Palace just last month,' she jokes.

Truth be told, Maisie has never returned to the country of her birth. Once or twice, she contemplated doing so. To see, touch and smell England once more would be a dream come true, but a large part of her fears that the changes would be too much to bear. Perhaps the meadows aren't as green as she remembers, or the sound of larks singing at twilight isn't quite as sweet. More importantly, it would have brought Maisie within spitting distance of the life she once lived in Paris, stirring up the old heartache.

There hasn't been a third husband. Though Maisie has dated other men over the years, nothing was ever serious or long-lasting. She tells herself it's because she was too busy being both mother and father to her children, and with work. Truthfully, though, Maisie has never really moved on from her first true love. Her mind drifts to him now, to those storm grey eyes and their time together, which was all too brief.

The driver leaves Maisie to her thoughts as the cab stop-starts, stop-starts the two miles to the pier. She ends up in her usual spot: a small bistro with a view of the little funfair reflecting off the gently lapping waters. This is her favourite part of the day, the no man's land between lunch and dinner, when usually she has the place to herself. This afternoon, however, someone else is already sitting at the best table.

The elderly gentleman stands when he spots Maisie approaching. He is small and slight with twinkling eyes.

'Maisie,' he says. 'Dear Maisie.'

She is immediately struck by his accent, the idiosyncratic melody of the Essex coastline which slipped away from Maisie long ago. Beaming, he opens his arms wide. As she sinks into his embrace, it feels like she's come home.

'Tommy,' she whispers.

She had put out feelers years ago to try to find him. Thinking he might have stayed on Canvey, she wrote to the island's tavern and church and shops to ask for any information they might have on him, with no success. Then *Time* ran a piece entitled 'Smashing through the Glass Ceiling: The End of Men in Power?', which featured Maisie, amongst a handful of other businesswomen. She thought it funny at the time because she's still the only woman in most meetings, and is often mistaken for the tea lady, so not that much has changed. But Tommy had seen a copy, recognizing her name, the details of her early life and even the photograph – or so he claimed – and he called Silver Kingdom's offices the very same day.

Time moves backwards as they stand hugging. They are the two children who ran free along the banks of Canvey Estuary, heaved buckets of cockles, chased wild rabbits, blessed dead squirrels and crabs and swans, steered Mr Sixpence's tiny boat between craggy rocks, planned their escape.

Eventually, they let go and sit at the table. The pink-haired waitress arrives to take their order, and, while they wait for the drinks to appear, Tommy reaches for Maisie's hand. His is knobbled by arthritis; hers is covered with dark brown blotches.

'I knew I'd find you one day,' Tommy says, looking very pleased with himself. 'That article about you couldn't have been more helpful.' He smiles. 'It seems you've had an interesting life, lived in a lot of places. That must have been nice.'

She squeezes his hand.

'Looking back, it does seem that way, doesn't it? But do you know, Tommy, mainly I always moved as a reaction to something. Going to America, leaving France. I would have stayed in Paris forever . . .' Her voice tapers out.

She had loved that city, the sophistication, the glamour and culture, but it was too painful to live there without Laurent, and one month after the funeral she had packed up and gone to Joliet, as she had originally planned. Leaving Amélie was a wrench, but the girl had her mother, and they still keep in touch to this day. Laurent's daughter became a sculptress, and is a grandmother to two boys herself now.

'Well, you made the best of it, did well for yourself, which is more than most can say,' Tommy answers. 'I always knew you had it in you.'

An instinct for survival is what Maisie holds within herself. In the thick of her grief at losing Laurent, she had funnelled all her energy into making a success of a new project on returning to America. It didn't take long for her friends from her time at Fairweather House to rally around, as though she had never been away. Deciding that she didn't want to deal with funfairs – or carousels – ever again, they started with ice-cream manufacturing, which blossomed into a conglomerate of foodstuffs. They make canned fruit, soup, frozen peas and TV dinners, and every one of them has reaped millions. Peggy Mae purchased the finest mansion in any southern state; Robert and Clara opened a chain of hotels; Eric travelled the world with a young man he was sweet on; Mrs Papadopoulos and her husband settled on a vast ranch in Illinois. As for Arnold, he followed Maisie to New York when the business was incorporated and became an influential patron of the performing arts.

Now Maisie dips in and out of meetings when the mood takes her, having handed over the reins to Milo many moons ago. Her boy has no recollection of James, no memories of waiting for Papa, his face squashed against the window, and is no better off than Joanna, who never even met her father. Laurent would have been proud of their child, not only because she's pursued a successful career as a biochemist but because of her kindness and dry sense of humour, which she gets from him.

She squeezes Tommy's hand again. 'We've both done very well for ourselves. We survived the Sixpences.'

Tommy nods his head from side to side, as if he's weighing up this statement.

'I'm not sure I would've, to be honest, not without you.' His eyes turn misty, as though he is also reliving the moment they were separated. 'But three days after you left, someone wrote a letter to the authorities about the poor conditions at the Sixpences', and the pair of them were arrested. The place was closed down,' he explains. 'The matron at the orphanage said the complaint came from a lady who was connected to some rich gentleman with a title. To be frank, I don't think anyone would've taken much notice otherwise.'

Maisie inhales sharply. Is he talking about Aunty Mabel? She feels grateful to the woman who saved her from the Sixpences, after having resented her for such a long time.

'What happened to you after that?' she asks.

'I'm a Barnardo's boy,' he replies. 'I was taken to the orphanage that day. It was a strict place but fifty times better than the shack – I was fed and clothed and kept warm, which was a blessing. And they trained me up and put me into service at fourteen.' He stares into thin air for a second. 'After the war, I became an omnibus driver, then worked my way up to a manager for London Transport.'

Tommy has been okay all this time. After decades of imagining the worst, she no longer need worry. Maisie feels a lump in her throat.

'It's all right, Maisie, it's all right,' he says gently, sensing her upset. 'I met my wife, Ada, early on. We've got four children. Funnily enough, our youngest granddaughter, Cecilia, has just been given the role of second dancer in the English National Ballet's *Swan Lake*.' He grins. 'Like my imaginary mother.'

She knows Tommy is trying to cheer her up. Smiling through the tears, she thinks of her own daughter, no nonsense and practical, just like Laurent.

'Well, my Joanna would never contemplate taking tea with a talking dolphin,' she replies, recalling one of her own made-up tales about her mother.

They both laugh. No one else would understand how these stories sustained them through the worst.

'Did you ever meet your real parents?' he asks.

Maisie shakes her head.

'Me neither,' he says quietly.

The drinks arrive, and they sit silently for a while, sipping, neither needing words. Maisie doesn't have the heart to tell Tommy that, unlike him, she has proof that her mother never forgot her – even after all these years, her protective instincts for him are fierce. Automatically, her fingers flutter to the tiny locket strung around her neck. She owns two Cartier watches, a whole safe full of jewels, tiaras, cars and several mansions, but this circle of tin containing a lock of blonde hair – her mother's hair – is Maisie's most valuable possession. Laurent had collected it from the slums and wrapped it up for her on the afternoon that he died.

She clears her throat.

'Tommy, do you remember our most precious treasure?'

He looks at her as though the question is ridiculous. 'Of course. I've loved carousels ever since. They're magical.'

Maisie couldn't agree more. Every carousel is special, but, decades later, nothing has ever beaten the exquisiteness of Gilbert Cloutier's creation.

'Well, I actually owned the exact carousel from that picture for a while. It was how everything started. It truly was gorgeous in real life . . . truly . . .' Her voice peters out.

'You never did,' Tommy replies, suitably amazed. 'I knew you had an amusement park but not that carousel.'

'To be honest, the thing caused all sorts of bother,' she admits. She hesitates, undecided whether to continue. But Tommy is like a brother. In actual fact, he *is* a brother, and she trusts him with her life. 'The truth is, and I've never admitted it to a soul, but . . . I set fire to it, in the end.'

It feels strange to admit this out loud after years of keeping the secret, like the truth is rusty and needs oiling. In theory, it was a resourceful plan: she lit a small fire within an earthenware pot, as she used to do at the Sixpences', settled it inside the carousel's metal control panel, and the embers smouldered for hours before finally cracking the container and catching to the fuel she had splashed around the carousel the previous night. It meant she was at Mr Peabody's office when the blaze took hold. If only she had been home earlier. Or one of the staff or Hugo had stayed at the house to supervise Nancy, as Maisie had assumed, and called the emergency services at the first sight of the flames, thus saving the rest of the park.

Laurent must have been blinded by love not to have suspected that the main reason Maisie delayed joining him in Paris was the guilt she felt for causing such trouble for the workforce. It's still there, their distress at the time haunting her after all these years. In the circumstances, assisting them was the least she could do. She helped the Ride Jocks and other employees find new jobs at other parks, filled out claims, badgered Hugo for compensation; he was no worse off after the fire since the company that had insured the amusement park eventually paid out. Maisie even donated a substantial portion of her own money until every single person was set up to her satisfaction. The Crew drifted away on the Illinois wind one blustery November day. 'Reckon we need to get moving again,' Lucky Nate had said.

Tommy leans forward and places one hand on her shoulder. 'You would've had your reasons,' he replies, always seeing the best in her.

She did. Of course, Maisie didn't mean for the flames to spread, or she would never have taken Milo back there. The explosion was unexpected: nowadays, everyone knows about the dangers of gasoline, but at that time Maisie had no idea what would happen; she was shocked when the unusually strong wind carried sparks to the other wooden rides, which easily caught on fire. Collateral damage. Maisie couldn't entrust the strange horse to Hugo. Obsessed with proving himself but never noticing anything, including his brother's imminent demise, he might have allowed people to start riding it again. She wishes now that she had done things differently. Several times Maisie was close to handing herself in to the police, but had changed her mind for Milo's sake.

Thankfully, Nancy was released without charge when the fluid in the fuel bottle was analysed and found to be what remained of her secret stash of vodka. They eventually found peace, the Randolphs, after the divorce: Hugo married Gloria the Money Girl and lived quietly at a restored Fairweather House, while Nancy left Assumption and bought a small apartment near the Met with her share of the divorce settlement.

All of them gone now, their stories faded to mist.

Tommy taps her hand. 'Shall we?'

She understands his question without further explanation. Helping each other up, they hold hands as they always did, heading towards the fairground. They arrive at the carousel. Maisie waits for Tommy to choose a horse, then, with some help from the woman operating the ride, she hoists herself on to the palomino pony beside him. When the music starts, excitement charges through her body. They circle and circle and circle again, both giggling. On the fourth rotation, Maisie's eyelids flutter closed.

You too shall fly, someone whispers.

In every direction, there is dark indigo blue dotted with tiny, sparkling stars. A breeze kisses her face, as warm as the heat of a summer afternoon. Maisie is rising and falling, half galloping, half soaring, gripping the reins of a caramel-coloured colt with golden eyes and a blue diamond on its forehead, its hooves thundering towards a ball of liquid silver light, towards Laurent, across a glorious midnight sky.

Acknowledgements

I am filled with gratitude for everyone who has helped to bring this book to life.

Hellie Ogden, my agent extraordinaire, who had me at 'I have a weird obsession with carousels.' Thank you for spotting what that first draft could become, for your enthusiasm and guidance, and the hours upon hours that you poured into this story. My admiration for you is boundless. And Ma'suma Amiri, assistant and all-round wonder – you are a joy. A big thanks to everyone else at WME, especially the amazing Laura Bonner for working her foreign rights magic.

Lily Cooper at Penguin Michael Joseph. You really are a dream editor – patient, wise, perceptive and possessor of a huge heart. I have loved every second of working with you. You assembled an incredible trio; Emily van Blanken, Clare Bowron, Donna Poppy. All of you – I am blown away by your brilliance.

Many, many thanks to the Penguin Random House network; the visionary Communications Team – Annie Moore, Sriya Varadharajan and Frankie Banks – for spreading the word; Kelly Mason on the sales side; Lauren Wakefield, the designer of the gorgeous front cover; Riana Dixon for the smooth running of the editorial process.

A shout-out to my friends, who have cheered me on throughout the long journey to publication: Amanda and Gerry, Cathy and Nick, João and Mario, Fatima and Fernando, Sonia and Keith, Celeste and Victor, Christina and Jim, Debbie, Sian, Celia, Trudy and Mario. Trudy, thank you for sharing your behind-the-scenes knowledge of amusement parks.

Lauren Hughes deserves a special mention as the first person to have assessed my writing. Getting published had seemed such a long shot back in 2021. But you convinced me that I wasn't wasting my time – and now here we are! Thank you, truly.

I have a mountain of appreciation for my family.

My father, Khalid. Charismatic, humorous, generous, and such fun to be around. Losing you inspired this story, and we all miss you very much.

The character of Maisie is based on two extraordinary women – my grandmother, Annie, who started her working life in the 1920s, at fourteen years old, as a maid in a Northumberland mansion. And my mother, Pamela, a trailblazer for women in the corporate world. I have an abundance of love and respect for you both.

My other grandparents – Walter, Zaib and Mohammad. Some of you I never met, but fragments of your stories are scattered throughout this book. And Aunty Eileen, the keeper of the Coate family history – you are a treasure.

My sister, Sarah. What happy hours we spent together, lost in our imaginations! Thank you for a wonderful childhood. My brother-in-law, Amit, and Jasmine and Marcus, my niece and nephew – you all hold a special place in my heart.

My children, Lucas and Ella. I am so lucky to be your mother. Watching you blossom into beautiful, creative and caring adults has been an absolute delight. Ella, thank you for all the input; this book wouldn't be the same without you.

To Amelia and Joe – I'm over the moon that you've joined this family! Emily, your help has been invaluable, and I am very grateful.

And Phil. Thank you doesn't nearly cover it. You are always there for me, through thick and thin, listening, caring, making me laugh. Your endless support means everything.